The Mysterious
Doctor Cornelius
1. The Sculptor of Human Flesh

The Mysterious Doctor Cornelius
1. The Sculptor of Human Flesh

by
Gustave Le Rouge

translated, annotated and introduced by
Brian Stableford

A Black Coat Press Book

Visit our website at www.blackcoatpress.com

ISBN 978-1-61227-243-6. First Printing. February 2014. Published by Black Coat Press, an imprint of Hollywood Comics.com, LLC, P.O. Box 17270, Encino, CA 91416. All rights reserved. Except for review purposes, no part of this book may be reproduced or transmitted in any form or by any means, electronic or mechanical, including photocopying, recording, or by any information storage and retrieval system, without permission in writing from the publisher. The stories and characters depicted in this novel are entirely fictional. Printed in the United States of America.

TABLE OF CONTENTS

CHAQUE RÉCIT EST COMPLET EN UN VOLUME

Exceptionnellement
10 Cent.

GUSTAVE LE ROUGE

LE MYSTÉRIEUX DOCTEUR CORNÉLIUS

L'ENIGME DU CREEK SANGLANT

10 Centimes
LE RÉCIT COMPLET

LA MAISON DU LIVRE 28 R. MONSIEUR LE PRINCE PARIS

Introduction

Le Mystérieux docteur Cornélius by Gustave Le Rouge (1867-1938), here translated as *The Mysterious Doctor Cornelius*, was originally published in eighteen weekly parts by the Maison du livre moderne in 1912-13. It proved to be the author's most successful work; two reprints of selected episodes were followed by a nine-volume reprint of the entire work in 1918-20, and it was reprinted again in 112 parts as a daily *feuilleton* in *L'Homme libre*, as *Les Lords de la "Main Rouge,"* in 1924-25, having by then been translated into Italian and Spanish. Another eighteen-part version followed in 1927. Because Le Rouge made a habit of selling the copyrights in his work outright, it is highly unlikely that he received any payment for any of these reprints, but they doubtless assisted in the maintenance of his reputation.

Interest in the work was revived in the 1960s, largely by virtue of the championship of Francis Lacassin, and several paperback versions followed in various formats, including a complete version in a massive "Bouquins" omnibus published by Robert Laffont in 1986, which also included the *Le Prisonnier de la planète Mars* (1908) and its sequel *La Guerre des vampires* (1909),[1] *L'Espionne du Grand Lama* [The High Lama's Spy] (1905), five short stories and a cycle of poems adapted from Le Rouge's work by the author's friend and first enthusiastic champion, the *avant garde* poet and novelist Blaise Cendrars.

The Bouquins volume also contains various supplementary materials by Lacassin, Cendrars and others, including a bibliography of works known to have been written by Le Rouge, but drastically incomplete; the full extent of his anonymous and pseudonymous work is unknown, but is generally believed to be vast, only a couple of his pseudonyms having been identified. Although Cendrars' most extensive account of his friend's life and endeavors is contained in a fictionalized autobiography, and is undoubtedly exaggerated—Cendrars, as a dedicated surrealist, was no fan of mere accuracy—there is no reason to doubt its allegation that Le Rouge's total publication ran into hundreds of volumes, the vast majority of which did not carry his own name, in addition to countless articles and short stories in periodicals.

By 1912, Le Rouge was already a highly experienced writer of popular works in the long tradition of French *feuilleton* fiction—having begun his career in that field, after a period of near-starvation as a Latin Quarter poet and publishing an assortment of short stories and items of non-fiction—by working in collaboration with Gustave Guitton on a series of sprawling endeavors, begun

---

[1] Both translated in *The Vampires of Mars*, Black Coat Press, ISBN 978-1-934543-30-6.

with what was intended to be a four-volume novel (it was actually split into eight by its publisher) collectively entitled *La Conspiration des milliardaires* [The Billionaires' Conspiracy] (1899-1900)[2]. Guitton and Le Rouge wrote three more long novels before going their separate ways, after which Le Rouge became far more successful than his former friend, whose solo career faded away and whose eventual fate—and, indeed, his entire life—remains mysterious.

Le Mystérieux docteur Cornélius is a deliberate return on Le Rouge's part to the milieu and genre of *La Conspiration des milliardaires*, with the exception that American billionaires are here the victim of a vast conspiracy rather than the makers of one. Whereas the earlier series had a band of American plutocrats hiring a scientific genius to provide them with the weapons necessary to conquer Europe and hence obtain economic world domination, in *Le Mystérieux docteur Cornélius*, the partners in a Trust monopolizing American production of corn and cotton become the targets of the insidious criminal association of the Red Hand, whose three mysterious Lords are the scientific genius Cornelius Kramm, his brother Fritz. and the renegade son of one of the billionaires.

The sympathy accorded by the overarching plot of *Le Mystérieux docteur Cornélius* to billionaires in general is an ironic reflection of literary convention. Le Rouge's own political sympathies were on the far left of radical socialism, but in his fiction he was consciously following in the footsteps of numerous French anarchists who had turned to popular fiction as a means of making a living—the most conspicuous examples being Jules Lermina and Michel Zevaco—and who embraced its conventional prejudices with an apparent wholeheartedness while retaining their tongues in their cheeks. The practice went all the way back to Romantic Republicans like Alexandre Dumas, whose fiction was content to embrace an apparent Royalism only subtly undermined by covert cynicism. Le Rouge's cynicism is so subtle as almost to qualify as perverse, but that was entirely typical not merely of him but of a substantial sector of the field of French popular fiction.

The narrative practice of foregrounding the lives of the improbably rich, in the context of a kind of pornography of envy, was already well-established in popular fiction by 1912, and has survived more-or-less unchanged into the present day, but its crucial counterweighting in *Le Mystérieux docteur Cornélius* with a curious kind of mirror-image, in the form of an aristocracy of crime, was a strategy that has undergone a much more extensive and elaborate evolutionary development. The notion of "organized crime" has now become so commonplace that it is not easy for modern readers to appreciate, without an imaginative leap, how unusual that concept was in 1912. It was not original, of course, and

---

[2] Translated in four volumes as *The Dominion of the World*, Black Coat Press: *1. The Plutocratic Plot*, ISBN 978-1-61227-095-1; *2. The Transatlantic Threat*, ISBN 978-1-61227-096-8; *3. The Psychic Spies*, ISBN 978-1-61227-097-5; and *4. The Victims Victorious*, ISBN 978-1-61227-098-2

Le Mystérieux docteur Cornélius has a much more remote but even more obvious model than *Le Conspiration des milliardaires* in Paul Féval's pioneering series of seven *romans feuilletons* featuring *Les Habits Noirs* (1863-74)[3], but Le Rouge's updating of the notion was considerably more adventurous and spectacular than any of the other revisitations of the idea produced before the Great War.

Cornelius Kramm is, in essence, an equivalent figure to Féval's Colonel Bozzo-Corona, and several other characters in the Le Rouge series also have near-equivalents either in the Colonel's coterie, or in the extensive cast of his victims and adversaries. The fact that Cornelius is an experimental scientist rather than a mere bandit, however, has numerous logical ramifications, which transform the fundamental nature of his conspiracy and its procedures. Arguable, they do not transform it nearly enough, because the logical ramifications in question are not extrapolated to what would nowadays be considered an adequate extent, but that is the inevitable fate of many pioneering enterprises; the writers who are boldest in taking first steps are often found wanting when it comes to developing more disciplined and far-ranging explorations. In spite of its limitations, however, the particular criminal conspiracy featured in *Le Mystérieux docteur Cornélius* does have some intriguing precedent-setting features.

Le Rouge follows, in a dutifully faithful fashion, the basic narrative pattern that Paul Féval had adapted and extrapolated from Eugène Sue's archetypal *romans feuilletons Les Mystères de Paris* (1842-43) and *Le Juif errant* (1844-45), in which villainous conspirators working covertly serve as levers of action and (more importantly) menace, while a complex multi-stranded story-line places the victims of their machinations in the narrative foreground, using the jeopardy of which they are initially unaware to generate suspense. Le Rouge deliberately aims for the same kind of complication and entanglement that Sue and Féval made into their hallmark, using particular episodes of action to suggest a much vaster pattern of activity that can only be vaguely glimpsed and tenuously grasped. The addition of a specifically scientific component to that pattern is a significant modification, not so much in matter of detail (in which the crudity of the series is painfully obvious to trained modern eyes) but in terms of the fundamental world-view of the series, which is an atypical but nevertheless intrinsic product of its era.

---

[3] Translated in Black Coat Press editions as *The Blackcoats: 'Salem Street*, ISBN 978-1-932983-46-3; *The Invisible Weapon*, ISBN 978-1-932983-80-7; *The Parisian Jungle*, ISBN 978-1-934543-03-0; *The Companions of the Treasure*, ISBN 978-1-934543-26-9; *Heart of Steel*, ISBN 978-1-935558-05-7; *The Cadet Gang*, ISBN 978-1-935558-45-3; *The Sword-Swallower*, ISBN 978-1-61227-024-1.

The notion of a criminal scientist employing his genius in the service of a vast criminal enterprise was not entirely new, and it must have seemed only logical in 1912 that anyone who was actually to undertake a large scale twentieth-century enterprise in plunder, making virtual war on a technologically-progressive society, would need scientific expertise in order to secure the necessary melodramatic inflation of its enterprise. That logic was, however, conspicuously lacking in much of the crime fiction of the era, and remarkably tentative in many of the instances in which it was manifest. Le Rouge is tentative too, but was nevertheless in the forefront of the early-20th century evolution of what was eventually to become a major literary mythology, fated to undergo an extraordinary elaboration and sophistication in the course of the century.

Although dismissive critical parlance tends to lump all antisocial geniuses together as "mad scientists," there are, in fact, several distinct categories of such alienated outsiders, and Cornelius Kramm is an archetype of "rational" unscrupulousness rather than irrational insanity; his ruthlessness, utterly untainted by sentimentality, is supremely orderly, without the slightest apparent hint of arbitrary delusion, paranoia, or even monomania. Admittedly, however—in consequence of the author's literary method—the reader never has any substantial access to the doctor's thought processes, so it remains possible that his apparent rationality is merely a cover for a mentality that is far stranger and more colorful in its intellectual riches. That possibility would not be out of keeping with the spirit of the exercise, given the deliberately deceptive narrative treatment afforded to the materially rich.

The format of Le Mystérieux docteur Cornélius is also somewhat unusual, and many of the work's idiosyncrasies are side-effects of the differences in strategy forced by producing a weekly part-work in substantial episodes rather than a more traditional serial. The individual parts of daily newspaper serials were generally between 1,500 and 2,000 words long, and when weekly periodicals ran serials they often retained that length or, at least, retained the basic philosophy of serial fiction, in which the entire work was supposed to be consistent and coherent. When episodes were considerably longer, as became standard in serials run by monthly periodicals, they were, effectively, slices of novels that had been carved from a whole, generally into two, three or four tranches. By contrast, the format and strategy of Le Mystérieux docteur Cornélius is much more similar to that of a contemporary TV drama series, in which each individual episode is encapsulated, but in which there is also a "running narrative" spanning the entire series. In essence, Le Rouge's enterprise is a hybrid of a segmental series and a true serial, and it was one of the first works to explore and experiment with the methodology of that kind of endeavor.

Inevitably, Le Mystérieux docteur Cornélius now seems painfully crude by comparison with the TV series that have now brought the methodology in question to a remarkable level of expertise, but it must be remembered that Le Rouge was a pioneer on largely untrodden ground, and that he was not working in highly-organized circumstances similar to those in which teams of modern TV script-writers operate. He was making up his story as he went along, working in real time, although one thing he probably did share with modern TV writers was the uncertainty as to whether his project might be abruptly cancelled part way through, or whether it might instead have to be extrapolated into a further set of episodes to meet reader demand. It is highly unlikely that he was able to determine in advance how many episodes *Le Mystérieux docteur Cornélius* would eventually contain, and he had somehow to cope with all the planning difficulties associated with that uncertainty.

What definitely would have been planned in advance was the length of each episode, of approximately 20,000 words (although the later episodes tend to fall increasingly short). It is worth noting that producing six episodes of a daily serial per week only required a writer to produce some 10,000 or 12,000 words in the week, and that Le Rouge was therefore committing himself to double the traditional burden. The great heroes of feuilleton fiction, Paul Féval and Ponson du Terrail, frequently had two serials running simultaneously, and occasionally more, so there is no reason why a hardened pro like Le Rouge should have had the slightest difficult grinding out 20,000 words a week, even if it was not the only work he was doing at the time—he was an active journalist who produced filler material for *Le Petit Parisien*, on a routine basis—but the mere fact that he had to do it every week with clockwork regularity, undoubtedly getting uncomfortably close to his deadline on many an occasion, must have generated particular strains, which often show through in the structure, pace and detail of the individual episodes.

One of Le Rouge's stratagems, in coping with these ongoing and regularly-repeated challenges to his ingenuity and imagination, was a kind of literary cannibalism. Not only did he routinely fall back on echoing the works of other writers, but he also re-employed motifs that he had previously used himself, and appearances strongly suggest that a handful of the episodes were originally independent short stories that were hastily revamped in order to fill a gap in the schedule of the new narrative. Indeed, Jean-Luc Boutel's excellent website *Sur l'Autre Face du Monde*—one of several invaluable internet enterprises making use of the collective expertise of hobbyist collectors and the new research facilities offered by *gallica* in the literary archeology of imaginative fiction—recently revealed that the very first episode is, in fact, a revised version of "Le Spectre mortel," a novelette published in *Le Globe Trotter* in November 1907 under the pseudonym of "Major Carl Bell." (The pseudonym has subsequently been found attached to a periodical version of another story that was also published under Le Rouge's own name.) Francis Lacassin observes in the bibliography he compiled for the Bouquins omnibus that several incidents from the earlier four-part serial *Le Voleur des visages* (1904) are recycled in the plot of *Le Mystérieux docteur Cornélius*, and the likelihood is that the stories contained in episodes 5,

10, 13, 14 and 16 all had some kind of existence prior to their readaptation to and incorporation within the ongoing enterprise.

Given all of this, it is hardly surprising that *Le Mystérieux docteur Cornélius* is, to say the least, patchy. Indeed, it is not far short of being a complete mess, and some readers might feel that all the excuses in the world cannot redeem its obvious flaws. Nevertheless, it remains a work of more than merely historical interest. It is undoubtedly primitive, and its habit of introducing ideas that are full of apparent potential and them ignoring that potential completely in subsequent episodes eventually becomes annoying as well as absurd, but its very discordance has a certain charm and esthetic appeal. It is not surprising that Blaise Cendrars loved it—or, indeed, that several of the apostles of surrealism loved *feuilleton* fiction in general, because it seemed to them to be almost a kind of "automatic writing," pulled straight from the subconscious wellsprings of imaginative inspiration without any elaborate intervention and processing by rational consciousness.

Gustave Le Rouge's work in general has a quality of raw immediacy that adds a certain fascination even to its frequent failures of logic and plausibility; seen as a whole, and from a certain distance, it becomes obvious that the individual episodes and underlying story of *Le Mystérieux docteur Cornélius* only move because everyone involved in the plot routinely behaves like a complete idiot, but that is probably not the right way to read and consider the work; it is, quintessentially, a narrative in which momentary incidents are far more important than the overarching plot, in which the narrative surge is everything, and the ideative background is only there to provide affective coloration, in the currency of ever-present menace and imminent peril. Its utter lack of sophistication is, seen from one viewpoint, its most crippling weakness, but there is an alternative viewpoint from which it becomes its most compelling charm.

This kind of fiction is not the sort that is produced in the first instance with a view to a second draft that will repair its faults—quite the reverse. Le Rouge sold his works outright as soon as they had materialized from his pen (unlike many *feuilletonists*, he did not dictate to an amanuensis), in spite of the fact that he realized early on in his career that it was economic lunacy to do that, because as soon as they were done, he wanted nothing more to do with them. He might well cannibalize their substance for other works in future, but they would be other works, not mere revisions done prior to publication, or between editions, in a quest for improvement. According to Cendrars, when the poet expressed amazement that his friend was not receiving any payment for reprints of his work, Le Rouge proudly proclaimed that he was, in consequence, a free man—by which he meant, we must presume, given the enormous amount of journalistic hackwork he produced, not that he was free from obligation to the people who paid him for work but that he was free from any further obligations *to the work*.

Le Rouge was, above all else, a spontaneous writer, who moved from inspiration to final product with the minimum possible intermediation—the complete opposite of a writer like Gustave Flaubert, who would search all day and all night, if necessary, for *le mot juste*, and experiment relentlessly with a host of alternatives before advancing his text. Perhaps Flaubert's is "the right way" to produce authentic literature, but it is not the only way to write, and if literary marketing history has demonstrated one thing above all others, it is that readers do not always appreciate that kind of narrative labor, and that many of them are extraordinarily stubborn in preferring the alternative. Like Eugène Sue and Paul Féval, in whose footsteps he was consciously following, Gustave Le Rouge was a writer who valued speed and volume of production far more than elegance and attention to detail, and he became one of the most inventive employers of the literary methodologies appropriate to that kind of production—and to his credit, he was far less dependent on repetitive formularization than most contemporary and subsequent writers of a similar stripe. He was a producer of hypotheses, not disciplined tester of developed theories, but in that capacity, he helped to provide raw materials in which later writers in the overlapping margins of crime fiction and speculative fiction were subsequently to find rough diamonds, and he was a paradigm example of sheer zest.

One thing that Le Rouge was careful to conserve, among so much that he simply threw in and threw away, while shaping the overarching plot of *Le Mystérieux docteur Cornélius* was Dr. Cornelius himself. He probably never intended to write a sequel to the series, although he would presumably have extrapolated the initial series further had he not run out of inspiration—or, more likely, received orders to cut and run from a publisher who saw sales inexorably dwindling—but he was careful nevertheless to leave that possibility open. Perhaps he was influenced in that by his awareness of the horrible difficulties that Paul Féval got into as a result of unwisely killing off his arch-villain in the first volume of what he did not know at the time would become a series, but the lesson Le Rouge took from the example was not a crude economic one; it was an awareness that there are certain kinds of characters that need to be immortal, and who never should be killed off, no matter what the conventional accountancy of moral credit and debit might prescribe. Some books never should be balanced, and *Le Mystérieux docteur Cornélius* is an archetypal example.

Much of Le Rouge's text is, of course, frankly ludicrous, especially its geography. American readers, in particular, will undoubtedly find his accounts of New York, Florida and San Francisco amusing in their frank absurdity. Its ludicrousness is, however, one of its most endearing features, and the casual flourishes with which he introduces bizarre new materials into his plot, as he strives with all his might to maintain its variety and impetus, is one of the story's principal sources of delight. In making such moves he sometimes copies blatantly from his models; his introduction of the Gorilla Club into the story undoubtedly echoes Paul Féval's introduction of circus performers into *Coeur d'Acier* (tr. as

Heart of Steel, q.v.) and their subsequent continual presence in the *Habit Noirs* series, but it is worth remembering that Le Rouge, unlike Féval, had apparently worked in a circus, and cultivated certain circus skills, and would very probably have drawn upon that experience even in the absence of the spur.

The most bizarre intrusion of that kind, Lord Burydan, who arrives in the plot a trifle belatedly, but eventually not only displaces its original hero (Harry) but eclipses him entirely, is, one suspects, a straightforward fantasy projection of a fragment of Le Rouge's own personality, ever-ready to go to imaginative extremes in order to avoid a menace far deadlier than the Red Hand or Dr. Cornelius: *ennui*. And that is, in essence, the purpose of the entire project: to provide immediate distraction at any cost. The mercurial aristocrat is, of course, only half of a double act, who can only achieve satisfaction and a heroic role in combination with his other half: Agénor Marmousier, the Latin Quarter poet driven by hunger to seek other employment, who eventually comes to treasure that new employment for its own absurd sake. Agénor fades away too, within the series of episodes, but he is dissolved rather than eclipsed, quietly reverting to his true role as part of the fabric and weave of the work, and, above all, of its coloration.

This translation has been made from the version of the text contained in the Robert Laffont "Bouquins" omnibus published in 1986. Although it is not entirely in keeping with the spirit of the enterprise, I have made the names of a couple of characters whose names are spelled differently in different episodes consistent, and have adjusted the plausibility of a few supposedly English names (substituting "Slug" for "Slugh," for instance, although it is not impossible that the author intended the name to be pronounced "slew"). I have also corrected a few minor errors of trivial nomenclature that might have originated from mere slips of the pen and have added footnotes to a few of the author's blunders and eccentricities, but I have left most of them devoid of comment, considering their erroneousness to be a component of the work's perverse charm.

Brian Stableford

1. THE ENIGMA OF THE BLOODY CREEK

I. The Stolen Ruby

Toward the end of the year 190**, a group of Yankee capitalists had decided to found a city in the Far West, in the foothills of the Rocky Mountains. A month had not gone by when the new city, still devoid of houses, was already linked by three lines to the railways network of the Union. From the beginning, it had been baptized Jorgell City, after the president of the Trust that had created it, the billionaire Fred Jorgell.

The workers came from everywhere; within the first two months, three churches had been built and four theaters were fully operative. Around an area where a few beautiful trees subsisted, in anticipation of a picturesque square, the steel carcasses of thirty-story buildings began to line up. It was a true forest of metal beams, resounding night and day to the rhythm of hammers, the grinding of winches and the gasp of steam-engines. In America, one starts building walls at the top, once the steel frame has been put in place and the elevators installed.

It was a fantastic spectacle to see those aerial lodges perched like birds' nests on the summits of giant steel girders, while the workers feverishly finished filling the interstices of the metal framework with rows of bricks, sometimes even with simple aluminum plate. Further away, entire edifices made of concrete were cast in a matter of hours, using the Edison method.

From the terrace of his palace, where he spent long hours, Fred Jorgell obtained an indescribable pleasure from seeing the new city emerge from the ground with a magical rapidity, hatched in the middle of the desert by the sun of his billions.

By virtue of a kind of superstition, the billionaire had wanted the first stone of "his" city to be laid on the anniversary of his daughter's birth, so that the first birthday of Jorgell City could be celebrated at the same time as Isidora's attainment of the age of twenty.

The celebrations were exceptionally, almost extravagantly, sumptuous, fully worthy of the Amphitryon's colossal fortune. After a dinner served in the winter-garden amid the clumps of lemon-trees, magnolias, jasmines and orchids, there was a ball on the lawns of the illuminated park; but the main attraction was the gifts sent to Isidora and exhibited in a small drawing-room adjacent to the winter-garden. They were regal in their luxury; there was a stream of jewels, the humblest of which must have cost a fortune.

Among all these marvels, a "pigeon's-blood" ruby stood out, whose size and gleam were incomparable. The gem in question would have been worthy of the diadem of an empress; none of the young billionairesses present possessed anything like it.

Skillful detectives and elegantly-dressed detectives mingling with the crowd of guests were there to keep watch on the treasures on display. The brilliant crowd that gathered in front of the great ruby did not take long to thin out, however. The precious stone had been admired, and people were no longer giving it any thought; the feverish tones of a fifty-piece orchestra were drawing the guests invincibly toward the ballroom. The domestics, confident in the vigilance of the detectives, had left.

Soon, the four policemen remained alone in the room with the gifts. In the midst of the general delight and agitation, they were beginning to get extremely bored; they were all yawning competitively.

"I have an idea of genius," one of them said, suddenly. "Since there's no one here, there doesn't need to be four of us."

"What are you getting at?" said the other three, very interested and drawing closer.

"It's quite simple. Two of us can perfectly well go and make a little tour of the buffet."

The proposal was adopted unanimously, by acclamation. A rota was arranged between the drawing-room and the buffet set up in the open in the garden. The detectives rapidly acquired the most joyful humor; they were no longer yawning. On the other hand, their faces became crimson, and, with each new trip to the buffet, they lost a little more of their impeccable correctness. Eventually, with their waistcoats unbuttoned and their ties loosened, they were whistling dance-tunes with a perfect ease.

A moment arrived when the two who had stayed to guard the ruby did not see their absent comrades, who had gone to get refreshments, coming back. Anxiously, they went in search of them—and, naturally, did not come back either.

The drawing-room was empty.

The party was in full swing, and the first rockets of the firework display were bursting over the lake when a rumor flew from one person to another, sowing consternation everywhere.

"The ruby's been stolen!"

"But that's impossible!" cried one young billionaire, the engineer Harry Dorgan. "There are only perfectly honorable gentlemen here!"

The fact was, however, correct; it was necessary to yield to the evidence. The great ruby had disappeared.

It was a trusted domestic, old Paddock, who had noticed the theft and had immediately informed his master.

The news threw the party into the greatest confusion. The dancing stopped; the orchestra stopped playing. Questions, exclamations of amazement and astonishment overlapped in a veritable hubbub.

"Does anyone know who did it?"

"The thief must be found!"

"Yes, yes! At any price."

"That's it—let's find the thief! None of us can be a suspect!"

"Shut the doors—we'll allow ourselves to be searched, if necessary."

"We can even be undressed," added one old lady, blushing modestly.

Fred Jorgell and Isidora were soon surrounded by a circle of guests who were loudly demanding an immediate investigation.

A search was undertaken for the detectives; they were discovered with difficulty, drunk on champagne, sound asleep and snoring in a clump of trees in the garden. They were thrown out scornfully, and Fred Jorgell promised them, by way of farewell, that he would see to it personally, the following day, that instead of being paid they would be sacked without delay.

That job done, the billionaire turned to the crowd of guests and demanded silence with an authoritative gesture.

"Ladies and gentlemen," he said, "I'm sure of the utmost probity of everyone here, and I'm equally sure of the honesty of all my servants. I don't suspect anyone—anyone at all. Permit me not to sadden this joyful gathering with the presence of policemen and the ignominious operation of a search. Will you please forget the larceny, which is, in any case, so far as I'm concerned, of minimal importance.

Isidora added, graciously: "It's a minor misfortune for which I'm already consoled. It's not necessary to interrupt our amusement for such a bagatelle." And the young woman turned, with a smile, to the conductor of the orchestra, who, raising his ebony baton, gave a signal to the fifty musicians installed on a leafy stage. They immediately attacked, in masterful fashion, a tango whose furious rhythm had soon dispersed the glittering crowd of dancers in a quivering swirl.

Isidora had accepted the hand of a young billionaire famous for his elegance, and set the example.

By the time a quarter of an hour had passed the theft of the ruby had been completely forgotten. The ball continued apace, with a joyful verve.

Among the few people who were not dancing was Isidora's brother, Baruch Jorgell. The billionaire's older child, Baruch had very emphatic features, a forceful jaw, thin lips and a scornful gaze. At first sight he gave the impression of being a very energetic person, but arrogant and taciturn. At that moment, he was sipping a glass of champagne with two individuals of grave expression, to whom he seemed to be showing a very particular deference.

"So, Doctor," he said to one of them, "I'll almost certainly come to see you tomorrow."

"Good," said the other, lowering his voice, "but I still have a few recommendations to make..."

"This isn't the right place to talk business," the third interlocutor objected.

"We can go into the garden," Baruch offered.

The other two agreed and the trio disappeared into a deserted pathway.

In the meantime, trusted servants had transported the precious objects presented to Isidora to the young woman's apartment. The small drawing room where they had been exhibited was now empty.

It was that that moment that a young man with a pensive expression went into it. Absorbed in his reflections, the newcomer was talking to himself, paying no heed to whether or not anyone could overhear him. "It's impossible," he murmured, "that the thief could have failed to overlook such a simple idea. If I'd had to take possession of the diamond I wouldn't have done otherwise. Let's see—it will be curious if I've guessed correctly..."

Carefully, the young man extended his hand beneath the monumental sculpted and decorated table on which the gifts had been exhibited. Suddenly, he uttered an exclamation.

"I would have bet on it! The thief has simply fixed the ruby under that table with a little glue. He was sure that no one would think of looking there."

Mechanically, he had taken hold of the precious stone, but, after due reflection, he put it back where he had found it, and ran out into the winter-garden, his face radiant with satisfaction.

A minute later, he accosted Fred Jorgell. "May I have a word, sir?" he whispered in his ear. "I have something very interesting to tell you."

"I'm at your disposal, Mr. Dorgan," the billionaire replied. "What is it about?"

"Why, the ruby, of course."

"You've found a clue?"

"Better than that—I know where the stone is. Come with me."

With an authoritative gesture, he drew the billionaire into the drawing-room and showed him the ruby.

Mr. Jorgell opened his eyes wide. "Thank you," he said. "I'm delighted that the stone has been found, as much for my guests as for my dear Isidora. He added, facetiously: "It's regrettable that your father, the honorable William Dorgan, is a billionaire—you'd make a first-rate detective, Harry."

"Wouldn't I just? It'll be a resource if things go awry. But we've only completed half our task. The ruby has been found; now it's a matter of pinching the thief."

"How are you going to do that?"

"It's quite simple. We have only to leave the ruby where it is. When our thief thinks the moment propitious, he'll come back to collect his booty."

"Perfect! I want to give myself the pleasure of contributing to the arrest myself. Let's hide behind the piano."

"God idea—and dim the electric lights."

Harry Dorgan turned the commutator; the room was invaded by darkness. Immobile, with their hands on the butts of their Browning pistols, the two improvised policemen waited patiently.

They did not have long to wait.

They had only been lying in ambush for a quarter of an hour when a person of tall stature slipped cautiously through the door, which stood ajar, and glided like a silent shadow over the thick carpet, heading slowly toward the table. His stride was uncertain and hesitant; at every step he turned round anxiously; one might have thought that a mysterious instinct was warning him of the presence of people spying on him.

Finally, reassured by the darkness and the silence, he became bolder. It was with a surge as rapid as the pounce of a wild animal that he reached the table and bent down in order to slide his hand underneath.

"There it is! I have it!" he stammered, in a hoarse voice.

For a second, in spite of the darkness the huge ruby gleamed between his fingers with a faint bloody light.

At the moment when Harry Dorgan leapt at is throat, however, while Fred Jorgell turned the commutator, inundating the room with dazzling light, two exclamations rang out simultaneously:

"Baruch!"

"Father!"

The man who was struggling in Harry Dorgan's steely grip was none other than Baruch Jorgell.

With an instinctive gesture, Harry had let go of his prisoner. There was a pregnant silence between the three men, which lasted for several seconds. The old billionaire was inert, astounded, having been struck full in the heart.

Livid with range and shame, Baruch looked at Harry and his father with a venomous expression; then, suddenly recovering his composure, he sent the ruby that he had been holding in his clenched fist rolling over the table, and marched toward the door.

His father barred his route. "You can't just go!" he cried, in a terrible voice. "No, you shan't go. Would you ring the bell, Mr. Dorgan, so that I can send someone to fetch the police."

Harry had moved forward. In a flash, he had glimpsed a means of saving the situation. "Sir," he said, turning to the old gentleman, "let's not exaggerate the extent of a joke that might have been a trifle reckless..."

Baruch had understood; he had only to seize the saving plank that was being held out to him. A honeyed smiled relaxed his featured, which lost their expression of inflexible hatred and harshness.

"Calm down, Father," he said, with a laugh that rang false, "and leave the policemen where they are, please. As Mr. Dorgan immediately guessed, it was a simple practical joke I wanted to play on Isidora, who is too vain and has too many trinkets. I admit that it was perhaps a trifle reckless, but all the humorists would have been with me. Having all the young and old ladies undressed by a detective would have been utterly hilarious. It would have been one attraction more, a veritable crowning glory for your party. How could you think that I, your son, wanted to take possession of a jewel that's no use to me, and would be impossible to sell? It's simply ridiculous."

He added that it was the drunkenness of the detectives that had given him the idea for the trick, to which he hoped that his father would not attach any more importance than he had attached himself.

He continued that speech for the defense for some time, to which Fred Jorgell and Harry Dorgan listened distractedly.

"From anyone else," said the old man severely, "I might perhaps be able to believe everything you've just said. Unfortunately, Baruch, I know you too well..."

"Father!"

"Well, so be it!" Fred Jorgell said drily, cutting of any further speech. "Let's admit the explanation that Mr. Dorgan has so kindly furnished. Now, I have a duty to let our guests know that the ruby has been found...but I can't tell everyone that..."

"Permit me to say," the engineer interjected, "that there's a simple means of getting out of the difficulty. We have only to suppose that one of Isidora's trusted chambermaids took the initiative, at the beginning of the party, of removing the great ruby to the safe. That seems quite plausible."

"Yes, that would fix everything," murmured the billionaire. "People would think that it was a simple misunderstanding." Then, addressing himself to Baruch, he said, in a glacial tone: "As for you, I need to have a serious talk with you. I'll expect you tomorrow evening, at nine o'clock, in my study."

"I'll be on time, Father," Baruch replied, arrogantly. He turned to Harry Dorgan and added, not without irony: "Good night, sir, and thank you very much for all your good ideas." He bowed and went out.

After having warmly expressed his gratitude to the engineer, Fred Jorgell asked him to maintain the most profound silence about the evening's events; then they both returned to the ball.

Harry Dorgan almost regretted having interfered in the affair of the stolen ruby; he took account of the fact that he now had a mortal enemy in the person of Isidora's brother—but he did not want to linger on that thought; he was pleased to be able to go and tell Isidora personally that the gem had been found.

Isidora welcomed him all the more because, among the numerous young men in her entourage, Harry was one of the few for whom she experienced a real sympathy.

When he left his father, Baruch had gone to meet the two gentleman with whom he had previously been in conversation in a deserted part of the garden.

"What's the news?" asked the older of the two, in a low voice.

"Nothing!" growled Baruch, with muffled anger. "It went wrong."

"That's regrettable," the other replied, coldly. "It was a beautiful stone."

"There's nothing to be done in that direction—but I have something else in mind."

"What?"

"Permit me to keep the secret until further notice."

"That's your business," replied the second gentleman. "You know the conditions on which we'll lend our support."

It was on this mysterious note that Baruch took his leave of his two interlocutors. He felt humiliated and exasperated. Furiously, he went to the small building situated at the far end of the park that served him as a laboratory and a library—for Baruch Jorgell, very ignorant in other respects, was a skilled chemist.

A short while after his departure, Harry Dorgan and Isidora found themselves at the buffet near the two gentlemen that Baruch had just left.

"Who are those two fellows?" he asked the young woman. "Their shrewd and cunning physiognomies scarcely appeal to me, I must confess."

"I think, Harry, that your suspicions are unjust," she replied. "Those gentlemen—they're brothers—are held in high esteem in Jorgell City. The older of the two, the one whose face is clean-shaven and wears gold-rimmed spectacles, is the famous Dr. Cornelius Kramm, the man they call the sculptor of human flesh."

"I've heard mention of his prodigious work; people speak very highly of him. And the other?"

"That's his brother Fritz, a rich art dealer."

Harry Dorgan left his enquiry there.

At that moment, the first rays of the sun pierced the cupola of foliage, paling the illuminations and displaying the wan and weary faces of the dancers. There was a general dispersal. While the exhausted musicians played one last piece, unenthusiastically, the billionaire's guests hastened to return to their automobiles, lined up in front of the front steps in the driveway.

The party was over.

II. An Inexplicable Murder

Fred Jorgell's study was fitted out with perfect comfort and marvelously well-equipped for the mighty feats of organization that the billionaire's vast enterprises required. Electric radiators and liquid-air ventilators maintained an even and mild temperature there in all seasons; five telephones and two wireless telegraph posts put him in rapid communication with all the cities in the world; admirable electric filing-cabinets contained countless industrial and scientific documents concerning the most various affairs.

The billionaire only really felt at home in his study, brightly illuminated by day by large windows overlooking the park and the city, and by night by mercury vapor lamps that emitted a soft blue-tinted light. It was from there that orders to buy and sell went out, which sometimes caused a considerable stir in stock markets the world over.

Nine o'clock had just chimed, and Fred Jorgell was busy sending a few urgent letters before going to his club when Baruch came in.

His expression quite calm, he bowed respectfully to his father and stood facing him, in the deferential attitude of a subordinate expecting a reprimand.

Momentarily, the father and son looked one another in the face.

It was Baruch who looked away first. "I've come, as you ordered me to do," he said obsequiously. "I await your orders."

That tone of feigned politeness had the effect of exasperating the old man, whose face went red and whose eyes flashed. "You're a thief," he replied, brutally. "I'm ashamed of having a wretch like you for a son. If you had a little courage, you'd have blown your brains out."

"I don't have the same prejudices as you on that subject," said Baruch, shrugging his shoulders with scornful irony. "I thought it was understood between us that the story of the great ruby was merely an amusing conjuring trick, a humorous joke."

"Do you think," thundered the billionaire, in a terrible voice, "that I was under that illusion for a single second? I know what you're capable of. I've seen your work before—remember the fake bonds you put into circulation!"

At that humiliating memory, the young man experience a stir of revolt; his fists clenched and his physiognomy took on a frightful expression of rage and hatred.

"I won't even try to defend myself!" he roared. "Yes, Father, it's perfectly true that when I hid the great ruby under the table, it was with the firm intention of taking possession of it."

"And you dare to admit it?"

"Why not? The only guilty party in this affair is you. Why leave me without money? I'm now twenty-six years old; I want to live my life! With two or three hundred thousand dollars—which is very little to you—I could launch myself into interesting enterprises. I'm as intelligent and as capable of directing a business deal as anyone in your entourage."

"You've scarcely proved it. You've devoured the fortune you inherited from your mother, and every time that I've confided any capital to you since then, you've dissipated it in a matter of weeks."

"Experience is always costly, but I've acquired enough now; I'm sure of myself, and I only ask to prove it. If, for example, forgetting all our old quarrels, you were simply to give me a hundred thousand dollars..."

"Not even fifty thousand! Not even twenty thousand!" cried the exasperated billionaire, so furious that, in his anger, he pulverized a fragile Murano cup full of rare stamps with his fist. The blood rose to his head; he was choking.

He rang in order to ask for a glass of iced lemonade. It was not until he had drunk it that he continued, slightly calmer. "Don't count in any fashion on my banknotes. I find your request singularly impudent, after what happened yesterday. All that I can do is not to cut off, as I intended to do, the allowance of a thousand dollars a month that I've been giving you since you've been here."

"I've spoken to you frankly, though," Baruch murmured, with a somber and menacing expression. "I was ready to be serious, honestly—too bad! Don't worry—this is the last time I'll humiliate myself by making such a request."

"What are your plans?"

"There's no point in communicating them to you."

The billionaire was more disturbed than he wanted to show by the simultaneously resolute and desperate tone in which his son had pronounced those last words. "Listen," he said, more quietly. "My resolution isn't irrevocable. I know that you're energetic and intelligent. Give me proof of your seriousness and good will, and I'll think about what I can do for you."

At that moment, Baruch was too irritated to understand the importance of that concession. "How long," he demanded, insolently, "do you expect me to await your pleasure and your whim?"

"That depends on you. For the moment, I'm prepared to forget yesterday's adventure, and that's already a considerable indulgence on my part. But take note that, if you don't give me entire satisfaction, I'll disinherit you pitilessly."

"There's no lack of people to encourage you in that, including that hypocrite Harry Dorgan, who, I perceived a long time ago, is paying court to my sister Isidora."

"Don't talk about Harry Dorgan," retorted the old man, vehemently. "I wish you were as serious as he is. Although he's younger than you, he's already running the electric plants of Jorgell City. He's a fellow with a great future."

"Indeed, for I can see that he's been skillful in capturing your trust."

"That's doubtless because he deserves it."

"I don't care, anyway," Baruch went on, shrugging his shoulders. "Let's get back to our business."

"I've just told you my decision."

Baruch looked at his father in a way that almost frightened him. "That's your final word, then? You're refusing to advance me the miserable hundred thousand dollars I've asked for?"

"I refuse. Accept the employment I'm offering you in my Trust; prove to me for a few months that you're capable of good administration, and my coffers will be open to you."

"All right, I won't insist. Perhaps I'll prove to you soon enough that I'm able to make my own way in life, without the aid of your money."

And Baruch left, slamming the door brutally.

The following day, however, he already appeared to have forgotten that violent scene. He appeared at the family table for lunch, as usual, and seemed very cheerful. In the afternoon, he went for a long walk in the park with Isidora, who was perhaps the only person for whom he had any real affection.

Fred Jorgell clung to the hope that the son who had already caused him so much disappointment would not be entirely lost to him, and that it would not take him long to revert to better sentiments.

The billionaire had just returned to is study after the evening meal when Isidora came in without knocking.

"Don't get up, Father," she said, from the threshold. "It's only me."

The young woman was wearing a China-blue crepe dress that discreetly brought out the richness and elegance of her figure. Her tawny blonde hair, in which a string of pearly gleamed, harmoniously framed a calm and symmetrical face that reflected honesty and generosity. Her large sea-blue, almost green, eyes were clear and bold without being impudent, and she possessed the fresh and velvety complexion that seems to be the prerogative of certain American young women. It was in a slightly emotional voice that she said to her father: "You seemed so careworn, even melancholy, that I wanted to come to see you."

"That's kind, my child; you know that your presence, a single smile from you, is sufficient to console all my sadness and heal all the wounds that I sometimes receive in the rude battle for dollars.

"It's necessary to believe," the young woman replied, coquettishly, "that my smile doesn't have its usual power today. Come on, be honest—something's upset you, as on the day of that massive Australian bankruptcy that you didn't want to tell me about."

The billionaire protested feebly: "No, I assure you, my child, that I don't have any serious anxiety."

"Do you have some reason to be displeased with my brother?"

Fred Jorgell frowned and shook his head sadly. "You're well aware, my dear Isidora, that your brother and I have never seen eye to eye. Baruch has an ingrate nature, from which I've never been able to extract anything."

"He seems to have become much more laborious, and especially more docile."

"Let's not talk about him, if you please. It's a subject of conversation that's disagreeable to me."

The billionaire had risen to his feet and was striding nervously back and forth in the large room. Isidora understood that there was no point in persisting. There was such a dissimilarity of character between the father and the son— such an antipathy, even—that they would doubtless never succeed in reaching an agreement.

"Well, so be it," she said, pouting. "Let's set Baruch aside and talk about the party the day before yesterday. You must have been content with it. Even my mot jealous friends have confessed that it was splendid."

"Certainly."

"There was only the incident of the ruby—a simple misunderstanding, fortunately..."

Fred Jorgell made a gesture of annoyance. "Don't talk to me about the ruby," he said, impatiently. "I haven't given it any thought for a long time. Anyway, if I need to tell you the whole truth, I've had an annoyance today, or, rather, a real anxiety."

"And you didn't want to tell me about it," the young woman murmured, in a reproachful tone.

"You can see that it's impossible for me to hide anything from you, but don't worry—it's nothing serious."

"What is it?"

"You know that I frequently have dealings with a textile-manufacturer in Buenos Aires, whom I've often mentioned: Pablo Hernandez. I recently sold him three hundred thousand dollars' worth of cotton of which he's taken delivery. He was supposed to pay me today and I haven't heard from him. That's all the more strange because Pablo is perfectly solvent and very punctilious."

"It is, indeed, very strange."

"The most worrying thing is that he telephoned my yesterday evening to say that he was on his way, bringing me the agreed sum..."

At that moment, someone knocked on the study door.

"Come in!" shouted the billionaire. "Oh, it's you, Paddock. Have you brought me good news?"

Paddock was an old Irishman, a steward, factotum and secretary as the occasion demanded; he possessed Fred Jorgell's full confidence. To the question asked of him he initially responded by shaking his head negatively.

"Pablo Hernandez?" asked the billionaire, anxiously.

"Dead. Murdered."

"But that's impossible!"

"I've seen his cadaver."

Fred Jorgell was violently distressed. "Pablo was a loyal friend," he said. "I'd gladly give the three hundred thousand dollars he owed me to see him still alive..." Then, with a feverish curiosity, he asked: "How was he killed? I want to know everything. I'll spend all the money it takes to have the murderers arrested."

"A strange mystery hangs over the death. Pablo Hernandez was found early this morning on the bank of the little marshy creek at the entrance to the wood on the far side of the factories. He'd been robbed of everything, but what is inexplicable is that his body bore no trace of any wound except for a slight bruise—a little dark patch—behind the ear. The automobile in which he'd arrived, alone, was a few meters away, intact."

"Has there been an investigation?" asked Isidora.

"Certainly," Paddock replied, "but it didn't reveal anything. Dr. Cornelius Kramm examined the body carefully, but it was impossible for him to reach a conclusion. He would have been tempted to conclude, if the victim hadn't been robbed, that it was a fatal apoplexy."

"That's an indecipherable enigma," the young woman murmured.

"The only possible explanation that anyone could suggest," the Irishman went on, "is that Pablo Hernandez had got out of his automobile to carry out some minor repair, and that while he was doing that, he was struck down by the apoplexy. Then a passer-by, some vagabond, who was the first to discover the body, took the opportunity to take possession of his banknotes."

During this explanation, Fred Jorgell remained pensive. "The bandits have pulled off a masterstroke," he said, slowly. "I'm certain that Pablo Hernandez had on his person, in various banknotes and bonds, the three hundred thousand dollars that he was due to pay me today. To me, the crime is evident. There was a veritable ambush."

Neither Paddock nor Isidora challenged that observation. They were both of the same opinion as the billionaire.

"Either way, it's a loss of three hundred thousand dollars for you," said Paddock, after a moment's silence.

"No—Pablo Hernandez was rich, very rich; I know that I'll be paid, but that's of scant importance. Three hundred thousand dollars wouldn't constitute an irreparable loss for me."

Isidora reflected. "Why," she asked Paddock, "has it taken so long for my father to be informed of the tragic death of his client?"

"That's quite explicable, Miss. The identity of the unfortunate Pablo was only recognized an hour ago. I've known since noon that a crime had been committed, but as brawls between Italian and Irish workers aren't uncommon in Jorgell City, I thought that it was a matter of a commonplace murder, and didn't pay much attention to it."

"That's all right, Paddock," said the billionaire, pensively. "Write a note for the newspapers, offering a reward of five thousand dollars to anyone who can provide valuable information pertaining to poor Hernandez' death."

The Irishman went out. Isidora would have stayed with her father, who seemed profoundly affected, for longer, but she understood that he wanted to be alone and withdrew in her turn.

After her departure, Fred Jorgell paced back and forth for a long time, with a nervous agitation, He was simultaneously anxious, irritated and sad. It had been a long time since the burden of his immense fortune and his responsibilities had weighed so heavily upon him.

III. The Brothers Kramm

At the same time that Fred Jorgell learned of the tragic death of his client Pablo Hernandez, Baruch emerged from the isolated building in which he lived by means of a door that let out into the street, to which he had the only key. He could thus go in and out as he pleased, without disturbing any of the servants.

Although it was marked on the official maps of the city, the street only consisted, thus far, of fenced-off plots and heaps of gravel. Baruch crossed it, casually jumping over puddles of water and pot-holes. For some while he followed the unfinished boulevard that traversed Jorgell City, illuminated at intervals by powerful arc-lamps. Finally, he stopped in front of a large cottage of severe appearance.

Baruch Jorgell had arrived at the house of Dr. Cornelius Kramm.

Dr. Cornelius was famous throughout America, but his marvelous cures were of a very particular kind. The doctor was the providence of all those persons, of either sex, who were afflicted by extreme ugliness or some physical blemish and who were able to pay his fees for a very expensive treatment. He straightened crooked noses, reduced the size of copious ears, enlarged eyes, tightened mouths, raised foreheads and rectified heights. In brief, by means of surgery, he treated living substance as a veritably plastic material, which he fashioned according to his caprice.

It was his incontestable dexterity that had earned him the bizarre nickname of "the sculptor of human flesh," by which was familiarly known.

Little was known about Dr. Cornelius' past. He had turned up one day, installed himself magnificently, and since then, thanks to clever advertising, successful cures and his very real knowledge, his reputation had grown steadily.

There was, however, a sinister rumor regarding his initial fortune. Ten years before, it was claimed, Cornelius had been associated, as a physician, with a mining company in the Matto Grosso in Brazil, which had employed more than five hundred black laborers. In spite of active and careful surveillance, thefts were quite frequent. One incident of that sort coincided exactly with the arrival of the doctor: a seven-hundred carat diamond disappeared and all the searches made had been fruitless.

A few weeks went by, and the theft was beginning to be forgotten, when an old black man fell ill and had to be transported to the hospital that Cornelius was running. The latter had no difficulty diagnosing acute peritonitis, caused by the presence of a foreign object in the intestine; he was about to carry out an operation when he remembered the vanished diamond. He was not unaware that the black workers often did not hesitate to swallow the stones they stole, in order to hide them more effectively.

28

Two days later, the patient died of an absorption of a prussic acid capsule prescribed "in error" and the doctor, as he had foreseen, found the seven-hundred carat diamond when he dissected the body. In that same month, the doctor handed in his resignation on health grounds, and left for Europe, where all trace of him was lost.

Franz Kramm's antecedents were also mysterious. He had made a fortune dealing in paintings and other works of art; that was all that could be precisely affirmed on his account. His enemies claimed that he had been part of an international gang of museum-burglars, whose receiver he had remained, but no one had ever been able to furnish proof of this slanderous assertion.

At any rate, those rumors did cause any prejudice against the two brothers; no one who has become rich has failed to be the target of denigration.

At the moment when Baruch rang the doctor's doorbell it as about ten o'clock in the evening; only a few beams of flight were filtering through the interstices of the tightly-closed shutters.

The domestic who came to open the door introduced the young man silently into a waiting-room furnished with severe elegance, already occupied by an individual clad in black who advanced courteously toward the visitor. It was an old Italian named Leonello, who had been in the doctor's service for many years.

"How can I be of service to you?" he asked Baruch.

"I want to see the doctor."

"Unfortunately, that's impossible. The doctor is working."

"He's expecting me," said Baruch, insistently. "Here's my card."

"A thousand pardons," said the Italian, obsequiously, after a glance at the card. "I'll tell him, that you're here."

Leonello came back a few moments later. There was a sarcastic expression on his fleshless face.

"My master will be very happy to receive you," he said, "but he cannot abandon the work to which he is devoting himself, so it will be necessary for you to accompany me to the laboratory."

"What is he working on, then?"

The Italian's shrewd features became even more ironic. "The doctor is busy with an embalming. It's a matter of poor Pablo Hernandez, whose cadaver was discovered this morning. The family telegraphed the doctor asking him to take the necessary measures, and you'll have the privilege of witnessing the operation."

"Thank you," Baruch stammered, his face covered with a mortal pallor, "but I don't care to see such a spectacle."

"I can understand that."

"Tell the doctor that I'll wait until he's finished."

"It might take a long time."

"Too bad—I prefer to wait."

Leonello disappeared. Baruch remained alone, fretfully, prey to anger and impatience.

Finally, the doctor appeared.

Dr. Cornelius Kramm was little more than thirty-six years of age, but his enormous and entirely bald head, his large gold-rimmed spectacles and his thin and clean-shaven face made him seem much older. His features were symmetrical and at first sight, he gave the impression of being a man of powerful intelligence, but his thin lips and his unquiet ferrety eyes, behind the crystal lenses of his spectacles, gave rise to an indescribable unease. He expressed himself with a glacial slowness and dryness.

The two men did not greet one another formally. Now they were free of witnesses, there was no need for banal gestures of politeness.

"For lack of the great ruby," Baruch said, "I have the bonds I mentioned."

"I know that better than anyone," Cornelius retorted, cynically, "since I've just finished embalming their previous owner."

Baruch did not flinch. "I'd like the money straight away," he said.

"So be it, then. Let's go to my brother's house."

Nothing further was said. Cornelius picked up a small electric lantern and guided his guest through the paths of the garden to an iron door that connected the properties of the two brothers.

Having gone through that door, they found themselves in a vast hall, literally crammed from floor to ceiling with heaped-up paintings and statues of all times and all schools. In an empty space contrived in the middle there was a desk, seats and a large safe sealed into the wall.

Cornelius and Bruch had hardly had time to sit down when Fritz, doubtless already alerted, appeared on the far side of the hall.

The dealer in curiosities was entirely different, in terms of physical appearance, from his brother the doctor. Whereas Cornelius was thin, emaciated and morose, Fritz was corpulent, rubicund, jovial and extremely polite in his manners and gestures. He was what we in France call a *bon viveur*.

His benevolent smile and his clear gray eyes full of frankness rendered him very likeable at first, but if one observed his over-developed jaw, his large ragged ears and his enormous short-fingered and round-thumbed hands attentively, one was much less reassured.

On perceiving Baruch, Fritz went straight toward him, holding out his hand. "Delighted to see you," he said. "Oh, I knew that your visit wouldn't be long delayed; I was almost expecting you."

Baruch breathed more freely; that cordial tone, real or feigned, put him at his ease.

"You've guessed what brought me," he said.

"Of course. You need banknotes."

"As you say..."

"Let's see the bonds."

Baruch took a fat morocco-leather wallet out of his overcoat pocket, but he blushed and became anxious when he suddenly noticed the name of Don Pablo Hernandez embossed in golden letters in one of the corners.

"That," said Cornelius, in his harsh and gruff voice, "is a little souvenir that I don't advise you to keep, Master Jorgell."

Fritz Kramm immediately intervened, with conciliating gestures. "All right—one can't think of everything, of course. But let's see the bonds." He took the wallet from Baruch's hands. "Oils, coppers and rubbers—excellent; the majority are on the rise; the man who bought them was far from being a fool. Except...look, not one is made out to the bearer. No one but me can negotiate those, and not without risk. Let's count up. There are three hundred thousand dollars' worth, so I can give you, as agreed, a hundred thousand dollars in bank-notes and gold."

Baruch made a movement of protest, which was quickly suppressed.

"I believe," Fritz continued, without giving him time to speak, "that my proposition is perfectly equitable: a hundred thousand dollars for me, who accepts the shares and obligations, which will be difficult to negotiate; a hundred thousand dollars for my brother, who has signed the medical report; and a hundred thousand for you, who..."

"I haven't made any protest," Baruch interjected, hurriedly.

"I believe that we understand one another perfectly."

With the scrupulous and placid gestures of an honest tradesman, Fritz went to the safe and took out a wad of banknotes, which he handed to Baruch.

"There," he said, with a broad smile. "The sum is all ready; count it. I think the number is correct, but anyone can make a mistake."

"No need," replied Baruch, stuffing the banknotes into his pocket. "Thank you. It's not impossible that I'll have further occasion to take advantage of your kindness."

"Entirely at your service."

Baruch took his leave.

Fritz insisted on escorting him to the door to the street, and they separated after having exchanged a firm handshake.

Fritz returned to his brother. When they were alone in the great hall with the paintings, facing the safe, they exchanged a singular smile.

"I believe we have him," said Cornelius.

"Oh, he's ours now," Fritz agreed, "well and truly ours. He's very head-strong, though; I fear that he might not be a docile instrument."

"Everyone becomes docile when they fall into our hands," the doctor affirmed, with a sinister grimace. "I can only see one dark spot in our plants—young Harry Dorgan."

"We'll think about that. It requires mature reflection. I think we've worked hard enough for one day." The two brothers left their conversation there and went their separate ways. Cornelius went back to his laboratory. Fritz changed his clothes in order to go out and spend the rest of the evening with a rich coal-merchant who was one of his best clients, to whom he had furnished an entire gallery of paintings.

In the meantime, Baruch had hailed a taxi and had himself taken to the celebrated Black Bean Club.

IV. The Black Bean Club

The Black Bean Club was an institution possessed of a very American originality. It consisted of forty active members, all bachelors, and a large number of honorary members, married or not. Every year, on New Year's Eve, after a splendid banquet, lavishly washed down with claret and extra-dry champagne, the *maître d'hotel* ceremoniously deposited on the table a silver-plated urn that contained thirty-nine white beans and one black one.

It was a solemn moment.

With eyes blindfolded, each of the members of the club, beginning with the president, took a bean from the silver-plated urn in turn. Whoever drew the black bean was required to marry within a year and, ceasing to be an active member, became an honorary member by right, but the club took responsibility for the cost of the wedding and the young couple, expenses throughout the honeymoon.

If the bride was poor—which rarely happened in that milieu, almost exclusively frequented by the sons of billionaires—the club's funds furnished a dowry.

This interesting association, which had come from a city not far away to establish itself in Jorgell City, was a great success; its members formed an elite into which it was difficult to be admitted.

Baruch Jorgell was only an honorary member, but as people played cards for high stakes at the Black Bean Club, he frequented it assiduously. Baruch was a gambler. He rarely won, though, for want of calculation and reflection; it was with a kind of feverish nervousness that he threw his gold in handfuls on to the green baize. He was ignorant or scornful of the skill of the old professionals who came to garner hundreds of dollars with an insignificant stake.

When Baruch went into the gaming room the session was very animated. There was a certain Mr. Stickmann there, who had arrived in Jorgell City not long before, who was betting with admirable audacity.

Arnold Stickmann, a young man with a fresh and rosy complexion, almost an adolescent, had made a reputation in the society of the Five Hundred by his elegance; in Chicago, and even in New York, he was a trend-setter. He was the man who had inaugurated cravats in gold cloth decorated with diamond florets; on another occasion he had innovated a suit in pink and violet metallic cloth; he had also launched sharkskin knee-boots in which each button was constituted by a small black diamond.

The portrait of that Yankee Beau Brummell was to be found in all the newspapers in the world, and skillful reporters went to interview his tailor, his boot-maker and his shirt-maker to try to find out what he would be wearing the following day. He had been seen to appear on the same day, alternately, in asbestos flannel pajamas, a green suit and a crocodile-skin waistcoat.

Stickmann was, in his fashion, a poet. He translated all his emotions and all his dreams into a new and original costume, meditated for a long time. In the slightest actions of his life he was scrupulously refined; every morning, his manservant scrubbed the gold coins that were to be placed in his purse, and he only ever had new and perfumed banknotes in his pocket.

Such was the man opposite whom Baruch sat down when he entered the Black Bean Cub's gaming room; they exchanged a rapid glance, and instinctively detested one another.

Arnold Stickmann had the bank. Baruch emptied a glass of champagne that a barman handed him and insolently threw a thousand-dollar bill on to the baize.

Stickmann dealt the cards with a sure hand. "Seven," he announced.

Baruch had drawn five.

Stickman collected the thousand-dollar banknote, which was slightly greasy at the edges, with an expression of disgust; in front of him, gold, chips and bills formed an enormous heap, a veritable small mountain.

Impassively, Baruch risked two more thousand-dollar bills.

He lost. His two banknotes went to increase the impeccable Stickmann's pile.

"Again!" said Baruch. And he threw successively on to the baize four, then eight, and the sixteen banknotes. He lost every time.

Very interested, the club's members had al stopped playing; they were following the battle raging between the two young billionaires passionately. Persistent bad luck dogged Baruch, and gold flowed through his fingers like water.

"Shall we have a game of fly?" proposed an old regular, suddenly.

The idea was welcomed with enthusiastic cheers.

"Fly" is an exclusively American game primarily played aboard transatlantic liners to while away the passengers' time.

Twelve of the club members each deposited a banknote on the table; a lump of sugar was placed on each banknote, and the entire audience remained plunged in a religious silence and complete immobility.

Suddenly, a fly that was buzzing around near the electric lights in the ceiling, attracted by the odor of the sugar, flew down. The gamblers and the spectators remained fixed in their statuesque rigidity.

It was an emotional moment. In the great silence, the breath of the gamblers, oppressed by anguish, was audible.

The little creature circled for some time around a tray on which bottles of champagne and whisky were set, and then headed straight or the sugar-lump placed in front of Baruch. The latter could not suppress an imperceptible shudder, which caused the fly to change course. It went to settle on the sugar-lump in front of Arnold Stickmann, who had not flinched.

"A winner!" cried the gamblers, loudly.

With a disdainful smile and a negligent gesture, Stickmann collected the eleven banknotes that were under the sugar-lumps.

The stakes were renewed, but five times in succession, Arnold Stickmann won. One by one, as they had the first time, the gamblers abandoned the game, amazed by that improbable good luck. Again, Baruch and Stickman remained alone, facing one another. There were ten thousand-dollar banknotes beneath each sugar-lump.

The witnesses of the scene were following its phases with that impassioned, almost unhealthy interest that the Yankees bring to every kind of game or sport. No longer playing, in order to leave the field open to the two adversaries, they laid side-bets in low voices.

"Two thousand on Baruch!"

"Two thousand on Stickmann—he's on a streak."

"The luck's bound to turn. Baruch will win!"

"We'll soon see."

"Three thousand dollars!"

"Done!"

In the meantime, the fly, which all gazes were following anxiously, amused itself by playing the coquette, so to speak; it circled around the vast room, drawing away and then coming nearer, only to fly up toward the ceiling again. For a moment, it even placed itself exactly between the two pale and tremulous gambles, as if to mock them.

Suddenly, it landed on Baruch's sugar-lump.

Finally, he had won. Avidly, he took possession of his adversary's stake; the latter was smiling with a detached air, like a man to whom winning or losing a wad of banknotes of any thickness was a matter of absolute indifference to him.

Baruch's supporters gained ground; the luck seemed to have turned. The game continued, as stubbornly as before.

At that moment, an argument broke out among the gamblers that nearly ended in evolver shots. Someone, without meaning any harm, had lit a cigar, the smoke of which was capable of influencing the insect at the moment when the destiny of the game was being settled. The unfortunate smoker, scolded by everyone, had to throw away his cigar and make his apologies

This time, Baruch put twenty bills under a sugar-lump, and won.

Still smiling, Stickmann took fifty banknotes out of a pigskin wallet. Without a second's hesitation, Baruch placed an equal number in front of him.

The game was becoming grandiose, but the fly, sufficiently gorged on sugar, had flown out of the open window. The players and side-betters were furious.

There as a moment of forced calm, but the flies asleep near the moldings in the ceiling did not manifest the slightest intention of disturbing their slumber, and the creature that had so far played such a sterling role seemed to have gone for good.

The conversations resumed their course, cigars were relit, and trays laden with glasses of extra-dry and incendiary cocktails were circulating.

There was already talk of playing something else—organizing bridge or poker tables—when, abruptly, with a joyful buzz, the fly, undoubtedly the same one, came back in triumphantly through the window and began to circle, uncertainly, above the gaming table.

"The quarter of an hour hasn't passed!" clamored the spectators, with one voice. "The bets stand; the game's on!"

Instantly, the cigars were extinguished, and in the room, so noisy a few moments before, the most religious silence and the most perfect immobility reigned. Everyone was thinking privately that it had been a long time since such a fine contest had taken place at the Black Bean.

This time, the contest was brief. After a minute, without the slightest hesitation, the fly settled on Baruch's sugar-lump. He won the fifty thousand dollars.

Stickmann handed them to him with the most gracious smile.

"My compliments, Master Jorgell," he said. "The evening's honors go to you. But don't you think we've played enough for one evening? For myself, I find my head's becoming a little heavy."

Baruch was astonished; he did not understand that sudden moderation. "I'm ready to continue," he said.

"No, that's sufficient for today. You'll certainly have another opportunity to give me my revenge. I'll be here for a fortnight, perhaps longer."

"As you please," Baruch murmured, nonplussed. "I dare say that one of these gentlemen will be delighted to take your place."

No opponent presented himself, however. With the particular superstition of gamblers they were all convinced that the luck had changed and that Baruch would win for the rest of the evening.

"Besides which, it's getting late," said Stickmann. "It would be wise, in my opinion, to go home to bed, after having drunk one last glass to the health of the fortunate winner."

That motion rallied all votes. The gaming room as deserted for the bar, and a joyous toast was drunk. Then the members of the club retired in small groups.

Bizarrely enough, Stickmann seemed to have suddenly recanted his aversion for Baruch. They conversed amicably for some time, and went into the elevator together.

As they were going down, Stickmann asked Baruch whether he had his automobile, and, on his negative reply, offered to give him a lift and drop him off at his door. Somewhat astonished by that kindness, Baruch accepted.

When they had taken their places in the luxurious electric coupé, the conversation did not take long to take a confidential turn.

"Listen, my dear opponent," said Stickmann, "I'm going to be entirely frank with you and tell you a secret."

"I'm listening," Baruch murmured, wondering what the other was getting at.

"As you know, I went to the party given by your father a few days ago."

"Indeed. I remember seeing you dancing a Scottish reel with my sister."

"That's precisely what it's about. I've never admired anything so much as the grace, charm and liveliness of that delightful young woman. I marveled at her intelligence as much as her beauty."

"And, naturally," Baruch put in, with a slightly ironic expression, "you're in love with her?"

"Madly in love! I intend to ask Mr. Jorgell for her hand in a few days."

"Good luck," said Baruch, still mocking. "But I don't see how I can be useful to you. As you probably know, I don't have any influence over my father, and very little over my sister."

"All that I'm asking of you, for your part, is not to be hostile to me."

"You can certainly count on my most benevolent neutrality, my dear Arnold. But I ought to tell you that Isidora has already refused a considerable number of brilliant suitors."

"That's no reason to hold back," the king of fashion replied, arrogantly. "Isidora will have to settle on someone, some day."

"Let's hope that it will be you. But I believe this is my destination. Don't worry—I'll keep your secret. A thousand thanks for your generosity, and we'll meet again at the Black Bean soon!"

The two young men parted, with every appearance of the utmost cordiality.

Stickman thought he had taken a step of very skillful diplomacy. In that, he was greatly mistaken. Baruch, who had previously had nothing against him but an instinctive antipathy, now detested him wholeheartedly. As he went back into the drawing-room on the ground floor of the pavilion in which he lived, he gave free rein to his bilious humor.

"The popinjay! The imbecile!" he exclaimed. "Does he imagine, then, that my sister will be immediately infatuated with him? He's doubtless counting on winning her heart by means of the excellent cut of his suits and the chic of his cravats. Isidora would have to be very stupid to grant her hand to that pretentious manikin, good for nothing, at best, but standing in a tailor's window..."

While talking to himself thus, Baruch had taken out of his pocket the banknotes that he had stuffed in pell-mell when he left the gaming room.

He counted them. There were a hundred and sixty—but that significant augmentation of his capital, rather than calming him down, further increased his ill-humor toward Stickmann.

""I understand now, why the clown refused to continue playing and let me take my winnings away. If anyone divines his intentions, I'll be the laughing-stock of the club members. Perhaps he thinks that I'll be grateful to him! I know that he detests me, deep down; he's scarcely addressed two words to me before."

Baruch was, before anything else, a proud man, and Arnold Stickmann, in thinking that he was being agreeable to him, had found a means of wounding his self-esteem to the quick.

The following evenings, at the Black Bean, the gambling was furious. Baruch was intent on proving to everyone that he was not, as people said, held in a state of dependence by his father, and that he had capital of his own at his disposal. He would have liked, in order to complete that demonstration, to lose a large sum playing against Stickmann, but the latter, faithful to the strategy that he had initially adopted, made every effort to let him win.

He's trying to humiliate me, thought Baruch, angrily, *to prove to me that he possesses a fortune of which he has free disposition, and business affairs that he administers himself, while I, thanks to my father's avarice, don't have any of that. He doubtless wants me to understand that, when he becomes Isidora's husband, I'll be able to count on his liberality. But he mustn't know me very well to make such a calculation, and I'm not a man to put up with insults for long!*

Meanwhile, the other members of the Black Bean did not have the same reasons as Arnold Stickmann to be careful of Baruch Jorgell; so, as they took advantage of his impetuosity and distraction, the wad of banknotes got thinner every day.

Soon, of the hundred and sixty bills, no more than thirty remained.

The proud Baruch did not want to believe the evidence of his own eyes that he was not rich enough to gable with opponents who almost all had billions at their disposal, and, instead of employing his money in some fruitful speculation, as he had originally planned to do, he played recklessly, without wanting to envisage the consequences of such conduct.

At the same time, Arnold Stickmann paid Fred Jorgell two or three successive visits. Nothing came of their conversations, but the king of fashion manifested a joviality and zest that were previously unknown. As for the costumes he inaugurated every day, they were in pastel shades, and dazzlingly chic.

V. A Sensational Mystery

With its clumps of orange-trees, jasmines, magnolias and orchids, its spurting fountains and its pathways carpeted with thick verdant moss, Fred Jorgell's winter-garden was a place of freshness and enchantment in all seasons. The palms and banana-trees there formed veritable arbors, whose broad leaves rose up to the crystal cupola in gilded arches.

Isidora spent long hours there in the company of a worthy Scotswoman, Mrs. MacBarlott, whose only function was to read to her and accompany her on her walks.

Every day, after lunch, they came to pay a visit to a large aviary of silver filigree filled with parrots, cardinals and other brightly-plumaged tropical birds. It was one of their favorite distractions.

They were occupied, one day, in reducing cakes to crumbs for their little feathered guests when Fred Jorgell suddenly appeared at a turning in a grove of Florida lemon-trees planted in superb Italian faience vases. Isidora immediately ran toward him.

"I thought you'd already gone back to your study," said the young woman. "Isn't it extraordinary for you, the ultimate businessman, to have time to waste in our company?"

"You know very well, my dear child, that I never have time to waste. Time is too precious a merchandise to be squandered. If I've come down, it's because I have to talk to you seriously.

"I'll leave you alone," said Mrs. MacBarlott, a well-brought-up individual.

"Isidora," the billionaire continued, "I have reproaches to address to you."

"To me?" said the young woman, in surprise. "If I've incurred your discontent, I assure you that it was entirely involuntary."

"Oh, it's not serious, and I wouldn't want to cause you and chagrin for so little. This is what it's about. I think that, for some time, young Harry Dorgan has been very assiduous in your regard."

"Oh, Father!" Isidora protested, her face coloring slightly.

"I hold Harry in great esteem as an engineer," the billionaire went on, more gently, "but I wouldn't want his visits to give rise to unfortunate interpretations. At this moment above all, I have particular reasons for your two names not to be linked in the mouths of gossips, as has happened in the past."

"I assure you," said Isidora, in a frank and calm tone, "that I have no reason to reproach myself for any flirtatiousness."

"I don't doubt it, but it's true nevertheless that Harry Dorgan is following you around like your shadow. He finds the means to be at all the receptions to which you're invited, and he dances and flirts with you, taking possession of you for entire evenings. At the theater, at concerts and at garden-parties, one is sure to see him at your side."

Becoming more animated as he spoke, the billionaire's face had become inflamed, and it was with great energy that the concluded: "Truly, it's becoming scandalous! It's necessary to put an end to it."

"Father," Isidora replied, with a little emotion in her voice, "I confess to you that I don't understand! You've come to talk to me as one takes to a French demoiselle, kept out of sight since birth in a convent and narrowly supervised in her slightest actions. As a daughter of free America, I've been brought up freely, and I hope to continue to use that liberty, since I've never made any bad use of it..."

"However..."

"I don't deny Harry Dorgan's assiduity, but if I like to have him around, it's simply because he's more intelligent, more cultivated and more likeable than all the sons of trustees who, emerging from the Stock Exchange and running after cottons and oils, no longer know what to say." In a deliberate tone, she added: "Besides which, haven't you told me yourself that you'd allow me perfect freedom in choosing a husband?"

"I haven't changed my opinion," stammered Fred Jorgell, with some embarrassment, "but I hope that it isn't Harry Dorgan that you've chosen."

Isidora could not help smiling on seeing her father's frightened expression.

"Don't worry," she said. "Harry Dorgan is a very likeable companion, but nothing more, so far as I'm concerned. I appreciate his conversation, nourished by serious reading, and I like his frankness, but that's all. If I'd decided to take him for a husband, you'd have been the first to know."

"I know that," said the billionaire, a trifle confused. "I've never doubted your honesty...but I have something else to tell you."

"I'll wager," the young woman replied, maliciously, "that you have some new suitor to propose to me?"

"That's true, in fact. I've received a proposal from a young man who, in my opinion, would suit you perfectly. His fortune is equal to yours, and he's already at the head of several important businesses."

"What about his physical appearance?"

"Grand elegant, distinguished intelligent—he'd be an ideal husband.

"If I accept him. What's his name?"

"Arnold Stickmann."

Isidora burst out laughing. "Well, no," she said, "the king of fashion won't be my husband, I can tell you that right away. I have a veritable aversion for young men who make clothes their predominant preoccupation. It's an indication of a profoundly egotistical character. I'd be obliged to be jealous of dandified waistcoats and cravats. Offer me someone else if you wish, but quite sincerely, the honorable Arnold Stickmann isn't my cup of tea."

The billionaire was direly irritated. He made a supreme effort to convince his daughter. "You know very well, my dear Isidora, that I would never try to marry you off to someone against you will, but if you wanted to give me pleasure, you'd consent to receive Mr. Stickmann's visits occasionally. I'm convinced that when you know him better you'll lose some of our prejudice against him."

"Futile, Father," said the young woman, frostily. "I've seen Mr. Arnold Stickmann often enough to have had time to form an opinion on his account."

The conversation as abruptly interrupted by the arrival of Mrs. MacBarlott, who came into the greenhouse like a whirlwind. The Scotswoman's face was distressed, and she was brandishing a copy of the principal local newspaper, the *Jorgell City Advertiser.*

"What's happened?" demanded Isidora, who had never seen her faithful companion in such a taste.

"It's frightful! Extraordinary! Read this…"

Fred Jorgell took possession of the copy of the *Advertiser* and went mortally pale on reading the headline printed in enormous letters:

ANOTHER CRIME IN JORGELL CITY
ARNOLD STICKMANN MURDERED

In spite of all his energy, it was with an unsteady voice that he read aloud the article printed on the first page of the local paper: "An odious murder has thrown consternation into our peaceful and hard-working city. The honorable Arnold Stickmann was killed and robbed last night. No clue permits the hope that he murderers will be discovered. Let us remember that this is the second murder in a month in Jorgell City, in the same mysterious circumstances.

"These are the facts in all their enigmatic horror:

"The unfortunate Arnold Stickmann had spent the evening cheerfully at the Black Bean Club in the company of his friends. He had won a considerable sum at baccarat and bridge; it was doubtless that fact, known to his murderers, that caused his death. Very happy with his gaming, Mr. Stickmann boasted rather imprudently about his winnings. It was common knowledge that the unfortunate king of fashion always had a large quantity of banknotes in his wallet.

When he left the club at about two o'clock in the morning, Arnold Stickmann climbed, as usual, into his automobile. According to the chauffeur, a trusted servant—whose talk was nevertheless carefully monitored—a breakdown occurred about half way between the club and the Chicago Hotel, where Mr. Stickmann was staying.

"The young billionaire did not have the patience to wait for the repair to be carried out. 'Return to the hotel without me,' he said to the driver. 'The weather's fine, and it wouldn't displease me to go a little way on foot, while smoking a cigar.'

"Jorgell City, as everyone knows, comprises two principal agglomerations separated by a low marshy valley still covered with thickets and traversed by a stream, over which a wooden bridge has been provisionally established. It is a little further upstream that the electrical plants have been established which supply light and energy to our city, under the competent direction of the engineer Harry Dorgan. Such was the place, absolutely deserted at that hour of the night, that Arnold Stickmann had to traverse in order to reach the agglomeration in which the Chicago Hotel is located.

"The night passed without Mr. Stickmann being seen to return; very anxious, the hotel manager immediately sent the deputy manager and two black men to search for him. It did not take them long to discover the cadaver of the unfortunate man lying a few meters away from the beaten track, under a bush—which explains why the chauffeur had not seen him when he returned to the hotel after finishing his repair.

"The body bore no trace of violence save for a small dark patch on the back of the neck. The wallet stuffed with banknotes had disappeared, but a large-caliber Browning pistol was found in a trouser pocket, of which the victim had not had the time to make use. The autopsy immediately carried out by Dr. Cornelius Kramm, assisted by Dr. FitzJames, has not yielded any conclusive result; although Dr. Kramm recognized the symptoms of a cerebral congestion, Dr. FitzJames observed a certain disaggregation of the tissues that are typical of cases of electrocution. Neither hypothesis is readily admissible.

"Let us have the courage to say that we are in the presence of a criminal armed with new means furnished by science, who murders his victims without leaving traces. If the authorities do not take the most energetic measures, we can expect a series of crimes that will leave the sinister exploits of Troppmann and Jack Sheppard far behind.[4]

"One circumstance that several people have noted is that the electric lighting went out last night and was lacking for almost half an hour. It is no doubt thanks to that propitious obscurity that the crime must have been committed."

Fred Jorgell dropped the copy of the *Advertiser*; he was overwhelmed.

---

[4] Jean-Baptiste Troppmann was a French murderer who slaughtered an entire family and achieved a certain celebrity because his execution, in 1870, was witnessed by the Russian writer Ivan Turgenev, who published his reflections on the event. Jack Sheppard was an English sneak-thief, executed (at the same age as Troppmann, 22) in 1724, who became a legendary figure because of his prison escapes, facilitated by the fact that he was so thin he could not efficiently be confined by handcuffs or leg-irons. His notoriety was boosted long after his death by W. Harrison Ainsworth's sensational novel based on his career, *Jack Sheppard* (1839-40).

"No one's life is safe here any longer," he stammered. "That poor Stickmann was full of joy and health the day before yesterday, when we were chatting together tranquilly."

Isidora was profoundly emotional. "Truly," she murmured, "I repent of sometimes making fun of the unfortunate man's pretentious mode of dress."

There were a few moments of anguished silence. There was something frightful about the mysterious death.

Mrs. MacBarlott, however, had picked up the issue of the *Advertiser* that Fred Jorgell had dropped and was scanning it distractedly.

Appended to article that had just been read out was a portrait of Stickmann, followed by his biography and a list of his assets and the shares in the Trust that he possessed.

"There's an interesting note in the stop press," said the Scotswoman. She read: "The municipality of Jorgell City is presently distributing posters advertising a reward of ten thousand dollars to anyone who can discover the authors of the two mysterious crimes. Let us not forget, in fact, that a few weeks ago Pablo Hernandez was found dead in identical circumstances. If the series of these unpunished murders continues, it is of such a nature as to seriously compromise the future of our nascent city by during away, perhaps forever, capitalists and workers. One of the most skilful detectives in Chicago has been summoned. No doubt his sagacious investigations will soon lead to the discovery of the murderer."

The Scotswoman had just finished reading when Baruch came in. He had also just learned about the murder, it seemed, and was holding a copy of the newspaper. "It's terrible," he said, sitting down beside his sister. And his emotion was certainly not feigned, for his pallor was livid.

"What's your opinion?" Fred Jorgell asked him.

"In truth, Father, like everyone else, I don't know what to think. It seems to me, however, that there must be a means of discovering the guilty party. There's an old juridical adage that says: 'Look for the person who profits from the crime.' Perhaps, by conducting a scrupulous investigation, it can be determined which of his enemies had the greatest interest in seeing him dead."

"Arnold Stickmann had no enemies," replied the billionaire.

"Then it's all the more extraordinary." Baruch got to his feet. "I'll leave you," he said. "I'll go in search of news." And he left, rapidly.

He had only taken a few steps along the street when he found himself in the presence of Fritz Kramm, the art dealer. They greeted one another and exchanged a few courteous phrases.

"I was just coming to see you," said Baruch.

"As it happens," Fritz replied, "I have a few words to say to you. Can you imagine that among the bonds that you passed on to me some time ago, there are a number that it's absolutely impossible to negotiate?"

"What are you going to do with them?"

"Nothing. I burned them, and for me, it's a simple loss."

"I understand. How much were they worth?"

"Five thousand dollars."

"I'll return them to you immediately. Let's go to your house, if you please."

"I see that we understand one another right away. That's perfect."

They went into the art-dealer's hall and, without delay, Baruch laid five thousand-dollar bills on the table.

"That's strange," said Fritz, examining the banknotes. "They're all new, and even perfumed. Arnold Stickmann only ever had similar ones in his wallet; it was one of his manias."

"I know," Baruch replied, without flinching, "but I won a great many of them from him at the gaming table."

"Be careful," Fritz murmured between his teeth, "that that kind of gambling doesn't end up ruining you." As his interlocutor remained silent, he added: "You know that a detective of superior ability has been summoned from Chicago?"

"Yes, I read it in the *Advertiser*, but whether he'll be as skillful as they claim, I doubt."

"I advise you to be prudent."

They separated on that recommendation, and Baruch went to the Black Bean Club, where he joined his condolences to those of Arnold Stickmann's other habitual adversaries at the tables.

A week went by; the investigation made no progress. Stickmann's enemies had been sought in vain; he only had friends. According to Baruch, who slyly put the rumor around, only one person could have had any interest in the death of the king of fashion, and that was Harry Dorgan, who, like Stickmann—as everyone knew—was passionately smitten with Isidora. But Harry was esteemed by everyone, and no one took that monstrous insinuation seriously.

VI. A Bloody Series

The arrival in Jorgell City of Mr. Curmer, the detective brought at great expense from Chicago, had been surrounded in profound mystery. It was desirable that he could carry out his investigation without being hindered by anyone, and above all without alerting the murderer.

Mr. Curmer, a pale and puny individual with a worried expression was staying in the most modest hotel in the city, where he had registered as a traveling salesman of leather and furs—an assertion justified by the presence of several suitcases stuffed with specimens. In order to conceal his true profession completely, he had visited the principal businessmen of the city and had even concluded a few transactions—which, he affirmed, encouraged him to prolong his stay in Jorgell City.

While playing his role as a commercial traveler to perfection, however, he collected information. Under the pretext that he was a stranger, he had the story of the mysterious murders at "the Bloody Creek"—that being the name given to the little stream in the valley since Arnold Stickmann's murder—repeated to him fifty times over by different people.

In spite of all his skill, the detective was soon obliged to recognize that he was dealing with an impenetrable mystery. What irritated him the most as that the bonds stolen from Pablo Hernandez had been found in St. Louis, in the hands of perfectly honorable businessmen, who had bought them a few days after the crime, before any prohibition could be placed on them. The people who had sold them had disappeared without a trace.

As for Arnold Stickmann's new and perfumed banknotes, Mr. Curmer had perceived those in the hands of numerous inhabitants of the city, but he could not build any hypothesis on that basis. The king of fashion had gambled for such high stakes at the Black Bean, and had made so many purchases in the city, that it was only natural that his money should have spread almost everywhere.

Mr. Curmer went to see Dr. Cornelius in order to obtain information about the autopsies; he revealed his name and profession and was welcomed admirably. Obligingly, the doctor even showed him photographs of the cadavers and fragments of viscera conserved in jars.

"I believe, Mr. Curmer," he said, "that you'll have a great deal of difficulty clarifying this bloody mystery. Neither I nor my colleague, Dr. FitzJames, who assisted me in the second autopsy, could discover the slightest trace of poison. On the other hand, the bodies bore no trace of violence."

"What about the black marks on the neck?"

"I'm unable to explain them. People struck by lightning sometimes bear similar marks; in addition, the brain and nervous system presented lesions similar to those causing apoplexy and cerebral congestion. The existence of a poison that escapes chemical analysis has to be admitted as a possibility."

While narrating these facts precisely, Cornelius took the detective through so many hypotheses that the latter remained almost completely in the dark, as hesitant as he was beforehand.

Before he left, the doctor asked Mr. Curmer what his personal opinion of the matter was.

"I believe," the latter replied, not wanting, out of professional pride, to confess his ignorance, "that we're in the presence of a very powerful and well-organized association of malefactors, which has a new and terrible means of committing murder. In my opinion, it must be an instantaneous poison that leaves no trace, launched from a distance by means of a dart, the contact of which produces the black mark left on the necks of the victims."

"That's rather ingenious," said Cornelius, "but it remains to be proven."

"I shall try to prove it. In any case, I'm certain to catch the murderer eventually."

"How?"

"I've notice one thing, which is that he never attacks people without money. It's known that I have none, so I can prowl in the vicinity of the Bloody Creek without danger, and I have a plan..."

"In your place, I'd keep it to myself," said Cornelius, tranquilly.

No one, therefore, ever knew what the detective's plan was. Two days later, Mr. Curmer was found dead on the bank of the Bloody Creek. His cadaver bore the fatal black mark on the neck and his convulsed features still expressed a superhuman terror.

This time, there was a veritable panic in Jorgell City. As soon as dusk descended, no one any longer dared to traverse the accused valley.

In spite of all the precautions, the public knew that he murdered man was a detective; the newspapers published his picture and the Chicago Police, informed of the circumstances of the murder, flatly refused to send another agent.

The death was a disaster for the nascent city. Several speculators sold their plots of land and buildings at a loss, and fled. Even the workers—Italians, Germans and Irishmen—deserted the accursed city. Legends were created. It was claimed that the banks of the Bloody Creek were haunted by a skeleton armed with a fiery blade; it had been seen dancing and performing frenetic contortions under the trees in the valley.

Jorgell City was in danger of being abandoned by its inhabitants before it was even finished. In vain, the alarmed municipal authorities promised rewards and organized hourly police patrols. The blow had struck home. For more than a hundred miles around, Jorgell City was reputed to be haunted.

Isidora was consternated; as for Baruch, while affecting a hypocritical chagrin, he was delighted by the difficulties that the paternal enterprise had encountered, and resolved to do everything possible to increase them. Prudently, he only gambled at the Black Bean rarely; he had invested his funds in a mining concern that offered high but reliable returns, and he was already obtaining very respectable dividends.

In the feverishly agitated life of Americans, a month is as long as a century. After that lapse of time, forgetfulness was already beginning to descend over the mysterious murders at the Bloody Creek. Workers and speculators flocked back again. It was possible to believe that the inexplicable and bloody nightmare was over.

Suddenly, there was a fourth mysterious crime.

A French banker visiting the town as a tourist had been introduced to the Black Bean Club. He had played a few hands, displayed banknotes a trifle imprudently, but had left very early. The next morning, his cadaver was found at the accursed spot, robbed. It was discovered subsequently that, in order not to denigrate "their" town, the members of the Black Bean had judged it superfluous to warn the Frenchman about the terrible danger he was running in traversing the Bloody Creek.

This time there was panic, an exodus of at least a third of the inhabitants to neighboring states. Henceforth, it was an established fact: Jorgell City was an accursed, uninhabitable city. Its founder was, quite rightly, desperate. He would have given a hundred thousand dollars to capture the bandits, to deliver the city conclusively from that murderous haunting.

Fred Jorgell, however, set out courageously to weather the storm. The diminution of his dividends did not prevent him from throwing parties as splendid as before, just as frequently.

In the course of one of those receptions, for which a performance by clowns and acrobats provided a pretext, Isidora and Harry Dorgan, who had not seen one another for some time, abruptly found themselves face to face at the corner of a path in the park, brightly illuminated as usual.

They greeted one another affectionately; they were both glad to find themselves distant from importunate eyes. They had begun to converse together when the sound of shrill voices not far away from them reduced them to silence. On the other side of the mimosa bush next to which they were standing a few of guests were casually exchanging their opinions.

Naturally, they were talking about the recent murders.

"After all," said one in a bitter voice, "there's never been a serious investigation; it was necessary to discover the person—and in my opinion, there can only be one—who profited from all these crimes."

"That's talking but saying nothing," said another.

"Pardon me," a third put in, "but I know someone to whom Arnold Stickmann's death was very useful."

"Who, if you please?"

"Young Harry Dorgan, of course, who's better placed, it's said, with Miss Isidora. If the king of fashion had lived, he's the one who would have married the charming young lady. The father had agreed to his request—I have that from a reliable source."

"You aren't, however," the first speaker said, "going to cast any suspicion on that honest young man."

"I'm not suspecting anyone. I'm stating a fact—a bizarre coincidence, that's all..."

Harry hastened to draw Isidora away from the idlers with the viperish tongues.

"Did you hear them?" he said, red with anger.

"It's shameful," the young woman murmured, very emotional, "but such slanders are too base to reach you and me. Let's not think about them anymore."

"On the contrary, I think about them a great deal. Those people have made me understand that it's up to me to clarify the mystery of the Bloody Creek. Henceforth, I shall have no other goal."

"Do that, my dear Harry, try to succeed," she murmured, in a tone softened by tenderness. "I'll help you and encourage you with all my strength."

"The true encouragement, the only efficacious one that you can give me, you know very well."

Isidora's cheeks reddened, and she lowered her eyes. "Shh!" she murmured. "Let's not talk about that. You know full well that my father won't refuse anything to the man who rids the city of the murderers."

"But what about you?"

"I follow my father's wishes," she said, smiling. "Ought I not to obey him in everything?" With a charming gesture, she held out her slender white hands. Harry Dorgan covered them with passionate kisses; he was mad with joy.

"Don't be astonished, Isidora," he said, as he withdrew, "if I don't see you for some time. For the success of the task I'm undertaking it's almost indispensable that people think that we're indifferent to one another, if not completely at odds."

"I'll do anything you wish," said the young woman, with an adorable gesture of submission. "Goodbye, Harry."

"Goodbye, my dear Isidora."

When he left Fred Jorgell's palace Harry Dorgan hurried back to the electric power plant near to which was the cottage in which he lived. Before going to bed, he went to cast a masterly eye over his machines. The gigantic dynamos were humming with an even rhythm; the watchmen were at their posts.

As he went through the garden that separated the plant from the factory he was accosted by an old Indian who was familiarly known as Old Kloum, whom he had taken into his service.

Kloum had renounced the costume of his forefathers a long time ago. He wore neither a head-dress of eagle-feathers nor a necklace of grizzly-bear teeth. He was modestly dressed in a blue overall soiled by machine-oil; his face, tanned like an old sheepskin, was furrowed by long horizontal wrinkles, and he wore two small gold earrings. The workers in the plant often mocked him because he claimed to have conserved the marvelous perspicacity of his ancestors, the scalp-hunters.

Sometimes, even Harry Dorgan had asked how it as that Old Kloum, with his Apache flair, had not yet discovered the Bloody Creek murderer. Kloum, who was blindly devoted to the engineer, contented himself with smiling silently on such occasions.

"Well," Harry said to the old man, "is it today that you'll bring me the scalps of the mysterious bandits?"

"No, Master," Kloum replied, looking a trifle guilty, "but I've discovered something important that no one else knows as yet."

"What?"

"Have you noticed that every time a crime is committed, the electric lights go out for a time in an entire sector of the city. The murderer must extinguish the lights before carrying out his coup. If we knew how he was doing it..."

The Indian's words were a flash of illumination for Harry Dorgan. He wondered how he had not noticed such a simple thing before. Many inexplicable things abruptly became clear to him.

"Thank you, Kloum," he said, excitedly. "Perhaps that's a good idea—I'll think about it. Here's a dollar for your trouble."

And he went into the cottage, wholly preoccupied with the new ideas that the Indian's observation had suggested to him.

Now he discerned a precise glimmer in the tenebrous mystery. Facts to which he had previously attached no importance appeared to him in their true significance. He recalled that on the very night of Mr. Curmer's murder, an entire district of Jorgell City had been deprived of light. Even the riveters who were finishing off the steel carcass of a fifth story had been abruptly plunged into darkness and had almost fallen.

The functioning of the apparatus was, however, perfect. Harry Dorgan was sure of his machines and no defect had been detected at the plant. What, then, had caused the interruptions?

What was evident and undeniable was that every time the electric lights had gone out, a crime had been committed the same night. There was an exact correlation between the two events.

It's certain, the engineer concluded, *that all the victims of the mysterious bandit were electrocuted. The dark patches found on their necks were the burns caused by an electric contact. I already know the most important thing; now it's a matter of determining the method that the murderer used. That, I'll find out!*

Harry set to work the following day.

First of all, he resolved to narcotize the vigilance of anyone who had an interest in tracking his actions and movements. A vague instinct told him that the Bloody Creek murderers were among the circle of his acquaintances; it was a matter of putting their suspicions to rest.

As he had warned Isidora, he suddenly stopped visiting the billionaire's palace, and he let it be known that he had fallen seriously ill. Only Isidora knew the truth, informed by a laconic note transmitted to her by Old Kloum.

Ostensibly, according to what his servants were able to report that they had seen, Harry was confined to his room, going to bed early, coughing and moaning. As soon as everyone was asleep, however, he got dressed, armed himself, and ventured forth into the derelict and fallow terrain, punctuated by small woods, which neighbored the valley of the murders.

He sometimes remained for hours hidden behind a coal-heap, under a bush or behind stacks of steel joists. He undertook those vigils several nights in succession, but without discovering anything new. He came back at dawn, furious and exhausted, covered in mud up to his shoulders, without having seen anything except banal drunken brawls.

He was sure of his facts, though. Dr. FitzJames, skillfully interrogated, had only confirmed his suspicions by repeating that the internal lesions observed in the victims' cadavers were similar in every way to those observed in cases of electrocution.

Furious at not having discovered anything, when he had thought he was on the brink of success, Harry fell into a state of irritation and nervousness akin to neurasthenia. His desire to capture the murderer became an obsession.

He did make some progress in his investigation, however. He understood why the victims had always been struck down in the vicinity of the Bloody Creek, near the bridge. It was because at that location the thick metal cable departing from the plant divided into two branches, one of which illuminated the eastern district and the other the western district of Jorgell City. It was evidently from one of those cables that the murderer drew the electric energy with which he electrocuted his victims. After that discovery, alas, Harry was not much further forward. He had not succeeded in determining the murderers' method of procedure.

The observations he had made, however, had permitted him to limit his surveillance to a narrow area. Exactly four meters from the wooden bridge there was an ancient cedar whose dense foliage firmed a comfortable observatory. Every evening, when he was sure that the lights were out in the servants' bedrooms, he slipped a formidable thirteen-shot revolver loaded with steel bullets into his pocket, which had a range of a hundred and fifty meters and was almost as accurate as a rifle. Then he moved through the darkness to the trunk of the tree, which he scaled cautiously, and remained for hours on end lying on one of the principal branches, completely hidden by the foliage.

Weeks went by, however, without any further result, and he needed all his patience not to abandon the arduous enterprise into which he had launched himself.

He had hours of discouragement, wondering whether the murderers, secretly informed of his enterprise, might be mocking him and abstaining from any further criminal enterprise until he was led by weariness to renounce the surveillance he was carrying out.

He was in that state of mind when, one moonless night, the obscurity of which was further increased by a thick fog rising from the marsh, he took up his habitual post.

Two hours went by. Numbed by the fatiguing position and the immobility to which he was constrained, he was beginning to yield to an invincible need for sleep. His eyes were closing when he suddenly shuddered. He had just heard a dry metallic click, coming from a few paces away.

That slight sound in the silence of the night woke him up completely. Now he was all eyes and ears, with his hand clenched on the butt of his revolver, ready to let himself slide down the trunk of the tree and launch himself forward.

The fog had dissipated slightly. Harry Dorgan thought he could see shadows moving in the bushes. He waited, his heard pounding.

He understood that the moment when he would know the truth was close at hand.

A minute went by, but nothing else happened.

Finally, footsteps sounded on the worm-eaten planks of the bridge.

A man came forward, lurching slightly as if intoxicated. He was carrying an enormous red morocco-leather briefcase under his arm. By the silhouette rather than the physiognomy the engineer recognized a certain Mr. Stewart, a trade association and land inspector, one of the most important people in the new city, whom he had often seen at the Black Bean Club.

Mr. Stewart came over the bridge, not without difficulty, making numerous sidesteps in either direction, seemingly completely drunk. He must have been, for him to have chosen such a route; Harry had often heard him express in a vehement manner his terror of the phantoms of the Bloody Creek.

At that moment, all the electric bulbs illuminating the western district of Jorgell City went out. Half the city was plunged into darkness.

His eyes bulging out of their orbits, his forehead damp with cold sweat. Harry Dorgan watched, dazed by horror.

He would have liked to cry out, to warn the unfortunate drunkard who was advancing, staggering, toward death, but his throat, contracted by a poignant emotion, would not let any sound escape. He made an effort to slide down the trunk of the cedar, but is limbs were paralyzed by an indescribable terror.

At that moment, Mr. Stewart reached the other bank of the Creek.

He took another step forward—and suddenly, out of the darkness, a shadow pounced.

Mr. Stewart uttered a cry of heart-rending anguish. His face was illuminated momentarily by a blue-tinted aureole, and he collapsed to the ground. The murder had already taken possession of his briefcase and was exploring his pockets. All that had happened with such rapidity that Harry Dorgan was still confused. A single gesture, and the victim had fallen like an inert mass, without even having had time to complete his final cry of agony. But the very horror off what he had just seen had snatched Harry out of his involuntary torpor. Within a second, he had recovered all his lucidity and composure.

With one bound he was on the ground, and firing a first revolver-shot at the murderer.

The flash of the gunshot showed him a tall man whose face was covered by a mask of brass wire with large goggles, like those worn by certain aviators.

He fired a second shot, but the murderer was already running away as fast as his legs could carry him, heading for the nearest clump of trees.

Harry Dorgan pursued him angrily, firing the thirteen cartridges of his revolver one by one. He only paused in order to reload, and then continued his pursuit.

The murderer seemed to have winged heels, but he gradually lost ground, slowed down by the weight of the briefcase, of which he had not let go.

Suddenly, the masked man stopped and rapidly bent down. Before being able to take account of his action, Harry received a heavy blow from a steel beam in his legs, and fell, his shin-bone and knees so painfully bruised that he feared momentarily that his leg might be broken.

It was only with great difficulty that he succeeded in getting to his feet. Limping lamentably and obliged in order to stay upright to lean on tree-trunks and fences, he could not take a step without experiencing stabbing pains. In the meantime, the murderer had disappeared in the direction of the western district of the city.

The engineer had been so gravely wounded that he nearly passed out several times before getting back to his cottage. When, at the cost of the most painful efforts, he succeeded in doing so, the interruption of the current had ceased; the powerful electric bulbs surrounded the tall buildings of the western district of Jorgell City in a scintillating swarm, as they did every night.

"The wretches!" he murmured.

He was at the limit of his strength. He fell unconscious on the stairs leading up to his room. It was there that his servants found him the following morning.

Dr. FitzJames, summoned in haste, confirmed that Harry's leg was not broken, but he had incurred such serious contusions that he would be confined to bed for a fortnight. He did not breathe a word of his adventure to anyone. He wanted the murderers to think that he was keeping silent for fear of reprisals.

As soon as he was able to get up, he went to see Fred Jorgell, with whom he had a long private conversation.

VII. A Tragic Night

It had been a long time since the engineer Harry Dorgan had appeared at any social gathering. The rumor went around that he had broken is leg falling off one of the iron ladders at the plant. Dr. FitzJames, who was caring for him, had testified to the exactitude of the fact, declaring that the engineer would be obliged to remain in bed for three weeks with his leg in plaster.

In reality, Harry was completely healed and was preparing his vengeance.

It was noticeable at this time that Fred Jorgell had modified his habits strangely. It was said, with a smile, that he was rejuvenated. Ordinarily so grave, so absorbed by calculations, he now spent almost every evening at the Black Bean Club, gambling for high stakes, drinking heavily and amazing the club's most determined high rollers with his verve and enthusiasm. It was affirmed that, having lost enormous sums in the foundation of Jorgell City, the billionaire was seeking to numb his pain, and that his ruination was imminent.

At any rate, he had no hesitation in talking about the murderers of the Bloody Creek, who had done such considerable damage to his enterprise—but to everyone's surprise, he now claimed that there had never been any murders, and that the victims were all poltroons and drunkards, who had died of congestion after having overdosed on whisky and champagne, until they could no longer stay upright.

In these incoherent speeches, no one could any longer recognize his habitual gravity and good sense; people even went so far as to say that the losses he had suffered had unhinged his mind. Those who laughed would have been very surprised had they known that in acting and speaking thus, Fred Jorgell as merely following a plan of conduct carefully developed with the collaboration of Harry Dorgan.

One evening—it was the exact anniversary of the death of the unfortunate Pablo Hernandez—the billionaire seemed full of joy; he had played numerous hands and had ended up breaking the bank; the extra-dry flowed abundantly. It was one of those brilliant evenings whose like had rarely been seen at the club since the disappearance of the elegant Arnold Stickmann. Fred Jorgell had won so many banknotes that, for want of room in his wallet, he had stuffed them into all his pockets.

The conversation, as was inevitable, turned to the murders of the Bloody Creek.

"There are no murderers in our city, I tell you," Fred Jorgell exclaimed, "And I'm so convinced of it that I'm willing to bet..."

There was a profound silence; the spectators were profoundly interested.

"I'm willing to bet fifty thousand dollars," the billionaire continued, pleased with the effect he had produced, "that I can go home alone, on foot, tonight, via the Bloody Creek, with all the banknotes I have in my pockets."

There was a momentary stupor.

"It's madness!" murmured the gamblers.

"We can't let him do it."

"It would be a crime."

"He's drunk too much extra-dry."

"He's unhinged..."

"No one wants to take the bet, then?" said the billionaire, slowly. "Is that right?"

"No one," replied Dr. Cornelius, who was present. "What you want to do is the ultimate in impudence. No one wants to be an accomplice to such folly."

The doctor, with everyone's approval, employed the most energetic demonstrations, but in vain. Fred Jorgell stuck to his plan intransigently.

"That's all right," he said. "If no one wants to take my bet, I'll go across the Bloody Creek anyway, on my own."

"At least let us follow you at a distance in an automobile," someone said.

"Never in this life. I declare that I would regard it as an unfriendly action to be escorted unwillingly, and that I would sever all relations with anyone who were guilty of it."

It was necessary to yield to that irrational obstinacy. It was well-known that the billionaire was endowed with the most despotic energy and that those who had attempted to cross him had always come out of it badly.

He left, therefore, with an enormous cigar between his teeth—delighted, he affirmed by the prospect of the walk in the fresh air that he was about to take.

For some time, from the height of the terrace, the members of the club followed his tall silhouette, which slowly decreased in the distance of the avenue under the harsh glare of the electric lights.

Under the pretext of visiting a patient, Cornelius left almost immediately after Fred Jorgell. Outside the club, he met Baruch, who was just going in, and they greeted one another ceremoniously.

"Are you going to the club?" the doctor asked.

"Yes."

"I'd advise you instead to undertake an excursion in the direction of the Bloody Creek. Someone laden down with banknotes is walking that way."

Baruch's eyes lit up with cupidity.

"And the person in question is in a state of inebriation, such that..." The doctor did not finish his sentence.

"What's his name?" Baruch demanded.

"There's no need to tell you his name; it'll be a nice surprise for you."

"Harry Dorgan, perhaps?"

"I don't want to tell you anymore. I repeat, I'll leave you the pleasure of the surprise." And the sculptor of human flesh drew away, laughing diabolically.

Left alone, Baruch, after a few moments' hesitation, retraced his steps, and then, hailing a taxi, had himself taken two-thirds of the way along the avenue leading to the Bloody Creek.

Throughout the time he had been in sight of the club, Fred Jorgell had followed the avenue in a straight line, but when he was sure that he could no longer be seen he went into a side-street that led to a path of fallow ground in the middle of which stood a long cabin. He took a key out of his pocket and let himself in.

In spite of its wretched exterior, the cabin was comfortably furnished inside. The billionaire groped for a candle, which he lit. He seemed abruptly to have lost the joviality and enthusiasm that the clubmen of the Black Bean had admired so much; his face no longer expressed anything but a profound sadness and an implacable resolution.

On the table placed in the middle of the only room was a sealed envelope. The billionaire opened it and read a few words written in pencil and signed "H. D."

I'm at my post, as I am every evening. If you decide to come, don't omit any of the precautions indicated.

"What a loyal and ingenious fellow that dear Harry is," he murmured. "I'll follow his instructions to the letter. A secret voice is telling me that the victims will be avenged tonight."

Fred Jorgell disposed of his banknotes, throwing them carelessly into a drawer in a sideboard. Then, underneath his clothes, he put on a kind of tunic of metal wires, which protected him from head to toe, like those worn by workmen in some electric plants, and he put on a kind of helmet fabricated on the same principle. Having made these preparations, he went out as mysteriously as he had come in, and headed toward the valley of the Bloody Creek.

When he reached the entrance to the bridge he thought it wise to adopt the slightly hesitant tread of an old gentleman who has drunk too much claret and extra-dry.

Scarcely had he reached the opposite bank when a tall man emerged from the darkness, brandishing some kind of club. Before the billionaire could adopt a defensive stance, he struck him lightly in the neck region, fortunately protected by the tunic of metal wires.

For a second, Fred Jorgell found himself surrounded by a veritable aureole of electric light. In spite of his protective armor, he had received a considerable shock.

"Help me, Harry!" he cried.

The engineer, hidden behind a bush a few paces away, had launched himself forward, brandishing his revolver in one hand and a powerful electric torch in the other, the dazzling light of which revealed Baruch Jorgell, who, his face livid, was standing face to face with his father, threatening him with his club.

"So you're the murder of the Bloody Creek!" cried the billionaire, in a terrible voice. "Kill him, Harry. Shoot! He's a wretch who doesn't deserve any pity!"

The shock had been too much for the old man; his head fell backwards; his arms beat the air, and he collapsed heavily, unconscious—perhaps dead.

"It's just the two of us now, blackguard!" proclaimed Harry Dorgan, in a menacing voice. Slowly and coldly, he took aim at the murderer, who was only a few yards away from him.

"One of us has to stay here," said Baruch, with a snigger. "If it's you, you'll be assumed to be the author of all these little electrocutions!"

For a second, Harry had time to see how the weapon that Baruch was brandishing was formed. It was a metal ovule equipped with a glass handle. From that ovule departed the supple and solid wire that extended to the bifurcation-point of the conductive cable. The ring that terminated the cable carried light and power to the western district of Jorgell City had been unhooked and replaced by the one that terminated in the wire attached to the club. It was, therefore, a force of several thousand volts that Baruch was directing against his victims.

With a rapid glance, the engineer had taken account of the danger he was in; hurriedly, he pulled the trigger of his weapon.

Baruch had ducked abruptly; the bullet whistled past his ear.

Before Harry had had time to fire a second shot, the murder had bounded toward him and grabbed his wrist. A frightful struggle began by the light of the electric torch, which, dropped in the grass, was still shining.

From the beginning, Harry had dropped his revolver, just as Baruch had dropped his glass handle. There was, in consequence, a battle of wild beasts, tooth and claw, over the body of Fred Jorgell.

At one moment, Harry felt Baruch's fingernails trying to gouge out his eye. To make him let go, he bit his wrist cruelly.

Soon, they were both splashed with blood.

Finally, Harry knocked his enemy to the ground with a formidable kick in the stomach.

Baruch lay still. The engineer thought he was victorious, and breathed deeply. He staunched the blood that was flowing from is wounds and rested for a few seconds on a heap of stones, so exhausted that everything seemed to be whirling around him, and he felt that he was about to faint.

That moment of weakness was fatal.

Baruch had not been as grievously hurt as the engineer had thought, but, having fallen to the ground, he had pretended to be unconscious. Then, profiting from the brief moment of respite that had been left to him, he had crawled unobtrusively to the revolver and taken possession of it.

As the unsuspecting Harry was trying to unbutton the collar of his shirt in order to breathe more easily, Baruch rushed him, knocked him down and, setting his knee on his chest, put the barrel of the gun to his head.

Harry felt the cold barrel against his flesh. He understood that he was about to die.

"Ha ha!" Baruch sniggered. "You've lost the game; it's necessary to pay up, and everyone will think that you're the murderer. Ha ha! It's a good joke!"

The wretch was deliberately prolonging his victim's agony, moving the barrel and the gun back and forth over his face. Suddenly, though, he shivered; he thought he had heard a noise in the distance.

"Let's go!" he said. "Must end it!"

And he pressed the trigger.

The gun did not fire. In the course of the struggle, gravel had been introduced into the mechanism of the revolver, which prevented it from functioning.

Baruch uttered an oath.

He was about to finish Harry off by some other means when all of a sudden, he got up precipitately and fled, with a howl of rage.

He had just perceived his father, who, armed with the electric club, was coming straight toward him. On coming round, he had perceived Harry Dorgan trapped beneath Baruch's knee, and the sight had been sufficient to return all his energy. He had got up, and his first action had been to take possession of the club. His soul closed to all pity, he wanted his unworthy son to perish in the same way that he had caused so many others to perish.

Baruch had fled as fast as he could, straight ahead, jumping over the hedges and fences in a kind of mad panic.

He did not stop until he reached the doctor's door. His instinct, that of a hunted animal, told him that he might perhaps find a refuge there.

In spite of the late hour, Baruch as introduced into the waiting-room, but the old Italian butler Leonello, on seeing that he was haggard and stained with mud and blood, frowned at him significantly.

"The doctor isn't at home," he said, dryly, "and I don't know when he'll be back. I advise you to come back tomorrow."

Baruch stammered a few vague words and ran to Fritz Kramm's house. That was his last hope.

"Say that it's a matter of the utmost seriousness," he said to the domestic who opened the door.

"You're in luck. Mr. Fritz hasn't gone to bed yet." Considering the visitor's strange accoutrement, he added: "Sir has doubtless been the victim of an automobile accident?"

"That's right," said Baruch, seizing that plausible excuse on the wing.

A minute later, he was introduced into the hall with the paintings.

Fritz Kramm examined him silently for a few moments, and then said, in a brusque and glacial tone: "I assume that you've let yourself get pinched, that you're being hunted, and that you want to take refuge here?"

In a few breathless, broken sentences Baruch recounted the drama of which the Bloody Creek, yet again, had been the theater.

"I ought to abandon you to your sad fate," said Fritz, after a pause, "because you're an incompetent. When one undertakes enterprises of this evening's sort, it's necessary to succeed, or not to get mixed up in them."

"But you can't remain indifferent to my situation."

"Why is that?" retorted the art dealer, in an indifferent tone. "My books are perfectly in order. I knew nothing about your actions. We have no connection between us. Nothing that you can say against me will compromise me."

Fritz remained plunged in reflection for a short while. Baruch waited in anguish for him to reach a decision.

"Listen," said Fritz Kramm, finally. "I'm going to help you one last time. Go into that room, where you'll find a change of clothes. As soon as you're ready, my automobile will take you to the nearest station on the line to Chicago. From there, you can reach New York and the Old World. Hide yourself as best you can—that's my advice." As Baruch thanked him, wildly, he added: "One last recommendation: in your own interest, don't address any questions to the man who'll drive you, and hide our face from him as much as possible."

A quarter of an hour later, Baruch Jorgell, enveloped in a long cloak, coifed in a wide-brimmed cowboy hat, and unrecognizable, took his place in a superb sixty-horse-power auto, which set off in fourth gear through the deserted boulevards of Jorgell City.

Three quarters of an hour after that, he caught a train at the little station of Ogstram, and two days after later he embarked in New York on the liner *Kaiser Wilhelm*, bound for Cherbourg. He was saved.

In any case, no further article had appeared in the newspapers on the subject of the mysterious murders in Jorgell City.

On the day after the drama of which the Bloody Creek had been the theater, Fred Jorgell, Isidora and Harry Dorgan met in the winter-garden. The billionaire had considered it his duty to tell his daughter the whole truth. All three of them had to deliberate as to what resolution to take on the subject of Baruch.

Isidora loved her brother dearly, so she had had a crisis of tears, followed by a long faint, when she learned about the atrocities he had committed. She cursed the fatality that had made her ask Harry Dorgan to discover the murderer. She remained sad and silent next to her father, without daring to look up at the engineer.

"I haven't changed my opinion," said the billionaire, bluntly. "Baruch is a wretch; I'll make my deposition to the constable, in order to have the murderer tracked by the police and condemned to execution. He deserves to be electrocuted more than anyone else."

"At least leave the poor boy the chance to repent and expiate his sins, Father," the young woman pleaded. "In my opinion, he committed his crimes while prey to the vertigo of some madness. It's not in a prison that he ought to be locked up, but a sanitarium."

"Isidora's right," said Harry Dorgan. "Such crimes are so monstrous that it's impossible that they were committed in full consciousness. Besides, think of the shame that will rebound on your name."

The billionaire stood up abruptly. "That last consideration settles it," he said. "I don't want Isidora to have to blush at having a murderer for a brother. We'll keep quiet, then, about last night's events. I can count on you, can't I, Mr. Dorgan?"

By way of response, the young man gripped the hand that the billionaire held out to him.

"As for the Bloody Creek," the latter went on, "I'll have houses built there. That's the best means of having the evil renown of the sinister place forgotten. As for my son, I want to live as if he never existed; I forbid his name ever to be pronounced in my presence."

Having said that, the old man got up and left abruptly. Harry and Isidora remained alone.

"Master Dorgan," the young woman said, in a voice full of sadness, "you know the promise I made to you. I shall keep it, but it will take some time for me to recover from the terrible shock I've had today. I'm too grief-stricken at present to think about happiness or believe in its future possibility."

"It's sufficient for me to have your promise," Harry stammered, in a voice strangled by emotion. "It's still a great joy for me. I'll wait for as many months, or even years, as necessary."

"Thank you," said the young woman, simply. "Here's the pledge of my promise." And she extended her forehead, which her fiancé brushed with a melancholy kiss.

N° 2. CHAQUE RÉCIT EST COMPLET EN UN VOLUME 25 Cent.

GUSTAVE LE ROUGE

LE MYSTÉRIEUX DOCTEUR CORNÉLIUS

LE MANOIR AUX DIAMANTS

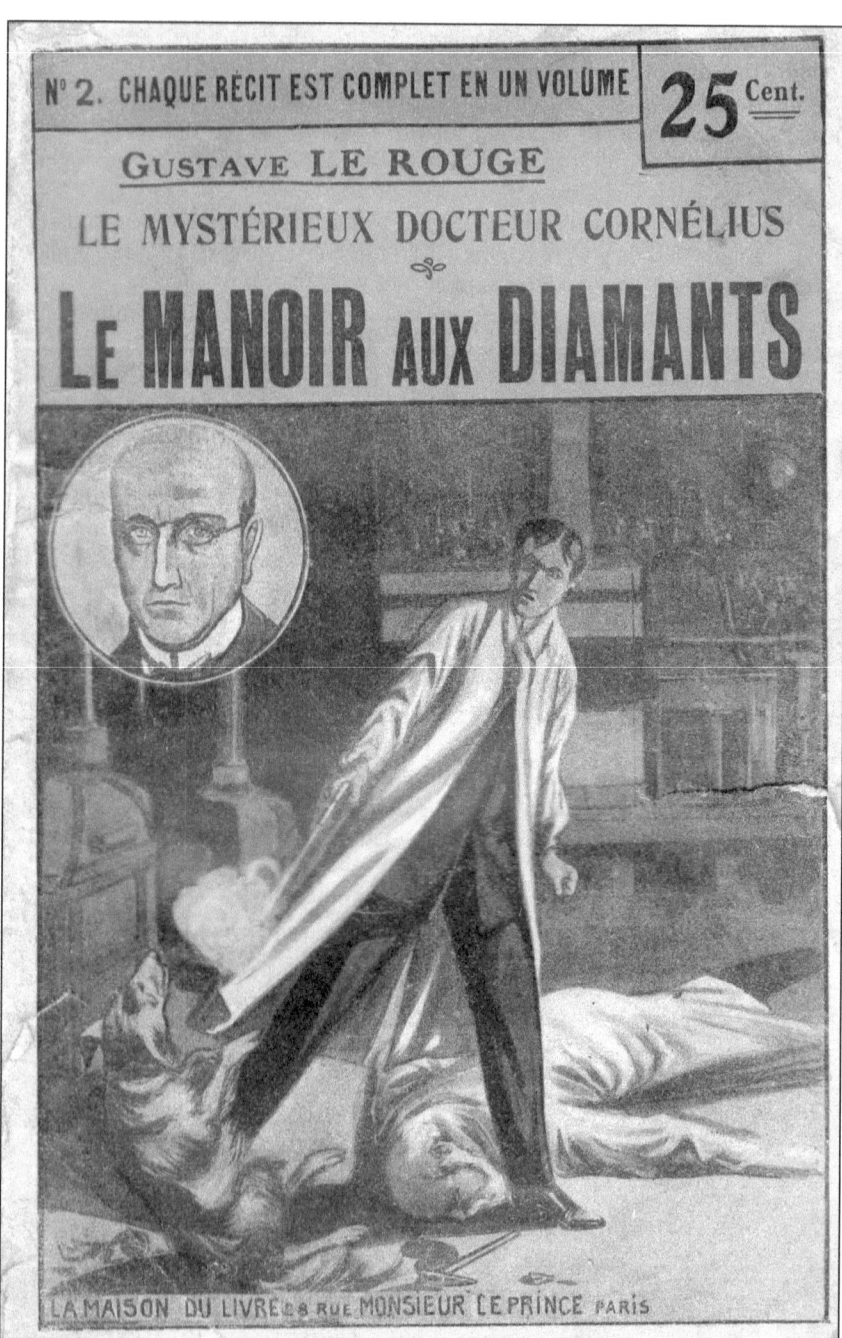

LA MAISON DU LIVRE 8 RUE MONSIEUR LE PRINCE PARIS

2. THE MANOR OF DIAMONDS

I. A Rescue

Monsieur de Maubreuil, the illustrious chemist to whom we owe the synthesis of the greater number of precious stones, the exact and inexpensive reconstitution of the most dazzling gems, was returning in his automobile to his property at Kérity, in a remote corner of the Breton coast, where he spent the greater part of the year.

Monsieur de Maubreuil was coming from Brest, bringing back several crates full of mineralogical specimens; he had left the city at about nine o'clock, after a summary dinner at a restaurant, and he expected to arrive home at about midnight.

The automobile, in the sparkling aureole of its headlights, was passing through the sleepy hamlets like a gust of wind, going up and down the slopes with vertiginous rapidity. Beneath the placid light of the moon, the forests, farms, fields and old châteaux succeeded one another like the décor of an incessantly-repeated dream.

The silence was profound, scarcely troubled from time to time by the cry of a night-bird or the grinding of some belated cart.

"What a delightful evening!" the old scientist murmured, with a blissful smile of satisfaction. "One can fill one's lungs as one breathes, and the sea breeze is charged with the odor of grass and wheat in flower..."

Abruptly, Monsieur Maubreuil left his poetic digression there. The powerful beams of the headlights had just shown him a somber mass lying across the roadway fifty meters in front of the auto.

Immediately, he slowed down, and sounded his horn several times.

"It's not moving!" he exclaimed. "But it's a man! Some drunkard, no doubt. I ought at least to deposit him on the bank, in order that he doesn't run the risk of being crushed."

The automobile had stopped.

Monsieur de Maubreuil got out and leaned over the man, who was lying inert in the dust—but he suddenly emitted a cry of amazement and terror.

A large pool of blood surrounded the body of the unknown man, whose thin and clean-shaven face had a death-like pallor.

"Whether there's been a crime or an accident," stammered the scientist, agitatedly, "it's necessary to help this unfortunate man. As long as he's still alive!"

Monsieur de Maubreuil unfastened the unknown man's outer garments—a green cape and the jacket of an elegant grey check suit—unbuttoned his shirt and observed that there was a large wound just above the heart, which appeared to be the result of the thrust of a knife.

The man was still breathing faintly, but it was the oppressed and wheezy breathing of a dying man.

The only scientist was in a difficult situation; he did not have any of the instruments he needed to hand.

But I can't abandon him like this, he reflected. *He'll be dead in two hours. There's only one thing to do, and that's to take him home, to the manor!*

Monsieur de Maubreuil was a cool-headed and experienced man; with the aid of his handkerchief and a little crème-de-menthe, a bottle of which he found in the trunk of the car, he bathed and dressed the wound summarily; then, not without considerable effort, he succeeded in getting the wounded man into one of the seats of the automobile.

Fortunately, he was not very far away from Kérity; the few kilometers that remained to travel were covered in a quarter of an hour.

"As long as he's still alive when we arrive!" Monsieur de Maubreuil repeated, while expertly maneuvering he steering-wheel.

He darted continual anxious glances at the wounded man, who was still unconscious, bounced about like an inert mass by the vehicle's jolts.

Finally, the automobile passed beneath the dense cover of an avenue of oaks, where the ground was carpeted with grass; then it stopped in a spacious courtyard, at the back of which stood tall buildings with turrets and pointed roofs; that was the manor-house.

At the strident appeals of the horn, lights appeared in the windows, and the somber façade lit up. A young woman hurried down the granite steps at the front door and ran to throw herself into Monsieur de Maubreuil's arms.

"Well, Father," she said, "have you had a good journey?" But she fell silent and her face was covered by a mortal pallor; she had just perceived the wounded man.

"My God!" she stammered. "A corpse!"

Monsieur de Maubreuil thought that she was about to faint, and he hastened to support her. "Don't worry, my dear Andrée," he said, swiftly. "The man isn't dead. I found him bleeding on the highway, and I picked him up—as, in truth, it was my duty to do."

The color reappeared in the young woman's gracious visage. "You did well," she said. "We'll care for him."

"As I say, he isn't dead, but he's not much better. Tell Oscar to make up the first floor bedroom as quickly as possible. Above all, don't be distressed. We'll save him, if it's possible."

During this conversation an adolescent of puny appearance, and slightly hunchbacked, emerged from the house and came to greet Monsieur de Maubreuil respectfully. By his side, a large black dog was barking joyfully.

"Down, Pistolet!" exclaimed the scientist.[5] "Yes, you're a good dog, you're glad to see your old master, but I haven't got time to pay attention to you today."

As a domestic, a robust Breton named Yvonneck, came from the other side of the courtyard to put the automobile in the garage, Monsieur Maubreuil said: "Leave it for now, and help Oscar take this wounded man up to the first floor, to the Red Room—that's the most urgent thing.

Yvonneck lifted up the unconscious man like a feather, and after having carried him carefully up the old sculpted wooden staircase he deposited him on the bed.

Without taking the time to change his clothes, Monsieur de Maubreuil had gone to fetch his medical bag and his case of pharmaceuticals. At the same time, his daughter Andrée brought an ample provision of gauze and bandages.

The old scientist was more anxious than he wanted to appear.

"We'll see whether the wound is serious," he said. "Unfortunately, it's close to the heart and the major blood-vessels."

There were a few minutes of anguish. Monsieur de Maubreuil had taken a little ebonite tube from his medical bag and was carefully sounding the wound. When he had fished that examination, his physiognomy expressed annoyance and disquiet.

"Well?" asked Andrée, anxiously.

The blade has passed within two or three centimeters of the heart and has scratched the aorta; it might not be mortal, but it's very serious. I'll put on a preliminary dressing, and tomorrow, we'll see."

The old scientist did not go to bed until he had made sure, by a series of judicious measures, that his patient would pass a peaceful night.

Early the next morning, he was at the bedside of the wounded man, over whom Oscar and Yvonneck had kept watch all night. He observed that his condition had not grown any worse during the night, but he remained plunged in a kind of coma due to the blood-loss that he had suffered.

The unknown man so strangely collected by Monsieur de Maubreuil was tall, with pronounced and energetic facial features and a prominent jaw. From the few words that escaped during the delirium of a fever, they divined that he was English or American, but his host forbade anyone to ask him any questions until he was completely out of danger.

One morning, when he came to make his daily visit, the old scientist had the satisfaction of finding his patient perfectly lucid—or, at any rate, entirely

---

[5] There is a character in the *Habits Noirs* novel *La Rue de Jérusalem* (tr. as 'Salem Street*, q.v.) named Pistolet, who plays a role analogous to the one to be played in the present series by Oscar Tournesol, but the name is more appropriately applied to a dog because there was a kind of pistol popularly known in France as a *chien*.

free of the disquieting coma. Raising himself up on his elbow, he looked in surprise at the old four-poster bed, the lampas curtains and the faded tapestries the made up the furniture of the Red Room.

"Where am I, Monsieur?" he asked, in a weak voice. "I'd be grateful if you could tell me. I vaguely remember being attacked, but then"—he put his hand to his head—"there's a kind of black hole in my memory. I don't know any more...I can't remember..." He was speaking in French, but with a strong accent.

Monsieur de Maubreuil hastened to reassure him, and told him how he had picked him up.

As he listened to the story, the unknown man's features expressed a profound emotion. With a gesture that was still indecisive, he took the old scientist's hand and pressed it between his own.

"I owe you my life," he stammered. "But for you I'd be lying dead on that deserted road, devoid of help. That's a service I shall never forget, and for which I hope to be able to recompense you some day."

"Don't think about that," replied Monsieur de Maubreuil, smiling. "Anyone else would have done the same for you in my place. Besides which, although I'm not rich, I have an adequate fortune."

"You haven't yet told me your name," the sick man put in, ardently. "At least let me know what to call my rescuer."

"My name is Gaston de Maubreuil. I'm a chemist and mineralogist."

"What! You're the illustrious scientist whose name is known throughout the world, whose admirable discoveries I've read about in the scientific journals of my native land, America?"

"I really wasn't aware that I was so well-known," said Monsieur de Maubreuil, modestly.

"I can assure you that I've followed all your work passionately, for I too am much occupied with chemistry—although I haven't, alas, obtained any result that can stand comparison with your admirable experiments."

Without his being conscious of it, the old scientist's vanity was delightfully tickled. "Since that's the case," he said, cheerfully, "I'm doubly glad to have saved the life of a colleague. Would it be indiscreet to ask your name?"

"Not at all," the wounded man replied, after a momentary hesitation. "I'm an American, and my name is Baruch Jorgell."

"Jorgell," repeated Monsieur de Maubreuil. "It seems to me that I've heard that name somewhere."

"My father is, in fact, one of the Yankee billionaires most often cited; he owns entire cities, but I've fallen out with him completely over questions of interest—the fact is, alas, all too frequent in families—and I left the United States with no intention of returning..." Baruch Jorgell interrupted himself abruptly, his physiognomy expressing a sudden anxiety. "Monsieur," he said, "I have every reason to suppose that I was robbed during the attempted murder of which I was the victim. Answer me frankly..."

"I can only tell you," the old scientist replied, "that I don't know anything about it. Your clothes are here, and no one has touched them."

Monsieur de Maubreuil went to open a large chestnut-wood cupboard and took out a pair of trousers, a jacket, a waistcoat, a cape and a leather belt with compartments, like those that emigrants use to carry gold and valuables. He deposited all these objects on Baruch's bed. "There," he said to the latter, "are all your clothes. I've refrained from searching them. You can verify for yourself whether or not you were robbed by your attempted murderers."

Baruch Jorgell explored the pockets with a tremulous hand and pulled out a large wallet. He opened it; it was empty. The purse connected to the belt by a steel chain was also empty, as was the belt itself. The bandits had only respected the waistcoat pocket, which contained some small change.

Baruch's face was woebegone. "I've been completely stripped bare," he said, in a strangled voice. "I don't have a single dollar left!" And he added, with a bitter laugh: "They've even taken my Browning. I don't even have the last resort of blowing my brains out!"

Monsieur de Maubreuil was sincerely afflicted by his patient's distress. He tried to bring him back to calmer sentiments. "Come on, my dear colleague," he said, affectionately, "Don't despair. What's happened to you is certainly very annoying, but you know our old French proverb: a wound in the wallet isn't fatal. Before anything else, recover our health. That's the most important thing. Afterwards, we'll see what can be done." As Baruch remained plunged in a somber silence, the old man went on: "Explain to me first how you were attacked. Can you remember?"

"Very precisely," murmured the young man, bitterly. "Oh, the story's very banal. I had gone to visit an Englishman, Mr. Bushman, whose property is a few leagues from here. He was supposed to give me a job managing a chemical factory that he's setting up, but we couldn't reach an understanding. I left Mr. Bushman's house at about half past ten. It was such a beautiful evening that I didn't want to go back by car, although the offer was made, and I decided to walk to the railway station."

"I remember that the weather that night was, indeed, beautiful."

"I was about half way along my route when half a dozen individuals dressed in rags, who had undoubtedly been lying in ambush waiting for me, emerged from a sunken road and fell upon me. I saw the blades of their knives gleaming, and felt a sharp pain in my heart...I don't remember anything more after that, until I recovered consciousness this morning, here in this room."

Monsieur de Maubreuil had listened to this story with profound attention. "As I said just now," he said, after a pause, "the essential thing is for you to get better. Afterwards, I'll do my best to find you a suitable job, by means of my connections."

"Thank you, Monsieur," Baruch murmured, dejectedly. "I'll never forget your generosity toward me, but I'm desperate, completely desperate."

"Wait a minute!" exclaimed the old scientist, with a benevolent smile. "I think I have a plan that will please you. You say that you're a chemist?"

"Certainly. I even had a fully-equipped laboratory in my father's house."

"Then it will work out marvelously. I'm astonished not to have thought of it before. I'm beginning to get old; I feel the need to have a collaborator, young and active, who loves science for its own sake, thanks to whom I can complete the program of discoveries that I've mapped out. What I propose to you, therefore, quite frankly and simply, is that you become that collaborator, Monsieur Baruch Jorgell."

Momentarily, the eyes of the convalescent lit up with a strange gleam. A grimacing smile contracted his features—but that strange sardonic expression only appeared on his face as a fugitive shadow. It was with the most obsequious and emotional tone of gratitude that he replied: "My dear Master, it would be a great joy for me to collaborate with your discoveries of genius. I shall try to render myself worthy of such a glorious distinction by my assiduity and my devotion, for want of the creative imagination that I doubtless don't, alas, possess..."

Monsieur de Maubreuil was radiant. "Enough compliments," he said. "That's something I detest more than anything else. Would you like me to tell you what it's necessary to do to be agreeable to me?"

"Anything that's in my power..."

"Well, try to get better as quickly as possible, and above all, no black ideas. You'll soon see that scientific labor gives more satisfaction than the greatest fortune can procure."

Then, as Baruch seemed inclined to continue the conversation, the old man said: "That's enough. All this talking must be tiring you out. Now, you must try to get some sleep, until Yvonnet brings you your broth and fresh eggs."

Monsieur de Maubreuil withdrew, leaving Baruch Jorgell to marvel at the new perspectives that his host's offer had just opened to his ambition, which was as ardent as it was unscrupulous.

II. A Colony of Scientists

A fortnight had passed. Baruch Jorgell was now completely recovered; a considerable weakness, and a little thinness and pallor were the only remaining traces of his injury. In the meantime, Monsieur de Maubreuil had discreetly made sure, via the United States ambassador, of the identity of his guest—who really was, as he had affirmed, the son of the famous billionaire Fred Jorgell, the founder of Jorgell City. At the same time, by means of a sequence of conversations, the old chemist was able to convince himself of the genuine scientific credentials of his future collaborator.

Every day he applauded the good idea he had had. Baruch was knowledgeable, intelligent and perfectly polite; the only reproach that could be offered to him was on account of his slightly misanthropic humor, but, as Monsieur de Maubreuil remarked to his daughter, it was quite natural that a man who had experienced such great misfortunes would not be overly cheerful.

On the day when he convalescent could finally go out, he old scientist and his daughter wanted to accompany him on a long walk and take him to admire the most interesting local sights.

The manor house—the Manor of Diamonds, as the local peasants called it—was built half way up a cliff and one of its façades overlooked the sea. On the other side there was verdant countryside, at the extremity of which the steeple of the little village church was visible.

After following the avenue of oaks for some time, Monsieur de Maubreuil and his daughter guided Baruch along a gently-sloping path that led to the top of the cliff, carpeted by short grass as velvety as moss.

There, all three of them rested for a few moments.

"Let's halt in the shelter of this furze with the golden flowers," said Monsieur de Maubreuil, "it's necessary not to overextend our strength, Master Baruch, and you're not yet perfectly steady on your legs."

"But it's going very well, I assure you," the American protested. "I'm completely cured now."

"Let's not push our walk too far," said Andrée. "I propose that we only go as far as Monsieur Bondonnat's. We haven't seen him for several days."

"An excellent idea," exclaimed the old scientist, joyfully. "I'll introduce Bondonnat to my new collaborator." Turning to Baruch, he added: "Perhaps I've told you already that we have a veritable little scientific colony here. My friend Prosper Bondonnat, the great naturalist whose name you'll certainly know, lives in a villa five hundred meters from the manor. He's established a laboratory there, which is certainly unique of its kind, and has brought with him his two most distinguished pupils, the engineer Paganot and the botanist Ravenel."

Baruch had become attentive. "I didn't know that there was such a seed-bed of invention in this remote region," he said. "I'd be delighted to be introduced to them and to hear about their current endeavors."

"Have a little patience, Master Baruch; we'll be at Monsieur Bondonnat's house in a quarter of an hour. That great white mass that you can see five hundred meters away, as if slotted into a fissure in the cliff in the midst of a green thicket, is our friend's villa." And Monsieur de Maubreuil added: "I believe, in any case, that Andrée will not be displeased to visit her friend the engineer."

The young woman lowered her eyes and blushed cherry-red. The engineer Antoine Paganot was almost officially engaged to Andrée, and Monsieur de Maubreuil was not at all hostile to that projected marriage.

Baruch darted a glance scintillating with jealousy at the young woman and his face, already pale, became even paler, but no one noticed the expression of hatred that had been momentarily reflected in his features.

They had resumed walking through the tall heather; after going through a hamlet inhabited by fishermen, and along a strand where blue thistles flourished, they reached the villa.

As soon as they had passed through the gate Baruch felt as if he were intoxicated by the embalmed and heady atmosphere that emanated from the gardens. One might have thought it a subtle but powerful aromatic extract of all known flowers. "It seems to me," he murmured, "that I'm going into a perfume factory."

"You're not mistaken," said Mademoiselle de Maubreuil, laughing. "Except that it's Nature herself who takes charge of distilling these perfumes…with Bondonnat's collaboration. But here's the man himself…"

As much as Monsieur de Maubreuil, with his long gray hair and unkempt beard seemed melancholy, Monsieur Bondonnat was jovial, smiling, and even light-hearted. The naturalist presented one of those beautiful scientist's physiognomies imprinted with so much bonhomie and serenity that age and worry do not seem to have any purchase on them. His high forehead was shadowed by snowy white hair; his bright blue eyes, sparkling with youth gave a cheerful charm to his grave, symmetrical, wrinkle-free features, framed by vast side-whiskers as white as his hair. He was dressed in a long laboratory smock, immaculately clean, and holding a pair of nickel-plated secateurs in his hand. He gave his visitors the heartiest of welcomes.

Already informed about Baruch's adventure, Bondonnat congratulated him wittily on the attempted murder of which he had been the victim "without which he would but have had the inestimable luck to become the collaborator of the great chemist Maubreuil."

"I'm delighted," he concluded, rubbing his hands, that our little colony has made a new and precious acquisition in the person of Monsieur Jorgell."

At that moment, Frédérique, he naturalist's only daughter, a childhood friend of Andrée de Maubreuil, came out in her turn to greet the visitors.

It would have been difficult to say which of the two young women was the more beautiful. They each offered, albeit in different genres, the most attractive and more gracious physiognomy. Andrée had ash-blonde hair; she was slim and svelte with two pale blue eyes that had a melancholy and dreamy expression. Fréderique's hair was an ardent blonde, almost red, and offered the rich complexion of Scandinavian beauties. There character was playful, almost boisterous; she was the gaiety of a house of scientists forever lost in abstract calculations.

"I must show you the gardens!" exclaimed Bondonnat, turning to Baruch. "I assure you that it's well worth the trouble."

Even though he had been used to the most grandiose luxury in the palaces of billionaires, Baruch could not help marveling in amazement. Surrounded on all sides by the rocky walls of the cliff, the gardens were divided up into terraces, where plants and trees from all nations and climates grew pell-mell, in a prodigious luxuriance of vegetation. Banana-trees, cacti and arborescent ferns were mingled there with holly-bushes, yew-trees and service-trees, and all those plants advertised an abnormal, almost miraculous force and vigor of sap. One might have thought it a magic wood, a section of virgin forest transported into that cleft in the rock by the hands of genies.

Delighted, Bondonnat rubbed his hands with a febrile vivacity; it was his tic. "What do you think of that?" he said, laughing. "My plants and I don't fear the rigor of the seasons. I've created a special atmosphere for them, rich in nourishing gases; the earth in which they're growing is saturated with formic acid, manganese and other substances that give them a formidable power of vegetation. From one day to the next the leaves sprout, the flowers blossom and the fruits ripen. The roots, thanks to special apparatus, are bathed by an electric current, which ensures a rapid, almost monstrous, growth.

"But will these experiments, assuredly marvelous, lead to any practical consequences?" asked the astounded Baruch.

Monsieur Bondonnat shrugged his shoulders. "That's very American," he said. "Time is money; you want a practical result. Personally, I love science for its own sake; we don't have the same way of looking at things. Besides which, soon enough, the practical results will be enormous. When one can, at insignificant expense, make fields and orchards produce four, five or six crops a year—perhaps more—poverty, misery and hunger will be banished from the globe. Everyone will be happy, since everything necessary to life will exist in an abundance of which nothing at present can give the slightest idea."

Baruch remained silent, alarmed by the prospect of a humankind brought back by the power of science to the legendary Golden Age.

The naturalist did not seem to perceive his interlocutor's confusion, and headed toward the greenhouses.

The visit to the greenhouses, and the explanation of the mechanism of the thermo-siphon that maintained a constant temperature there, took up more than an hour. Baruch Jorgell went from one astonishment to another, and from one amazement to another; he seemed to be living a fantastic dream.

What astonished him more than anything else was the simplicity and bonhomie of the scientists, who unveiled to him in total confidence secrets that would each have been sold in America to some Trust for millions of dollars.

He was about to ask what the purpose was of the enormous metal tubes that he could see raised up vertically at the top of the cliff, when a tall, thin and stiff young man, to whom a prominent hooked nose gave him a physiognomy reminiscent of Don Quixote, emerged from the villa and came to accost Monsieur Bondonnat.

"Messieurs," said the naturalist, "Monsieur Roger Ravenel, one of my most devoted collaborators."

When the introductions were concluded, Roger Ravenel told Monsieur Bondonnat that two fishermen from the nearby hamlet wanted to speak to him.

"I can't help wondering," he said, "what these people can have against me. I know that they hold me in low esteem."

"Is that possible?" asked Baruch.

"I have the honor of telling you that this villa—like the Manor of Diamonds, by the way—is reputed to be a den of lunatics, or rather sorcerers. The people of this backward region are convinced that we're Satan's henchmen, and what is reported about our little experiments has done nothing to modify that opinion."

"Well, Father," said Frédérique, "let these worthy people come in; I'm as curious as you are to know what they want with us."

At a sign from Monsieur Bondonnat, Roger Ravenel went away; he came back a minute later, pushing in front of him, almost forcibly, two sailors shod in sabots and clad in filthy and greasy reefer-jackets. They were two veritable seadogs, with tanned faces reddened by harsh weather, and gnarled hands blackened by tar. They came through the enchanted garden looking around with expressions of suspicion and dread.

Having arrived two paces from Monsieur Bondonnat they stopped, berets in hand. There were sly smiles on their aged faces, wizened by the sea-winds.

"Messieurs," said the naturalist, with his habitual courtesy, "to what do I owe the pleasure of your visit?"

The two sea-dogs, looking at one another with the same embarrassed smile, did not breathe a word. One might have thought that they were mute.

Frédérique had come forward, trying to assume a severe expression, although she felt a strong desire to laugh. "Come on, Père Yvon," she said, addressing the older of the fishermen, "are you afraid of me and my father? Stop twisting your beret in your fingers and explain what brings you here."

Old Yvon, thus put on the spot, finally overcame his timidity and, not without uttering a preliminary cough, began: "Mamzelle knows me well; she's often bought bass and crayfish from me."

"Well?" demanded the naturalist.

"Well, when I'm not fishing, I cultivate the land; I have a small field. My wheat is ripe, and, well, there's going to be a big storm before long. That's why I've come to see you."

"I can't understand what they want," murmured Bondonnat, discouraged..

Monsieur de Maubreuil intervened. "It's obvious," he said. "These worthy folk are convinced that you're a sorcerer, and that you can make rain and good weather at will. They've been delegated to beg you to save their crop by driving away the storm."

"That's it," approved old Yvon, delighted to have been so comprehensively understood.

Bondonnat seemed to be amused by the fishermen's request, but then, looking at the sky, where the heavy afternoon heat had amassed thick black clouds that were gradually invading the blue sky, he said: "Hmm! I believe that there will indeed by a considerable downpour in the near future. I'm willing, my good men, to try to drive that big soot-colored nimbus out to sea, but I can't guarantee that I'll succeed..."

"Will it cost very dear?" asked Yvon, with a residue of suspicion.

"Not a sou—but everyone, please follow me. I'm delighted to have the opportunity to allow you to witness an experiment that promises to be interesting.

Bondonnat was heading toward a corner of the garden, from which a slender aluminum and crystal tower rose up parallel to the rock, which was nothing other than an electric elevator. Everyone took their places within it, and thus attained the top of the cliff, where the flattered earth formed a spacious circular pathway surrounded by a high wall. It was on that pathway that the gigantic tubes were installed that had previously attracted Baruch's attention.

From that point they had a view over the entire landscape, suddenly darkened by an accumulation of clouds the color of soot and lead.

"I can see," the naturalist said, "that there's no time to lose, but where's Monsieur Paganot? It's him that the matter concerns particularly."

The engineer, the naturalist's second collaborator, emerged at that very moment from a glazed cabin placed on the far side of the circular arena and was rapidly apprised of the situation.

"We still have time," he declared, after having examined the condition of the sky, "but these two brave mariners will need to help me load the cartridges."

"We've both served in the navy," old Yvon declared.

"Then all will go well."

"What's going to happen?" asked Baruch, very intrigued by these preparations.

"It's simply a battle in which we're about to engage with the tempest," said Frédérique. These tubes are hail-cannon invented by my father, whose power and radius of action are enormous. They're loaded with melinite bombs, which administer a considerable shock to the layers of air. The devices employed in

Champagne and the Bordelais region are mere children's toys compared to these."

"It's thanks to this peaceful artillery," added Monsieur de Maubreuil, "that my friend Bondonnat maintains a special climate in these gardens."

While these observations were being exchanged, the engineer Paganot—a type-specimen of the classical scientist with his clean-shaven face and naïve expression—with the help of the two mariners, loaded melinite cartridges into the automatic chargers of the eight cannons that raised their tapered barrels toward the sky.

The visitors had taken their places on a stone bench some distance away from the cannons.

"Everything's ready," declared the engineer. We can fire for ten minutes without interruption."

"Fire!" shouted the naturalist, gravely.

A formidable detonation rang out.

Sheaves of flame sprang from the mouths of the cannons. The summit of the cliff was crowned with a cloud of smoke, and the echoes of the cannonade's rumble reverberated from the rocks in the distance.

In the region, for several leagues around, there was a general alarm. Some people thought that a munitions dump had exploded; others that large scale military maneuvers were taking place; a few, on seeing the melinite bombs explode in the bosom of the torn clouds, imagined that they were watching a simulacrum of aerial warfare. Soon, however, it was realized that the detonations were departing from the cliff, aureoled with tongues of fire and crowned with a plume of white smoke.

The frightened people took refuge in their houses, bolting their doors, repeating, while shaking their heads anxiously: "It's those accursed sorcerers at the villa up to their devilries again. They'll end up bringing some calamity down on the country. What a shame it is that the government protects such rogues!"

Finally, the cannonade ceased. When the breeze had dissipated the smoke of the explosions, the sky seemed almost completely clear of the cloud that had previously obstructed it. The nimbus and cumulus were fleeing in complete disarray toward the open sea. The black balls that had been hoisted on the semaphores to announce the tempest had disappeared. The people of the nearest village were heaping the sheaves of their miraculously-preserved crops on to carts.

"Bravo, Father!" said Frédérique, planting a kiss on the old scientist's forehead. "We've won the battle!"

"And without doing much harm!" he replied, cheerfully. "I'm quite content with my artillery campaign!" Turning to the two fishermen, who were so bewildered that they could not say a word, he added: "Remember one thing, my friends, which is that there no devilry at all in everything you've just seen. I haven't employed any other means in putting the clouds to flight than the shock caused by the detonations. The true sorcery is knowledge of natural phenomena."

The two mariners stammered vague thanks, but in the rapidity with which they withdrew, their dread was manifest; they had not lost any of their prejudices.

Monsieur Bondonnat was warmly congratulated by his friends and they went into the villa, where lunch had been prepared.

Baruch remained pensive; he was taking account of the extraordinary good luck from which he had benefited in penetrating into a society of scientists whose smallest discovery represented a fortune. Instead of being touched by the trust they were manifesting toward him, however, he promised himself to exploit all the secrets he might discover without the slightest scruple.

The afternoon was drawing to its close, however. After lunch, Monsieur de Maubreuil took his leave of his friends and returned with Andrée and Baruch Jorgell to the Manor of Diamonds.

It was the following day that the American was to assume his functions and begin working in the chemist's laboratory.

III. The Manor of Diamonds

When Baruch Jorgell went into Monsieur de Maubreuil's laboratory for the first time he was literally dazzled. The laboratory comprised two vast rooms that occupied an entire wing of the manor. The first was entirely furnished with large glass-fronted cupboards that contained mineralogical specimens and a complete assortment of chemical products; the other comprised the laboratory itself, properly speaking, and was almost entirely occupied by a powerful electric furnace.

Baruch had often visited laboratories of an almost similar kind, but he stood ecstatic before the showcases of precious stones. There was a treasure of inestimable value therein. It was a veritable stream of sparkling gems, so numerous that their contemplation eventually wearied the eyes. Rubies, sapphires, diamonds, amethysts, topazes, aquamarines, corundums, emeralds and opals were methodically piled up in large cups, symmetrically arranged.

"You're looking at my pebbles," said Monsieur de Maubreuil. "I posses about seven hundred varieties, and within that number there are some that are very beautiful—but we'll do better than that. At the moment, I'm occupied with the synthesis of diamonds; crystalline carbon is the only gem that I haven't yet succeeded in reproducing in a satisfactory manner."

"Have you already obtained some results?" asked Baruch, prodigiously interested.

"Bah! It's hardly worth the trouble of talking about it. I've fabricated minuscule diamonds, but they were all yellow, discolored or flawed. What I want is to produce, at will, without the slightest risk, gems as large and as clear as the Regent or the Koh-I-Noor." He added, in a melancholy tone: "I have a personal interest, a passionate interest, in the solution of that problem. I want the stones for which people presently pay hundreds of thousands of francs to become as common as roadside pebbles."

Baruch was surprised by the almost hateful vivacity with which the scientist pronounced that sentence.

"One might think, my dear Master," he said, "that you detested precious stones."

"That's not entirely accurate, but you'll understand soon enough. It's time to take you into my confidence. Since we're going to be working together, I ought to give you an explanation right away."

The chemist sat down at a table covered with stacks of paper, in an old leather armchair with winglets, and the American sat down opposite him.

"In spite of my wrinkles and my gray hair," Monsieur de Maubreuil went on, "I'm still young, but my life has been replete with disappointments. Without a fortune, I contrived to create for myself a certain notoriety in science. I revised, with the aid of the most exact observations, geological theories that had been almost immutable since Lamarck and Cuvier. Firstly, I demonstrated the existence of a central fire, maintained in a solid state by the enormous pressure of centripetal force. But several of my discoveries were disputed, and others stolen from me. I never acquired the status that was my due."

"My dear Master..." Baruch began.

"There's no need to offer me compliments or condolences; I'm philosophical. I'd easily be consoled for those disappointments if I hadn't had to undergo crueler ordeals. I had married a young woman as poor as myself, and initially had to suffer many privations that he mediocrity of my situation imposed upon us. Unfortunately, I must confess, Madame de Maubreuil loved jewels passionately; she suffered from being unable to deck herself in veritable rubies and diamonds, and being obliged to content herself with imitations..."

"I'm beginning to understand," murmured the American.

The chemist resumed, effortfully: "It was that unfortunate coquetry that made me launch myself wholeheartedly into the synthesis of gems." His gaze shining with somber enthusiasm, his voice rose in pitch. "I wanted to strip those miserable pebbles of all their prestige; I wanted kennels and stables to be paved with rubies, and no one to be stupid enough to prefer a diamond, no matter how beautiful it might be, to a dew-drop shining in the calyx of a flower! What sapphire is worth as much as a periwinkle in a wheat-field, what amethyst as much as a sprig of violet exhaling it sweet odor amid the moss? Hating stones, I began to love flowers madly, and that's doubtless one of the reasons for me friendship with the botanist Bondonnat. Then again"—the chemist's voice trembled slightly—"our wives, who were childhood friends, died in the same year, carried off by a typhus epidemic just as successful experiments were beginning to bring my glory and fortune. I'd never been so happy!"

Monsieur de Maubreuil remained silent for a time, lost in his memories.

"I nearly went mad," he continued, after a pause. "For a long time I was obsessed by the idea of building my wife a mausoleum of emerald and sardonyx, even of diamond...I was inconsolable. However, the friendship of Bondonnat and the care it was necessary to devote to the education of my daughter provided a diversion for my grief. Andrée and Frédérique were brought up together, like two sisters, between flowers and books, in the midst of nature and science."

"My dear Master," said Baruch, feigning a tenderness that he did not feel at all, "I'm profoundly touched by the confidence you're showing in me, and I'll try to justify it. But ne last question, if I wouldn't be indiscreet—what gave you the idea of installing yourself in this remote spot?"

"It happened quite naturally. It was Bondonnat who discovered this delightful solitude. He had no difficulty persuading me to leave Paris, which, with its autobuses and its Metro, is definitely becoming a city unfavorable to intellectual endeavors. I bought this manor, which had almost fallen into ruins, and restored it. Here, I'm perfectly tranquil."

"And very near to your friend."

"Precisely. He brought his two most distinguished pupils, the engineer Paganot and the naturalist Ravenel, and the four of us—the five of us, now you're here—for a true scientific colony in the midst of this primitive region..."

After these confidences, which, in his confident honesty, Monsieur de Maubreuil had thought necessary, the two scientists examined the electric furnace constructed in refractory brick and infusible metal plates, which could produce extremely high temperatures of several thousand degrees, thanks to which the crystallization of gems could be obtained.

The chemist already knew that his new collaborator was quite familiar with questions of electricity, of which, he affirmed, he had made a special study in Jorgell City, a city founded in the Far West at the foot of the Rocky Mountains.

In that regard, Monsieur de Maubreuil asked the American innocently what were the causes of his quarrel with his father, the billionaire.

"They're quite simple," Baruch replied, with a constrained expression. "My father engaged the considerable fortune left to me by my mother in speculations, and was able to arrange things so as not to render me an account of them. We had a violent confrontation, and I proudly refused the meager allowance that he offered me by way of alms, so I left for Europe with the twenty thousand dollars that remained to me. You know the rest."

Monsieur de Maubreuil was content with this rather vague explanation, and he began to discuss the conditions in which they were to make a new and crucial experiment in the synthesis of diamond.

The afternoon as well advanced and the technical discussion was reaching its conclusion when Andrée appeared on the threshold of the room with the showcases. "I believe, Messieurs," she said, "that that's enough for a first session. You mustn't overtax yourselves, and the dinner-bell will be sounding in half an hour."

"Undoubtedly," said Monsieur de Maubreuil, approvingly. "A tour of the garden, by way of an aperitif, seems entirely appropriate to me."

"No," said André. "I have something rather curious to show you—or rather, not me but Oscar, my favorite page."

"What is it?"

"I can't tell you—it's a surprise."

Baruch did not let such a good opportunity to inform himself about the residents of the manor go to waste. "Isn't Oscar the young man who cared for me at the beginning of my convalescence?" he asked. "He seems to be a very devoted servant."

"I beg your pardon," said Andrée, "but Oscar isn't a domestic; I regard him almost as a relative."

"In reality," Monsieur de Maubreuil explained, "the little hunchback who answers to the singular name of Oscar Tournesol is a child that we found one morning half-dead of cold at the door of the house in which I was then living, on

76

the Quai des Tournelles in Paris. We kept him; he's very devoted and very docile, and I haven't despaired of making a scientist of him some day."

"Oscar Tournesol is indeed a singular name!"[6]

Tournesol is only a nickname," said Andrée, "and our protégé owes it to the color of his hair, which is a bizarre yellow color, certainly unique."

Baruch bit his lip. He was secretly humiliated by the manifest resemblance between his own present situation—that of the son of a billionaire—and that of the street-urchin taken in by the old scientist's charity. From that moment on he conceived a mortal hatred for Oscar, but he concealed his impression and asked, with a feigned indifference "What did your protégé do, then, before having the good fortune to encounter you?"

"He had run around the streets of Paris," Andrée said, "hawking newspapers on the terraces of cafes, selling Armenian paper,[7] little fur monkeys in fairgrounds, or olives from a cedar basket."

"I'm curious to see this phenomenon, and to study him more closely than I was able to do during my convalescence."

"You'll see that he's a very likeable and intelligent boy."

During these explanations they had left the laboratory and they arrived in a large sandy area at the entrance to the garden. Oscar was there in company with his dog Pistolet. The latter, at the sight of Baruch, uttered a dull growl—he appeared to have an instinctive antipathy toward the American—but a caress from Andrée quickly calmed him down.

"Well?" asked Monsieur de Maubreuil. "What's this famous surprise that Master Oscar has in store for us?"

The little hunchback—Oscar Tournesol was sixteen years old but looked twelve, at the most—had a mischievous smile, and pointing at Pistolet, who was now standing motionless and attentive, he said: "I've simply taught Pistolet to read."

"You're joking! That's impossible. What can have put such an idea into your head?"

Oscar handed Monsieur de Maubreuil an old issue of a magazine, in which an article had been circled in blue pencil.

"Look," he said, simply.

The old scientist read aloud: "An English scientist, Mr. Newcome, has succeeded, by dint of patience and ingenuity, in teaching his dog, an English griffon of remarkable intelligence, to read and understand a certain number of words. Mr. Newcome had an alphabet of movable wooden letters constructed, and, thanks to a great deal of coaxing with the aid of sugar-lumps, has succeeded in

---

[6] *Tournesol* usually means sunflower, but it can also mean litmus.

[7] "Armenian paper" was blotting-paper infused with a solution of benzoin resin, which enjoyed enormous success in France in the 1890s as a domestic deodorizer.

associating in the animal's memory certain ideas and words. Thus, when the dog wants something, such a sugar, he is obliged to form the word 'sugar' with the aid of the movable letters placed in front of him. It is the same for all the objects of which the dog has need. Mr. Newcome, who has presented his pupil at the Royal Institution in London, does not despair of one day being able to initiate him in abstract ides."

The old scientist added: "Very curious. Has Oscar obtained such fine results as the English scientist?"

"Not yet," Andrée replied, "but Pistolet is making progress day by day."

"You can judge his knowledge for yourselves," said the young hunchback proudly, taking twenty-four wooden letters from a box, which he threw pell-mell on to the sand of the path. "Pistolet, what are you going to have for your dinner this evening?"

The animal barked briefly, furrowed his bushy brows with an expression of comical gravity, and hen, scattering the letters with his paws unhesitatingly chose an M, then an E and then an A. Within a minute, he had lined up correctly on the sand the four letters of the word MEAT.

"No, Pistolet," said Oscar, with an expressive mime, pronouncing the syllables very clearly, "You're not having meat, you're having *soup*."

The dog uttered a discontented growl, dispersed the word he had formed with his paw, and then began barking dully, turning his back on the spectators.

"You see, m'sieur!" cried the hunchback, triumphantly. "He doesn't like it, but he understands—he understands very well."

"That's marvelous!" declared Monsieur de Maubreuil. "Pistolet fully justifies everything that has been written about the psychology of animals. My compliments, Oscar—but you must have had a great deal of difficulty in arriving at that result."

Not as much as all that. I've been training Pistolet for a little more than a month, giving his lessons twice a day."

"Does he know many words?" Baruch asked.

"Seven or eight, Monsieur," Oscar replied. "What it has been most difficult for me to get into the dog's head is the idea of a walk. It required a lot of patience. I've observed that when I pick up my cane, Pistolet, divining that I'm about to go out, barks with joy. I've therefore been able to get him to formulate the letters of the word *walk* every time he sees me pick up my cane. I only permit him to come with me when he's lined up the letters of the word faultlessly. He learned fairly quickly to make up the word himself when he wants to go for a walk. Then, gradually, I got him accustomed to no longer taking any notice of my cane. Now, Pistolet only attaches its true meaning to the word *walk*, detached from any other object."

André was delighted with Pistolet's achievement. She had Oscar instruct him to form the word *sugar*, and she gave him several lumps that she had brought for that purpose.

At that moment, the dinner bell resounded in the tranquil evening atmosphere, and everyone, including the canine phenomenon, headed for the dining-room.

On the way, Baruch attempted to stroke Pistolet, but the dog recoiled, showing his teeth and barking furiously. The American was definitely antipathetic to him. Andrée and her father were astonished, for they had a certain confidence in Pistolet's instinct, and the dog had never reacted in that fashion to any of their friends.

The dog had scented a mortal enemy in Baruch and, as we shall see, his marvelous instinct was not mistaken.

IV. The Furnace

It was the evening on which the experiment for which Monsieur de Maubreuil had been preparing for more than a month was to take place. Like all true scientists, the old chemist, on the brink of that decisive attempt, was not without emotion. Leaning on the window-sill of the laboratory, he was pensively watching the darkness gradually descend over the sea and the countryside, from which mysterious rumors were rising.

"Will I finally succeed?" he wondered, for he thousandth time. From memory, he ran through the mental calculations that he expected, this time, to produce an infallible result.

Suddenly, the screeching of a flock of seabirds that was settling on the strand to feed cut through the silence of the evening. Although he was exempt from all superstition, the chemist could not help shuddering, but he quickly overcame the impression of vague and unhealthy terror.

"Come on," he said to himself. "It's time."

Going into the first room, he called: "Baruch!"

"Here I am, my dear Master."

"Switch on the electric lights; we'll go to work, if you please."

At that moment, someone knocked lightly on the outer door of the laboratory. Without waiting to be given permission to enter, Andrée burst into the room with the showcases and threw herself into the old scientist's arms.

"God night, Father—I'm going to spend the evening with Frédérique at the villa.

"Go, my child, but don't stay out too late. Although it's not far, I don't like to think of you wandering over the heath and the strand, like a Breton fairy. We're going to be working late this evening, and I won't be in bed when you get back."

"What new prodigy are you preparing now?"

"I'm still on diamonds, my dear. I haven't yet obtained what I want, but I'm firmly convinced that we're nearing the goal. Perhaps, tomorrow, I'll be able to show you brilliants more beautiful than those of the Queen of England or the Empress of Russia."

André had been brought up to hate gemstones. "You know, Father," she said, "that I prefer flowers to any jewels."

"Well, we'll have the most beautiful flowers in the world, and we'll give the diamonds to your friend Frédérique. But once again, don't be late!"

"Good luck, and don't worry—I'll be back early. Am I not, in any case, under the protection of my faithful Oscar, armed with his lantern and his holly stick?" With her finger she pointed at the paltry silhouette of the hunchback, hiding in the doorway.

During this conversation, Baruch Jorgell had gone back into the second laboratory, as if he were avoiding the presence of the young woman.

For some time, there had been a covert coldness between Andrée and her father's collaborator. In spite of all his dissimulation, Baruch had been unable to conceal the discontent and jealousy caused to him by the assiduity of the engineer Paganot with regard to the young woman. Briefly, he had nurtured the idea of becoming Monsieur de Maubreuil's son-in-law, and he was both infuriated and humiliated by the polite indifference that Andrée testified to him. With her feminine intuition, she had divined, without perhaps quite being able to take account of it, that her father's collaborator was an enemy even more dangerous than he was hypocritical.

Monsieur de Maubreuil was the only one—his scientific ingenuity being ignorant of the treasons of life—who professed a complete sympathy is Baruch's regard. Having only praise for him from the point of view of scientific work, he mistook the American's taciturnity for melancholy, and his slyness for seriousness.

Meanwhile, André had already gone down several of the steps of the monumental granite stairway with wooden banisters when Monsieur de Maubreuil shouted to her from the landing at the top: "Give my best wishes to Bondonnat. Tell him I'll come to see him at lunchtime tomorrow. If I succeed, I'll bring Frédérique some diamonds of my manufacture."

Monsieur de Maubreuil came back in pensively, prey to a vague and ominous presentiment.

For a long time, with his forehead applied to the window-pane, his eyes followed the lantern-light that appeared and disappeared between the clumps of gorse on the cliff, like a glow-worm. Finally, it disappeared into the kind of phosphorescent aureole that was suspended over Prosper Bondonnat's electric gardens. André had arrived at his friend's house.

"Let's go!" he called to the chemist, pulling himself together. "Enough dreaming—to work!"

"Everything is ready, my dear Master," Baruch replied, obsequiously.

In the light of the electric lamps, the gems in the display cases launched scintillating gleams; one might have thought them the fulgurant eyes of demons, intensely radiant, almost alive in their immobility.

Monsieur de Maubreuil went into the laboratory and approached the large porcelain table that occupied the center, cluttered with a host of flasks, retorts and test-tubes. With a pair of tongs, Baruch opened the heavy doors of the electric furnace that occupied one entire side of the room, protected by thick metal plates reinforced with fireproof bricks.

Monsieur de Maubreuil's melancholy physiognomy was brightened by a smile.

"This time," he declared, "I believe I'll succeed. Failure is impossible! We're going to make big diamonds, true diamonds, in as much quantity as we wish."

"Even Moissan,[8] the greatest chemist in France," said Baruch, "has only obtained tiny ones. The largest were the size of a pin-head, and he distributed them as curiosities to the pupils at his lectures."

"That's doubtless because he wasn't working with sufficiently considerable masses."

Baruch smiled sardonically. "I don't doubt that we'll succeed," he said, "but it will be so much the worse for the jewelers and shareholders in diamond mines."

"I don't have any scruples in that regard," the chemist relied tranquilly. The disappearance of war from human affairs will one day ruin the cannon-founders and the manufacturers of melinite, just as the disappearance of disease will pit pharmacists and druggists out of business. I don't see any great evil in it; the activity of human labor can be directed toward more genuinely useful objects."

Baruch Jorgell made no rely; his attention had just been attracted by a square metal apparatus attached to the wall opposite the gigantic electric furnace.

"That's a recording microphone!" he said.

"Yes," said the chemist. "I set it up this morning to record the special sounds produced by the matter in fusion at the moment of crystallization. There might perhaps be something to learned from that."

"Perhaps," the Yankee murmured, becoming pensive.

Now silence reigned in the laboratory. On the table, Baruch arranged the various crucibles that were filled with metal bars sprinkled with extremely dense carbon dust. Into others Monsieur de Maubreuil introduced blocks of graphite, and he adjusted the nozzles of an apparatus through which carbon dioxide, raised to a high temperature, would be transmitted into the very heart of the molten mass.

Baruch devoted himself with methodical slowness to the task that had been allotted to him. When he thought that the chemist was no longer observing him, however, his gaze scintillated and his face contracted in a frightful rictus.

Monsieur de Maubreuil was brimming over with enthusiasm. His features had lost their dull and melancholy expression. With his long gray hair swept backwards and his unkempt beard, he was moving back and forth with a busy and joyful fever.

In less than half an hour the final preparations were concluded. The crucibles, filed and their lids sealed, were lined up symmetrically on the central table.

---

[8] Henri Moissan (1852-1907) was one of several French chemists who attempted to use electric arc furnaces to manufacture diamonds, with limited success.

"We're nearing the goal!" exclaimed Monsieur de Maubreuil, excitedly. "We're finally about to realize the infantile dream of ancient humankind, infatuated with those useless shiny stones. The stones that we shall make will far surpass King Solomon's bowl, hollowed out, the rabbis say, from a single emerald, and the giant ruby that, according to what I've read, is presently the property of your father, the billionaire Jorgell!"

Baruch's expression was charged with hatred. "Never talk to me about my father," he stammered, in a tremulous voice. "We have nothing in common. You know how he robbed me."

"Forgive the allusion, my dear Baruch," said the old man, affectionately. "I had no intention of upsetting you; I forgot that those memories are painful. But let's get back to our diamonds. Now it's a matter of putting the crucibles in the furnace."

Without a word of response, the American opened the heavy doors of the electric furnace again, inside which he lined up the heat-resistant receptacles.

There was nothing more to do now than unleash the current of several thousand volts, powerful enough to reproduce the crystallization of the carbon mixed with the metal in the crucibles.

The doors were hermetically sealed. The solemn moment had arrived.

"Go!" ordered Monsieur de Maubreuil, gravely.

Baruch operated the switch, releasing the formidable current.

Almost instantaneously, a terrible heat spread through the two rooms. The gigantic furnace doors turned red; the floorboards and the furniture creaked and split, and on the table, although it was situated several meters away from the furnace, items of glassware shattered.

Inundated with sweat, their faces congested, although they were only dressed in laboratory smocks made of coarse cloth, Monsieur de Maubreuil and Baruch had to go into the room with the display cases, where the heat was less intense.

They were both breathless and semi-suffocated.

From time to time Baruch went back into the laboratory, consulted the apparatus situated near the furnace with his gaze, and then came back hurriedly, half-stifled by the intolerable temperature of the room.

Rare words fell into the great silence.

"How many degrees?"

"Three thousand."

"Good."

Then there were three thousand five hundred, four thousand, four thousand five hundred.

The atmosphere became as unbreathable as that of a liner's engine-room; the floor-tiles were warped and charred two meters from the stone slabs on which the electric furnace was installed. The timber framework of the old manor seemed ready to come apart; one of the window-panes split with a sharp tearing sound, like a cry of agony.

"Five thousand five hundred!" Bruch announced.

"That's enough!" stammered Monsieur de Maubreuil, sponging his brow. "It's sufficient now to maintain that temperature for half an hour."

The American moved the commutator. In the reddish light emitted by the incandescent doors, his gaze flashed. One might have thought that, in that fiery atmosphere, he was at ease in his own element.

"I can't do any more," murmured Monsieur de Maubreuil. "Let's go get a little air on the landing."

They went out, delightedly breathing in the cooler atmosphere of the staircase.

The Manor of Diamonds seemed to be asleep; the Breton domestic and the electrician who looked after the machines installed in the basement were in bed on the far side of the château. In the silence, one could only hear the creaking of warping wood, mingled with the rumble of the sea and the wind whistling over the heath.

"I'm afraid that Andrée will have bad weather for her return journey," Monsieur de Maubreuil said suddenly.

"Don't worry about that," said Baruch, with a strange intonation.

"It's true that my friend Bondonnat will have her escorted back by one of his collaborators, or better still, will telephone me to say that he'll keep her until tomorrow morning."

"You'll see."

"I know, but it troubles me. I almost wish that my daughter were here to witness our triumph or failure..."

"The half-hour is almost over, you know," said Baruch, suddenly, darting a glance at his chronometer.

"Let's go back up!" exclaimed the aged scientist, precipitately, abruptly snatched back to the preoccupation of his experiment.

They both went back up to the laboratory in haste and went into room containing the ardent furnace again. At the precise moment, Baruch cut off the current. Then he opened all the doors and the windows protected by solid steel bars.

The cool humidity of a slow west wind refreshed the suffocating atmosphere of the laboratory delightfully. The furnace lost its fiery glow and began to cool down slowly.

"Shall we open it?" said Monsieur de Maubreuil, with feverish impatience.

"Let's try," the American agreed, no lees impatient. And, arming himself with long steel pincers, the drew nearer to the furnace—but the heat was too intense; it was necessary to wait a little longer.

The old chemist could hardly contain himself. He strode back and forth in the two rooms of the laboratory, mechanically repeating equations and formulae—the very formulae of the synthesis of diamond, of which, now that the experiment was nearing its end, he was no longer so certain.

"As long as I'm not mistaken," he murmured.

In the meantime, Baruch had closed the doors and windows again.

Both of them, as if yielding to an invincible attraction, had drawn nearer to the electric furnace.

"I hope," said Monsieur de Maubreuil, agitatedly, "that the current has accomplished its mysterious task this time. The crystallization ought to be perfect, or it will be the despair of chemistry!"

"That's what we'll see in a moment; we can open up now."

Baruch had picked up his pincers; the heavy metallic bolts were drawn; the crucibles appeared beneath the profound vault, in a nimbus of pink vapor.

"If we've failed…!" stammered the chemist, his heart palpitating with anguish.

Teeth clenched, Baruch lifted up each crucible in turn with his pincers and came to deposit them on the porcelain table. Soon, they were all lined up there.

With a smaller set of pincers, the American tried to open one of the crucibles, which was still red hot, but the operation was not easy.

"Get a hammer and break it!" exclaimed Monsieur de Maubreuil, incapable of waiting a minute longer.

Baruch took hold of a heavy steel hammer with a short handle and, with a brutal gesture, shattered the crucible into smithereens. Every fragment of fireproof earthenware seemed to be coated with a dazzling layer of diamonds. They were sparkling with a thousand fires, in the midst of the acrid vapor that was still being exhaled.

The American stood there, mute with amazement. The fortune displayed before his eyes was inestimable; there were raw crystals there the size of an apple, for which empresses and queen would have competed to pay millions.

Very pale, Monsieur de Maubreuil, considered the gems with an ecstatic smile.

"Diamonds!" he exclaimed, with nervous laughter. "But that's all over. They're no longer worth anything. Who wants them? I'll manufacture them in hundreds, in thousands. People will fill carts with them, load them on to wagons, cover houses with them, pave streets with them. Ha ha!"

He stride back and forth through the laboratory, gesticulating, having reached the summit of exaltation.

"Let's go, Baruch!" he said. "Let's not lose a minute. It's necessary to see what there is in the other crucibles."

If Monsieur de Maubreuil, entirely given over to the joy of a long-awaited triumph, had looked at Baruch Jorgell at that moment, he would have been frightened by the sudden transformation that had overtaken his features. Of the man of the world, the polite Yankee, always grave and even a trifle sad, nothing any longer remained. Jaw jutting, teeth clenched and eyes bulging, Baruch had acquired in a second a fearful expression of cupidity and bestial ferocity.

"Break the crucibles, then!" the chemist repeated—who, literally hypnotized by the diamonds, saw nothing and hard nothing in the delirious joy of his success.

"Which one?" asked Baruch, raising the hammer.

"That one!" said the chemist, leaning over to point at the largest of the crucibles.

The heavy mass fell with a dull thud.

Struck on the back of the head, Monsieur de Maubreuil fell without uttering a sound, and collided with the red-hot all of the electric furnace.

"Die, then, you old fool!" roared the murderer. "The secret of making diamonds is mine!"

The face of the unfortunate chemist had turned violet. His eyes turned up in their orbits, his features conserved in death a frightful expression of stupor and anguish.

Baruch contemplated the disfigured cadaver of his benefactor for some time with cynical composure, and then turned away with a shrug of the shoulders.

"Now," he said, aloud, as if he were addressing an invisible interlocutor, "it's necessary not to hang around here!"

With a rapidity and a precision that denoted an abominable resolution, he broke the other crucibles one after another, plucking out the largest diamonds, which he piled up as he went at a corner of the table. The sparkling pyramid grew incessantly, sparkling with a thousand fires.

"There are millions there!" the murderer muttered, with a sort of avaricious fervor.

And he stood there, ecstatic, forgetting the time, where he was, and the terrible risk he was running.

Suddenly, he shivered. It seemed to him that someone had knocked softly on the door.

He listened, his ears anxiously attentive to the noises outside.

The sound became clearer. It was someone scratching softly, as when one fears being indiscreet.

"Andrée!" he murmured, in a low voice. "It's her, coming to discover the result of our experiment. Too bad! Woe betide anyone who comes to surprise me at such a moment!"

With grim courage, he took a large-caliber Browning from his pocket and opened the door abruptly.

He was nearly knocked over by Pistolet, who launched himself into the room with a single bound, barking furiously.

Baruch's rage was at its peak. "So it's the wretched dog that gave me such a fright!" he growled. "But it'll pay me now for my stupid alarm."

And he fired at point blank range.

Pistolet fell, gasping, with pink foam on his mouth.

Baruch was now prey to the species of panic that invariably takes hold of murderers after the crime. He had finished emptying the crucibles. Precipitately, with crazed gestures, he rushed to the display cases of the first room. Recklessly, he scooped up the most beautiful gems, neglecting the stones of little commercial value, such as, for instance the amethysts and topazes, in favor of the rubies and emeralds, whose price, in certain cases, is inestimable.

He added that booty to the heap of diamonds and parceled up the lot in his laboratory smock.

He completed that work with jerky movements, interrupting himself continually to consult his chronometer.

"She must already have come back," he stammered, in a low and halting voice. "She shouldn't have come back! My hands are already steeped in blood. I'll go on until the end!"

He gripped his Browning with a convulsive pressure.

Suddenly, he put his hand to his head in a wild gesture. "I mustn't forget the essential thing," he said, in a dull voice. "The formulae! I can't go without them!"

Not without a grimace of horror, he went to the cadaver, and rummaged in the waistcoat pocket where the chemist usually carried a minuscule notebook. It was in there that the savant briefly noted down his most important daily finds.

The notebook containing the formulae was not there.

Baruch looked around wildly. On the metallic plate of the furnace, at ground level, he perceived a square pile of black ash, which still retained a few flecks of gilt. That was all that remained of Monsieur de Maubreuil's notebook, which had fallen from his pocket on to the hot metal plate when the murderer had struck him.

"Too bad!" Bruch muttered, with a sort of dejection that might already have been the commencement of remorse. "I'll rediscover the exact figures with a little trial and error. I no longer have time now to do anything but save myself."

The murderer washed his blackened hands, put on a coarse reefer jacket and a traveling cap, stuffed his booty hastily into a valise that he had hidden the day before in the room with the display-cases, and fled without daring to look back, without even switching off the electric lights or closing the door. He was able to get out of the Manor of Diamonds by the small door that opened on to the strand. He had not encountered anyone.

V. In the Torment

Baruch Jorgell had one of those natures of an almost animal energy, for which scruples and remorse never last long. Once on the strand, where the rising tide, driven by a furious west wind, was advancing with menacing rapidity, he breathed freely. The rain that was falling in large drops pictured him an indescribable relief, refreshing his feverish brow,

"All the events of my existence, until this very moment," he exclaimed, have been nothing but a bad dream, a hideous nightmare! I want to forget them, never to remember them again! I'm rich now. Life will be beautiful henceforth, and the struggle interesting! Full steam ahead!"

Triumphantly, he lifted up the heavy briefcase at the end of his arm, which contained his bloody fortune.

Going along the shore in the direction opposite to that of the naturalist's villa, he scaled the cliff by a narrow path. After walking for half an hour he reached a fisherman's cottage with walls of granite and clay and a thatched roof, near to which, in a narrow cove of the bay, two or three boats were bobbing in the eddies of the ebb-tide.

The rain had changed into a heavy downpour; the sky was veiled with thick black clouds fringed with livid silver, like mortuary drapes borne away by the furious blasts of the wind. In spite of his energy, Baruch felt himself invaded by a malaise.

With his ears buzzing, and echoed footsteps sounding behind his own, he fled, ever more rapidly, not daring to turn around.

He recovered some assurance on perceiving the tremulous light shining in the windows of the small house.

He thumped on the worm-eaten door with his fist. "Hey, Père Yvon!" he shouted. "Are you there?"

The door opened slowly. Yvon—the same man who had come to solicit the aid of Monsieur Bondonnat's hail-cannon—appeared in the gap in the smoky aureole of an oil-lamp.

"Bonsoir, M'sieur Jorgell," he murmured.

Without replying to the old man's greeting, Baruch had barged into the only room. Breathless and steaming with water, he sat down on a stool, his precious valise between his legs, facing the hearth. He had mastered his agitation abruptly. It was in a tranquil voice that he said: "Bad weather today, my worthy Yvon. My word, if I'd known that it would be bowing like this, I'd have put off my journey till another time."

"Monsieur is joking," said the old man, winking mischievously. "I've never known such fine smuggling weather! We'll be in Jersey before daylight, provided that the wind doesn't change."

Baruch appeared to be playing his part resignedly. "Oh well, too bad!" he declared. "Since the wine's open, as they say in France, it's necessary to drink it. Is your boat ready?"

"Yes, everything's ready."

Once or twice already, Baruch Jorgell had made the voyage to Jersey in the company of Yvon, in the utmost secrecy. He had been able to persuade the honest fisherman that he was amusing himself running contraband without Monsieur de Maubreuil or Monsieur Bondonnat knowing what he was doing.

Père Yvon, with an appearance of reason—for he had never studied the subtleties of morality—was convinced that stealing from the State was not theft.

Baruch had every interest in leaving the old sea-dog his illusions; he feigned a certain awkwardness at the word contraband. "Let's not talk about that," he murmured, perfectly simulating embarrassment. No one can hear us can they, Père Yvon?"

"Don't worry."

"Whether I'm after contraband or not is nobody's business. I need to go to Jersey on business, that's all."

With a mechanical gesture, Baruch clinked a few gold coins in his pocket.

"Understood," sniggered the old sea-dog, "it isn't me who'll have anything to say if an honest man like you goes in search, among our good friends the English, of tobacco or lace for Mademoiselle Andrée, without disturbing the customs."

At the allusion to Mademoiselle de Maubreuil, Baruch became livid. The conversation, which Père Yvon would have like nothing better than to prolong, was annoying him beyond expression. Hardly listening to the old mariner, who expressed himself slowly, drawing methodical puffs from his black and juicy earthenware pipe, he lent an ear to the drumming of the rain on the windows, the strident plaint of the wind raging over the heath and the dull murmur of the surf on the shingle. He seemed to make out, through those confused rumors, cries of agony, heart-rending appeals for help, and the gallop of a pursuit.

"Let's go!" he cried, getting to is feet agitatedly. "Let's hurry, Père Yvon, or we'll miss the tide."

"There's plenty of time," replied the old fisherman, calmly.

Baruch made no reply. He understood that in order to gain time, it was necessary not to answer the old chatterbox, but he was fidgeting. At any moment, he knew, his crime might be discovered. Time was of the essence.

Finally, after having drunk a bowl of cider in small sips, Yvon slowly put on his oil-cloth overcoat, but on his hat and sea-boots, which came up to his waist.

"We're off," he said, once these preparations were complete.

"It's not too soon," Baruch grumbled, his patience at an end.

Yvon turned the key in the door of his hut and went on ahead. Baruch followed him, almost bent double by the weight of his valise full of stones, with his cap pulled down over his eyes and his reefer-jacket turned up to cover his ears.

As they arrived on the edge of the sand, the murderer thought he could make out a plaintive barking in the murmur of the wind and the rain. He shivered from head to toe. He was in haste to be far away from the scene of his crime.

It was with a sigh of relief that he sat down in Yvon's boat, which the latter had hauled to the bank.

Although he seemed awkward and inert on land, once he was aboard the old mariner became decisive and agile. In the blink of an eye, they were ready to set to sea. With the sail hoisted, Yvon sat down in the bow of the boat beside his passenger, and, taking the tiller, set a course for the mouth of the large bay, signaled by the fires of two small lighthouses.

The fishing-boat flew over the crests of the waves. As long as they were in the shelter of the cliffs bordering the coast, the force of the waves was not too evident, in spite of the wind and the rain.

With an indescribable satisfaction, Baruch Jorgell saw the gray line of the coast melting into the darkness. Only the lights of the naturalist's villa and the Manor were shining there, like two bloody patches

As soon as the boat, the *Rose-Adélaïde* of Kérity had doubled the point and emerged into the open sea, however, she was gripped by a squall. A wave half-filled her with water, and she leaned over in a disquieting fashion. Yvon only just had time to slacken the mainsail, only retaining the jib, the small triangular sail at the front.

Soaked to the skin, clinging to the bench in the bow, Baruch Jorgell was mad with fear. His teeth were chattering like castanets. Alone with the old man in that fragile boat, like a nut-shell, already full of water, he imagined that the final catastrophe could only be a question of minutes. He would have given his valise full of precious stones to find himself safe on land.

Yvon was not in the least disturbed. As taciturn, once at sea, as he was loquacious on land, he held the tiller in a firm hand and paid no attention to his passenger.

Lifted up like a feather by the breath of the storm, the *Rose-Adélaïde* progressed with frightful velocity. She flew like a meteor. Already the lighthouses were no more than little blinking dots on the horizon.

Suddenly, a white light appeared between the high waves to port, very close to the *Rose-Adélaïde*.

"A thousand thunders!" howled Père Yvon. "It's the customs cutter! No one but them can be out and about in this weather!"

"Well, too bad!" stammered the American, who had just been inundated from head to toe with sea-water. "Hail the customs men. Perhaps they can row us ashore."

The murderer was already calculating that from the nearest port, he would probably still have time to catch a train before his crime was discovered.

Yvon, however, was not in the least disposed to summon the greencoats to his rescue. "No chance, my dear Monsieur," he replied, in a slightly mocking tone. "You should have told me that you were scared, and I wouldn't have taken you with me in my boat. For my count, I've no intention of letting the revenue men interfere in my affairs. How do I know what merchandise you have in your valise?"

Baruch Jorgell had no reply to that. In the panic of the fear that had gripped him, he had not thought of that.

"Help me, then," said Yvon, rudely. "If you don't want to drink the big cup, take the tiller for a moment and hold it steady."

Baruch obeyed without saying a word. He had no idea what the old fisherman intended to do.

The latter, in spite of the sea-water that was inundating the frail vessel, and in spite of the waves that were lifting them up to mountainous heights only to plunge them down again as if into a ravine, precipitated himself toward the rigging of the mainsail between to enormous waves. Bracing himself against the two sides of the boat, he hauled on the ropes with all his might.

The veil began to extend, with a furious flap that nearly capsized the boat.

"Stop! What are you doing?" Baruch shouted, fearfully.

Yvon did not even deign to reply. He finished hoisting the sail, which he secured solidly; then, snatching the tiller from the hands of his consternated passenger, he took control of the rudder again.

The howling wind was engulfed in the canvas, now stretched to breaking-point, lifting the *Rose-Adélaïde* in a furious bound, which flew like a seagull over the summits of the monstrous waves, lunging with vertiginous speed into the heart of the storm, in pitch darkness.

A minute later, the white light had disappeared.

Baruch had collapsed on to his bench, exhausted. Now, in the livid crest of a foaming wave, he seemed to see the melancholy face of Monsieur de Maubreuil.

VI. After the Crime

Three months had gone by since the crime that had thrown the entire scientific world into mourning. Monsieur de Maubreuil was now resting in a little cemetery on a hill facing the sea, in the shade of old mossy apple-trees.

In spite of the sagacious investigation mounted by the local magistrates, with the aid of the finest sleuths of the Sûreté, and in spite of the considerable rewards offered by Mademoiselle de Maubreuil and Monsieur Bondonnat, who had furnished useful information to the police, the murderer had not been found.

The old naturalist, who had agreed to serve as Andrée's guardian, had welcomed the young woman into his home. He had even insisted on taking responsibility for Oscar, and claimed to have discovered in the young hunchback the most fortunate aptitude for Science.

Nothing had changed in the villa with the fantastic gardens, where Prosper Bondonnat and his two collaborators, the engineer Antoine Paganot and the naturalist Roger Ravenel, were transforming the most diverse specimens of the vegetable kingdom at the whim of their caprice. As before, the days went by peacefully in experiments, conversations and labor.

The Manor of Diamonds, whose doors and windows remained closed, gradually resumed the dismal appearance of a building in ruins.

As before, Andrée still went for walks along the shore and in the gardens of the valley, arm-in-arm with her friend Frédérique. Now, though, pale and thin, dressed in black, she never smiled. The character of her beauty had been transformed; her soft blue eyes had taken on a pensive and melancholy expression and her physiognomy was imprinted with a meditative gravity.

Frédérique manifested the most fraternal devotion to her friend; the two young women were never apart. In any case, habituated by their education to a sedentary life and serious occupations, they were never bored.

Both of them were occupied with an indefatigable activity in searching for Monsieur de Maubreuil's murderer. Every day, they conducted a copious correspondence. In spite of these efforts, the investigation made no progress.

Only one thing was known for sure, which was that Baruch Jorgell had gone back to America.

A few days after his return from Jersey, Père Yvon had been stricken by remorse. He had gone to find Monsieur Bondonnat and had confessed to him frankly how, thinking that he was only dealing with an inoffensive smuggler, he had furnished he murderer with the means to escape.

"If I had known that," murmured the old mariner, regretfully, and ashamed of his naivety, "I would have strangled the swine with my own hands."

Very sadly, Monsieur Bondonnat had only been able to find one response. "I don't hold it against you; I know that you're an honest man—but how unfortunate it s that you let the wretch escape!"

After Yvon had given him that information, Monsieur Bondonnat had immediately telegraphed the Constable of Jersey, with whom he was personally acquainted. That was how it was discovered that Baruch had succeeded in reaching New York. The arrest warrant transmitted to the chief of police arrived three days too late.

Andrée had sworn, however, that the case would never be "filed." She multiplied the offers of rewards in America and had them advertised temptingly. Every day she received a veritable heap of cuttings from newspapers.

Antoine Paganot and Roger Ravenel, as well as Frédérique, were helping Mademoiselle de Marbreuil in the work of keeping the investigation going. The naturalist and the engineer were occupied in that fastidious work when the engineer Paganot suddenly uttered a cry of surprise, pointing to the headline of an article in the *New York and Chicago Review* that he was in the process of scanning.

"Look," he said. "Here's something that concerns us: *The billionaire Fred Jorgell and his criminal son.*"

"Unfortunately," said Roger Ravenel, "My English isn't very good."

"Oh, I can take care of that." He began to translate the text from the open magazine, summarizing the less interesting passages.

The first paragraphs of the articles contained biographical details about Fred Jorgell; his story was similar to those of many of the emperors of the dollar. Once a barman aboard a luxury train on the great Pacific Line, an abattoir worker in Chicago, a newspaper seller in Boston, a cowboy and a prospector, Fred Jorgell, thanks to his energy, his prodigious business sense had, step by step, rapidly become one of the kings of corn, a very important item of commerce because it was used in the manufacture of whisky. The American periodical gave precise details on the Trust that he had recently organized for the monopolization of cultivation in the central and northern states of the Union. All his competitors had been swiftly driven to the wall by the formidable speculator. Finally, very recently, he had founded a city in the solitudes of the West, baptized with his name, Jorgell City, about which sinister legends circulated.

The second part of the article was devoted to personal details regarding the billionaire and his private life. Although he was over fifty, he was still in his prime. Only sleeping a few hours a night, dictating hundreds of letters every day, leading several complicated enterprises from the front, his sobriety was exemplary; he only drank water, never went to the theater and lived more simply than the least of his overseers. Although quite charitable, he was said to be incapable of any enjoyment or cheerfulness.

He had not always been thus, but that misanthropy was due to a series of domestic misfortunes that did not seem to have finished yet. Firstly, he had lost his wife, whom he adored, and had been left a widow after three years of marriage. The affection of his daughter, the charming and distinguished Isidora, had brought him precious consolation, but his son, Baruch had caused him great distress. Since infancy he had showed the most vicious tendencies, revealing himself to be brutal, a gambler and a wastrel. Later, in consequence of events that remained obscure, Fred Jorgell had expelled the unworthy son from his roof, and no more mention of him had been heard in America.

It was now known that he had then taken refuge in France, where, having been rescued and saved from death by Monsieur de Maubreuil, he had murdered and robbed his benefactor. That discovery, made public by the steps taken by the French consulates in New York and Chicago, ad caused an enormous scandal in the society of the Five Hundred. All the detectives in the Union were now launched in pursuit of Baruch.

Fred Jorgell, with typical Yankee energy, had declared to several interviewers that if his son was guilty, he would not make any attempt to preserve him from punishment, not even to find him a defender or lessen the rigors of his imprisonment.

As soon as these facts were known in America, singular rumors had begun to spread. It was affirmed with considerable plausibility that Baruch was the author of a series of mysterious murders of which Jorgell City had been the theater, and which had remained inexplicable and unpunished. The billionaire's son was now revealed as one of the most redoubtable bandits that had ever been featured in the annals of crime.

Finally, it had just been announced that, yielding to the pressure of irritated public opinion, Fred Jorgell had sold the block of shares that gave him four-fifth of the ownership of Jorgell City and left the city. A number of notable inhabitants, including the famous Doctor Cornelius Kramm, his brother Fritz Kramm, and the engineer Harry Dorgan, had followed the example of the founder and had, like him, come to take up residence in New York.

The engineer Paganot had just finished translating that article, which threw new light on the sinister personality of Baruch Jorgell, when Andrée and Frédérique, accompanied by Monsieur Bondonnat, came into the drawing-room where the two young men were sitting. The three of them had been taking a walk in the gardens when the post has arrived.

The engineer began re-reading the article from the *New York and Chicago Review* for the benefit of the newcomers. He had almost finished when Andrée de Maubreuil interrupted him, her blue eyes illuminated by a vengeful flame.

"Yes," she murmured. "What the American magazine says is perfectly true. The information correspondents at every point with what Baruch told my father. The wretch always talked about his grim hatred of the billionaires. I remember now that he manifested considerable embarrassment every time he was asked questions regarding Jorgell City."

"Monsieur de Maubreuil was so discreet," observed Frédérique. "He never told us anything about his collaborator's antecedents."

"I hope it won't be long before he's caught," said Roger Ravenel.

"I'm going to write a letter to the consul in New York right away," said the old naturalist. "He's an old friend of mine. Come and find me in ten minutes, my dear Andrée; I'll show you what I've written."

Bondonnat shut himself up in his study, where, as had been agreed, his ward did not take long to join him.

Andrée found the old scientist with a screwdriver and a wrench in his hand; he was finishing setting up a delicate mechanism.

"The letter to my friend the consul is finished," he said. "I'll give it to you to read; just give me a minute."

"Don't disturb yourself. But what is this elegant apparatus, so neatly nickel-plated?"

"Don't you recognize this kind of microphone? It's provided with an improved mechanism invented by your friend Paganot."

Andrée blushed slightly, but Monsieur Bondonnat did not seem to have noticed.

"Thanks to this apparatus," he continued. "The story of the fairy Keen-Ear, who could hear the grass grow, will soon be more than a fairy-tale."

"What are you going to do with it? I can't really see what use a microphone will be in your horticultural experiments."

"You'll understand. I'm going to install one in each of my greenhouses. They'll be provided with recording apparatus, and will register all the almost-imperceptible sounds produced during the processes of germination and flowering of plants. I'll be able to make some curious deductions from that, perhaps a new law.

Andrée de Maubreuil reflected. "I've seen a similar apparatus in my father's hands," she murmured, with a sigh.

"Come on, don't be sad," said Monsieur Bondonnat, emotionally. "I've promised you that I won't neglect anything to avenge my unfortunate friend, and I'll keep my word."

The young woman's physiognomy had become more serious. "My dear guardian," she said, "I have something to ask you. I'd like to visit the Manor of Diamonds with you; I haven't dared return there since the murder."

"My child," the old man replied, a trifle dubious, "don't you think it would be preferable to postpone that funeral pilgrimage until another time? You'll revive your grief."

"I want it always to remain as sharp. I want my father to be avenged."

"Well, so be it; I understand the sentiment that's guiding you. I'll do as you wish—but there doesn't seem to be any point, it seems to me, in taking Paganot and Ravenel.

"You're right—but Frédérique and Oscar can go with us."

"We'll leave right away. Since it's decided, it's best not to put off the visit.

Monsieur Bondonnat put on his broad-brimmed felt hat, picked up his cane with an ivory handle, and, a quarter of an hour later, he was heading for the Manor of Diamonds, accompanied by the two young women.

By virtue of a sentiment that Andrée respected, Oscar wanted to bring the dog Pistolet with him, the latter having now recovered from the wound he had received on the night of the murder.

The morning was radiant; the heather was a dark purple color and the golden furze had not yet shed its flowers. The sea, as calm and clear as a mirror, came to expire at the foot of the pink and blue granite of the cliff. Seagulls of various species were tracing broad circles against the pale blue sky.

In the bright sunlight, the old manor, set between the ancient oaks of the avenue that shaded it, seemed even more solemn and morose. The panes of the large Gothic windows seemed to be covered with gray dust, like eyes devoid of thought. Moss had grown over the doorsteps; sea-grass was growing and the thistles of the strand were swaying their downy heads in the flower-beds in the garden.

Monsieur Bondonnat took a large key out of his pocket and tried to open the door, but the rusty lock grated, and when the heavy oak battens finally moved back, with a sonorous noise, repeated by the echoes of the vestibule, Andrée shivered, imagining that she was hearing a long and plaintive moan.

The two young women, linking arms with Monsieur Bondonnat, instinctively huddled closer to him, tremulously.

The acrid and funereal atmosphere of empty houses took them by the throat. Large spiders had woven their webs in the corners. Crystals of saltpeter were scintillating along the walls and granite vaults.

They all traversed the vestibule in silence, climbed the stiff and massive steps of the stairway, without saying a word. Finally, they arrived at the laboratory door and went into the room with the display-cases.

The room was exactly as the murderer's flight had left it. The police, during their searches, had not disturbed anything. The pillaged cupboards remained open, still bearing the traces of seals. In the second room, the items of metallic apparatus were rusted or stained with verdigris; on the porcelain table the debris of the crucibles broken by Baruch's hammer were still sparkling with the meager gems left behind. A fine dust had settled over all the objects, as if a snow of forgetfulness had fallen over the past.

As he went into the laboratory Pistolet uttered a long and lamentable howl. He ferreted around everywhere, anxiously, stopping in front of the electric furnace, at the very spot where Monsieur de Maubreuil had fallen beneath the blows of his murderer—but he always came back to the place, still marked by a bloodstain, where Baruch had felled him with two shots from his Browning.

Andrée, who had been containing herself with difficulty for several minutes, abruptly burst into tears and threw herself into the arms of Monsieur

Bondonnat and Frédérique. "Poor Father," she murmured, through her tears. "With what solicitude, a few hours before falling under the blows of a murderer, he told me not to be late. Who knows? Perhaps he'd still be alive if I hadn't gone out that evening..."

"Don't think that," said the old scientist, authoritatively. "We know now that Baruch Jorgell wasn't committing his first murder, and that he'd been premeditating the crime for a long time. If you had stayed, he would have killed you too!"

"To shed the blood of his benefactor—the man who had saved him from death!" murmured the young woman, horrified. "It's abominable!"

Again she melted into tears; silence reigned.

In the meantime, Oscar Tournesol had been searching in all directions, blackening his fingers with the dust that covered everything. "Monsieur Bondonnat!" he exclaimed, suddenly. "Look!"

He was pointing, amid the apparatus, at a recoding microphone similar, but for a few minor improvements, to the one that Andrée had just seen in the old botanist's study.

"What do you mean?" asked Frédérique

"But if...yes, I understand!" exclaimed Monsieur Bondonnat. "That apparatus must have been switched on at the time of the murder. It's almost impossible that it hasn't recorded my unfortunate friend's last words."

"My God! Is it possible?" Andrée exclaimed.

"We'll certainly find a precious clue there," added Oscar, proud of the idea that he had had.

Without losing a moment, Monsieur Bondonnat cleaned the recording microphone carefully. He made sure that its mechanism was intact. It had not suffered any damage.

"It's in working order!" the old scientist declared, solemnly. "Listen to the voice of an incorruptible witness!"

Prey to a poignant emotion, the little hunchback and the two young women had drawn closer; their hearts were pounding.

In the profound silence of the abandoned laboratory, the nasal voice of the apparatus emerged. One of the metal scrolls unwound slowly, reproducing the voice of the unfortunate scientist like a distant echo.

Andrée de Maubreuil was stirred by an indescribable emotion on hearing that voice, which seemed to be speaking to her from beyond the tomb.

"*Diamonds!*" murmured the apparatus, in a distant voice as feeble as a breath. "*But that's all over. They're no longer worth anything. Who wants them? I'll manufacture them in hundreds, in thousands. People will fill carts with them, load them on to wagons, cover houses with them, pave streets with them. Ha ha!*"

There was nothing more funereal than the microphone's quavering laughter, which seemed to be coming from the distant regions of Death.

Now the apparatus continued to repeat the slightest sounds of the laboratory on the night of the crime, reproducing all the phases of the experiment. They all listened with a feverish anxiety to that scarcely-perceptible whisper, which revealed the most poignant of tragedies to them.

The microphone recited the formulae that Monsieur de Maubreuil had repeated to himself as he paced back and forth in the laboratory.

"In that case," Monsieur Bondonnat exclaimed, "the secret of the synthesis of diamonds isn't lost!"

"What does that matter?" said Andrée sadly. "Listen—the terrible moment's approaching."

But at the moment when the apparatus repeated the dull sound of Monsieur de Maubreuil's body falling to the floor, the murderer's cry of triumph and his frightful snigger, it was more than Andrée could bear, and she fainted into Frédérique's arms.

When she came to, the microphone was no longer functioning.

Bondonnat rubbed the young woman's temples with vinegar while Frédérique made her breathe smelling-salts. Pistolet, his eyes moist, gently licked his mistress' hands. Oscar had gone to fetch help from the villa.

"Thank you for looking after me, my dear friends," Andrée stammered, with a heart-rending smile. "I couldn't sustain that cruel ordeal to the end. I am, however, glad to know the whole truth. Now, the murderer must be punished."

As soon as she had recovered completely, Andrée de Maubreuil went back to the villa on the arm of Monsieur Bondonnat and his daughter—but the shock had been too great; she had to go to bed. Frédérique undertook to serve as her devoted nurse.

A week later, the old naturalist received a letter from New York. It was signed by the French consul, and informed him that, after having believed that they were on the point of arresting Baruch Jorgell, the detectives had suddenly lost track of him. One hypothesis was that he had succeeded in reaching Australia. According to other information, the murderer had entered into an association with a New York gang, the Red Hand, which had furnished him with the means to hide.

VII. Tracked

Dinner was coming to a conclusion at the "family hotel" run by Mrs. Griffon on Thirtieth Avenue, New York.

The venerable lady, having dispensed plum cake and marmalade with a parsimonious hand, lifted up the crystal bell covering a heady Canadian cheese, the violent odor of which had the effect of driving the majority of the guests into the "parlor" where tea had been served.

Mrs. Griffon was getting ready to follow them and take a well-earned break reading the evening papers, which were generally filled with exciting new items—the lynching of negroes doused in gasoline and burned alive, stirring electrocutions, conflagrations in thirty-story buildings, the sensational arrests of pickpockets or the murderers of billionaires—when a shabbily-dressed individual with a long and slightly hooked nose surmounted by a pince-nez with smoked lenses came into the dining-room. When he thought he was unobserved, he darted a rapid glance around him, over the top of his lenses.

"You're late again," said the lady sharply. "You know that one of the rules of my establishment is exact punctuality." After a pause full of menace, she added: "And a perfect regularity in payment."

The newcomer bowed his head humbly and sat down at the table while a "waiter" with threadbare waistcoat brought some oxtail soup with beans and a large joint of cold beef, appetizingly pink.

"A thousand pardons, Madam. Very sorry to for the delay in settling my little bill, but I am, as you know, a dealer in chemical products, and I've just concluded an important sale this evening. Tomorrow, Saturday, I'll collect the commission, which will be more than fifty dollars, and my first concern will be to pay you."

Mrs. Griffon, a worthy Scotswoman who had been living in New York for ten years, seemed entirely reassured by her client's affirmations. "I know," she said, "that the rewards are irregular in your game, and until now you've always been able to pay on time..." Then, changing her tone and unfolding a large copy of the *New York Times*, she added: "By the way, did you know that they're on the track of Baruch Jorgell, the billionaire's son who killed an old French scientist to steal his diamonds?"

At these words the guest reddened, his eyes fluttering behind the lenses of his pince-nez. It was, however, with a perfect indifference that he replied: "Baruch Jorgell? I don't know the name. You know, anyway, that I'm so absorbed by business that I don't have time to read the papers."

"Look," said Mrs. Griffon. "Here's his picture." She laughed sonorously. "And what's very amusing," she added, "is that he resembles you slightly."

"That's quite possible," the diner replied, not without an imperceptible shudder.

To put an end to the conversation, which seemed to be annoying him prodigiously, he unfolded a copy of the *New York Herald* himself and absorbed himself in reading it. Mrs. Griffon did likewise, but soon, recalled to the sentiment of her professional duties, she went into the parlor to take her customary place between the piano and the table where the teapot was set.

Her interlocutor hurried through his meal and hastened to go out. He seemed distracted and preoccupied. In the street, he bumped into a stout gentleman with white side-whiskers who was coming out of a bar whose display-window was sparkling with mirrors and electric light.

"You might be more careful," said the fat man, jovially. And, looking at the brightly-lit face of the man who had bumped into him, he added, thinking that it was an excellent joke: "Just because you look like Baruch Jorgell, the billionaire murderer, that's no reason to be proud and go jostling passers-by."

He was bewildered that the man to whom he was speaking only replied to his witticism with an oath, and hastened to disappear into the crowd.

The evening was well-advanced. Electric cabs were going at top speed along the vast avenues, already deserted. Mrs. Griffon's client, wandering like a soul in torment, headed for the Chinese district.

He felt so weary, so desperate and so tormented that the idea had occurred to him of numbing his chagrin by going to smoke opium in a den he knew that was mostly frequented by immigrants.

On the way he patted his waistcoat pocket, which contained the only dollar he had left.

"To possess millions" he muttered, furiously, "and not to be able to touch it! It's enough to drive one mad!" And he brandished his fist as if to threaten an invisible adversary.

He arrived in the Chinese district. He was about to go into a sordid and sticky alleyway, poorly lit by a smoky gas-lamp, when his attention was suddenly attracted by a gathering, in the midst of which a dozen policemen armed with night-sticks were moving.

Gripped by curiosity, he slipped into the crowd, and, addressing a street-porter of Herculean dimensions who was holding forth in the middle of the group, he asked him what was happening.

"Police raid," the man replied, laconically.

"It's believed," added another, "that Baruch Jorgell, the billionaire murderer, has taken refuge in the Chinese quarter."

"Thank you," murmured Mrs. Griffon's boarder, between his teeth—and he drew away from the Chinese quarter rapidly. He walked with a long stride, turning round instinctively, as if to check that he was not being followed.

He stopped in front of a cinematograph hall into which a noisy crowd was flocking. For some time he followed with a distracted gaze, through the vast window that occupied the entire façade, the advertisements in large luminous letters that succeeded one another at five minute intervals, with alternations of profound obscurity and dazzling light.

Suddenly, a flamboyant sentence in bloody letters appeared on the dark background: BARUCH JORGELL, MURDERER OF AN ILLUSTRIOUS FRENCH CHEMIST: EXACT RECONSTITUTION OF THE CRIME.

The man hesitated momentarily. An irresistible desire to see the sensational film had taken hold of him. He took a few steps toward the entrance of the hall, but when he arrived in front of the kiosk where tickets were being sold, he made an abrupt about-turn and fled.

For an hour he walked straight ahead, crossing unfamiliar streets, avenues and squares at random. On a quay where hundreds of dock-workers were busy unloading a liner, he seemed to come to a sudden decision.

He went into a bar and ordered a whisky cocktail, and then a second and a third. When he had paid, he had nothing left but a little loose change.

The alcohol that went to his head in ardent gusts seemed to have calmed him down momentarily. He breathed in the cool evening air delightedly.

"Bah!" he murmured. "Perhaps I'll have a good idea."

He went slowly back to Mrs. Griffon's family hotel, where he occupied a small room under the eaves.

He got up very early the next morning, hoping to get out of the establishment without being seen, but he had counted without his hostess. The Scotswoman had got up even earlier than her boarder. She was already in the parlor when he came in.

"Good morning," she said to him, amiably.

"Good morning, Mrs. Griffon. "I hope you slept well?"

"Admirably." Then, abruptly changing her tone: "I hope I can count on you this evening?"

"Understood. You can make up my bill. As soon as I've got my commission, my first concern will be to pay you."

Reassured by the sincere tone in which this promise had been made, the Scotswoman took her leave of her debtor, who went out into the street as quickly as possible.

Outside, he mingled with the multitude of workers who were hurrying toward offices and factories, but it was visible in his indolent stride that he had no objective.

With the few cents he had left he drank a cup of coffee and ate a sandwich in a bar in the open air, and then headed for a small public library situated in Brooklyn, which was usually only frequented by a dozen unemployed old man. He sat down in the darkest corner and, with his head in his hands, in order that people could see as little as possible of his features, he plunged into reading a translation of one of Berthelot's books on chemistry.

He remained thus all day, apparently completely absorbed with the study of the synthesis of organic compounds. At six o'clock, however, the library closed, and he found himself back on the street.

Night was falling rapidly, and a fine rain had begun to fall; all along the immense avenues, lines of scintillating electric bulbs lit up. The man shivered with cold in his threadbare jacket. He was hungry.

"No more credit at Mother Griffon's!" he said, with a bitter laugh. "And not one dollar left! I might have been able to make my money last for one more day, but what's the point? A little sooner or later—what does it matter?" He ground his teeth with rage. "Not to be able to spend a farthing and to die of hunger, when one possesses millions! What a stupid situation!"

He continued walking slowly. His anger was suddenly succeeded by a profound dejection.

"Where to now?" he murmured, discouraged. "I'll be picked up as a vagrant, identified, searched, and then..."

At that moment, a newspaper-hawker passed close by, howling at the top of his voice on behalf of the evening edition of the *New York Advertiser*. Mechanically the man put his hand into his waistcoat pocket. His finger encountered a single cent, the last that remained to him.

"I never felt so rich," he muttered, ironically.

He threw the copper coin to the hawker, took the issue of the *Advertiser* that was held out to him, and started scanning it distractedly by the light of a gas-lamp.

An enormous headline immediately attracted his attention: *NEW DETAILS OF THE MURDERER BARUCH JORGELL.*

He shrugged his shoulders and was about to throw the paper away, angrily, when his eyes fell upon another article at the foot of the front page, which immediately attracted his keen attention:

DR. CORNELIUS KRAMM'S LATEST MIRACLE

Since the eminent practitioner justly nicknamed the sculptor of human flesh left Jorgell City to take up residence in New York in his sumptuous establishment on Tenth Avenue, he has not let a day go by without effecting some miraculous cure. This is the latest in the series.

Everyone has read in our columns the story of the exploits of the honorable Colonel MacDolmar during the recent American expedition to the Philippine islands. Everyone knows that the heroic soldier was obliged to retire following a particularly serious injury; shrapnel had carried away his nose and half of his right cheek, disfiguring him atrociously. The princes of science had declared unanimously that it was impossible to remedy such a mutilation. Colonel MacDolmar was reduced to wearing a kind of silver half-mask of the most dis-

graceful appearance and had been obliged to resign himself to remaining thus disfigured for the rest of his life.

Recently, on the advice of a few friends, the Colonel had the idea of consulting Dr. Cornelius Kramm, and on the basis of the assurances the latter gave him, confided himself entirely to his care.

After a month of treatment, the result has surpassed all expectations. Of the frightful mutilation, nothing any longer remains but a slight white scar, circular in form. The illustrious doctor has succeeded in completely rebuilding the missing nose and cheek. Once again, he has justified the bizarre and glorious nickname of the sculptor of human flesh.

Colonel MacDolmar, so completely healed that he has actually become engaged to a young and charming heiress, has rewarded Dr. Kramm for his care with the donation a check of considerable value.

The man read that clever advertisement for a second time, and immediately made a resolution.

"I'll go!" he exclaimed. "It's the only hope I have left. Cornelius Kramm is the one man who can save me...if he wants to."

The unknown man carefully folded up the copy of the *New York Advertiser* and set out at a deliberate pace for Tenth Avenue.

After walking for half an hour, he stopped in front of a luxurious property surrounded by high walls and closed by a monumental wrought-iron gate.

As he was about to press the button of the electric bell, the nocturnal visitor recoiled instinctively. He had the vague sensation that he was about to penetrate into the lair of some ferocious wild beast, from which he might never emerge.

"Come on!" he murmured. "I must!"

He rang the bell.

A servant dressed in black with woolen stockings, glacially polite, opened the door and looked the newcomer up and down suspiciously.

"What do you want?" he demanded.

"I'd like to see Dr. Cornelius Kramm."

"Impossible, Monsieur. It's necessary to request an appointment in advance, by letter."

The visitor appeared to be extremely annoyed.

"It's a very serious matter," he stammered, "that can't be delayed..."

"I'm sorry, but my orders are strict."

"Wait!" cried the unknown man, with a sort of despair. "I'm a friend of the doctor. It's absolutely necessary that I speak to him. Give him this note on my behalf, and I'm sure that he'll see me."

He had torn a page out of his notebook; he scribbled a few lines on it and held it out to the hesitant domestic. "There! Give that to the doctor."

The Irishman hand taken the piece of paper with an ill grace. He took the obstinate visitor to a small waiting-room, where he left him.

He came back a few minutes later, with a surprised expression.

"The doctor," he said, in a much more respectful tone, "has said, exceptionally, that he agrees to see you, sir. Would sir care to follow me?"

He preceded the visitor to a luxurious drawing-room ornamented with paintings by Old Masters, bronze statues and Louis XIV furniture of imposing magnificence.

The Irishman disappeared. Almost immediately, a small door concealed in the ebony woodwork opened silently. An individual with a bony face, and cruel staring eyes like those of a bird of prey, behind large spectacles with gold rims, came in slowly.

The two men looked at one another silently for a short time. One might have thought that each of them was reluctant to speak first.

"Why are you here, Baruch Jorgell?" said the doctor, finally, in a grave voice. And as the murderer remained silent, having suddenly gone mortally pale, the doctor repeated, in the same solemn voice: "Why are you seeking refuge in my home, Baruch Jorgell?"

"Where do you expect me to go?" exclaimed Baruch, with the energy of despair. "Where else can a wretch like me find shelter? Remember that once..."

Cornelius imposed silence on him with a gesture. "Once isn't today," he said. There's no connection between us. You might cause me serious annoyance."

"I don't have any money, or shelter; I'm being hunted everywhere, tracked like a wild animal."

"You might have been followed here. Policemen might be outside, waiting for you. I might compromise myself without saving you. Go away."

"You can't send me away like that! It's impossible!" Swiftly, he added: "Anyway, I'm in a position to reward the favor you're about to do for me."

"Yes," said the other, sarcastically. "I can guess how. With the French chemist's diamonds, no?"

"Look," aid Bruch, simply. Unbuttoning his coat, he detached a heavy leather belt from beneath his waistcoat. He unbuckled the clasps, and emptied its contents on to the table-cloth.

Enormous diamonds, rubies and emeralds spread out. The display was dazzling.

Cornelius looked at the gems covetously.

"You see," said Baruch, incisively. "Well, I have a great many secret pockets in my overcoat and waistcoat."

"A true fortune, indeed," said Cornelius, with biting mockery. "Unfortunately, it will be difficult to negotiate, especially in your situation. It's a rather original situation to be dying of hunger when one has such stones in one's pocket."

"Don't mock me. I've let you see my booty. You know me. I'm at your mercy."

"That's my opinion too," the doctor sniggered.

"I'm reduced to the worst extremities, desperate, almost devoid of strength, so weary of living on expedients with millions around me waist that I'm resigned to anything. I've almost got to the point of saying: 'Hand me over to the law and keep my diamonds. Anything rather than continuing to live like this.'"

"Well, no!" exclaimed Cornelius, abruptly, his skeletal face grimacing with a kind of smile. It's not up to me to judge you. Not only will I not turn you in, but I'll give you shelter and associate you with grandiose enterprises. You realize now, don't you, that your fate is completely in my hands?"

"You don't have to spell it out," Baruch replied, in a surly tone. "I know that I'm at your mercy."

"Of course," said the doctor, whose owlish eyes were scintillating. He continued, in a softer tone: "I won't abuse the situation, but I want you to understand that it's in your interest to do whatever I say. We'll be collaborators and accomplices."

"I'll obey—I have no alternative. But what do I have to do?"

"I don't know exactly myself. I simply want to find a use for the qualities of energy, audacity, coolness and intelligence that your latest adventures have brought out. In a few months, perhaps in a few days, I'll have found the idea I'm looking for."

Baruch uttered a profound sigh. He felt as if an immense weight had been lifted from him.

"And the diamonds?" he asked, after a pause.

"Have no fear in that regard. The diamonds will be cut by Dutch jewelers in my brother's workshops; then they'll be placed in antique mounts and sold at full price, believe me! My brother will release them gradually through his European branches."

"And how much will they bring me?"

"I could say nothing. A life saved and impunity are worth more than the most beautiful diamonds in the world—but don't worry. I repeat, I won't abuse the situation. I'll give you an exact account of all your stones; the sale price will be shared between you, me and my brother. That's quite natural, I think."

While speaking, Cornelius Kramm amused himself by picking up the scattered gems one by one and building a kind of pyramid that sparkled in the light of the electric bulbs, but he interrupted that occupation abruptly and turned to Baruch Jorgell, who was standing there pensively.

"You must need money?" he said.

"I've already told you that I don't have a dollar left."

"Here's a thousand-dollar bill—but it's probable that you won't have the opportunity to make use of it for some time."

"Why is that?"

"Because it's indispensable to your safety that you don't leave here until you receive further instructions. It's necessary for you to be forgotten, and for your individuality to be completely modified..."

Cornelius broke off. A loud burst of laughter had just resounded from the far side of the room. An elegantly-dressed gentleman with smiling and affable features advanced toward them. It was Fritz Kramm, the famous art dealer, the doctor's brother.

"When it comes to modifying people's individualities," the newcomer said, laughing, "that's my brother's specialty." Greeting Baruch with perfect ease, he added: "Delighted to see you, Master Jorgell."

Baruch sighed. He felt his heart gripped by anguish. Since he had entered the dwelling of the sculptor of human flesh, he had understood that his destiny was no longer in his own hands.

The two brothers conversed together for a while in low voices; then the doctor, coming back to Baruch, simply said to him: "You can make yourself at home now. Until tomorrow—I have to go out this evening. I'll give the servants orders with respect to you."

The two brothers withdrew.

Completely reassured, Baruch Jorgell slept soundly in a comfortable room overlooking the gardens.

He was sure that the New York police would never come to look for him here.

3. THE SCULPTOR OF HUMAN FLESH

I. The Hand Strikes

Eight men with hirsute beards of criminal appearance were sprawled idly around a large fire of brushwood, silently smoking a short-stemmed blue clay pipe, while a sheep, spitted on a long pole balanced between two forked branches, finished roasting in the flames.

The place where they were sitting was in a rugged gorge in the Californian Sierra, surrounded on all sides by sheer accumulations of rock covered in meager vegetation. A thin trickle of fresh water emerged from a cavern, near which stone bottles full of wine and whisky were piled up pell-mell, along with rifles, swords, pick-axes, spades, ropes and various other objects.

It would have been difficult to tell, at first glance, whether one was in the presence of a camp of gold-prospectors or a lair of bandits.

The second hypothesis would have been correct. The Black Canyon—that was the name the ravine had been given because of the dark color of its basalt rocks—had served for a long time as a refuge for a band of the thieves known as "tramps."

The tramps are the vagabonds of the New World, wandering incessantly from State to State, working for a few weeks in mines or large-scale agricultural enterprises, to depart afterwards at hazard, following the whim of their caprice, In France such travelers are usually inoffensive, only indulging in insignificant thefts, but it is not the same in America, where the cities are often separated by enormous distances, and where immense tract of wilderness exist; the tramps frequently form bands of audacious highwaymen.

The central authorities are almost powerless against them. They stop trains, pillage and set fire to isolated farms, rob travelers, and in the immense deserts of the West they constitute a redoubtable peril. Sometimes, they even form perfectly organized associations that terrorize an entire region, holding it to ransom.

It was to one of these associations that the eight individuals presently gathered in the Black Canyon belonged.

They were all wearing similar costumes: broad-brimmed hats, loosely-fitting waistcoats and trousers of coarse cloth, and stout knee-length boots, not forgetting brightly-colored belts through which were passed large-caliber revolvers and long daggers known as Bowie knives.

They all seemed to be waiting impatiently for the roast to be ready.

"I believe we can sit down at table," declared one of the tramps, suddenly. He was a man of athletic build whose gray beard came down to his belt. "For myself, I'm diabolically hungry."

Setting an example, Slug—that was the name of the man with the long beard—took out his Bowie knife, carved a large slice of bloody mutton, which he spread on a piece of biscuit, and set about eating it heartily. The other imitated him, and the animal's corpse was soon no more than a carcass, almost as well-cleaned as if the great red-brown vultures that were circling overhead had taken charge of the task.

When everyone had sat down and a bottle of whisky had been passed from hand to hand, the pipes were lit, charged with the harsh wood-cutter's tobacco known as "log cabin" and they chatted.

"I believed," said Slug, studying the sky, where large coppery clouds were accumulating, "that there's going to be a heavy downpour before nightfall. That'll be a stroke of luck."

"Why's that?" asked a young red-haired tramp, who answered to the name of Jackson.

"Because heavy rain doubles our chances," Slug replied, sententiously. Even if it only rains for a couple of hours, the bog in the defile will become impracticable."

"So the big job is today?" asked another. "You've had orders?"

"Yes," said Slug, proudly taking a greasy piece of paper from his pocket, which was covered with hieroglyphic symbols. "This is a letter that a cowboy gave me this morning while I was taking a turn around the mountain. It's signed by the Red Hand, and it's from the boss."

There was a profound silence at these words, which combined respect and curiosity. The seven tramps had drawn nearer to Slug, impatient to know more.

"What does it say, exactly?" asked Jackson.

"Yesterday, or even this morning," Slug replied, swelled up with importance, "I wouldn't have been able to tell you; now, it's different. I'll give you all the details. A fortnight ago, you saw a carriage going past hitched to four horses and escorted by a dozen armed cowboys and mounted policemen."

"Yes," Jackson replied. "And we asked why we weren't allowed to attack it—for the carriage to be escorted like that, it must have contained something precious,"

"It didn't contain anything at all—but today, it'll go along the same route, through the defile at the foot of the Black Canyon, and today—listen to me carefully—it's loaded with gold!"

The bandits' eyes sparkled with avarice beneath their bushy eyebrows.

"Yes," Slug went on "It contains the farm rents of the three large estates on the far side of the sierra, which belong, as you know, to William Dorgan, who's a partner with Fred Jorgell in the Corn and Cotton Trusts. Oh, I'm well-informed. I even know that one of William Dorgan's sons is leading the escort."

"As for that..." said one of the bandits, miming taking aim with a rifle.

"Well, no—that's where you're mistaken," said Slug, swiftly. "It's necessary to make sure that Joe Dorgan doesn't receive the slightest wound. He has to be taken alive; it seems that his capture is the most important part of the expedition. It would be better to let the money and the policemen go than not to make sure of his person. Is that understood?"

The seven tramps nodded their heads by way of assent, but they remained thoughtful.

At that very moment, large drops of rain flew through the air, and a heavy rainstorm soon began to descend. The tramps had to seek refuge in the grotto that served them as a storehouse. There, the rifles and revolvers were carefully checked and loaded, and Slug made sure that each of his men had an adequate supply of cartridges.

The rain had become torrential. Nothing any longer remained of the fire but a few blackened twigs, which the cascades tumbling down the rocks carried away to the bottom of the valley.

Slug rubbed his hands. "All this water," he said, "will accumulate in the bog in the defile; the carriage won't get out of that."

Suddenly, dominating the racket of the squall, three rifle shots rang out, repeated for some time by the echoes of the mountain.

Slug had gone slightly pale. "The bosses' signal," he murmured. "I need to go."

"When will you be back?" asked Jackson, also slightly nervous.

"I don't know. Wait for me. Don't do anything before I come back."

In the blink of an eye, he had slung his rifle behind his back, thrown an ample Mexican serape over his shoulders and had pulled his hat down over his eyes. Then he slid through the gap in the basaltic rocks and disappeared.

Left alone and watching the rain fall, which was covering the desolate landscape with a misty veil, the tramps waited silently, prey to a vague anxiety. Each of them felt a need to talk, but none of them dared speak first.

Finally, an old tramp named Bishop said in a slow voice: "I knew a Dorgan some years ago, who was also the son of a billionaire, but he wasn't called Joe, he was called Harry."

"It's not the same one," said Jackson. "It's his brother. I happen to know that the billionaire William Dorgan has two sons, Harry and Joe."

"It's Harry that I knew—the engineer. He was running the electric power plant in Jorgell City at the time. He was a good guy. I wouldn't like it if anything bad were to happen to his brother."

"Since the orders are not to do him any harm at all, you can sleep easy."

The conversation lapsed there, and no one dared strike it up again. Darkness was beginning to fall and the rain had not stopped. The tramps wondered, with a strange unease, what had become of their leader, and their anxiety was increasing when Slug reappeared. He was streaming with rain from head to toe, but his face was radiant.

"Everything's okay," he said, "but we don't have any time to lose. We need to have a bite to eat—we might have a long time to wait. Open a tin, let's have a little corned beef and a shot of whisky, and we'll be on our way."

Slug was obeyed precisely. In no time at all the tramps had eaten and gathered up their equipment, ready to leave. The return of their leader and the good of which he was giving evidence had animated them with a new ardor, but no one had dared to ask him any questions.

In water that came up to their knees the eight bandits followed the rugged slopes of the Black Canyon, which the rain had turned into a torrent, for some distance. They climbed over a mass of bizarrely-tormented rocks and came out into a defile bordered to the right and the left by imposing basalt walls.

"There's no other road," Slug declared. "They'll have to come through the defile, and we'll take them there. Once they've set foot in the bog I defy them to take another step. That's the moment we have to wait for before attacking. Then you open fire. Shoot at the horses first."

"Okay," said Jackson, "but how are we going to recognize Joe Dorgan. It might be that, without intending to shoot at him…"

"Never!" aid Slug, embarrassed by the objection. "I'm not exactly sure what to do—we'll have to try to recognize him by his costume."

"It seems to me that the simplest thing to do would be to shoot the policemen first. There'll be no mistaking them because of their uniforms."

"Yes, that's right—oh, one more thing that I forgot. Two envoys of the Red Hand might perhaps be taking a hand in the affair—it's necessary not to shoot them either."

Slug repeated these carful instructions to each of his men individually, and then posted each of them in a crack in the rock, where, through the profound darkness, further augmented by the rain, it would be impossible to see them.

An hour went by, slowly. In the holes where they were lying in ambush, the tramps felt fatigue and numbness grip them. Slug was extremely nervous, and noticed angrily that the rain was no longer falling as heavily.

"That's bad luck," he muttered between his teeth. "If the convoy's much later, the moon will be shining and the water will have time to drain away."

Impatience was beginning to get the better of him when he suddenly made out the faint sound of trotting horses.

Another quarter of an hour went by; the sound got closer and a dark mass, flanked by two red gleams of lantern-light, was silhouetted in the mist.

The carriage was now clearly visible, along with the dozen mounted guards accompanying it. The leader, cursing and complaining about the impossible route, forced the horses to follow the trail, which the rain had rendered similar to a pond—but when the carriage reached the deepest point, its heavy wheels stuck in the mud, and it was impossible to make further progress.

"We won't get out of this!" moaned the leader. "We're stuck in the mud all the way to the axle."

As if that statement were a signal, eight gunshots burst forth simultaneously. Three policemen fell to the ground, their skulls traversed by bullets; others were wounded, more or less seriously.

"The tramps!"

"The Red Hand bandits!"

"Help!

"We're doomed!"

All those cries erupted confusedly, and there were a few moments of terrible chaos, further augmented by the whinnying of a mortally-wounded horse.

One vibrant voice rose above the tumult, however; it was that of a rider who had so far remained behind the carriage. "Courage, my friends!" he cried. "If we weaken, we'll be wiped out to the last man. Take cover behind the carriage and return fire vigorously."

The bandits fired a second volley, but the policemen, following the advice of the rider—who was none other than Joe Dorgan—had had time to take refuge behind the carriage, and none of them was hit this time.

The policemen fired in their turn in the direction from which the bandits' gunfire was coming. A cry of pain responded to the discharge of the rifles. It was old Bishop, who, struck full in the chest, had just fallen out of the gap in the rock where he was ensconced.

"One less!" said Joe Dorgan. "Hold on! We'll end up getting the upper hand—they aren't as many as us."

The battle continued furiously, but the tramps, who, following Slug's orders, still remained hidden, had a considerable advantage over their adversaries. They could take aim accurately, while the policemen could only fire approximately and dared not quit the protective rampart that the carriage had become.

The battle might, however, have lasted a long time if Slug had not decided on a new tactic.

One tramp—it was Slug himself—suddenly bounded out of the darkness and plunged his Bowie knife to the hilt in the throat of one of the policemen, and fired almost instantly, blasting out the brains of another. Then he threw himself backwards, crawling toward the rocks.

"My friends," Joe Dorgan shouted, "let's abandon the money and beat a retreat!"

The men of the escort would certainly have liked nothing better than to obey, but all their horses had been killed or wounded, and flight, in those conditions, was almost impossible.

Nevertheless, they made the attempt.

By this time, there were only five of them, including Joe Dorgan. As soon as the battle began the lanterns had been broken, and the scene of the drama was only illuminated by the livid and intermittent flash of rifle-shots. The fugitives hoped to escape by courtesy of the darkness.

Two of them, going on ahead, slipped outside the protective shelter of the carriage. They had not gone two yards when they fell to the ground, shot dead.

"Forward!" cried Slug. "There are only three left!"

At this injunction, the tramps emerged from their holes, a Bowie knife in one hand and a revolver in the other.

In the blink of an eye, the fugitives were surrounded. Two revolver shots rang out. Jackson had just blown out the brains of the two policeman.

Joe Dorgan was left alone.

Browning in hand, he fought like a lion. He killed one of the tramps who tried to grapple him around the waist, and wounded Jackson in the shoulder, but he was bound to succumb to the force of numbers. Ten robust hands grabbed his arms and immobilized him. His Browning was torn out of his hand and he was tied up.

"Miserable murderers!" he howled, struggling. "Kill me, then, if you dare!"

No one deigned to reply.

"The battle's won now!" Slug shouted. "Give the wounded a few good thrusts with a Bowie knife, to take away any desire they might have to testify against us."

"That's already done," muttered an old tramp with a gray beard whose hands were dripping blood. Now it's a matter of getting the dollars out of the box."

The bandits had already surrounded the carriage when two riders emerged abruptly into the defile. By the light of the moon—which, now that the rain had stopped, was shining through the clouds—the tramps saw that the two newcomers were wearing masks over their faces.

Respectfully, Slug had hastened to meet them, and took hold of the bridles of their horses.

"The Red Hand's orders have been carried out faithfully," he said, his tone full of humility.

"That's good," said one of the men. In a low voice, he gave a few orders to Slug, and handed him a rather voluminous package.

Slug unwrapped the parcel. It contained a square flask and a wad of cotton wool.

Slug carefully soaked the cotton wool in the liquid contained in the flask, then, approaching slyly, he put it over the prisoner's face. Joe Dorgan uttered a dull groan; the insipid odor of chloroform filled his nostrils. He lost consciousness.

Immediately, Slug and one of the masked men carried him away carefully, and tied him securely to a horse that the emissaries of the Red Hand had taken care to bring with them and had left some way behind.

All that was done with extraordinary rapidity, under the stupefied gaze of the tramps, so intimidated by the presence of the "big bosses" that they had forgotten the carriage and the dollars.

The two masked men were preparing to climb back into the saddle when Slug thought he ought to ask for instructions regarding the carriage.

"Stupid question!" said one of the unknown men, impatiently. "Share it out according to the usual rules. We'll collect the Red Hand's share at a time to be arranged. And above all, no errors in the counting. We know the exact figure."

The unknown men mounted up. Placing the horse to which Joe Dorgan's inert body was tied between them, they disappeared at a gallop through the northern extremity of the defile

After having ridden for three hours in succession in the most profound silence through the roads carved into the mountain, they finally reached a properly constructed highway equipped with odometric markers and indicative signposts. Their horses were white with foam when they dismounted in front of a wretched inn constructed with badly-squared tree-trunks A silent stable-hand took their horses away after helping them to transport Joe Dorgan's body to a stone bench near the door.

No light appeared in the hovel's windows. The two men, who had now taken off their masks, paced up and down in the courtyard, chatting in low voices.

An hour went by. The emissaries of the Red Hand were beginning to show signs of impatience when the sound of an automobile became audible in the silence of the night.

Ten minutes later, a superb hundred-horsepower vehicle with luxurious bodywork, fitted out for long journeys, stopped in front of the inn with all its headlights on.

Like the servant who had taken charge of the horses, the chauffeur did not say a word. Silently, the two bandits and their prisoner, still inanimate, were installed in the interior of the vehicle, which immediately sped away in fourth gear.

Three days later, the same mysterious automobile, now covered with a thick layer of mud and dust, came into New York a little after midnight, and, after having traveled along Tenth Avenue at low speed, stopped in front of a luxurious property surrounded by high walls and closed by a wrought-iron gate. To one of the columns supporting the gate a black marble plaque was fixed, with an inscription in golden letters: *Dr. Cornelius Kramm.*

The chauffeur gave three blasts of the horn, regularly spaced. Both battens of the gate immediately opened, and the automobile was engulfed by the interior of the property.

The following day, news of the drama of which the desert near the Black Canyon had been the theater burst like a thunderbolt in New York, where the billionaire William Dorgan and his two sons were held in particularly high esteem.

By way of documentation, we shall reproduce one of the numerous articles that the *New York Herald* published on that subject:

A frightful crime has just thrown the State of California into consternation and put the family of one of our honorable fellow citizens, William Dorgan, in mourning. His younger son, Joe, has disappeared in tragic circumstances, and everything indicates that he has fallen victim to the bandits of the Red Hand.

Joe Dorgan, who, although only twenty-six years of age, had already given proof of brilliant talents as an administrator and a financier, had been charged by his father with recovering considerable sums due from the farmers of the immense estates that the billionaire possesses in the province of California. That region still has entirely desert regions entirely deprived of roads and railways, where public services are only organized as yet in the most defective fashion.

Joe Dorgan, who had completely his tour successfully, was returning with his escort, comprised of twelve mounted policemen. The money he had collected was contained in one of those robust carriages that are the only ones able to travel the rocky roads of the sierra. It was while passing through a defile, which recent storms had rendered almost impracticable, that the convoy was attacked.

Cowboys returning from one of the regional fairs found the atrociously-mutilated bodies of the twelve policemen next to the staved-in carriage and the disemboweled horses. One horrible detail is that each cadaver bore on the cheek the imprint of a hand crudely drawn in blood. The bandits of the Red Hand had left their sinister signature.

In spite of extensive searches, the body of the unfortunate Joe Dorgan has not been recovered. One dare not hope that he has been taken prisoner; it is supposed that the tramps must have thrown his body into one of the gulfs of the sierra. A company of mounted police is presently scouring the desert region, but thus far, the searches have only resulted in the discovery, in a rugged ravine known as the Black Canyon, of one of the lairs of the evil band, where an abundance of weapons, munitions and provisions of every sort were found. The hunt for the bandits continues, directed with indefatigable activity by the engineer Harry Dorgan, the victim's brother, who immediately traveled to the area.

We shall take advantage of this opportunity to give a few details of the Red Hand, the vast association of malefactors who, for several years now, has been terrorizing the western and central States of the Union. The Red Hand, powerfully organized and possessing, we are assured, ramifications all over the world, bears little resemblance to the famous Italian organization with the same name. Those making it up are almost all of American, German or Irish nationality. It includes among its ranks allies belonging to all classes of society—even, it appears, bankers, businessmen, physicians, officers and senior policemen in our

*big cities. That is what explains the inconceivable impunity from which the ma-
jority of its members has thus far benefited.*

    *All the efforts made to exterminate these wretches have failed pitifully, but
the limit has been reached. The crime that we have just related, which surpasses
all the others in audacity and horror, ought to open the eyes of the public authorities. We hope that a special law will be voted by the Senate in Washington
and that extraordinary credit will be put at the disposal of the police in order to
track down the Red Hand's lairs and affiliates.*

II. In Living Flesh

Dr. Cornelius Kramm was one of the most fashionable physicians in New York, and his establishment was scarcely frequented by anyone but billionaires, or at least multimillionaires. His enigmatic and sardonic physiognomy was displayed on the front pages of specialist periodicals as well as large-circulation dailies. His pamphlets, *The Esthetic Rationale of the Human Body* and *Scientific Means of Prolonging Youth in Men and Women*, were ardently read and commented on by scientists and socialites alike, and were universally appreciated.

At any rate, Cornelius Kramm was no ordinary physician. He left the vulgar work of curing disease to his colleagues; he only occupied himself with healthy people who were afflicted by some physical imperfection. In that field of endeavor he was worked virtual miracles.

Among a hundred others, the case of the brave Colonel MacDolmar, wounded by shrapnel in the Philippine War and deprived of his nose and half his face, was often cited. Dr. Cornelius had restored that wrecked physiognomy so effectively that scarcely any trace of the frightful mutilation remained. Thus, Dr. Cornelius Kramm was routinely designated by such nicknames as "the rejuvenator" or "the sculptor of human flesh." It was affirmed, doubtless with some exaggeration, that he was able to make a blind, toothless, wrinkled and jaundiced old spinster into a fresh and rosy young woman; many people were convinced that his power was unlimited.

The doctor, who had lived for some time in a new city in the Far West, had settled permanently in New York, where he owned an Academy of Beauty—an "Esthetic Institute," as they say in America—equipped according to the latest gifts of science and the supreme refinements of modern comfort.

Cornelius Kramm lived alone; his only family was a brother a little younger than himself, Fritz Kramm, who was a large-scale art dealer.

For several weeks the doctor had had as a guest a young American of a taciturn and misanthropic bent, whose was not—apparently, at least—undergoing any treatment, for he was endowed with a robust constitution and was in excellent health. He occupied an isolated room on the second floor of one wing of the house, completely isolated and overlooking the gardens. He only came down in the evenings to smoke a cigar while taking a long walk in the shade of the gardens, almost as vast as a park. Sometimes, too, he went to join the doctor in one of his laboratories, and had long conversations with him.

The individual who led this almost eremitic existence appeared to be perfectly satisfied with his situation. When he was alone, he plunged himself with extraordinary ardor into the most recent treatises on chemistry and physiology; that work possessed such an attraction for him that he was never bored for a moment, and only took as much exercise as was necessary for his health.

Another bizarre feature of that reclusive existence was that every morning, an old Italian named Leonello, who had been in the doctor's service for many years, came to the recluse's room and took one or several photograph of him; he had accumulated about a hundred of them, in all possible poses: full face, in profile, sitting or standing, naked or fully-dressed.

That formality was not to the taste of the man who was its object and he had sought in vain to know why his image was being thus multiplied in the most diverse aspects. To all his questions, Leonello replied with evasive statements. Once, the young man attempted to refuse to pose, but the old Italian had only had to say, very courteously, that it was the doctor's orders; the recalcitrant photographic model had not persisted and had posed with a good grace in front of the lens of a powerful apparatus that produced life-sized prints of a perfect clarity.

One evening, when the strange guest of the Academy of Beauty was walking slowly along the shady paths of the garden, contemplating the star-filled sky with a pensive gaze, he thought her heard footsteps behind him, but was reassured when he turned round to find himself face to face with Leonello.

"Are you taking a little walk, as I am?" he asked the old Italian.

"No," the other replied, with an obsequious smile. "I was looking for you."

"The doctor wants to see me?"

"Precisely."

"I'm delighted. I'll join him immediately. Tell me, is he in his study or the laboratory?"

"I'll take you. He is indeed in the laboratory, but not the one you know."

"Give me directions."

"There's no point; you wouldn't be able to find it without me, so it's preferable that I accompany you."

"All right, I'll follow you."

"Take note that the laboratory to which I'm taking you is rigorously proscribed to everyone, even the doctor's closest friends, who do not know of its existence as yet. It's a great favor that he's doing you in admitting you to it."

While he was speaking, Leonello and his companion had gone into the main building and into a long corridor with marble floor-tiles, which mercury vapor lamps illuminated with a soft blue-tinted light. They stopped at the cage of an elevator.

"The doctor's laboratory isn't on the ground floor, then?" said the unknown man, surprised.

"No," said the Italian, tranquilly. "It's a subterranean laboratory." And he pressed the control button.

The elevator set off, and stopped in a kind of vestibule with ceramic walls that were absolutely bare, into which thick doors lined with leather opened. A rhythmic sound of piston-rods testified that the basement must contain powerful machinery.

"We've arrived," said Leonello. Pushing one of the doors, he stood aside to allow his companion to go in first.

As he emerged from the semi-darkness of the vestibule, the doctor's guest was dazzled.

He found himself in a vast room with a dome-like vault, the walls of which were entirely covered in white porcelain. Under the blinding electric lights, a confused mass of strange apparatus extended as far as the eye could see. On pedestals there were barbarously colored life-size anatomical models devoid of skin; cages mounted on glass floors according to the Arsonval method,[9] which permits an invalid to be surrounded by beams of electric radiance; armchair equipped with jacks, by means of which limbs could be immobilized or distended; and in one display-case there was a group of wax automata, colored so artfully as to give the illusion of life. Finally, in one corner, on the marble floortiles, semi-dissected cadavers were lying, in a state of perfect conservation, doubtless due to powerful antiseptics.

The atmosphere of that fantastic laboratory was saturated with an extraordinary balsamic odor that seemed singularly vivifying, the absorption of which doubtless formed an integral part of the treatment to which invalids were submitted.

On perceiving the newcomer, Cornelius Kramm had set down a test-tube into which he was in the process of decanting the contents of a flask, and came forward, smiling as amiably as was possible, given his sinister physiognomy.

"Good evening, my dear Baruch," he said, indicating a seat. "I'm delighted to see you. I've permitted myself to disturb you this evening because I need to have a serious chat with you."

"You have a splendid laboratory here," murmured Baruch Jorgell, more emotional than he wanted to appear.

"Yes, isn't it?" the doctor replied, negligently. "It cost me a great deal, but in terms of its installation the laboratory has the advantage that I'm perfectly tranquil here. I could, if the whim took me, skin one of my clients alive here, and let him howl as much as he pleased; no one would hear a sound."

"That is, indeed, convenient," Baruch murmured, less and less reassured.

The doctor had perceived his interlocutor's disturbance; a mocking smile tucked up his thin lips; his rounded, lashless eyes, like those of a bird of prey, sparkled behind his gold-rimmed spectacles.

"Don't worry," he sniggered. "I only indulge in experiments in vivisection very rarely, and even then, it's always in the interests of science."

"What do you want to talk to me about, then?"

---

[9] Jacques-Arsène Arsonval (1851-1940) was the great pioneer of the field of electrophysiology: the study of the effects of electricity on living organisms. In 1892 he was appointed as the director of a new biophysics laboratory at the College de France.

"I'll get to that. Do you remember, my dear Baruch, the situation you were in when you arrived here?"

"I remember that I had good reasons for coming. I'm obliged to you, and I'll never forget it, but there's no use talking about the past."

"On the contrary, it's very useful. I understand that certain memories are painful to you, but it's indispensable hat there should be no species of misunderstanding between us."

"Go on," said Baruch, unable to help going pale.

"When you came to me asking for shelter, you were accused of having murdered a French chemist, Monsieur de Maubreuil, whom you had robbed of his diamonds; you were being hunted everywhere; your description had been posted, there was a price on your head and hundreds of detectives were at your heels."

"That's true," the murderer replied, having had time to recover his composure. "You saved me; I'm not seeking to deny it. You even mentioned at the time an association between us and your brother that might lead to 'grandiose results'—your word. Since then, however, you haven't said any more about it."

"Well, the moment has come to acquaint you with those plans, which, as I told you, are grandiose—I don't take back the word. I'll get to the point. Let's see: between the two of us, are you enthusiastic to conserve your present physiognomy?"

"My physiognomy?"

"Yes—by which I mean the color of your hair, the expression of your face, the color of your skin: in brief, everything that constitutes your physical personality."

"I don't care about it in the least. I suppose you want to dye my hair and put on make-up to render me unrecognizable."

Dr. Cornelius shrugged his shoulders. "Dye and make-up—what a joke!" And he added, in a grave tone: "It's not a matter of that. The changes that you will undergo will be so radical and profound that you'll be a veritably new man."

"Impossible!"

"It's very possible. The experiment is certainly bold, but it doesn't involve any serious danger. My brother Fritz explained to you the other day some of the means that I employ to achieve my objectives; you've been able to observe that they're very ingenious and extremely simple."

"But why a complete transformation?" Baruch murmured, his heart constricted by a vague anguish. "Wouldn't a little retouching be sufficient?"

"No, not retouching! I see that I'll have to spell it out. One evening— today, for example—you'll go to sleep in the skin of Baruch Jorgell, notorious criminal, wanted by the police of the entire world; and when you wake up, you'll have become, thanks to the magic of Science, one of the most brilliant members of the aristocracy, of the Five Hundred, the fortunate son of a billionaire father."

Baruch thought for a moment that the doctor had gone mad. "It's a dream," he murmured. "Science can't and never will be able to effect such a metamorphosis."

"Ha ha!" sniggered Cornelius. "If you think that, you don't know the resources of *carnoplasty*—a science that I've created in all its aspects. It's not for nothing, believe me, that they call me the sculptor of human flesh!"

Baruch Jorgell trembled in every limb. He already believed that he was to be subjected to an atrocious experiment, dissected while alive.

"I'd rather stay as I am," he stammered, in a voice choked by fear.

The doctor had risen to his feet, his face radiant with pride. "I could proceed without your permission," he said, "but I'd rather employ reasoning to convince you. When I've explained, you'll understand where your true interests lie." Abruptly, he added: "You know Joe Dorgan, the billionaire's son?"

"Quite well," said Baruch, surprised. "We took some of the same classes at Boston. Since then I've lost sight of him; I'm more familiar with his brother Harry, the engineer. He ran the power plant at Jorgell City, as you know, and courted my sister Isidora—that one I detest mortally."

"It's not a matter of him," the doctor put in, dryly. "It's a matter of his brother Joe. Be aware of the fact that there's a certain resemblance between you and Joe Dorgan. You're almost the same height and build. It's that resemblance that I'll guarantee to render as complete as possible. After a few weeks of treatment, it will be definitive."

"Including the face?"

"Even the face."

"Then there'll be two Joe Dorgans?"

"Not at all—because, thanks to science, the real Joe Dorgan will have taken on the exact physical appearance of the excessively famous Baruch Jorgell. Do you understand now? You'll pass your somewhat spoiled personality, as one does a fake coin, on to an obliging neighbor, who will give you his in exchange. It's quite simple."

Baruch was literally astounded.

"It's frightful!" he said. "It would be wonderful if it were possible, but I can see a thousand difficulties—to start with, Joe Dorgan wouldn't want to wear my false personality. He'd put up a devil of a struggle! He'd demand an investigation. The truth would come out."

Cornelius sniggered briefly.

"That's an eventuality that will never materialize," he said. "I give you my word that Joe Dorgan won't raise the slightest protest, for the very god reason that he'll have completely lost his memory of past events."

"Even if that's the case," Baruch replied, energetically, "and even if I succeed in putting on the exact appearance of Joe Dorgan, I couldn't simulate his voice, his gestures, his opinions or his thinking."

"All that is possible," the doctor continued, enthusiastically. "I have simple means of giving you Joe's voice and gait, even his gestures; you'll know the slightest memories of his past and his most secret thoughts. You'll posses his soul, to the extent that such a thing is realizable."

Baruch Jorgell recoiled in fear, his teeth chattering in terror. He understood that Cornelius was not lying, and that what he had announced he was going to do, in spite of any resistance. "What kind of man are you, then?" he stammered, wildly.

"Oh, nothing but a simple scientist—a very modest scientist, I assure you. There's no sorcery in the procedures I employ. I've simply perfected certain formulae in current use. When I've published the book about carnoplasty that I'm writing, the prodigies I accomplish, which excite so much astonishment, will be within the range of all physicians."

In spite of all Cornelius' eloquence, Baruch remained hesitant. "Well, no," he said, abruptly. "I refuse."

"As you wish," sniggered the doctor. "You're perfectly free, after all, not to accept my offer. You understand, though, that since you're opposing one of my projects—and your own interests—I can no longer keep you here. You'll leave here today, and once outside, you know what awaits you: prison and the infamous electric chair."

Baruch ground his teeth like a wolf caught in a trap. "I'll do as you wish," he muttered, effortfully. "I'm at your disposal. Oh, I knew you'd make me pay dearly for the service you've rendered me."

"I'm delighted to see you become more reasonable, but I repeat, it's wrong for you to be alarmed. Your life isn't in danger and you won't experience any pain. When I've succeeded, you'll be the first to heap me with blessings."

"I doubt that very much, but since I have to serve as the subject of this frightful experiment, start as soon as possible. I've made my decision."

"I know that you're courageous; we'll begin this evening, then. I'm glad to observe that you're in a perfect state of health, for tonight will be employed in operations that will require a certain measure of endurance on your part."

"I'm ready," the murderer murmured, resignedly. "But where's the man whose place I have to take?"

Cornelius Kramm pressed a switch. A curtain slid along its rod, uncovering an extension of the laboratory where there was a bed surrounded by a network of electric wires. On the bed lay a young man of almost exactly the same height and build as Baruch, but whose physiognomy more no resemblance, even distant, to the latter's. He seemed to be sleeping peacefully; his eyelids were closed and there was a vague smile on his lips.

While asleep he was recounting things in a low voice that were doubtless very interesting, for a recording phonograph was placed next to his bed on a small table.

"I have the honor of introducing to you the honorable Joe Dorgan," said Cornelius, sarcastically. "As you can see, he's admirably disposed to submit to the experiment we're about to undertake."

"But how did he get here?" Baruch asked, with a secret thrill of fear.

"Don't worry about that," said Cornelius. "What is interesting for you to know is that for more than a week, Joe Dorgan has been plunged into a hypnotic trance. I've given his orders to recall all his childhood memories and recount them, with the most trivial details, and the most minute accuracy. All of that will be scrupulously noted, in order that you might profit from it whenever you wish.

As Cornelius Kramm initiated him into the practical means of realizing his audacious plan, Baruch Jorgell gradually overcame his terrors. "Will it be necessary, then," he asked, "for me also to expose details of my memories and my projects to you?"

"Not at all. That will be completely unnecessary. Haven't I just told you that Joe Dorgan will lose all memory of his past life? When plastic surgery has given him an exact external resemblance to you, he'll undergo a small operation to the larynx to give him your voice, then a slight prick in the brain to relieve him of his memory."

"Why not simply make him disappear?"

"Fritz asked me the same thing, but I don't want that. First of all, the existence of a false Baruch is a guarantee of safety for you. Then again, I have my self-respect as a scientist. It pleases me to toy with difficulty and succeed in achieving a double transformation that the whole world would regard as implausible, or even impossible."

"Perhaps you're right. When the pseudo-Baruch has been well and truly electrocuted as Monsieur de Maubreuil's murderer, no one will ever think to search for me in the skin of Joe Dorgan."

"Don't forget that, thanks to me, you'll become William Dorgan's heir. One might say that you were born under a lucky star. Rejected by Fred Jorgell, you've immediately found another father, no less a billionaire than the first, in the person of William Dorgan." Cornelius Kramm added, sarcastically: "From now on, my dear Baruch, you'll be able to show your gratitude to your friends in a regal fashion."

"And I won't fail, you can be sure of that."

"If you were to fail," the doctor went on, with a muted threat in his voice, "It would be most imprudent on your part. My brother and I are not men who can be mocked with impunity."

"I never had any such intention!" Baruch protested, vehemently.

"Come on, calm down. We have complete confidence in you—otherwise, as you can imagine, it would be easy enough for us to choose someone else.

We've wasted enough time in explanations. We need to get to work immediately."

"I'm at your orders," said Baruch, calmly—and after contemplating his own features, which he would never see again, for one last time, in the full-length mirror handing on the wall, he sat down intrepidly in the large metallic armchair that Cornelius indicated to him.

The latter took a bottle from a cupboard and brought it close to Baruch's nostrils. The latter immediately fell into a deep sleep.

III. Another Man's Skin

The long and delicate operations by means of which Dr. Cornelius Kramm intended to bring about the strange metamorphosis lasted for several days, and were undertaken methodically.

Firstly, with Leonello's aid, the doctor took molds of his two subjects, and the two molds, mounted on pedestals, were reclad, thanks to color photography, with exactly lifelike complexions. With the aid of injections of warm paraffin wax beneath the epidermis, he provided Baruch's slightly thin features with the roundness that Joe's face possessed; by means of a skilful resection of the cartilage, he rectified the form of the nose. The resemblance of the two physiognomies began to appear in a striking fashion.

With his skeletal arms bare to the elbows, Cornelius toiled with a feverish ardor. Reshaping the living substance itself, adding and subtracting according to need, he truly merited his nickname.

When he had completed the initial sketch, with the aid of the scalpel and injections by means of a hypodermic syringe, he armed himself with a microscope. By means of pink and pale brown pigments, he reproduced the slightest flaws in the epidermis. No artist had ever put so much care into perfecting his work.

The hair and beard demanded laborious work in themselves. Hairs, measured to the centimeter, were depilated electrically, one at a time, from areas where they were too thick. In the places where they were too thin, Leonello made use of a special needle to plant the required number, as hairdressers do in cases of incurable baldness.

As for the teeth, the operation presented little difficulty; imprints in wax were taken from both patients by Cornelius; with the aid of a few strokes with a file and a few implants, a perfect result was obtained. The exact shade of the hair was produced by an indelible dye. The doctor had made a special study of alkaloids that have the property of modifying the color of the eyes; he decided that, in order to endow Brauch with Joe's dark eyes, internal treatment was indispensable.

Once these tasks were complete, Cornelius stood for some time in contemplation before his work.

"The resemblance is perfect!" he proclaimed, proudly. "It's impossible to do better. Now the proof is complete; I possess the secret of molding the human face to my whim, my fingers modeling living flesh like clay!"

Leonello extracted him from that lyrical enthusiasm. "Master," he said, "the work might be regarded as almost complete with regard to Baruch, but he's still more corpulent than Joe."

"It's easy to remedy that imperfection. By submitting the subject to a high-tension electrical current, an abundant transpiration will be produced. Like certain jockeys on the eve of a race, Baruch will grow thinner instantaneously, so to speak, or at least in a matter of hours. You can take care of that."

The singular treatment indicated by Cornelius was a complete success.

When Baruch came to, he experienced a strange and dolorous sensation. It seemed to him that he had been asleep for years. He felt a dull ache throughout his body, and he was as weak as an infant.

He opened his eyes and recognized, with a kind of stupor, that he was in his room.

Gradually, he recovered consciousness of himself. He remembered his visit to the subterranean laboratory, the strange pact that he had concluded—and then a kind of mist clouded his memories.

He tried to move.

He could not budge; his entire body was imprisoned in powerful elastic bandages and molds that immobilized him. His face was covered by a steel mask that tugged dolorously at his eyelids and the corners of his mouth.

He made an effort to escape the vice-like grip that held all the parts of his body, but could not do it. He uttered a dolorous groan. It was then that he perceived, a short distance away, the obsequious face of the laboratory assistant Leonello.

"Don't move," said the Italian. "I'm happy to tell you that the experiment undertaken by my illustrious master, Dr. Cornelius Kramm, has succeeded brilliantly. In a few weeks you'll be completely healed and can return to the palace of your father, Mr. William Dorgan, who is inconsolable over your loss."

Baruch's head reeled, vertigo invading his anemic brain. So the sculptor of human flesh had carried out his frightful promise to the letter. He was gripped by an irresistible desire to see his face. He could not bring himself to believe that Leonello was telling the truth.

"A mirror!" he stammered. "I want a mirror..." But he fell silent abruptly, gripped by a mad terror. It was no longer his own voice that he could hear; he no longer recognized its intonations.

"Stay calm," said Leonello, swiftly. "The doctor has recommended that you don't talk, and that you remain completely still. He's even forbidden you to eat for some time yet. I'll nourish you myself with the aid of liquid aliments."

Baruch uttered a stifled groan, whose significance Leonello understood. "Don't worry," he said. "It won't last long and you'll be well looked after. I shan't leave your bedside. I'll be here night and day, ready to divine whatever you might need. I understand what you want. You want to see your new physiognomy—it's a perfectly legitimate desire, after all, and I'll satisfy it right away. I'll free you—but just for a moment."

With infinite precaution, Leonello loosened the fastenings of the mask, removed it, and brought a mirror close to the patient's face.

Baruch Jorgell uttered a cry of amazement.

The astonished and melancholy face that was looking at him from the depths of the mirror was no longer his own. He had before him the features of the young man he had seen asleep in the subterranean laboratory before his metamorphosis: the features of Joe Dorgan.

He could not bear to contemplate that physiognomy—which was, henceforth, his own physiognomy—for long.

He closed his eyes; it seemed to him that he had just seen a ghost.

"Have you seen enough?" asked the Italian, ironically. "I hope you're content with your new face. I'll put your mask on again now."

Baruch made no gesture of protest; he allowed it to be done meekly. He felt madness invading his skull. He tried to go to sleep in order to stop thinking. Doubtless thanks to the narcotic drugs that he had been obliged to absorb, he fell into a profound slumber.

When he woke up the next day, he experienced the same painful sensations as the previous day, albeit to a lesser extent. During the time he remained awake, however, he was prey to a mortal ennui. He received a visit from Dr. Cornelius that day, accompanied by Fritz Kramm, who was frankly ecstatic about the marvelous result.

"It's astonishing," he declared. "I would never have believed that one could achieve such perfection in resemblance. It's truly prodigious."

"Except," Cornelius Kramm sniggered, "that it's not very agreeable for the person who submits to such an operation—but that's perfectly understandable." And as a flash of hatred passed through the eyes of the convalescent, still reduced to silence and immobility, he added by way of palliation: "But what a triumph when the treatment is finished!"

"It would, indeed, require a very shrewd detective to unearth Baruch Jorgell from beneath the skin of Joe Dorgan, which his double has put on like a new suit..."

"And which suits him marvelously."

"He certainly looks younger."

"More elegant!"

"More distinguished!"

"One can never be too elegant and distinguished when one's the son of a billionaire."

Baruch, who was forbidden to open his mouth, was put to the torture by these ironic consolations.

Leonello, meanwhile, left no stone unturned in trying to soothe the convalescent's lack of patience. He explained the progress of the healing process every day, and gave him the most devoted attention.

The days went by. Baruch Jorgell was devoured by ennui and impatience.

Finally, little by little, the wounds closed, the flesh violently brought together knitted, and one item and a time, the apparatus was removed. Baruch was able to get up and to take solid food.

For the murderer, thus miraculously metamorphosed, it was a true joy when the doctor permitted him to go down into the garden, supported by Fritz and Leonello.

He was completely cured, no longer experiencing any extreme weakness, but he was assailed by strange sensations. He was out of place in his new physical envelope; his body, retouched, so to speak, and remolded by the sculptor of human flesh, felt uncomfortable, like a garment that was too tight. His limbs vacillated; his gestures were uncertain, hive voice hesitant. He felt throughout his person the strange numbness of someone emerging by virtue of a miracle from a coffin.

"You're not yet accustomed to your new envelope," said the doctor who observed him attentively. "You still retain a certain awkwardness, a certain heaviness in your gestures and attitudes, which will soon disappear. In any case, I'm in a hurry to complete your cure."

"Why is that?"

"It's necessary for you to go to work." As Baruch manifested a certain astonishment, he went on: "Don't you remember what I said to you? Obviously, it's already a great deal to possess a physical resemblance to Joe Dorgan, but that's not all. You already have his voice; you require his speech, his thoughts, his gestures, tics and manias—everything, in sum, that constitutes a personality."

"But how can I do that?" Baruch asked, who had not yet had time to think about that in his mental confusion.

"I've thought of everything. In my subterranean laboratory there are several thousand phonograph scrolls that Joe was kind enough to dictate himself, and which contain everything we need. It will require a complete abstraction of your old self, and to for you habituate yourself to certain words and phrases. Do you have a good memory?"

"Not bad."

"Then all will be well."

"Permit me one more question," said Baruch, marveling. "That's all very well for words and phrases—but what about mannerisms and gait?"

"Everything's been anticipated, nothing left to chance. I've taken care to film Joe Dorgan in all his attitudes, standing, walking, lying down, sitting, eating and reading. You'll only have to imagine for a while that you're an actor, studying your part conscientiously."

"I'm sure I'll succeed," said Baruch. "I'll put all the time that's necessary into it—I want the adaptation to be perfect."

As Cornelius had foreseen, within a few days Baruch had forgotten his suffering and his seclusion, and was proud of having emerged alive and victorious from such a fantastic experiment. He showed all the more enthusiasm because he had initially been so hesitant.

From the next day onwards, he went down to the subterranean laboratory early in the morning and stayed there until the evening, working with a kind of fury to engrave in his memory, in an indelible fashion, the victim's attitudes and his very thoughts. He resumed work the following day, untiringly.

While the calm voice of the phonograph repeated the phrases, cheerful or sad, joking or serious, extracted from Joe Dorgan under the influence of hypnotic power, Baruch repeated them word for word, trying hard to reproduce the exact intonation. At other times, facing a cinematographic apparatus supervised by Leonello, he studied and reproduced the habitual gestures and facial expressions of his involuntary double.

There was something terrible about that phonographic phantom capering on the white screen in monochrome, while Baruch, his face contorted, strove to reproduce all his attitudes exactly.

From time to time, the Kramm brothers subjected their accomplice to a kind of examination. The doctor rubbed his hands, more satisfied every day.

"You're doing well," he said. "It's almost perfect. A few more hours of conscientious work, and you'll be completely Dorganified."

Baruch Jorgell was a scoundrel devoid of any kind of scruple; he had never felt remorse and had consented without hesitation to commit a further crime, but as he penetrated more deeply, with the aid of the phonographic conversation that he was obliged to learn by heart, into the thought of his victim, he felt a kind of embarrassment, akin to the commencement of shame.

Joe Dorgan had had an exemplary youth. As soon as he had completed his college studies at Boston, like his brother, the engineer Harry Dorgan, who was two years younger,[10] he had become a valuable collaborator for his father. Very charitable, very sober and very hard-working, Joe had no vices; he was a loyal and honest friend.

On observing all these qualities, which he was obliged to assimilate whether he liked it or not, the murderer was prey to a cold rage. "Why," he cried, angrily, "Am I obliged to play this terrible role? Cornelius is a wretch! One might think that he were seeking to amuse himself by making me play the hypocritical role of a petty saint. But patience! The time is approaching when I'll be able to recompense myself for this abominable constraint!"

Grating his teeth, forcing himself to ape the honest man, Baruch got back to work, and his exasperation increased by the day.

Soon, however, another phenomenon emerged.

Spending all day in the subterranean laboratory filled with strange machinery, grimacing manikins and half-dissected cadavers, the murderer fell prey to

---

[10] Joe was previously reported to be the younger brother, but becomes the older from this point on.

128

frightful nightmares. His sleep was populated with variegated masks. The atmosphere, saturated with electricity and charged with gases with penetrating odors, gradually infected his brain; he realized that if his sojourn in that accursed place were to be prolonged, he would go completely mad.

When, in the evening, the enervations of fatigue set in and he happened to glance at himself in a mirror, he recoiled in fright. "It's terrible," he stammered, shivering in his every limb. "I'm becoming the authentic phantom, the living specter of my victim!"

Sometimes, at dusk or in the morning twilight, it was no longer Joe's face that the mirror reflected back to him; it was a face that was grave and sad beneath the long gray hair that crowned it: the vengeful face of Monsieur de Maubreuil, the French chemist he had murdered in order to steal his diamonds.

"Back, phantom!" he cried, his teeth chattering.

And, white with fear, he hastened to cover the mirror, or turn it to face the wall.

IV. A Revenant

A few months before Joe Dorgan's disappearance, the excellent Mrs. Griffon, who ran an honorably-stocked boarding house in New York, had experienced a bitter disappointment.

A traveling salesman of chemical products—that, at least, was how he represented himself—had succeeded, thanks to false promises, in obtaining credit for several weeks. Then, abruptly, one Saturday, on the very day that he was supposed to settle his bill, he had disappeared, and since then, no one had had any news of him.

For an entire week, Mrs. Griffon had filled the hotel parlor with her lamentations.

"What a crook!" she exclaimed, indignantly, in talking about her boarder. "It's shameful, to deceive my trust like that, unworthy of a true Yankee!" And she concluded, dolefully: "I've had a lesson there from which I'll profit: never again will I give credit to anyone; I've sworn a solemn oath."

Mrs. Griffon might perhaps have resigned herself to that misfortune if some of her clients had not put a malign insistence into reminding her that the bad payer who had taken flight had borne an undeniable resemblance to the famous Baruch Jorgell, the murder of a French chemist. And they displayed before her, as if taking pleasure in it, copies of newspapers and magazines reproducing the murderer's photograph.

"You see, Mistress," they repeated, "you missed a superb opportunity there to get your hands on a reward of several thousand dollars."

"Then, you think that that mild young man really was the murderer of Monsieur de Maubreuil and a diamond-thief?"

"We're perfectly sure of it," clamored the chorus of boarders. "Just look at his picture."

And, in fact, there was a perfect resemblance between the celebrated murderer and the indelicate debtor...

After long reflection, she decided to go to the police station and make a formal declaration. She expected to be complimented for her zeal. To her great surprise, she was given a rather poor welcome by the chief of detectives.

"You'd have done well not to disturb yourself, Madam," he cried, furiously. "It's not today that you should have come. What were you thinking? You have at your table, every day, a rogue whose head is worth its weight in gold; you even remark naively that he resembles the portrait published in all the papers, and you only have the idea to come and see me when the bird has flown? Truly, it's unforgivable."

"But I didn't know! Do you think, sir, that if I'd known...? I even gave him credit..."

"You were stupid. Naturally, he didn't pay you?"

"No, sir."

"You're too naïve. He did well—you only got what you deserved. Now the murderer in on his way to some foreign land, or has gone to ground in some remote spot. We'll never find him!" As he showed the manageress of the boarding house out, he added, with a very ungracious expression: "The trail's gone cold—very cold, by now—and it's your fault. A pleasure to see you, Madam!"

She was in a very bad mood when she got back to the hotel.

The step that Mrs. Griffon had taken was not entirely useless however. Her deposition was reproduced by several newspapers, which brought a host of reporters to the hotel, desirous of knowing the slightest details about the famous Baruch Jorgell: his habits, his favorite games and the brand of his favorite tobacco.

Avid for exact information, the newspapers published full-length portraits of Mrs. Griffon and photographs of her parlor and dining-room.

After the reporters and the amateur detectives came the curiosity-seekers. There was an uninterrupted procession of idlers, delighted to visit the famous criminal's room and sit down in the very place where he had taken his meals. The hotel was never empty.

Since success had come, the proprietress had taken on a new importance in her own eyes. In the parlor where she presided over the distractions of her guests every evening she took her stance in her armchair beside the piano in the manner of a great lady; now, it was only after being begged for a long time that she consented to tell new guests the hundred-times-repeated story of the murderer Baruch Jorgell, who had doubtless come to kill her.

"In sum," she concluded, "I only escaped death thanks to the protection of Providence."

And the entire audience shivered as they thought about the peril she had run.

For her, the solemn moment of the day was the one she devoted to reading the newspapers, in which exciting accounts were rendered of crimes, suicides and lynchings, in which the rich imagination of the reporters did not spare improbabilities.

But it was destined that Mrs. Griffon would not be long delayed in playing a leading role herself in one of the police tragedies that exercised such a powerful attraction upon her.

One evening, Mrs. Griffin, enthroned in her usual place between the piano and the tea-table, had just finished reading a long article devoted to Joe Dorgan, whose cadaver had not yet been discovered, when the electric bell of the outside door resounded precipitately.

"Toby," Mrs. Griffon ordered the waiter who had just served the tea and stale cake, "see who's at the door. If the person is of respectable appearance, show them into the waiting-room."

"Very good, Madam."

"I don't know," she added, "who can be presenting themselves at this hour."

Toby went out. He came back almost immediately, his face pale and his entire body agitated by a tremor of horror.

"What's the matter?" demanded Mrs. Griffon, majestically.

"Madam…Madam…!" stammered the waiter, inarticulately.

"What's the matter?"

"Madam..." Toby repeated, fearfully. The poor devil was so terrified that nothing more could be extracted from him.

Mrs. Griffon was more deeply disturbed than she wanted to appear. "Something extraordinary has happened," she murmured. "I'll go see for myself what intruder can have given Toby such a fright."

Slowly, to show that she was fully in control of herself, she folded up her newspaper, adjusted her pince-nez, and marched to the door in a deliberate manner.

She did not have time to go into the next room. She was almost knocked over by an individual with a distraught expression, in dirty and creased clothes, who came into the parlor like a gust of wind. He darted a glance around full of supplication and horror.

The newcomer had raised his head and was stammering incomprehensible words. His bony, emaciated face appeared in the bright light.

Mrs. Griffon, along with all the other people present, emitted a cry of fright. One old lady fainted; others took refuge behind the piano. As for Toby, he had disappeared under the table.

"Baruch Jorgell!" someone shouted, in the midst of an indescribable din.

"It's him! How dare he come back here!"

"He's going to kill us all!"

"Help!"

"Murder!"

Mrs. Griffon had remained standing still momentarily, as if frozen by amazement, but in the general panic she was the one who regained her courage first and understood, with admirable self-composure the necessities of the situation.

"Ladies and gentleman!" she commanded, in a thunderous voice. "Shut the doors and prevent the murderer from doing any harm, before he has time to make use of his weapons!"

It must be said that Baruch Jorgell did not appear at all redoubtable. He continued looking around with a vague and unconscious gaze, as if he had suddenly fallen into the hotel parlor from the moon.

At the masculine and comforting voice of Mrs. Griffon, the most cowardly recovered their courage. In the blink of an eye, Baruch, who had not raised a hand to defend himself, was grabbed by ten vigorous arms. He was knocked to the ground, solidly tied up with the curtain-cords and deposited in an armchair, without ceasing to roll his bewildered and bleak gaze around him.

After that brilliant capture, the entire assembly uttered a triumphant hurrah.

Mrs. Griffon was radiant with joy and pride. "Now, Toby," she said, with an admirable simplicity, "will you please fetch two policemen."

I shall take my revenge valiantly, she thought. *When I went to give information, I was poorly received. We'll see what they have to say this time.*

Her gaze brooded upon the wretch extended in the armchair as if he were a treasure. His own eyes were now welling with tears.

"It's really him, though," she murmured. "I recognize him—but one would think that he's lost his mind; he has an idiotic expression. It's God's punishment; remorse has doubtless addled his brain."

The hotel's boarders now formed a large circle around the murderer, whom they contemplated with wide eyes. So this was the cunning bandit, the murderer covered with crimes who had defied the police of the two worlds! A profound silence reigned in the parlor.

In spite of the gravity of the circumstances, Mrs. Griffon could scarcely hide a smile of satisfaction. Like the milkmaid in the fable, she was already counting up all the profits and advantages that such an important capture were going to bring her.

First of all, the reward, which was about to drop a thick wad of banknotes into her coffers; then there was the increasing and naturally gratuitous advertising from which the boarding-house was about to benefit. And was not all of that very little by comparison with the value of the glory of having rid society of a criminal of that magnitude? She could already see her picture appearing in pride of place alongside that of Baruch Jorgell.

On reflection, she thought that, with a view to future interviews, it might be as well to proceed with an initial interrogation, before the reporters and detectives had deflowered such a sensational subject.

"Ladies and gentlemen," she said, with as much gravity as if she were presiding over a court of law, "Does it not seem to you to be indispensable to address a few questions to the murderer?"

"Yes, of course, it's absolutely necessary," cried all the boarders, with one voice.

Baruch Jorgell, whose lamentable face was bathed by a torrent of tears, darted the gaze of a hunted beast around him.

"Infamous rogue," she said, "is it to murder me—me, whom you cheated unworthily, by abusing my generosity—that you've returned to this honest house?"

"There's no doubt about it," said Toby, who had emerged from underneath the table, where he had taken refuge.

"Silence!" said Mrs. Griffon. "Let the accused answer."

Baruch Jorgell did not emerge from his stupid dejection, however. To the reiterated questions of the proprietress of the family hotel, he only replied with inconsequential words.

"Yes, yes…I don't know…no…" he stammered, like a man making an incredible effort to remember.

At first, that was all that could be got out of him. However, by dint of tormenting him with multiple and reiterated questions, Mrs. Griffon ended up understanding that unknown individuals—doubtless accomplices—had brought the murderer to the door of the boarding house and had fled after pressing the doorbell.

"Tramps!" he stammered. "The Red Hand…yes!"

"He's trying to make us understand," said Mrs. Griffon, "that he belongs to the bandits of the Red Hand. It's doubtless because of that that he escaped the searches for such a long time."

"There's nothing to understand," said one of the boarders. "One would think he'd become idiotic, completely idiotic."

"All murderers end up like that. They drink gin or ether to escape remorse and end up losing their minds." She continued, in a tone full of sagacity: "Shall I tell you what's happened? It isn't difficult to deduce. Hunted everywhere, he must have found shelter with the malefactors of the Red Hand, and they must have rewarded themselves for their hospitality by stealing his diamonds. Once they'd robbed him they got rid of him by bringing him back here."

"Why here rather than somewhere else?" someone asked.

"Perhaps he still has the diamonds?" Toby hazarded.

"That's true," replied Mrs. Griffon. "We haven't searched him."

"Perhaps," observed one of the boarders, "we don't have the right to do that?"

"As if!" retorted another. "As long as the search is carried out in the presence of honorable witnesses, it's perfectly legal."

"As legal as can be!"

"Let's search him!"

"Right!"

This motion was adopted unanimously, and Mrs. Griffon ordered Toby to explore the captive's pockets.

The improvised detective set to work before the anxious gaze of the audience. He deposited his finds as he went along on the lid of the piano. A Bowie knife of respectable size, a Browning, a block of tobacco and various other objects were seized, one after another, and finally, a wallet was found that contained a few banknotes and papers in the name of Baruch Jorgell.

"You see!" cried Mrs. Griffon. "There's no possible doubt about it—it really is Monsieur de Maubreuil's murderer."

But the audience had not yet reached the end of its excitement. Toby suddenly extracted from the lining of the waistcoat several colorless and transparent stones.

"I can assure you," said one of the boarders, who was a professional broker of precious stones, "that those are the most beautiful uncut diamonds that I've ever seen."

These interesting investigations were doubtless about to continue when two policemen abruptly irrupted into the parlor. After brief explanations they put handcuffs on Baruch Jorgell and led him away, each supporting him with one arm, for he seemed to be incapable of standing up. All the people present were invited to come to the police station to make their statements.

On the way, a terrible argument broke out between Mrs. Griffon, who wanted to claim the whole of the reward, and her boarders, who contended that they all had a right to a share. The police chief, to whom the case was submitted, declared that Mrs. Griffon would first be compensated for the money that was owing to her, and that she would have, in addition, the largest share. That compromise arrangement was agreed by everyone.

Baruch Jorgell was locked up in a solidly-barred cell and, when all the statements had been taken, the guests all returned to the boarding house, where Mrs. Griffon, in honor of such a memorable occasion, offered a bow of punch to all her residents.

V. Perplexity

The arrest of Monsieur de Maubreuil's murderer generated considerable publicity in America and throughout the world. Again Baruch Jorgell's picture appeared in the dailies and the magazines, this time flanked by that of Mr. Griffon and her boarders.

The event produced such a sensation that the abduction of Joe Dorgan, which still remained enveloped an impenetrable mystery, was almost forgotten.

Baruch had now taken his place in the ranks of illustrious criminals, and his biography was sold in small booklets illustrated with crude drawings. For some time, he was fashionable; his portrait was seen mounted on brooches and bracelets displayed in jewelers' windows. The enthusiasm of the idlers changed into a veritable delirium, however, when it was perceived, after the initial interrogations, that Baruch was counterfeiting madness, or, at least, stupidity, in an admirable fashion.

The most skillful magistrates and the wiliest detectives could not succeed in getting more out of him than fragments of sentences, inconsequential phrases whose ensemble presented nothing intelligible.

"What a great actor!" cried the idlers, admiringly. "He's turned them over, the lawyers, eh? You'll see that it will be impossible to get any confession out of him, and that the jury will be obliged to acquit him. Needless to say, you have to come to America to find criminals with that kind of strength."

After wasting a lot of time, the district attorney in charge of the sensational case was obliged to recognize that the accused was not in possession of a sound mind. The most eminent specialists in the Union were summoned as expert consultants. After a summary examination, they declared unanimously that Baruch Jorgell, afflicted by grave cerebral lesions, was utterly irresponsible.

This conclusion caused profound public disappointment. It was widely rumored that the murderer's father, the billionaire Fred Jorgell, had paid the doctors to save the life of his worthless offspring. The prison was besieged by a crowd whose members were talking about nothing less than lynching the murderer; it required two detachments of mounted police to reestablish order.

In any case, it was absolutely false that Fred Jorgell had paid the doctors summoned as experts; the billionaire, as he had loudly declared, had not wanted to do anything to save his son from punishment. He was glad, however, because of his daughter Isidora, that Baruch had not been condemned to execution. Then again, he preferred to think that his son had acted under the influence of madness than to supposing him entirely conscious of the monstrous crimes he had committed.

American law is opposed to condemning an insane person to death. In the presence of the formal declarations of the doctors, the jury rendered a verdict of not guilty by reason of insanity, and the court decided that he would be committed to a lunatic asylum—which is what madhouses are called on the other side of the Atlantic.

It seemed thereafter that the world was in haste to let silence fall upon the affair, which remained shrouded in profound mystery. Baruch Jorgell who had been taken to Greenaway Lunatic Asylum, was soon completely forgotten—but not by everyone.

There was still one person who was interested in the wretched madman; that was his sister Isidora. Soon after the trial, the young woman had a quarter of the monthly allowance she received paid to the director of the asylum, in order that her brother could have a private room and would not be subjected to any privation.

Isidora, who had a personal fortune that she had inherited from her mother, of which she had personal control, had not told her father about her intention; she knew that the billionaire would never forgive Baruch, even on his deathbed, and that he had forbidden the name of his unworthy son to be spoken in his presence.

Isidora, in contrast to many young women of the society of the Five Hundred, solely concerned with sumptuous clothes and new jewels, devoted a great deal of her leisure time to serious reading. Fred Jorgell adored his daughter and had such confidence in her judgment that he would not undertake any important operation without having consulted her. There was no example of Isidora having advised her father to undertake a poor speculation.

At present, Fred Jorgell was engaged, albeit courteously, in a financial battle against William Dorgan. After having been partners for a long time in the Corn and Cotton Trusts, each of them wanted to become the sole master of the market. It was thanks to Isidora that the struggle between the two magnates had not taken on a harsher character.

Isidora had been engaged to the engineer Harry Dorgan. The departure of Baruch, driven away by his father after the mysterious crimes whose author had been discovered by the engineer, had caused the projected marriage to be postponed. The enormous publicity given to the murder of Monsieur de Maubreuil had caused the marriage to be put off again, indefinitely. In spite of Harry Dorgan's persistence, Isidora had not wanted to consent to it. When the children of billionaires marry in America, it is the rule to publish portraits of the young couple, and Isidora could already see, in her mind's eyes, on the front page of every large-circulation daily, the pictures of "the murderer" and "the murderer' sister."

"Let's wait," she had said to the engineer. Meekly, Harry Dorgan had yielded to her reasoning, and he was still waiting.

That semi-rupture would not have prevented the two young people, who could have met one another frequently in the drawing-rooms of the Five Hundred, from maintaining a keen and profound affection. After the noisy publicity given to the assassination of Monsieur de Maubreuil, however, Isidora had re-treated into absolute solitude. She spent entire afternoons walking in silent medi-tation through the long pathways bordered with orange-trees in the paternal park. She liked to isolate herself in the shade of a grove of venerable cedars, where there was a moss-covered marble bench.

Isidora often fell into strange reveries. By dint of reflection, she had been struck by the obscurities and contradictions that surrounded the crime and the criminal. She scented a mystery therein; she thought that the law had been much too hasty. She was intimately convinced that the truth of the sinister drama was much more complex than the detectives and the reporters, in haste to find a plausible explanation, had imagined.

With a dolorous anxiety, the young woman had read the interrogations of the sheriffs, the reports of the alienists and the accounts given to interviewers; that reading had left her very perplexed.

Certainly, she knew, Baruch was devoid of any kind of scruple, and even of any moral sensibility, but his intellectual health had been very robust and powerfully energetic.

There's an inconceivable enigma in this, she thought. *If my wretched brother had completely lost his memory, he would never have remembered the way to the boarding-house. He wouldn't have remembered it at all. Why didn't he recognize Mrs. Griffon or give any evidence of the fact that he had ever known her? Another enigma: what had become of the diamonds? How is it that there has been no trace of them anywhere? Gems that are a little larger than ordinary size are well-known to jewelers. As soon as a diamond of unusual size comes on to the market, it's immediately identified by special publications edited in London and Paris. It's necessary, therefore, that these diamonds must be in someone's possession—in the hands of an accomplice, or several accomplices. If so, why aren't the police looking for those accomplices?*

That problem became, for her, a piercing obsession. It was necessary for her to know the truth, at any price. She took a desperate resolution. Accompa-nied by her Scottish governess, Mrs. MacBerlott, she went to the lunatic asylum situated in a suburb four miles from New York.

Like everything one encounters in America, the madhouse offered a strik-ing contrast between luxurious comfort and savage negligence. One entire wing of the buildings was constructed in marble and polychromatic ceramics, with bay windows with dazzling glass. It was there that the administrators were in-stalled, the doctors and a few rich clients—former speculators for the most part, whose brains had been unhinged by overexertion. The poor lunatics were exiled to badly-built wooden huts, from which howls and lamentations rose up all day long.

As she went through the solid gate with the gilded lances that served as an entrance to that pandemonium, the governess could not repress a vague appre-hension, and the director scarcely reassured her with his warm welcome.

Dr. Johnson, a Yankee of funereal gravity, was not unaware that he was in the presence of Miss Isidora Jorgell, the billionaire's daughter, and he put himself entirely at her disposal.

VI. In the Lunatic Asylum

The director of the asylum felt a certain pride at possessing in his establishment an individual as notorious as Baruch Jorgell, whose crimes had occupied the entire world.

"Mr. Jorgell," he declared, "is surrounded by the most devoted care here; he is visited by celebrated alienists, among whom I can cite Dr. Cornelius Kramm. He was here the day before yesterday."

"Does he think," asked Isidora, emotionally, "that any hope can be maintained, if not for a complete cure, at least for an amelioration of the patient's condition?"

"I want to be frank with you, Miss; the doctor does not hold out any hope. Baruch Jorgell is stricken by a complete amnesia, and the alienists are in accord in deeming that the amnesia in question must have been caused by a violent shock, which produced a lesion that will certainly be incurable...barring a miracle."

Isidora uttered a profound sigh and silently followed the doctor along a sandy path bordered with trees in pots.

"You'll be able to observe," the director went on, "that the accommodation works are proceeding with the most fervent activity. A few months from now we'll have to hand the very best of everything discovered for the cure of the mentally ill: large gardens for the treatments of fresh air and physical exercise, operating theaters, electrical baths, radium baths and solar baths, nor forgetting the refrigeration room, indispensable in the treatment of hypochondria and acute neurasthenia."

Perceiving that Isidora and the governess were only listening distractedly, he added, with a smile full of promises: "Perhaps you'd like to see some of our patients? It's a favor that I don't often grant, and we have some very interesting cases here!"

"No thank you, sir," the young woman replied, coldly.

"I can assure you that you're missing an opportunity," he replied, insistently. "We have the aviator Nelson here, for example, who believes that he has been changed into an airplane, and had to be carefully watched to make sure that he doesn't climb up to the roof in order to take off; the automobile man who goes around all day swaddled in pneumatic tires and has to be prevented, with great difficulty, from drinking gasoline; and the cat man, who refuses any other nourishment than cream and raw liver, who spends all his time mewling, purring and scraping his fingernails of a plank. We also have...."

"I don't doubt," the governess interjected, "that all these patients are very interesting, but Miss Isidora has no interest in seeing those unfortunates, the sight of whom would only sadden her profoundly. She has come purely to visit her brother, and for that alone."

"Very well," murmured the director, slightly vexed but the poor response to his offer. "I thought it would be agreeable to you, but since it isn't, let's say no more about it. I'm unfortunately obliged to leave you for an urgent meeting, but here's the chief warder, who will serve as your guide."

And Dr. Johnson, after a ceremonious bow, entrusted the two women to the care of an athletic individual dressed in a yellow uniform with metal buttons and coifed in a bizarre soft leather helmet. He was the chief warder.

Isidora asked a few questions about her brother's condition, but the warder had precise instructions as to how to reply to the relatives of rich clients.

"Mr. Jorgell," he said, in an obsequious tone, "is as well as can be expected. We have only to congratulate you on his behavior. As for the care with which he is surrounded, you know, Miss, that the motto of the establishment is *tenderness, humanity and comfort.*"

The man in the yellow uniform was careful not to mention the straitjacket, the cold showers and the whip, which he had no scruples about using when the patients showed the slightest inclination to be turbulent.

They had arrived at a high wall in which there was a little iron door fitted with a judas-hole. The warder took a bunch of keys from his belt and introduced the visitors into an enclosure whose soil, covered with meager grass, nourished a few stunted trees. This was doubtless the "vast garden" propitious for fresh air cures and physical exercise that the director had mentioned, Isidora thought, with a constriction in her heart.

Some thirty paying patients were, some prey to a dismal depression, others walking with a jerky step with emphatic gesticulations, under the alternately fixed and roaming gaze of four warders: the special gaze of jailers always wary of being unexpectedly attacked.

It was with great difficulty that Isidora recognized her brother.

She contemplated fearfully that dull gaze devoid of warmth, that thin face ravaged by remorse and malady, and the discolored lips like those of an old man. A fearful, stooped individual devoid of any precise age, his limbs agitated by a perpetual tremor: that was all that remained of the robust and energetic Baruch.

"I can't get used to the idea that that's my brother," the young woman murmured, with poignant sadness.

"It's really him, though," said the governess. "But how depleted he is—no more than a shadow of himself!"

Isidora took the hand of the madman and sat down beside him. "It's me, your sister Isidora," she said, forcing herself to smile. "How are you?"

Baruch raised his eyes to direct a gaze at the young woman from which thought was absent, and withdrew his hand fearfully.

"Come on, Baruch," said Isidora, with obstinate tenderness, "make an effort. Look at me! Isidora—doesn't that name remind you of anything?"

"Nothing," he muttered, in a hoarse voice. He was now looking at the young woman with a gaze that was slightly less extinct, through which something akin to a fugitive flash of thought passed. Then he put his hand to his head in a lamentable gesture.

"I can't remember any more," he stammered. "I don't know any more. What do you want with me? I'm very unhappy! Oh, very unhappy!"

Isidora turned away to hide the tears that rose to her eyes. She was running out of courage. She made one supreme effort, however; she did not want to go away without taking a little hope with her.

"Tell me your name," she demanded.

"I don't know..."

He hid his head in his hands and it was impossible for Isidora to get anything else out of him.

During that heart-rending scene, the governess had remained silent. She was invincibly attracted by the grimaces of an old gentleman who was prowling in the vicinity, walking on all fours and arching his back. He was the man who imagined that he had been changed into a cat. Suddenly, he began mewling in such a lugubrious fashion that the good woman felt frightened in spite of the presence of the warders.

"Miss Isidora," she said, "I think it's best if we go. The haggard expressions of all these unfortunates make the blood run cold. Perhaps our presence is annoying them. Let's go."

"You're right," the young woman murmured, sadly.

"Let's go," the Scotswoman repeated, fearfully, drawing nearer to her mistress. "That gentleman's frightening me with his mewling." She pointed at the madman, who had stopped a few yards away from her.

"We're going," said Isidora. "Perhaps it's better, after all, that Baruch has lost all memory of the past..."

They both hastened to leave the sinister garden and get out of the house of dolors. They got back into the automobile that was waiting for them, which transported them rapidly in the direction of New York.

Isidora took a long time to recover from the terrible emotion she had just experienced.

"It's strange," she murmured. "I can't imagine that it's my brother Baruch that I've just seen. It seems to me that it's him, but not him: that the unfortunate that we've just left is merely a grotesque and pitiful caricature of the Baruch of old."

"Certainly," said the governess, "the illness has changed him a great deal."

"But then, there are things I can never explain. At certain moments I wonder whether my brother is really capable of all the crimes of which he's been accused. One can't say that he's mad, and he's no longer idiotic, since he can take account of his situation and is suffering. This visit has broken my heart..."

Isidora returned sadly to her father's palace, but her melancholy and her preoccupation had increased. She shut herself away thereafter in a retreat more profound than ever.

Every month, courageously, she went to the Lunatic Asylum and observed with despair that Baruch's condition had not changed at all. His intelligence and his memory remained plunged in the darkness of oblivion.

VII. The Fire in Thirtieth Avenue

Until the day when his son Joe had been abducted, and doubtless murdered, by the tramps of the Red Hand, William Dorgan would have been able to consider himself one of the luckiest billionaires in the entire United States. Very prudent, he had only ever bet on sure things in the great battle of dollars, and his fortune had grown from year to year, without upsets, with a wise slowness. It was sufficient for him to take an interest in an enterprise for its success to be assured.

He had been as fortunate from the viewpoint of family life as that of business. His two sons gave him full satisfaction. He was sure of leaving behind him heirs worthy of his fortune and his reputation for probity.

William Dorgan was English by birth, and, as such, he loved comfort and good food. He was not one of those billionaires who work sixteen or eighteen hours a day without granting themselves the slightest distraction, living more miserably than the humblest of their employees. He was hard-working, but in a reasonable fashion, and it would have required an extraordinary catastrophe to force him to delay his dinner time. His cook was famous and all those who had had the honor of sitting down at his table declared that William Dorgan was a *bon viveur*, a good companion and an excellent fellow.

Physically, the billionaire offered a merry expression, a broad rubicund face framed by curly white hair. His features radiated generosity and a perpetual smile played over his fleshy kips. Affection sparkled in his bright gray eyes, as bright and lively as those of a mischievous schoolboy. Very simple in his manners, very liberal and very cheerful, William Dorgan unfailingly attracted the sympathies of those who had dealings with him.

Joe's disappearance had been a bolt from the blue.

In a matter of days, William Dorgan had lost his appetite, and had grown thinner; he neglected his business; nothing interested him any longer. One hope remained to him however: that the engineer Harry might find his brother.

Harry, in fact, in spite of the fruitlessness of his searches, was not discouraged. At the head of an elite troop, he continued to search the defiles and caverns of the mountain, the usual refuges of the tramps. As he had explained to his father, it seemed inadmissible to him that bandits as intelligent and as pragmatic as the companions of the Red Hand would have stupidly murdered a man whose ransom value was colossal.

William Dorgan had ended up sharing the engineer's conviction; he had even published in all the newspapers his willingness to pay any sum at all provided that his son was returned to him. But those promises, like Harry's searches, had not yielded any result.

Time passed without anything new materializing. William Dorgan had fallen into a state of neurasthenia, or, in older parlance, overwhelming spleen. He no longer went out, and paced back and forth in his study all night long, like a wild beast in a cage.

The billionaire's residence, at number 299 Thirtieth Avenue, was a luxurious edifice pretentious in its architecture, based on that of certain castles in the south of England constructed in the reign of Elizabeth. There were turrets everywhere, bell-towers, and arcades florid with sculptures. The dwelling pleased its owner so much that he had never wanted to leave it, even though it was built in one of the less aristocratic districts. It was, in fact, surrounded on three sides by immense dockyards, some enclosing bales of cotton and others construction timber belonging to various Trusts.

During the night, these dockyards were under the surveillance of six guards who took turns to make hourly patrols. One evening—it was a Saturday, and the workers had gone home early—at about ten o'clock, two of the guards, whose turn it was to make the round, emerged from the hut that they occupied in the courtyard of the dock and went into the cotton warehouse, equipped with a shielded lantern and each armed with a Browning.

In the most profound silence, the two men advanced into the middle of the vast warehouse. All around them, the bales of cotton formed regular cubes, between which narrow passages were fitted.

"I think, Slug," said one of the men, suddenly, in a low voice, "that it'll be today."

"You think so?" said the other, with a bizarre smile.

"Yes. I have a presentiment. And then, certain clues..."

"Your presentiment isn't mistaken. Look." And he took from his pocket a piece of paper on which a few lines were scrawled in hieroglyphic characters, and which had for a signature a hand crudely drawn in red ink.

There were a few moments of silence.

"It's astonishing," murmured the first speaker, in an unsteady voice. "I'd rather be in the desert, in the Black Canyon, my rifle in my hand, with our friends the tramps, than doing this job."

"What do you expect? I share your opinion, but, after all, we have to do what the bosses say. Besides which, I've received precise instructions. We're not running any kind of risk."

"Are the drums here?"

"Yes, since yesterday. The Red Hand got them in without anyone knowing. I couldn't say how myself. Now, to work—ten minutes delay could compromise everything."

Slug—the leader of the tramps who had murdered Joe Dorgan's escort—had bent down. He moved aside several bales of cotton and exposed a dozen drums similar to those used to contain oil.

"You see," Slug said. "All that we have to do is pour the contents of these drums over the bale."

"Then set fire to it?"

"Not at all. It will catch fire all by itself."

"Impossible!"

"It was explained to me that it's a chemical compound that contains phosphorus. When the liquid has evaporated, everything goes up in flames."

"That's terrible. Let's hurry. It seems to me that we might be roasted alive."

Slug made no reply, but he began to sprinkle the liquid contents of the drums over the cotton bales, with a haste that proved that he shared his accomplice's anxieties.

In less than a quarter of an hour, the two bandits had finished their criminal work. Then they slipped precipitately out of the dockyard, traversed the courtyard breathlessly and went out into the street, not without having taken the precaution of closing the exterior door behind them.

"Oof!" said Slug, once they were outside. "I'm glad that's finished. I don't like these tricks. I'd rather do battle with mounted policemen than do what we've just done again."

"Where do we go?"

"Follow me—someone's waiting for us; we need to give an account of our expedition."

The two bandits, who seemed to be in a hurry to get away from the theater of their exploits, headed at a run toward the city center, and did not take long to lose themselves in the Saturday night crowds.

At the very moment when the tramps had finished emptying the last barrel of incendiary liquid over the cotton bales, William Dorgan was walking back and forth agitatedly in his bedroom, situated on the second floor of the house. He was holding a letter he had received an hour earlier, from his son Harry.

The young man informed his father that the investigation had made no progress, even though the enquiries of the mountain policemen had extended all the way to the Mexican border. No serious trace had been found, in spite of the gold that had been distributed prodigally. The tone of the letter expressed profound discouragement.

"I'm desperate," murmured the billionaire, dejectedly. "If even Harry is losing hope, there's no resource left. Poor Joe!"

The old man could not hold back a profound sob. The engineer's letter slipped out of his hand.

A domestic had come in on tiptoe and had deposited a heap of letters and telegrams on a side-table. William Dorgan had watched him do it with a distracted gaze, as if absent-mindedly.

"Is that the post from San Francisco?" he asked, anxiously.

"No sir. You had a letter from Mr. Harry in the last batch; there can't be another one today."

The billionaire dismissed the man with a vague gesture and plunged back into his melancholy meditations.

"Poor Joe, my poor boy," he stammered, his throat squeezed by anguish. The stifled sobs continued. He went to the window, opened it very wide, and breathed in the icy night air gratefully.

In front of him, New York extended beneath a sky inundated with harsh electric radiation, with its monstrous perspectives of giant bridges and skyscrapers thirty or forty stories high; a menacing rumor, like the distant growling of thousands of wild beasts, rose from the enormous city.

William Dorgan stood motionless, unable to help being distracted from his dolor by the spectacle of the immense panorama of all that human activity.

"What good is this monstrous material progress?" he sighed. "Will anyone ever find a means of preventing people from suffering...?"

But his sentence was interrupted by a cry of stupor and fear.

Abruptly, with the suddenness of an explosion, and immense sheet of livid flame had just spring forth, rising up to the clouds, illuminating with a violent light the entirety of a vast horizon of monuments and houses.

"There's a fire in the docks!" the billionaire shouted, terrified.

Almost at the same instant, however, a second column of flames, as high as the first, rose up toward the sky.

A second later, a third nucleus of conflagration burst forth with the same suddenness and the same inexplicable violence; there was now a veritable sea of fire, with reddish waves and surf of russet smoke, undulating mightily in the evening breeze, and the billionaire's house, surrounded, was like a reef lost in the middle of a blazing ocean. The Gothic turrets and sculpted balconies stood out sharply against an apocalyptic backcloth. It had taken less than a minute for the cataclysm to erupt. There were entire blocks of houses on fire; an entire district was burning.

William Dorgan had recoiled from the window, driven backwards by the ardent breath of the blaze; already the windows of the house were breaking with a dry crackle, their frames already ablaze.

Losing his head, obedient more to the instinct of a panicked animal than to reason, the billionaire ran out of the room. The stairway was already full of smoke and the cage of the elevator was like the ardent mouth of a furnace.

"Help!" he cried, in a voice that resembled a howl. "Help! Help!"

Acrid fumes gripped his throat; he had to take refuge in the room, where the paintings were cracking and curling under the effects of the heat, and the disjointed parquet was already emitting thin jets of steam. He was blinded by the light of the flames, half-suffocated by the burning atmosphere filling the room. He could not find a way out; he understood that he was doomed.

Meanwhile, an immense clamor of desolation went up from the great city, wrenched from its pleasures by the red horror of the blaze, which was visible ten miles out at sea. Fire engines raced in dozens to the theater of the disaster, finding a path with difficulty through the crowds that two battalions of mounted policemen could barely contain.

It was soon obvious, however, that all efforts to ward off the scourge that had been unleashed on such a vat scale would be futile. It would have been necessary to pour an entire river on the blaze, alimented by so much highly combustible material. Fifteen-story skyscrapers were burning, but the jets of the most powerful pumps were incapable of rising above the eighth story. The rescuers were only thinking of one thing: to limit the spread of the fire, sacrificing one district completely in order to preserve the others; even that task seemed to be bristling with insurmountable difficulties.

Soon, a sinister rumor began to circulate through the crowd.

"The Red Hand! It was the Red Hand that set the fire!"

"All of New York is going to burn!"

"Two banks have been pillaged."

"The police are in cahoots with the bandits. We're doomed!"

There was panic. Many people hastened to their homes and the residents of buildings organized themselves into groups armed with revolvers and clubs, ready to defend their domiciles against the fire-setters.

Here, there and everywhere, groups of courageous rescuers precipitated themselves into the flames to pull out women, children and the sick. The crowds encouraged them with resounding cheers. It was not until the following day that it was perceived that the houses visited by these intrepid citizens had been comprehensively plundered.

In other places the panic had produced terrible stampedes; onlookers, especially women, had been trampled underfoot. The numerous cadavers that were found the next day had all been stripped of their jewelry and valuables.

Idlers gathered opposite William Dorgan's palace; it was not a banal spectacle to see a billionaire roasted alive in his palace; everyone wanted to witness such an event.

Many of William Dorgan's friends had brought extendable ladders and other rescue equipment, but no one dared risk themselves in the furnace. In any case, no one could be sure that the billionaire was not dead already.

Suddenly, a group of men cut through the crowd; among them were Dr. Cornelius Kramm, his brother Fritz and a young man who seemed to be prey to a violent emotion. Those three individuals seemed to have a great authority over the multitude. In a matter of minutes, under their direction, a huge iron ladder was extended along the façade of the house, the windows of which were now vomiting torrents of smoke mingled with flames.

The young man was wringing his hands in despair.

"My God!" he repeated, "Work quickly! As long as it's not too late!" And he stimulate the zeal of all those around him with carelessly-distributed banknotes.

Rapidly, he put on an incombustible asbestos costume and one of the helmets equipped with mica goggles, of which the firemen in certain American cities make use. Then he shook the hands of the Kramm brothers and launched himself forth up the ladder. In a few strides he reached one of the balconies of the house and, breaking the window with his fist, penetrated into the furnace.

The crowd uttered a long cry of admiration and fear, and then fell silent. All hearts were beating with the same anguish.

A minute went by, as long as a century. The young man did not reappear.

"I fear," Fritz murmured in his brother's ear, "that we waited too long."

"No," the doctor replied. "All my precautions have been taken; I can guarantee success."

Once he had reached the balcony, the mysterious rescuer, who seemed perfectly familiar with William Dorgan's house, went straight to the bedroom.

He arrived there at the moment when the crazed billionaire, his hair on fire and half-asphyxiated, had just taken refuge in a fitted closet, which—by a chance that subsequently seemed providential—had been entirely lined with sheet metal because important papers were stored there. In there, it was as if William Dorgan were inside a vast safe. Henceforth, he was no longer running the risk of being burned alive, but he only had a minimal interval before he was completely stifled.

The man clad in asbestos opened the closet door, seized the old man by the arms and carried him to the balcony against which he had leaned the iron ladder.

There he paused for breath; the most difficult part of the task was complete.

"Who are you?" stammered the billionaire, in a feeble voice.

The unknown removed the asbestos mask that was covering his features.

"My son! My dear Joe!" stammered the billionaire.

After so much violent emotion, however, the shock had been too much. William Dorgan fainted in the arms of the son who had so miraculously emerged from his captivity to save his life.

The members of the crowd began to applaud loudly, quivering at the drama that had just been played out before their eyes in a matter of minutes.

In the meantime, Joe Dorgan had attached a solid rope under his father's arms, thanks to which the old man, still inanimate, was carefully lowered down to the street. He had scarcely reached the ground when the house collapsed into the flames, with a dull explosion.

When William Dorgan came round, he found himself in one of the most comfortable apartments of the Atlantic Hotel. Dr. Cornelius and Joe Dorgan were mopping his brow with a counter-irritant solution and making him breathe smelling-salts.

When he opened his eyes, his first glance met his son's eyes, and immediately his face lit up with a smile. Contentment is the most powerful of remedies. A moment later, he was able to speak.

"My Joe is found!" he exclaimed. "I don't care about all the rest. Come into my arms, my son, that I might clasp you to my heart."

"Father," murmured the young man, profoundly moved, "I'm glad to have arrived in time to snatch you from the jaws of death."

The father and son embraced tenderly.

"My poor boy," the billionaire repeated. "If you knew how we've wept! Your brother Harry has been admirable. At present, he's still searching the rugged gorges of the Mexican sierra."

"Dear Harry—how happy he'll be to see me returned, safe and sound."

"You'll tell us all your adventures—but perhaps we ought to take precautions to make sure that what remains of the house isn't pillaged."

"Don't worry about that. Fritz Kramm has taken charge of the necessary measures. By now, the ruins of the house ought to be surrounded by a cordon of policemen, who won't let anyone near it. To make sure of their vigilance, I had fifty dollars given to each man, and promised them a similar sum tomorrow."

"All is for the best, then," said the billionaire. "My most important files are in armored safes that won't have suffered any damage in the fire. My fortune is on deposit in the State bank. As for the loss of the house, I consider it insignificant. I'll build a more luxurious one. Let's not think any longer about anything but rejoicing in your return. Have a bottle of old port sent up, and while we're drinking it, you can tell us the story of your adventures—for the moment, that's what interests me the most."

Joe Dorgan—or, rather, Baruch Jorgell disguised with the features of Joe Dorgan—then began to tell a story whose slightest details had been concocted in association with his two accomplices.

"You remember, Father," he said, "that in making my annual tour of your properties in the state of California, I had to bring back a considerable sum of money—a particularly difficult transport in a country devoid of roads and police, since it consisted mostly of coins and silver ingots. Following your recommendation, I had myself escorted by a dozen mounted policemen."

"That wasn't sufficient," Dr. Cornelius Kramm put in.

"That's true," said the narrator, "but it was all that was available, and I was told that the region had been tranquil for a long time. During my tour I didn't see anything worrying; as I'd been told, the region appeared to be entirely safe. It wasn't until we were going through the sinister defile at the Black Canyon that I perceived, when it was too late to turn back, how dire my error was. In the middle of the night, in a terrible rainstorm, the carriage carrying the money became bogged down in a narrow passage hemmed in on both sides by walls of rock from whose heights a single man could have kept an entire army at bay.

"It was an ideal place for an ambush. The tramps, who must have been lying in wait for us there for days, killed all my men one by one with rifle shots. Soon, in spite of desperate resistance, I found myself alone. The bandits tied me up, and I suddenly smelled the insipid odor of chloroform. A cold pad was placed over my nostrils and I lost consciousness.

"When I came round, I found myself in a desolate ravine surrounded in all directions by precipices, which must have been the crater of an extinct volcano. I was given a little roasted meat to eat and whisky to drink; then I was tied to a horse again and we set off on the march..."

"How is it," William Dorgan asked, suddenly, "that your brother Harry's searches, which covered a vat region bush by bush, had no result? That's what I can't fathom!"

"It's easily explicable. My captors seemed to be admirably well-informed. While my brother Harry was limiting his searches to the region near the Black Canyon, the tramps, covering several hundred miles by means of forced marches, had traveled a long way northwards, skirting the Rocky Mountains, where they were always sure of finding shelter in case of an alarm. I was able to convince myself, in the course of that obligatory journey, of the power of the Red Hand. Everywhere, the tramps found food-supplies and guides; sometimes we even received hospitality at farms of perfectly honest appearance. Finally, we made a definitive halt in a wooded valley to which access was only gained via a narrow path that ended at a furious torrent, over which the trunk of a fir-tree had been thrown by way of a bridge."

William Dorgan was all ears as he listened to this fantastic tale. "But in the end," he asked, impatiently, "how were you able to escape?"

"I'll get to that. The leader of the tramps, an old bandit condemned to death several times over, had decided that I would write to you myself to demand that you pay a hundred thousand dollars for my ransom."

"You had to write."

"Never! The tramps would have doubled their demands and wouldn't have released me once the sum was handed over. Then again, it's not in my character to give in to threats, under any circumstances. Furious at that refusal, the tramps decided to tame my by means of hunger; they put me on a diet of dry biscuit and water, while alongside me the brazenly scoffed beef and mutton stolen from the 'squatters' of the prairie, which they washed down with large draughts of whisky, and even wine. Many a time, my nostrils tickled by the perfume of a roast, I was on the point of giving in."

"My dear Joe," the old man exclaimed, "you conducted yourself in an admirable fashion." Moved by that heroism, he seized the hands of the man he took to be his son and squeezed them affectionately.

"Meanwhile," Baruch continued, "the bandits fell out. Following the classic procedure, some of them wanted to cut off my ears to send them to you, instead of the letter, and thus hasten the payment of the funds; others wanted to wait a little longer. Many fights resulted, with revolvers and Bowie knives. It was in the course of one of those bloody brawls that I succeeded in cutting my bonds without being detected. When night came, I crossed the footbridge, not without taking the precaution of tipping it into the torrent thereafter. The bandits were unable to pursue me. I heard their cries of rage, and their rifle-bullets whistled overhead.

"Eventually, I reached the clearing where the gang's horses were pastured. I leapt on to the best after chasing the rest into the woods, and after riding for three days I reached a small railway station lost in the middle of the prairie. I jumped on to the first train heading for New York. There, two gentlemen who had seen my picture in the papers generously lent me money to pay for my ticket and get a little nourishment in the restaurant car. At a station where there was a sufficiently long halt I sent you a telegram."

"I must have received it," murmured the billionaire, "but I was in such a state of chagrin and prostration that I hadn't had the courage to open the letters and dispatches that reached me shortly before the fire broke out."

"It doesn't matter, since I'm here. When I arrived in New York I jumped into a taxi and arrived just at the moment when the house was enveloped by a sheet of flame. You know the rest, but I ought to put it on record that I was only able to procure the necessary rescue equipment thanks to Fritz and Cornelius Kramm. I scarcely knew them, from having met them some time ago at Fred Jorgell's receptions, but they remembered me, and they put themselves at my disposal with real devotion."

The billionaire thanked the doctor warmly, assuring him that henceforth, he would have no other physician.

Baruch Jorgell was radiant with joy, and his admiration grew for Cornelius, whose docile instrument he had so far been. From now on, thanks to the skillful staging of the fire, it was impossible for William Dorgan not to be absolutely convinced that he had recovered his son Joe.

While the real Joe languished in a lunatic asylum, Monsieur de Maubreuil's murderer and his accomplices were going to be able to share William Dorgan's billions.

4. THE LORDS OF THE RED HAND

I. The Saturday Nightmare

Leaning on one another's arms, two young women were walking slowly in the gardens created at Kérity-sur-Mer in Brittany by the famous naturalist Prosper Bondonnat. When they reached the end of a magnificent pathway lined by rhododendrons, they sat down on a rustic bench shaded by the dense foliage of a linden tree. Both seemed to be prey to a somber preoccupation.

"My dear Andrée," said the one who appeared to be the older of the two, suddenly, "I can assure you that you're wrong not to be frank with me, who loves you as much as if you were my true sister. I'm sure that you're hiding something from me."

"No, Frédérique," Andrée replied, seemingly annoyed, "you're mistaken; I'm not hiding anything from you."

The statement had been pronounced in a constrained and ill-humored tone that did not deceive her adoptive sister. "Do you think, then, that I haven't perceived your pallor and your sadness?" she went on, forcefully. "For some time now you've been considerably changed, and I'm not the only one who has noticed that change."

"Who do you mean?" asked Andrée, her forehead covered with a fugitive blush. "Monsieur Bondonnat, perhaps?"

"You know very well that my father, always preoccupied with his experiments on vegetables, is the most distracted of men. It's not him that I'm talking about, but one of his collaborators—and you have no need to ask which of them, do you?" And as Andrée lowered her head, blushing more deeply, she continued: "You're not unaware that Roger Ravenel will become my husband at a more-or-less distant date—I don't make any secret of it; I'm not as sly as you. Nor are you unaware that Monsieur Paganot has the most respectful admiration for you."

"So it's Monsieur Paganot who has charged you with extracting my secret?"

"So you do have a secret, you see!"

"Oh, a sad secret," murmured Andrée, in a melancholy tone.

"It doesn't matter. You have one. Trust me, tell me about it in all sincerity, and I'll find a means of putting Monsieur Paganot's mind at rest without betraying you."

Andrée threw her arms around her adoptive sister's neck. "You're right, my dear Frédérique," she said. "You're my only friend, my veritable sister, and I'm sorry I tried to hide something from you."

"It's never too late to put things right," said Frédérique, smiling. "Go on—I'm all ears."

"The story I have to tell you is very sad—even terrible!" The young woman had suddenly gone pale; all her limbs were trembling. "I'm obliged," she went on, lowering her voice involuntarily, "to talk to you again about the abominable catastrophe that caused my father's death."

"Speak, no matter how painful I find the memory of Monsieur de Maubreuil's death."

"You haven't forgotten that it was on a Saturday that my father was murdered in a cowardly fashion by the American he had been imprudent enough to take on as a laboratory assistant."

"The wretched Baruch Jorgell, now confined in a madhouse."

"Well, I now have the conviction that my father hasn't been avenged. I even doubt that it's the real Baruch Jorgell that has been locked up in the Lunatic Asylum. Every Saturday, at the same time as my father was killed, I'm tormented by a frightful nightmare. And it isn't an ordinary nightmare; I've been forced to recognize that there's something mysterious and inexplicable about it."

As she pronounced these words, Andrée's face expressed the most vivid and intense terror. Frédérique was no les emotional than her friend. She waited anxiously for the strange story to continue.

"The most extraordinary thing of all," Mademoiselle de Marbreuil continued, "is that in my dream I see people who are unknown to me, but who are always the same. First, there's an old man with rosy cheeks and a cheerful expression, and curly white hair, and two young men who are doubtless his sons. All three live together amiably, but I divine that a secret animosity exists between the two brothers..."

"Thus far," said Frédérique, "there's nothing very terrible. I've often seen unknown faces in my own dreams..."

"Wait a little; it's here that the nightmare becomes frightful. I see the one that I think of as the older brother again. In this phase of my dream he's alone in a luxurious apartment, the furniture of which I can almost describe. He's alone and looking into a large mirror, and it isn't his features that are reflected in the mirror, but those of Baruch Jorgell, the murderer. Gradually, the face of the man who's there, grimacing fearfully, becomes similar to that of the reflection that is frightening him. It's Baruch that I have before my eyes, as, if, suddenly, the correct gentleman, the elder brother that I saw at first, had changed his face."

"But you're going mad, my poor Andrée!" exclaimed Frédérique, disturbed by the fantastic story.

"That's not all, Mademoiselle de Maubreuil went on, with a gesture of horror. "Afterwards, I have to witness the murder of my father, exactly as it must have happened. I see all the phases of the drama; I see my father radiant with the joy of finally having solved the problem of synthesizing diamond. He leans over toward a crucible, and it's then that the murderer strikes him with a hammer...

"I wake up bathed in cold sweat, shivering all over. That's it with regard to sleep for the rest of the night. I think I'll fall ill, that I'll die, if that frightful haunting continues to weigh upon me..."

Andrée fell silent, and her wild eyes retained a kind of reflection of the horror of those visions.

"And it's every Saturday?" asked Frédérique, who had become pensive.

"Every Saturday. The dream is always identical and, so to speak, divided into three parts, as I've just described it."

"It's frightful! I'm no longer astonished by your sadness and pallor. We have to try to find a remedy for it—but how?"

"I must say," said Andrée, "that over time, the nightmare has lost much of its intensity; it still occurs, but I no longer wake up covered in cold sweat, as at the beginning. It's not until the morning that I remember having dreamed. It's as if a secret voice were repeating to me every Saturday: *don't forget!*"

"Do you know what we ought to do?" said Frédérique, gravely. "We ought to tell my father everything."

"I've thought of doing that, but I've never dared. He'd think that I'm crazy!"

"Not at all. He's made a study of telepathic phenomena; he doesn't form an opinion about any fact before having observed it for himself. He'll find a natural explanation for the haunting that's tormenting you."

"Well, I'd prefer that," said the young woman, abruptly making a decision. "It seems to me that I'll experience a great relief when I've unburdened myself of this obsessive secret."

"If that's the case, put the plan into operation immediately. The first step is the important one. Don't wait for hesitation to get a grip on you."

The two young women went through the gardens, passed the greenhouses with sparkling windows where Prosper Bondonnat was experimenting with the influence of colored light on the development of vegetation and went into the villa.

Monsieur Bondonnat's dwelling, built on the edge of the sea in an indentation of the cliff, was cited as a model of comprehensive scientific comfort and modernism. The walls of all the rooms were lined with large ceramic sheets of fired sandstone or porcelain, all the colors of which had been harmoniously combined, and which left no refuge for microbes.

In Bondonnat's home, the heating system did not employ wood or coal, but electric radiators distributed about the rooms, ornamented with delicate arabesques. It was sufficient to turn a switch for the temperature of a room to be increased. In summer, invisible ventilators spread cool and perfumed air in profusion. In the dining room thin sheets of water flowed murmurously down the porcelain walls, spreading a delightful freshness.

Andrée and Frédérique found the old scientist in his study, from which one had a view of the gardens limited by a high cliff, the summit of which was crowned by hail-cannon and other complicated and singular machinery, which Bondonnat used in his experiments. In the distance, one could make out a château whose roof had caved in; it was there that Monsieur de Maubreuil had been murdered, and the local people, who avoided it fearfully, affirmed that it was haunted by the victim's specter.

Bondonnat, who was occupied in examining tiny specimens of plant tissue with a microscope, interrupted his work on seeing the two young women come in, and asked them cheerfully why they had come to disturb him in his "dear studies"—but he suddenly became grave when Andrée had told him the object of their visit, and he listened in attentive silence to Mademoiselle de Maubreuil's story. He remained perplexed, seeking in vain to explain why the terrifying nightmare was reproduced with such perfect periodicity.

"This is," he said, finally, "an extraordinary case of telepathy, and I agree with Frédérique. Baruch isn't mad, and it can't be him who is locked up in the Lunatic Asylum. When, my dear child, did you first become the victim of this nightmare?"

"On the very day that we heard about the arrest of the murder in a boarding house in New York."

"That proves that you're not the victim of an ordinary hallucination. I ought to tell you that I followed the progress of Baruch's trial with great attention, and the manner in which he was arrested has always seemed inexplicable to me. A drama must have unfolded over there in America of which we know nothing. I need to think about this matter very carefully."

"But do you think, Father," Frédérique asked, "that Andrée will continue to be obsessed by this frightful vision?"

"I think that the Saturday nightmare will pursue her for a long time yet, but, as the facts seem to indicate, its violence will be gradually attenuated, if Andrée has sufficient courage no longer to be frightened by it, and to consider it simply as a warning of some mysterious occurrence."

"There's one thing about my dream that's utterly incomprehensible," said Andrée, whose emotion had gradually calmed down. "It's the transformation of the man, which abruptly changes his face."

"There's only one way to explain that, which is to suppose that the murderer has succeeded in modifying his facial features thanks to surgery. That has been done on occasion. Then, when the murderer is alone, he sees his true face again—but that's a hazardous and rather vague hypothesis."

The two young women said no more, and Bondonnat lapsed into silence too. In spite of the reassuring explanations he had just provided, he found himself very embarrassed; he had never encountered such a case.

Suddenly, however, his face cleared, and it was with a smile of mischievous benevolence that he said to his daughter: "Would you do me the favor of leaving Andrée and myself alone for a moment, my dear? We need to talk."

"All right," said the young woman, "I'll go. I don't need to know your secrets." And she withdrew.

"My child," said the aged scientist when he found himself alone with his ward, "I've been meaning to have a serious talk with you for some time. I had a long conversation yesterday with my collaborator, Antoine Paganot, and he has asked me formally whether you will consent to become his wife."

"What did you reply?" Andrée stammered, blushing with emotion.

"In my capacity as your guardian, friend and adoptive father, I've effectively replaced poor Maubreuil with regard to you; I believe that I said what he would have said himself. I hold Monsieur Paganot in high esteem; he's an honest man and a first-rate scientist. I therefore told him that, for my part, I was all in favor of the union, but that before giving him a definitive response I had to consult the principal interested party. You know me too well not to know that I will do nothing to influence the decision."

"I esteem Monsieur Paganot as much as you do," the young woman murmured, with embarrassment. "He has great qualities..."

"I can see that we understand one another," said the old man, smiling.

"I know that my father liked Monsieur Paganot a great deal. That's one reason for me to ratify that choice you've made."

"Then I can tell my collaborator that his request is agreed?"

"Certainly."

"But I hope that it isn't simply out of respect for your father's wishes and deference for me that you're giving your consent?" Bondonnat added.

"No, I have a strong sympathy for Monsieur Paganot," Andrée replied, swiftly, "and I wouldn't want any husband but him." Then, slightly ashamed of the spontaneous impulse, in which she had exposed the depths of her heart, she lowered her eyes in confusion.

"Very good!" exclaimed the old scientist. "You've spoke frankly; I congratulate you for it. I'm certain, in consequence, that you won't be marrying against your wishes."

The young woman's only response was a smile more eloquent than any words.

"The marriage pleases me all the more," the naturalist went on, "because I've also decided, for my part, to grant Frédérique's hand to Monsieur Ravenel. The two weddings can take place on the same day, and in that fashion, I won't be separated from my two most cherished collaborators; we'll continue to live as a family, as in the past. Embrace me, my child; I'm happy today—truly, very happy."

Andrée threw herself into her guardian's arms. "How can I ever repay you?" she murmured.

"I forgot one more thing," the old man interjected, suddenly. "As soon as you're married, I want us to go to America."

"I'll do anything you wish."

"The voyage is indispensable. I want to know the truth about Baruch. I want to carry out a serious investigation myself, on the spot. I need to get to the bottom of things, on principle. It's only in America that we'll obtain a definitive explanation of the Saturday nightmare that has caused you so much torment. I'll only make one recommendation to you, which is not to say anything about the voyage until I give you permission."

At that moment Frédérique came back into the study.

"The confidences are concluded," said the naturalist, cheerfully.

"It's not too soon!"

"Andrée will let you in on the secret herself. It's good news that I wanted to have the pleasure of giving to her personally. Go and continue our walk. I need to get back to work."

The two young women left arm in arm, and a few minutes later, their joyful voices were resounding in the gardens of the villa.

II. The Lords of the Red Hand

Joe Dorgan had just returned to his room after having taken care of a voluminous correspondence when the telephone beside his bed rang loudly.

"Hello?"

"Hello!"

"Is that you, Mr. Dorgan?"

"Yes, Who's this?"

"Dr. Kramm."

"Very good. I'm listening."

"Can you spare an hour or two this evening?"

"Yes."

"I'll expect you, then. We need to talk. Fritz will be here."

"See you soon."

The young man hung up the receiver, slightly anxious at the late communication, but Dr. Cornelius was one of his best friends, a man to whom one did not refuse anything.

Joe Dorgan put on a Swedish overcoat and a broad brimmed hat and slipped the Browning into his pocket from which he was never separated. At the same time, he put a sizeable wad of banknotes into his wallet.

When these preparations were terminated, he left the room and took his place in an elevator that deposited him in the large vestibule on the ground floor.

In the vast sandy courtyard there were two electric automobiles, headlights illuminated. Joe Dorgan climbed into one of them.

"Stop at the end of Thirtieth Avenue," he said to the chauffeur.

"Very good, sir," the man replied, obsequiously.

The automobile pulled away, went through the gate, which had just opened silently in response to the chauffeur's horn, and traveled at top speed along the deserted avenues of New York.

A quarter of an hour later, Joe Dorgan got out and, after ordering the chauffeur to wait for him, he went along Thirtieth Avenue on foot, with his hat pulled down over his eyes and the collar of his overcoat turned up over his ears, hugging the walls like a man afraid of being recognized.

On the way, he noticed that the rare passers-by, muffled like himself up to the eyes and taking the same precautions, were hastening in the same direction as himself. After walking for about twenty minutes, he stopped in front of a property bordered by high walls and closed by a wrought iron gate. On one of the columns supporting the gate there was a black marble plaque on which was inscribed in golden letters: *Dr. Cornelius Kramm.*[11]

The young billionaire rang the bell and was immediately let in by a smiling old man severely dressed in black from head to toe, who greeted him with the marks of the most profound respect.

"Good evening, Leonello," said Joe, negligently. "Is the doctor well?"

"Marvelously. He's waiting for you."

"Where?"

"Come with me."

"Is it far?"

"A few steps."

Guided by Leonello, Joe Dorgan traversed the garden, went through a small door half-hidden by ivy and found himself in a deserted back street bordered with sordid buildings.

They walked silently for a few minutes; then Leonello stopped and knocked four times on the door of a wooden building on the edge of a plot of derelict ground surrounded by a fence.

The door opened by a crack; the two men slipped silently inside into a low-ceilinged room poorly lit by the tremulous glow of a rusty oil-lamp suspend from the ceiling by iron wire.

"Here's the doctor and his brother," said Leonello, indicating two men sitting at a small table covered with papers, who had not even raised their heads on hearing the door open.

The old man disappeared.

Joe nearly uttered an exclamation of amazement. The two people with whom he was face to face were wearing rubber masks pierced with eye-holes, thin enough only to conceal in part the play of the features.

"Is that you, Cornelius and Fritz?" the young man asked, anxiously.

"It is," replied one of the men, with a sarcastic laugh. "Don't worry—it's not for your benefit that we're in disguise."

"I'll breathe easy! You're hideous in those masks. Why this late meeting? Has something serious happened?"

"No—if we've asked to you come it's to give you one more proof of our complete confidence..."

At that moment, four regularly-spaced knocks sounded at the exterior door.

---

[11] The reader will perhaps remember, although the author has obviously forgotten, that Cornelius Kramm's house was previously reported to be situated on Tenth Avenue, while Thirtieth Avenue was cited (perhaps somewhat inconsistently) both as the location of Mr. Griffon's boarding house and William Dorgan's dockland "palace."

"They're here!" murmured Cornelius. "it's necessary that no one sees you in our company. Come this way—hurry! Listen and watch; you're about to be party to one of our most important secrets."

Cornelius had drawn the young man into a dark corner of the room. Before Joe Dorgan could recover from his surprise, he found himself enclosed in a narrow hiding-place little more spacious than a cupboard. Holes had been bored at eye-level in such a fashion that he could see and hear.

The panel that sealed the covert had hardly had time to close when Fritz Kramm opened the door. A man clad in rags came into the low-ceilinged room. He seemed very intimidated, and, holding his cap in his hand respectfully, he darted fearful glances at the two brothers.

"Here it is, Milords," he said—and he took a piece of paper from his pocket on which a few hieroglyphic symbols were traced. At the bottom a hand crudely drawn in red ink was visible, and a smaller hand in the left-hand corner.

Cornelius and Fritz examined the piece of paper carefully, while the man waited humbly.

"It's two hundred dollars," said Cornelius finally.

"Two hundred dollars," Fritz repeated. And he pulled a small stack of gold coins out of a box placed beside him. The man took it and went to the door without saying another door, moving backwards and bowing.

Scarcely a minute had gone by since his departure when another visitor was introduced. It was a middle-aged man, fairly well dressed, whose manners advertised a certain education. Like the wretched individual who had just left, he seemed ill at ease and penetrated by a respectful terror.

Bare-headed and silent, he presented Cornelius with a piece of paper exactly similar to the other, bearing the two hands drawn in red ink.

"Five hundred dollars," said Cornelius Kramm, in a blank and toneless voice, as if faded.

"Five hundred dollars," Fritz repeated.

The man took the banknotes that were handed to him and retired without having said a word.

Scarcely had he disappeared than he was replaced by a uniformed policeman who collected a thousand dollars, then an elegant female socialite who received seven hundred, and a minister, who got two thousand. For two hours, there was an uninterrupted procession of individuals belonging to all classes of society and who each collected a more or less considerable sum of money. The pieces of paper bearing the double seal of the Red Hand now formed a voluminous stack beside Cornelius Kramm, and the box containing the cash was almost empty.

From the depths of his hiding-place Joe Dorgan watched, wide-eyed. He had calculated that nearly two hundred thousand dollars had just been distributed that evening. A kind of vertigo took hold of him; he scarcely glanced at the more or less bizarre faces that succeeded one another in the low-ceilinged room, which faded away as if in a dream, with almost identical gestures.

Suddenly, however, his attention was caught by a kind of broad-shouldered Hercules with enormous fists, who had just come into the room with a kind of arrogance. He looked around with an expression of impertinent curiosity. He had left his cap on his head and was whistling through his teeth.

"It's customary to take your hat off in the presence of the Lords of the Red Hand," said Cornelius, gravely.

The man took off his cap, impressed in spite of all his audacity.

"I don't much like these famous lords whom no one has ever looked in the face," he sniggered. "But I don't care as long as I get what's due to me." And like those who had preceded him, he handed over his piece of paper, stamped with two red hands.

"Five hundred dollars," said Cornelius coldly.

"Five hundred dollars," Fritz repeated, holding not a banknote.

The Hercules took it angrily and crumpled it between his fingers before sticking it in his waistcoat pocket. His face was red, the veins in his temples swollen.

"Five hundred dollars!" he exclaimed, giving the table a thump with his fist that made the worm-eaten board creak lamentably. "Is that all I get for having risked my skin a hundred times over emptying bankers' safes during the big fire? I want at least ten thousand dollars, you hear? The work's worth that—and I won't go without getting them. Jack Simpson isn't afraid of anyone—not even the Lords of the Red Hand. You can't intimidate me with masks and play-acting! Come on, I want my money, right away!"

"Jack Simpson," Cornelius replied, very calmly, "you've just insulted the Lords of the Red Hand. It's not the first time something similar has happened, and you'll be punished for it."

"We'll see about that!" the bandit ranted. "I'm not afraid of half a dozen like you two! Nobody cheats me. Give me my dollars, or I'll shoot!"

Matching action to his words, Jack Simpson brandished an enormous Browning, taking aim at Cornelius' head.

The doctor remained impassive, but already, without the athlete perceiving it, he had pressed a copper stud fixed in the parquet with his foot.

From the depths of his hiding place, Joe Dorgan had watched the scene unfold, and was ready to fly to the aid of the Kramm brothers, when two men as robust as Jack Simpson leapt upon him with lightning rapidity. One of them crushed the wrist that held the Browning with his fingers, while the other seized the athlete by the throat.

"Accursed dogs!" howled Simpson, struggling desperately—but all resistance was futile; in a matter of seconds, the colossus was floored, tied up and gagged.

The two men disappeared as rapidly as they had arrived.

Cornelius and Fritz conversed for some time in low voices.

"Jack Simpson," said the doctor, finally, in the same tranquil voice, "you have insulted the Lords of the Red Hand. Prepare yourself to suffer the punishment you have incurred."

The colossus writhed in his bonds as if to ask for mercy, and his face expressed an unspeakable terror. That face, contracted by a mute supplication, had an eloquence to make one shiver...

Cornelius called out: "Slug! Jackson!" The two men reappeared. "Take this brute away," he ordered. "Put him in a safe place. Tomorrow, I'll tell you the decision of the Lords of the Red Hand in his regard."

Slug and Jackson lifted the colossus, effortlessly, on to their shoulders and carried him away to a side room; then the procession of visitors continued.

Finally, Fritz Kramm declared, yawning, that the session was concluded, and went to fetch Joe Dorgan from his hiding place.

The young billionaire was very impressed by what he had seen and heard during those two hours. "The organization of the Red Hand is a marvel!" he declared, enthusiastically. "In spite of everything you've told me, I would never have believed that one could contrive such administrative precision in a society of that sort.

"You haven't seen anything yet—but with the kind of fellows we have under our orders, it's sometimes necessary to show them the fist. You've just had an example."

"But they don't know your real identities?"

"We'd be lost if they suspected. Everyone imagines that the Lords of the Red Hand are numerous, and we arrange things so that they persist in that belief."

"But your retreats must be known—this house, for instance..."

"Has been rented for a fortnight only, under a false name, and we'll never return to it. The next quarterly share-out will take place in another district of New York."

"So you issue dividends every three months, like the big banks?"

"Yes, it's necessary. Today, I've shared out the profits originating from the big fire lit be the Red Hand, which consumed, as you now, an entire district of New York..."

"It seems to me," Fritz Kramm suddenly interjected, "that it would be much better to chat elsewhere than here."

"That's true," the doctor agreed. "There's nothing to keep us in this hovel, and it might even be imprudent to stay here any longer."

Fritz and Cornelius took off their rubber masks, carefully tidied up the pieces of paper that would doubtless help them to make up their accounts, and got ready to leave.

"One more question," said the young billionaire. "What will become of Jack Simpson, who had the audacity to insult the Lords of the Red Hand?"

"His case is clear," muttered Cornelius. "I've learned, in addition, that he's been in communication with Police Headquarters. We need to make an example of him."

"Will he die?"

"There's not a shadow of doubt about it. His corpse will be found tomorrow on some deserted avenue, his cheek marked with the bloody hand that is the Association's signature."

The young man could not help shivering.

"Examples are necessary," the doctor continued, as if he had read his interlocutor's mind. "If we didn't act thus, it wouldn't be long before we were sold to the police, and the association would no longer exist. I wanted you to see that, now that you too are a Lord of the Red Hand. You'll soon find that there's a certain pleasure in exercising that formidable and mysterious power. In sum, it's a royalty like any other."

While talking, the three bandits had arrived at the little garden door, which Leonello opened silently for them.

"That's enough talk of the Red Hand," said Fritz Kramm, curtly. "Now we're going to occupy ourselves with our friend's business—which is, henceforth, ours too."

"And for that," added the doctor. "We'll be much more at ease is my subterranean laboratory."

They went into the luxurious building that stood in the middle of the gardens and took their places in an electric elevator that was engulfed in the depths of the earth.

A few minutes later they emerged into a room with ceramic-lined walls. It was the vestibule of the laboratory.

III. The Hallucination

The Kramm brothers and their accomplice were now in a vast vaulted room illuminated by numerous electric lamps, in which a host of strange machines and items of apparatus of unknown function was accumulated.

They took their places in comfortable armchairs around a small table on which the officious Leonello deposited a bottle of extra-dry champagne and three crystal goblets, as well as a box of Havana cigars.

"This laboratory," Dr. Cornelius said, his eyes, like those of a bird of prey, scintillating behind his gold-rimmed spectacles, "must bring back a few memories for you."

The young man had gone pale. "Yes," he murmured, "it's here that I experienced what were probably the most poignant emotions of my life."

"I hope that you don't regret having confided yourself to my care. When you came in here, you were Baruch Jorgell, wanted for the murder of a French scientist, Monsieur de Maubreuil; when you left, your name was Joe Dorgan, the son of a well-known billionaire. Thanks to surgery, the carnoplasty of which I'm the pioneer, you've completely changed your physiognomy. I've rendered for you the miracle of magicians who effect the transmigration of souls from one body to another. Who knows whether there might not be a kernel of truth behind those legends? One day, perhaps, the true story of Baruch Jorgell becoming Joe Dorgan might pass for a legend."

"Why remind me of all that?" Baruch murmured.

"Because," said Fritz, "my brother is legitimately proud of an operation that has succeeded so well. It's necessary to overcome that weakness. Anyway, in this laboratory no one can hear us; we're absolutely at home here."

"Let's talk seriously," Cornelius put in. "The interests of all three of us are now completely associated, and it's absolutely vital that I know exactly how Baruch has been playing the role of Joe in the three weeks since William Dorgan recovered his son."

"Admirably—even the engineer Harry has been deceived. No one has the slightest suspicion. Besides, I'm doing everything I can to maintain the illusion. I'm continuing in the greatest secrecy the internal treatments that ought to render the changes that the doctor has effected in my personality definitive. I've adopted the same tastes and he same opinions as my involuntary twin; I even play the same games..."

"What about the childhood memories?" asked Cornelius.

"I make use of them discreetly, putting in the occasional anecdote, and so far I'm sure I haven't made any mistakes. Mind you, one thing that irritates me terribly is being obliged to retell, wherever I go, the story of my pretended captivity. I've recounted that anecdote at least two hundred times."

"Everything's gone according to plan, then," said Fritz. "Now, though, it's necessary for us to consider, once and for all, what's the best way for us to exploit the situation."

"I've already thought about it, and my plan is made. We won't be able to make any attempt on William Dorgan's billions so long as my so-called brother, Harry, is there to watch me. It's necessary, first of all, that he fall out with his father."

"That might be difficult to contrive," muttered Cornelius.

"Difficult, yes, but not impossible. The engineer is very proud, very stubborn; he can't stand contradiction. At the slightest remonstrance from his father, whom he loves very much, I'm sure he'll become headstrong and go to seek his fortune elsewhere. To get to that point, however, I need time. For the moment, I'm being zealous, working very hard; I've realized that that's the best means of gaining old Dorgan's confidence."

"Continue to do that," said Fritz. "I'd prefer to succeed in that fashion than by employing violent means. There'll always be time to have recourse to that."

The three bandits continued their reflections for some time, wondering how much longer they would need to wait before getting their hands on William Dorgan's billions.

It was Baruch who broke the silence first. "You mentioned violent means just now," he said, abruptly. "If you take my advice, you won't ever resort to that."

The brother Kramm exchanged a rapid glance.

"Why is that?" asked Cornelius.

"I've given it a great deal of thought. We now have enough capital to act overtly. Let's avid compromising ourselves with unnecessary crimes."

"One might really think," Fritz mocked, "that in putting on Joe Dorgan's features, you've inherited his virtuous theories."

"Would you like me to be frank?" Baruch continued, without responding to the sarcasm. "Well, you ought to abandon this Re Hand, which will do you a bad turn sooner or later."

"That's impossible at present," Cornelius replied, seriously. "It's the Red Hand that procures us most of our resources. It's thanks to its affiliates that my brother's warehouses are filed with paintings and *objects d'art* stolen from all the museums of Europe. It's the Red Hand that furnishes me with the enormous sums of money that I need for my experiments. I'm not yet rich enough to be able to do without it."

"Then again," said Fritz, "isn't it something to command an army of audacious malefactors who have a finger in every pie in all the States of the Union? Thanks to the Red Hand, I have a police force that keeps me up to date with everything; there's nothing that I can't undertake. You've been able to judge that for yourself. I can, with the most complete impunity, burn cities, rob banks, hold the rich to ransom..."

"You'll be betrayed sooner or later."

"I'll be able to get out in time—but for that, my brother and I will each need our billion, securely invested."

"Perhaps that will come very quickly, thanks to Baruch," said Cornelius. "Thus far, the affair has gone admirably. Here's to Baruch!"

The three bandits clinked glasses and emptied them in a single gulp; then silence reigned again in the laboratory, all three of them falling back into their reflections.

"I believe," said Cornelius, eventually, "that it's time for us to part. We don't have anything left to say."

"Pardon me," said Baruch, with a certain hesitation. "One more word, if you lease. I showed you the positive side of my situation just now, but I haven't told you about my own suffering..."

Cornelius Kramm shrugged his shoulders. "Bah!" he said. "It's nothing. Your new personality is doubtless rubbing at the seams, like a new suit, but it will become more supple with time. By dint of repeating your role, you'll know it so well that it will be an integral part of you. You'll even get to the point, I'm convinced of it, of completely forgetting that you were once Baruch Jorgell."

"Oh, as to that, never! I have terrible reasons for believing that I'll never lose my memory of the past."

"What do you mean?"

"Even if you consider me to be weak in the head, as if afflicted by mental illness, I ought to confess to you that I'm haunted by horrible visions, by atrocious nightmares. If I believed in remorse..."

"Science doesn't recognize that," snigger he doctor. "You're simply a victim of hallucinations, to which time, physical exercise and a few sedatives will soon put an end. Would you like me to give you a prescription?"

"Wait...it's just that these hallucinations, as you call them, are of a very particular sort. First of all, they translate themselves into a fear of mirrors; I experience intolerable suffering in their presence. I'm like the man featured in fantastic tales who had sold his reflection. I'm attracted in an invincible fashion to mirrors, but when I look into them, I seem to see, grimacing through the physiognomy of Joe Dorgan, my true face—Baruch's face. And that attraction, I feel, has its dangers, for there are moments when my present features, under the contortions of the fear, reassume something of their former appearance. And yet, it's necessary that I study myself carefully every morning, to see whether any modification has been produced in my features, to make sure that I still resemble Joe Dorgan. It's terrible! Mirrors attract me, but I'm afraid of the reflection they send back..."

"All this isn't very serious," said the doctor. "I can only see a little nervousness, caused by stress and fatigue."

"If it were only that, I'd agree with you, but my illness is more complicated, and also more terrible. Every Saturday...and it was on a Saturday that I killed Monsieur de Maubreuil"—the murderer's voice did not tremble as he pronounced that phrase—"the hallucination takes on a sharper form."

"Go on," said Cornelius, suddenly attentive.

"It always begins in the same fashion," Baruch continued, "and goes through three phases. Always the same. Every Saturday, when I'm taking tea with William Dorgan and his son, as a family, I see before me, quite clearly, the living phantasm[12] of Mademoiselle de Maubreuil; she looks at me with an expression that is both desperate and menacing. To begin with, she's only a kind of vaporous fog, and indecisive patch of light, but as I look at her—and it's impossible for me not to look at her—her features are accentuated, and she takes on form; it seems to me that I only have to reach out me hand to touch her; I tremble in case she advances toward me, and yet she always remains standing behind William Dorgan's chair. The hallucination reaches such a degree that it's impossible for me to follow the conversation. I'm obliged to make some excuse and flee..."

"You must have been amorously attracted to the young woman?"

"That's true, but she rejected me brutally—and perhaps it was also for that reason that I was so pitiless toward her father."

"This is suggestion at a distance," Cornelius Kramm explained, albeit without conviction. "You think about her and she thinks about you; provided that one has a certain degree of objective force...have you read the book *Phantasms of the Living*?"

"No, I haven't...but that's only the first phase."

"Let's hear the second," said Fritz, with a certain affected negligence. "This is very interesting."

"I flee, and take refuge in my room, and here I'm obliged—obliged, you hear?—to place myself in front of the large looking-glass...and it's no longer

---

[12] The author inserts a note at this point to define "living phantasm"—which is rendered in that fashion in the original—as the spectre of a living person. The phrase is doubtless given in English in the text because the first major publication of the Society for Psychical Research founded in England in 1882 was a massive collection of reports of *Phantasms of the Living* compiled by Edmund Gurney, F. W. H. Myers and Frank Podmore. Gurney also published an essay on "Hallucinations" that is probably relevant to this episode, which attempted to explain such phenomena by means of a theory of telepathy, and he conducted extensive experiments on the subject using hypnosis to try to establish telepathic links and induce hallucinations. Le Rouge was familiar with these endeavors—he cites the first-named book a few lines further on, although he translates its title into French on that occasion—and took them very seriously; he published an occult theory of his own in his long essay *La Mandragore magique* (1912), presumably written immediately before he began *Le Mystérieux docteur Cornélius*.

the reflection of Joe Dorgan that is grimacing in front of me but that of Baruch Jorgell...Baruch the murderer! At that moment, I feel that my face has become itself again, that the mask has fallen..."

The murderer had paused momentarily; he wiped his brow, which was covered in cold sweat.

"Which is annoying," grumbled Cornelius. "If such hallucinations were to take hold of you often, it could comprise the resemblance obtained with such difficulty, and spoil my masterpiece..."

"Why does Baruch go back to his room?" objected Fritz Kramm. "In his place, I'd go to the theater, a bar—anywhere—and not come back till daybreak; that's the best way to escape all these visions."

"I've tried," Baruch replied, waspishly, "but at the time in question, whatever I do, an invincible force draws me back to the accursed mirror, in front of which I'm constrained to stand, and soon—this is the frightful thing—I see slowly imprinted, in the changing mist of reflections, the melancholy face of Monsieur de Maubreuil, with his gray hair and his forehead wrinkled by insomnia. He's clad in his laboratory smock, stained by acids, just as I saw him *the last time!*"

Baruch had pronounced those final words in a hollow tone; his eyes turning up in their sockets, he extended his arms forward, as if, at that very moment, the vengeful image were standing before him. The Kramm brothers looked at him, also prey themselves to a secret fear.

"I can see," said Cornelius, in a doctoral tone, "that your nervous system is depressed, somewhat deprived of phosphorus; you need to take phosphoxyl, a marvelous remedy that has a powerful tonic effect on the cerebral cells. But I hope that you've finished with all your phantoms?"

"No," said Fritz, more calmly. "We need to hear about the third phase."

"That's perhaps the most terrible," said Baruch, shivering. "This is what happens: the atrocious struggle against the specter that haunts the depths of the mirror abruptly comes to an end. I snatch myself out of the haunting and I throw myself on the bed, fully dressed. I'm exhausted by fatigue, physically and mentally, and I go to sleep immediately, almost instantaneously—a leaden slumber. My eyes have scarcely closed when the obsession takes the form of a nightmare and I see myself in Monsieur de Maubreuil's laboratory, assisting in the synthesis of diamond..."

"And no doubt," Cornelius put in, with a horrible laugh, "the unexpected death of Monsieur de Maubreuil. I deduce that you wait for Saturday evening without any impatience."

"It's my terror all week long. And yet," Bruch added, with a sort of rage, "I have will-power; I'm a strong-minded man, you know, and no one has ever been able to hypnotize me!"

"What is most obvious in all that you've just told us," the doctor declared, "is that you're very ill, and in everyone's interest, it's necessary not to let the neurosis take you over. If you don't resist courageously, your phantoms will never leave you. Like Banquo in *Macbeth*, you'll see the specter of your victim sitting at the table, in your place. Shakespeare described those sorts of hallucination very well. How long have you been suffering this neurosis?"

"Since the day of Joe Dorgan's arrest in the New York boarding house, disguised with my appearance. The obsession began with a simple dream, which, from one Saturday to the next, has taken on a more piercing acuity."

"That's because the neurosis has increased and been exacerbated week by week," explained Cornelius Kramm. "But why didn't you tell me sooner?"

"I hope to be able to master it myself, but I've realized that it's impossible."

The doctor took a notebook from his pocket and scribbled a prescription rapidly. "Here," he said. Phosphoxyl, lecithin, valerianate of iron.[13] Absolute abstention from alcoholic liquors, walks in the open air, long sleep, moderate exercise. Follow that regime obstinately, and I'm sure that your Saturday nightmares will have completely disappeared before long."

"I hope so...but what if the treatment doesn't work?"

"Tell me, and we'll try something else."

"What!" exclaimed Fritz Kramm, darting a glance at his chronometer. "Two o'clock already. It's high time we were gone."

The three accomplices hastened toward the elevator.

Five minutes later, Baruch and Fritz emerged from the gate of the establishment together.

"By the way," said the art dealer, suddenly, handing Baruch a heavy envelope. "I have something to give you."

"What is it?"

"A few banknotes—your share, as a Lord of the Red Hand, in that last dividend distribution."

"I don't see how I've deserved it..." the young man stammered.

"It doesn't matter—take it anyway. You're a Lord of the Red Hand, that's sufficient. Remember that it isn't always those who sow and reap the wheat that eat the bread."

Baruch did not insist. He shook his interlocutor's hand distractedly and went back to his automobile, whose chauffeur was patiently waiting for him at the corner of Thirtieth Avenue.

---

[13] Extracts of the plant valerian were used in herbal medicine as a sedative; however, the salts of valeric or pentanoic acid, a more specific extract from the plant, actually have an irritant effect, so this might not have been the wisest prescription.

IV. The Trust

American billionaires—kings of steel, oil or cotton—are almost all at the head of a Trust. A Trust is a monopolization throughout a region—and, if possible, the entire world—of one of the products of primary necessity.

The functioning of the redoubtable financial mechanism in question—forbidden by law in every country except America[14]—is very simple.

Let us take an example. Let us suppose, for instance, that it is a matter of oil. Several speculators sign a treaty of association pooling their gigantic capital, and then they buy, at any price, the mines, the distilleries, the storage depots and sometimes even the railways lines that give access to the oil-producing regions.

As one might suppose, there are proprietors that resist, and who refuse to sell their factories and their mines at any price. Then the Trust has recourse to other means; it floods the market with low-price oil. The isolated industrialists cannot provide it on such good terms; they are ruined and obliged to capitulate.

The most glorious Yankee billionaires would be considered in France as simple criminals and sentenced to many years in prison, but in America that brigandage is permitted, and has become current practice.

In the end, a time arrives when the Trust is the owner of the entire production of a country. Then master of the market, it can double, triple or quadruple prices as it wishes, and realize, to the detriment of consumers, who cannot defend themselves, fantastic benefits.

The goal of the Trust directed by William Dorgan was the monopolization of cotton and corn, the two principal objects of agricultural production in the United States.

However, Fred Jorgell, the father of the murderer Baruch, had formed a counter-Trust, and as the capitals engaged in the struggle were almost equal on either side, the two billionaires had not thus far dared to engage in an all-out battle; they shared the market in cotton and corn, and their antagonism maintained a certain equilibrium in prices.

Baruch's arrival in the home of William Dorgan, who believed him to be his son Joe, abruptly modified that state of affairs. Until then, the billionaire had been afraid to a decisive battle that might as easily ruin him as multiply his capi-

---

[14] Although the first American anti-Trust law, the Sherman Act, had been passed in 1890, it required strengthening, in order to be effective, by the Clayton Act and the Federal Trade Commission Act of 1914. When Le Rouge was writing this episode in 1912, therefore, the nexus of US anti-Trust legislation was still incomplete. Le Rouge had probably read *Le Talon de fer*, the French translation of Jack London's *The Iron Heel* (1908), a dystopian novel that explains the logic and iniquities of Trusts in great detail.

tal tenfold. Contrary to the opinion of the engineer Harry, who was in favor of moderation, Baruch set out to persuade William Dorgan that it was necessary to go forward and engage in an all-out battle.

"My brother Harry doesn't understand business," he repeated. "Besides which, it's no secret that he's passionately in love with Isidora, our rival's daughter."

Baruch wanted to ruin his true father, Fred Jorgell, against whom he had sworn a mortal hatred, and in his rancor, he did not neglect any argument in convincing William Dorgan.

"Audacity," he said, "always audacity. Don't wait for Fred Jorgell to go on the offensive. I'm sure that he's only practicing moderation because he's preparing some trap."

"That's not what your brother Harry says."

"Harry, I repeat, has every interest in protecting the man he believes to be his future father-in-law, but I know from a reliable source that Fred Jorgell will never give his daughter's hand to the son of his financial adversary."

"Besides which," the billionaire replied, "I don't much like the idea of my son marrying the sister of a murderer."

Little by little, Baruch took possession of William Dorgan's mind, and Harry, almost always traveling or busy setting up factories on behalf of the Trust, was not there to defend his ideas.

Hesitant at first, the billionaire ended up being persuaded that Baruch was right, and, insensibly drawn along, he entered into the dangerous path of all-out competition. Purchases of land and planted crops succeeded one another rapidly.

At first, the unsuspecting Fred Jorgell did not retaliate, but, abruptly snatched out of the false sense of security into which he had allowed himself to slip, he riposted vigorously, returning blow for blow. He also set about acquiring, by the liberal disposition of banknotes, all available land and crops. At the same time he lowered the prices of sacks of corn and bales of cotton to an almost derisory level. The two competitors bought dear to sell cheap, and their capital—and that of their shareholders—decreased rapidly.

After a few weeks of that hectic duel, the situation did not seem to have been modified. William Dorgan and Fred Jorgell were, as one says in certain contests, neck and neck.

William Dorgan began to repent of having followed his son's advice. He became anxious, and lost his appetite; his face, once pink and chubby, became pale and furrowed by wrinkles.

"I ought to have listened to Harry," he often said to himself. "He was right. But now I've set the machine in motion, it's necessary to go on to the end."

With regard to Harry, Baruch gave proof of a diabolical ingenuity. When the young man expressed surprise at the excessive thrust that the contest had taken on, he replied, hypocritically: "It's not Father's fault; it was Fred Jorgell who went on the offensive first; we've been forced to defend ourselves."

"That astonishes me," the engineer murmured, very perplexed. "I didn't think Fred Jorgell was as avid for gain."

"You can see for yourself that our enemy's moderation was merely a clever tactic."

"I need to clear this up; it's impossible that Fred Jorgell's character and plans have been modified so abruptly, without there being any reason..."

Baruch feared above all else that Harry might discover the truth, and he always arranged things so that the engineer, called away by some urgent dispatch, was obliged to depart in haste for the South or the West, to install a steam-mill or some other agricultural endeavor, the supervision of which kept him a long way from New York.

In the meantime, Baruch was the sole master of the situation. He had acquired an absolute empire over his supposed father; the old man, drawn into a whirlwind that he could not master, scarcely dared raise a few timid objections to the audacious projects of the son in whose intelligence he had a blind faith.

In spite of that weakness, the billionaire could not help suffering terrible anxieties at the thought of the total ruination that might one day fall upon him. He understood that in spite of all Baruch's fine talk, the situation was going to intensify, and could only end in a catastrophe.

In spite of the hallucinations that were tormenting him, however, Baruch deployed an extraordinary activity and zeal, and had prepared, in the greatest secrecy, a veritable *coup de théâtre*.

One morning, after a night anxiously spent studying statistics relating to plantations and the mercurial vagaries of the market, William Dorgan went to find Baruch.

"My dear Joe," he said, sadly, "until now I've followed your ideas blindly. Like you, I believed in the ultimate triumph, and spent millions without counting them."

"It was necessary," Baruch replied, his eyes sparkling with a savage energy.

"But where have we ended up?" said the old man.

"Wait!"

"I've been waiting too long. Every day you tell me that Fred Jorgell is on the point of capitulating."

"I'm firmly convinced that he can't hold out much longer."

"That's possible, but he might hold out long enough to witness my ruination. Do you know that my reserves are exhausted, while his seem almost intact? Why didn't I listen to your brother Harry? Today, I bitterly regret not having followed his advice. Do you know how much liquid capital I still have at this moment?"

The billionaire had spoken in a voice tremulous with emotion. Baruch was still perfectly calm, his expression cheerful, almost ironic. "I don't know exactly, Father," he replied, with an affected negligence, "but what does it matter?"

"What do you mean, what does it matter? We scarcely have twenty million dollars still disposable—only enough to continue the battle for one more month!"

"Twenty million dollars, yes—that's very little by comparison with the figure in the calculation I've made."

"I don't understand your tranquility at all!" exclaimed the billionaire, beginning to get angry. "So you realize that we're heading straight for catastrophe, for an irremediable collapse?"

"I think, Father," said Baruch, who had not lost his calmness for a moment, "that you're exaggerating the danger somewhat."

"I'm not exaggerating at all! I'm seeing things as it's necessary to see them. How bitterly I regret having followed your advice, abandoning myself to your inspirations!"

"They were, however, excellent—and they still are..."

"Don't talk like that. Do you know what I'm going to do? I'm going to telegraph your brother Harry right away to come back immediately, and we're going to try to arrange a cease-fire, to make an agreement with Fred Jorgell, if he's prepared to consent to it."

Baruch had stood up, his gaze gleaming with a somber fire. "You're not going to do that, Father!" he declared, imperiously.

"Are you going to stop me? Are you determined to ruin us?"

"Listen to me," the bandit replied, gravely. "Before addressing such stinging reproaches to me, it would be as well to consider where I deserve them. From the very start, I knew perfectly well that we would have to sustain a gigantic struggle for a long time."

"You knew that? And you let me get up to my neck in the mire?"

"You'll understand. Our reserves, that no longer amount to more than twenty million dollars, would only permit us to hold on for a month at the most, it's true. But what would you say if I had the means to resist victoriously for another six months, perhaps a year?"

"Oh, if you could say that! That would be certain victory, Fred Jorgell would be completely crushed—but is it possible that you've been able to find the capital?"

"Nothing is more certain; it's a surprise that I've been saving up for a long time. I've explained our situation to our excellent friends Fritz and Cornelius Kramm, and they've consented to take an interest in your Trust. The doctor is barely a millionaire, but the art dealer is very rich; in any case, they have friends whom they'll be able to persuade. It's agreed that they'll make an initial investment of ten million dollars, which will be repeated if the need arises."

"But that's magnificent!" exclaimed William Dorgan, enthusiastically. "Fred Jorgell is doomed—he's in the drink! We'll triumph all along the line."

"You can see that you were right not to listen to my brother Harry. With his policy of moderation at any price, it's us that would be going under."

"My dear Joe," exclaimed the billionaire, emotionally, "I've never doubted your talents as a speculator. I've followed you to the end, and I'm proud of not having doubted you!" After a moment, however, with a residue of doubt, he added: "I hope that you've taken precautions, that you haven't been content with verbal promises?"

"Not at all," said Baruch, proudly. "Everything is in order; the contract has been signed with the group of shareholders that the brothers Kramm are heading. The funds will be made available when we wish. I kept what I was doing the secret from you until everything was settled in order not to give you false hope."

"Now I'm unburdened of all my anxieties," said the billionaire, cheerfully, all of his good humor having returned. "You've brought off a masterstroke there, and I congratulate you very sincerely. I'm growing old, you know, and I think it will soon be time for me to retire and leave the direction of the business to you. As for your brother Harry, he really is too timid; he doesn't understand speculation at all—he'll have great need of your lessons if he's to succeed..."

"I'd like nothing better than to give him good advice. We'll talk about it again, although he won't take it very well...but I have to go; Cornelius and Fritz Kramm are coming to dinner, and I only just have time to take a bath and get dressed to be ready in time..."

The billionaire and his pretended son separated, each as satisfied as the other by the fortunate event that had just modified the chances of their battle with Fred Jorgell in their favor.

It was not without difficulty that Baruch had convinced the Kramm brothers to become William Dorgan's benevolent shareholders, but he had ended up making them understand that it was where their true interests lay, and they had arranged things so as not to run any risk in the operation. Thanks to minutely-verified information, they knew that Fred Jorgell had reached the limit of his resources and that he had tried to find new capital in vain. His shareholders were weary of incessantly venturing further sums with a view to a result that the energy of his adversaries rendered problematic.

Although he hid his situation, Fred Jorgell's back was to the wall, and to play against him was almost a sure bet. Furthermore, Baruch crimes and the reprobation that surrounded his name had gradually hollowed out a void around the billionaire, and had distanced some friends from him who would otherwise not have failed to come to his aid.

Baruch had demonstrated to his accomplices that the sole means of getting their hands on William Dorgan's billions was ostensibly to support him, in such a way as to take away all his suspicion. The influence of Harry Dorgan over his father, once all-powerful, would thus be completely neutralized, and Baruch had not despaired of causing a fatal quarrel between the father and the son in the near future.

In any case, the bulk of the capital that the Kramm brothers were putting at William Dorgan's disposal was not coming out of their own coffers; they had found obliging shareholders among the rich clients of the sculptor of human flesh and the billionaire collectors of Old Masters with whom Fritz was in routine communication. The sum personally furnished by the two brothers came from the sale of a portion of the diamonds stolen from Monsieur de Maubreuil. Those diamonds had been cut by Dutch jewelers in the hire of the art dealer, and then inserted in antique mounts and cleverly sold to various European potentates.

In that circumstance, Fritz had made use of a novel trick; the newspapers had reported that a poor ditch-digger in Philadelphia had discovered a treasure of inestimable value in the foundations of an old house, comprised of all kinds of jewelry ornamented with diamonds of an extraordinary size and beauty. The archeologists consulted had declared that the jewels must have been hidden during the War of Independence, perhaps in the era of the filibustering pirates. It was soon known that the famous art dealer Fritz Kramm had acquired the antique treasure for a fabulous sum.

As can easily be guessed, the ditch-digger from Philadelphia was an accomplice of Fritz, an affiliate of the Red Hand, and the discovery of the treasure was a cleverly staged deception of which the world was the dupe. Henceforth, the stolen diamonds had an admissible provenance, and the advertising cleverly generated around the discovery enabled them to fetch unexpectedly high prices.

Such, therefore, was the origin of the sums invested by the three bandits in William Dorgan's Trust.

The latter was radiant. Saved from catastrophe by a stroke of luck that he could not explain, he went forward audaciously, buying more plantations of cotton and corn every day. At the same time, those two kinds of primary merchandise were subjected to substantial falls in price.

According to an ancient proverb, strokes of luck come in threes, and the billionaire had proof of that when the shares he had in the copper mines of Colorado suddenly increased in value and he acquired a considerable sum from the expropriation of some land that he owned in the suburbs of New York.

In addition, the yields per acre of cotton and corn promised to be more abundant than ever before, and demand in the world market was almost double that of previous years. When William Dorgan became the absolute master of the market, and could raise prices at his whim, he would be able to count his profits in millions of dollars.

Fred Jorgell's defeat was regarded as certain in well-informed financial milieux, and the most well-heeled shareholders would not have risked a hundred dollars in the enterprise he directed.

Baruch was triumphant. He was, therefore, about to be able to satisfy his rancor. Delightedly, he saw the moment approaching when the father who had cursed him and kicked him out would be completely ruined.

V. On the Eve of Ruin

Fred Jorgell had foreseen the catastrophe that was threatening him for some time, but he understood that all his efforts would come to naught, and he had resigned himself in advance to his ruination.

In any case, after the murder committed by his son Baruch, following a series of other crimes that remained unpunished, the speculator's character had been abruptly modified. In a matter of weeks he had aged several years; his hair, already graying, had gone completely white; his thin face had elongated further and his eyes, sunken in their hollow orbits, shone with a disquieting gleam. His affection for his daughter, the utterly good and charming Isidora, was the only sentiment that could still bring an occasional melancholy smile to his lips.

Baruch's arrest and trial had been like dagger-thrusts in his heart; he had never recovered from them, and his energy and intelligence had suffered from the terrible chagrin he had experienced.

Since that disastrous day, nothing he had done had succeeded; it seemed that ill luck was pursuing him doggedly. Although he possessed, in the highest degree, the business sense and special knowledge necessary to the launching and direction of large-scale enterprises, all the speculations that he undertook had led to losses of various magnitudes. Despairingly, he saw that the Trust in cotton and corn, the enterprise on which he counted most, was also about to conclude in a cataclysm. In vain he had tried to find capital, but doors closed before him as if in response to a mysterious word of command.

Fred Jorgell continued the struggle, as a kind of point of honor, as if to maintain an illusion, but he sensed that he was doomed. Proud by nature, he did not want to make anyone party to his apprehensions. All day long, at the Stock Exchange, in the presence of his peers, he affirmed loftily that everything was going well; he even simulated cheerfulness, and spoke about considerable reserves that he had in various banks in the Union, and thus succeeded in maintaining the illusion for a few other people.

In the evening, however, once he was alone in his study, he let himself collapse dejectedly into an armchair, no longer having the courage to calculate or to plan, even striving no longer to think. That was the hour in which he tasted, in his sadness, a kind of tranquility very similar to that of a condemned man in his cell—but it was also the hour in which he received a visit from his dear Isidora.

Smiling and consoling, the young woman came in on tiptoe and came to plant a silent kiss on her father's forehead; and then they talked.

"What's new?" Isidora asked. She was the only one who knew about her father's chagrins.

"It couldn't be any worse," the billionaire replied. "William Dorgan isn't letting up or showing me any mercy. Soon, I won't be able to continue the struggle any longer; I'm already beaten."

"I don't understand. Haven't you told me a hundred times that you had nothing to fear from that Englishman, whom you regarded as perfectly honest?"

"William Dorgan is no longer the same. He's suddenly become intractable, disloyal and perfidious. I no longer recognize him."

"What can have caused that change?"

Fred Jorgell made an angry gesture. "The cause is easy enough to find. It's Joe Dorgan who's exciting his father against me. It's only since his return that everything has been spoiled, He's conceived a mortal hatred for me, and I can't divine the cause of it."

Isidora reflected. "Even if we have Joe Dorgan against us," she said, after a momentary pause, "we know that the engineer Harry is entirely devoted to us."

"Yes, but unfortunately, Harry's influence over his father is now almost negligible. Joe has acquired such an ascendancy over William Dorgan that the engineer no longer counts, so to speak."

"In any case," said the young woman, insistently, "Harry has always been perfectly honest. I know that he's personally desolate because the struggle between you and his father has become bitterly intransigent."

"Of course! I'm not unaware that he's entirely on our side, and it's not difficult to guess why."

Isidora turned away, blushing. "You're doubtless alluding," she said, in a weak voice, "to the marriage plans that Harry and I once made. I won't deny that I still have a sincere affection for him, and it's very unfortunate that terrible circumstances prevented that marriage..."

Fred Jorgell stood up, a trifle emotional. "I can see that you love him as much as you did at the beginning."

Isidora nodded her head affirmatively, and her eyed filled with tears.

"All these misfortunes were caused by that infamous rogue Baruch!" cried the billionaire, furiously. "But for him, I'd have been calling you Mrs. Dorgan for a long time, the two Trusts would have been fused and I wouldn't be two fingers away from ruin. You must understand that the marriage can never take place, now..."

"Who can tell?" stammered the young woman, in a tremulous voice. "Circumstances might change..."

"Don't nurse any vain hope. Even if Harry Dorgan—and I believe he's capable of it—consents to accept as a wife the sister of a murderer...I'm calling things by their name, bluntly...I'd be the first to refuse your hand to the man who's in the process of stripping me of my last dollar!" With a bitter laugh, he added: "Besides which, I won't have a dowry to give you; you'll no longer be an eligible match for the son of a billionaire."

"So the catastrophe is imminent?"

"We're already there!"

"Father!" cried the young woman, courageously, "I'm ready to bear anything, provided that I'm not separated from you. But at least give me the final mark of confidence of telling me the date on which the final collapse will occur. I need time to prepare myself."

The billionaire had gone pale; he seemed hesitant. "My poor Isidora," he finally contrived to articulate, "we have another month before us: one month, no more."

"But that's a great deal! A lot can happen in a month. In that short space of time, the face of things might change."

"I no longer have any hope of that."

"Is there no means of avoiding ruin, then?"

"Yes, there might be one—but to make use of it I'd have to implore the pity of William Dorgan and his son, both of whom I detest, and that I'll never do."

"What would that means be?"

"It would be necessary for me to start right away selling all my land, all my factories, all the stock and merchandise in my Trust. That way, I'd only lose half my fortune and I'd still have enough to try something else. If I don't sell immediately the word will get around—it's already beginning to spread in spite of all my precautions—that I'm losing my battle against William Dorgan. Then, people would take advantage by buying my merchandise and land at rock-bottom prices, and nothing would remain of my capital but wreckage, scarcely enough not to die of hunger."

Isidora was devastated. "Father," she murmured, "you taught me a long time ago not to fear poverty. If you're ruined, you'll be able to start all over again."

"It's too late for me," said the billionaire, somberly.

"It's never too late—haven't you told me that a hundred times yourself? I only regret that you didn't think it necessary to warn me about the true state of affairs."

"My child, it's better that I acted as I did; I've spared you many unnecessary tears."

Isidora remained silent. She wondered anxiously whether there was anything she could do to ward off the imminent ruination.

If only, she thought, *I'd been able to see Harry Dorgan, perhaps he would have indicated a means of sorting everything out. Yesterday's newspapers announced the departure of Joe Dorgan and his inseparable friends the Kramm brothers for a long tour of inspection in the South and the West. Temporarily free of the baneful influence of Joe, William Dorgan might perhaps be accessible...*

Entirely given over to her preoccupations, Isidora left her father sooner than usual. Energetic and stubborn, like the true Yankee she was, she had determined to do her utmost to save her father—but when it came to thinking of practical means of putting her plan into action, she found herself in great difficulty. She knew that her father would never forgive her for visiting William Dorgan, and she dared not write to Harry, who would have deemed such a step "improper."

She could not shut her eyes that night; it was not until daybreak that she fell into a fitful sleep, without having found a solution to the vexing problem.

She was woken up by her companion, Mrs. MacBarlott, whom, in spite of her recognized devotion, she had not informed of her troubles.

"Good morning, Miss," said the Scotswoman, cheerfully. "I hope you slept well."

"Not very well," murmured the young woman, whose pale face retained the traces of insomnia and whose beautiful eyes were surrounded by dark rings.

"My dear child!" cried Mrs. MacBarlott, solicitously, "I can see that you've had a bad night. You seem very nervy. Take my advice and have an electric bath, which will take away your fatigue, and then we can go out on the Hudson in a motor boat. The weather's magnificent; the fresh air will do you good..."

"I'll follow your advice," the young woman murmured, with a slight yawn. "The sea breeze will rectify my nerves. I'll be ready in three-quarters of an hour...until then..."

VI. On the Hudson

After getting out of the automobile that had rapidly transported them to a quay on the Hudson, Isidora and her companion took their places in the electric launch that they employed in their habitual excursions on the river. It was an elegant craft entirely constructed in teak, in the centre of which there was a cabin similar in its disposition to those seen on Venetian gondolas.

The two women sat down on velvet cushions with golden buttons while the chauffeur took up his position at the stern.

Almost soundlessly, the launch slid between the numerous vessels anchored in the immense estuary, which bore the flags of all the nations of the world. There were huge clippers laden with timber that had come from Canada, and iron steamboats belching torrents of black smoke, while a population of stevedores belonging to all races busied themselves, to the blasts of sirens and factory whistles. One might have thought it the activity of a monstrous ant-hill.

Soon, however, the launch had left behind the industrial districts bordered with soot-blacked factories spitting out their nauseating vapors almost dolorously into the clouds; the banks of the Hudson were now populated by villas and gardens.

Delightedly, Isidora breathed in the atmosphere freshened by the breeze, and listened distractedly to Mrs. MacBarlott's chatter.

Like many old woman, Mrs. MacBarlott had a hobby, which was totally inoffensive. She collected portraits of celebrated actors and actresses. Her gallery, which included several thousand photographs and cuttings from illustrated newspapers, was considered to have a real documentary value.

"I'm expecting a sizeable package from Rome and Paris," she said, "which will complete my collection..."

Isidora whose thoughts were elsewhere, was preparing to reply with some polite phrase, when she suddenly noticed, fearfully, that the launch had just gone into a branch of the river between two islets. At the entrance to the channel there was a large placard bearing this warning in black and red letters: *DANGER: THIS CHANNEL IS RESERVED FOR THE EXPERIMENTS OF THE ENGINEER HARDISON.*

The chauffeur had not noticed the placard, and the launch continue to fly at top speed beneath the shade of the tall trees that grew on the banks of both islets.

"Turn round!" ordered the young woman, pointing at the danger warning.

The chauffeur realized then that he had committed an imprudence by virtue of his negligence. He tried to circle around, but it was impossible; the channel was not broad enough.

Isidora had gone pale, but she had not lost her composure. Without knowing exactly what danger the engineer Hardison's experiments might pose, she thought that the simplest thing would be to land on the nearest bank.

"Put into shore!" she ordered.

The chauffeur tried to obey, but he could not reduce the vessel's speed rapidly enough, which advanced by another ten meters by virtue of its acquired momentum. A boom, masked until then by a clump of trees, appeared abruptly. There were five people there, who, at the sight of the launch, exhibited signs of a violent terror.

"Get back!" they shouted, waving their arms. "Now—or you're doomed!"

"Too late!" cried one heart-rending voice.

At the same moment, a jet of liquid erupted from the surface of the channel with the noise of a muffled detonation, capsizing the launch along with its passengers.

The engineer Hardison, well-known in America for his discoveries in the field of explosives, was in the middle of experimenting with a new torpedo charged with a powder of his own invention. Ill-luck had determined that the chauffeur would not see the danger sign, and the launch had arrived just as the torpedo was about to explode.

Already, however, one of the witnesses of the scene, without even taking the trouble to take off his clothes, had dived into the water, and after having dived twice had brought the unconscious Isidora back to the bank.

It was the engineer Harry Dorgan, whom, by a strange coincidence, the inventor Hardison had invited the day before to witness his experiments; he was the one who had uttered the cry of anguish on observing the young woman's peril.

In the meantime, Hardison and his friends had jumped into a dinghy and had fished out Mrs. MacBarlott and the imprudent chauffeur of the launch, easily enough.

The three victims were laid down to the grass in front of the engineer's workshop, and energetic care was lavished upon them: the application of powerful revulsives, artificial respiration and massage.

It was the Scotswoman who recovered consciousness first, as soon as reinvigorating "lavender salts" had been waves under her nostrils. After half an hour, the chauffeur was similarly recalled to life.

Only Isidora's condition continued to cause anxiety. The young woman's forehead had struck the nickel-plated edge of the launch; her temples were bloodstained and her face had a corpse-like pallor.

The inventor Hardison was distressed.

"It's still lucky," he stammered, almost as pale himself as the victims of the accident, "that the effect of my torpedo was limited to the vertical direction. Otherwise, the launch would have been literally pulverized."

On his knees beside the woman who had once been his fiancée, Harry had bandaged the head-wound and had just observed, with an infinite joy, that her heart was still beating feebly. The rapidity with which Isidora had been rescued had been such that asphyxia had not even had time to begin its work. It was necessary to attribute the young woman's unconsciousness to the serious contusion she had received, and doubtless also to the shock of fear she had felt.

Initially reassured by that idea, Harry fell back into panic on perceiving that Isidora was not coming round in spite of his care.

"She's dead!" he cried, with an immense despair. "And I'm one of the people who have killed her."

It was at that moment that Mrs. MacBarlott, whom a glass of whisky had put back on her feet, advanced tragically toward the inanimate body of her mistress and cried, in a lamentable voice: "You've killed Miss Isidora! What am I going to tell Fred Jorgell, my master, my benefactor, who entrusted the care of his only child to me?" Suddenly, though, she recognized the engineer and fell upon him. "Why, it's you, Harry Dorgan," she murmured, with an expression of sadness and reproach, "who've put torpedoes in our path. Oh, I'd never have thought it of you! I imagined, like everyone else, that you had an old and sincere affection for Miss Isidora...so the father's ruining us, and the son..."

Harry Dorgan was both furious and desperate. "But I had nothing to do with the accident," he replied. "On the contrary, I'm the one who has just saved Miss Isidora from death!"

The young woman opened her eyes languidly, look round with an expression of profound dejection, and then, recognizing Harry Dorgan, she smiled weakly and made as if to take the young man by the hand.

"She's alive! We'll save her!" cried Mrs. MacBarlott. "A doctor! She needs a doctor!"

Almost at the same moment, an individual dressed entirely in black advanced at a measured pace; it was the doctor so impatiently awaited. He increased his pace as soon as he was informed that the client for whom he had been summoned was the daughter of a billionaire.

After making a rapid examination, he declared pedantically: "Her general condition is certainly worrying; the nervous depression is considerable; ulterior accidents are perhaps to be feared with regard to the heart. However, for the time being, I don't believe that the patient's life is in danger..." In the midst of the general attentive silence, he added: "The first thing to do is to transport the patient to a place where I can lavish my care upon her."

"I have my automobile!" aid Harry Dorgan.

Isidora was carefully deposited on the vehicle's eat; the doctor and Mrs. MacBarlott placed themselves to either side of her, while Harry sat down facing her.

A few minutes later, they halted in front of a pharmacy where the doctor had a cordial potion mixed before his eyes, two spoonfuls of which he gave to his client. The effect of the elixir was immediate. Isidora recovered consciousness again and the automobile set off again at top speed. The doctor rubbed his hands, without trying to hide the satisfaction he felt.

"That's what I thought," he murmured, self-importantly. "The prostration phase has concluded, the unconsciousness is dissipating, even the pallor is disappearing gradually. As for the wound on the temple, it's nothing serious. I'm sure that after two weeks of treatment, I'll have the charming Miss Jorgell back on her feet..."

The doctor continued to perorate as the automobile went through the outlying districts of New York City. Suddenly, it stopped in front of an edifice with Gothic turrets and luxurious and complicated sculptures.

It was William Dorgan's residence, which the billionaire had had rebuilt in a less dangerous location immediately after the great fire that had destroyed it. In his emotion, Harry had not given his chauffeur any address, and the latter had quite naturally brought his master home.

But Mrs. MacBarlott had stood up.

"You must understand," she said to the engineer, "that Miss Isidora, however serious her condition might be, cannot receive hospitality from her father's most obstinate enemy."

"But..." Harry stammered.

"It's impossible, I tell you—absolutely impossible."

At that moment, however, either because the effect of the potion that had momentarily reanimated her had worn off or because the emotion caused by the sight of her former fiancé' residence had been too much for her, Isidora uttered a profound sigh, collapsed into her companion's arms and lost consciousness again.

"Let's leave questions of propriety there," Harry exclaimed, energetically. "First of all, it's necessary to think of Isidora's salvation. It would put her life at risk to go any further."

"What does the doctor say?" demanded the Scotswoman, nonplussed.

"After this further loss of consciousness," the physician declared, gravely, "I won't answer for anything if the patient has to submit once again to the jolts of transportation."

Mrs. MacBarlott remained silent. The omnipotent authority of the Faculty was not to be set in the balance against the necessities of protocol.

A few minutes later, Isidora was carefully deposited on a bed in a spacious chamber lacquered in light blue and pale green, whose spring-like décor was perfectly suited to the individual who was about to become its inhabitant for several days.

While the doctor, who was more anxious than he wanted to appear, gave Isidora a further dose of the potion, the Scotswoman hurried to the telephone to tell Fred Jorgell what had happened.

The billionaire let out a string of typical Yankee oaths on learning about the accident that had befallen his daughter, but his wrath no longer knew any bounds when he learned that Isidora had found shelter in the home of his enemy William Dorgan.

"My God!" he roared into the apparatus. "You stupid woman! You should never have let such a thing happen! Now I'll be forced to thank a man I detest!"

"It was necessary, sir," said Mrs. MacBarlott, apologetically. "The doctor..."

"Shut up! I ought to send you back to Scotland!"

Mrs. MacBarlott heard nothing more. Fred Jorgell had slammed the receiver down.

Ten minutes later he presented himself, in person, at William Dorgan's home, very calmly, only thinking about one thing: the danger that was threatening his child.

When Isidora came round, she observed with surprise that she was in a room that was completely unfamiliar; it was with nothing less than amazement that she saw at her bedside William Dorgan, Harry Dorgan and her father, who seemed to be talking to one another in low voices, with a certain cordiality.

She thought she was dreaming. She tried to speak, but Harry, smiling, put a finger to his lips, while Mrs. MacBarlott gave her a potion. She drank it in tiny sips, without trying to comprehend such a strange situation; almost immediately she fell into a peaceful sleep.

"Now," declared the doctor, who was standing discreetly to one side, "All will be well. Tomorrow, Miss Jorgell will almost have recovered from that terrible shock. Her cure will merely be a matter of care."

"And I promise you, Mr. Jorgell, that she won't lack that here," said Harry energetically.

The two billionaires could not help smiling. They went out together, and William Dorgan escorted Fred Jorgell ceremoniously to his automobile.

When they were about to part, they shook hands.

"I'm very grateful for what you've done for Isidora," said Fred Jorgell, his expression a trifle constrained.

"My conduct is quite natural, it seemed to me," William Dorgan replied. "Isn't my son one of the people responsible for the accident?"

"Don't say that—he's the one who saved her. That's something I'll never forget, regardless of our financial rivalries."

The dialogue continued for some time in that coldly courteous tone, and then the two billionaires took their leave of one another.

The next day, as the doctor had predicted, Isidora was much better. She was able to take a little light nourishment and received a visit from her father, who went away completely reassured this time. That day, the two billionaires spoke for longer than they had the day before; they both had a deep sympathy for one another and they were both experiencing a secret remorse with regard to the animosity that had divided them.

Harry spent the greater part of the afternoon in Isidora's room, where the Scotswoman—who had not left her side for an instant—was caring for her with the utmost devotion.

Harry had brought a stack of illustrated magazines and new books, and in spite of the opposite of Mrs. MacBarlott, who claimed that he was trespassing on her prerogatives, he wanted to read them to the convalescent himself. Then they both lapsed into a conversation full of charm. They knew that it was no longer permissible for them to make plans for the future, but they abandoned themselves joyfully to reminiscences.

"Isidora," said Harry, after a long pause, "do you remember how happy we once were?"

The young woman uttered a profound sigh; her beautiful faced reddened. "Alas," she murmured, "why is it necessary that our dreams of old have become unrealizable?"

"Why should they be unrealizable? The promise I made to you, to have no other wife but you, I shall keep, I swear to you once again, even if you marry someone else."

"I've resolved never to marry."

"You don't love me anymore, Isidora?"

The young woman's eyes filled with tears. "My heart hasn't changed," she stammered in an almost-inaudible voice, "but circumstances have rendered the marriage impossible. Why did my brother have to be such a wretch?"

"He's not relevant. It's as if he never existed."

"And that rivalry that has made our fathers bitter enemies, irreconcilable enemies..."

Isidora was in one of those moments when the heart overflows, like an over-filled cup, in which secrets seem too heavy for further discretion; she knew that the loyal Harry was incapable of betraying her confidence.

"Listen," she said, abruptly making her decision, without paying any heed to her companion's alarmed expression, "it's best that you know everything. My father is within an inch of ruin, because of the incessant war that Mr. Dorgan has been waging against him for months."

And without trying to hide anything, she described Fred Jorgell's true situation.

The engineer listened to that confidence with a somber expression, his eyes lowered.

"You can take it from me, Isidora," he replied, "that I had nothing to do with all that. My father is being badly advised by my brother Joe and the Kramm brothers; they've inspired all kinds of disloyal or excessive resolutions in him. I don't know how it happened, but I no longer have enough power over my father to counterbalance that baneful influence."

186

Harry remained lost in his reflections for some time. He seemed hesitant.

"Isidora," he said, finally, "I have too much affection for you not to make a supreme effort on your father's behalf."

"Have you any chance of success?" the young woman asked, palpitating with an anguish that she did not try to hide.

"I don't know, but at the moment there's a favorable opportunity that might not occur again for a long time. Our enemies, the Kramm brothers and my brother Joe, whose bitter hatred has caused all this evil, are away from New York, making a tour of the corn and cotton plantations owned by the Trust. My father is free of their pernicious advice for a while. I'm going to do something—but I can't tell you anything more today..."

Isidora dared not ask the engineer for explanations, but she had regained her courage; she knew that Harry, in order to please her, was ready to try anything. A mysterious voice told her that the banal accident that had put her in communication with William Dorgan and his son once again might have unexpected and providential consequences.

That evening, she went to sleep less tormented by anxieties regarding the future; feeble as it might be she had a hope.

When he left Isidora, Harry Dorgan had gone directly up to his father's study, where he had found him in a bad temper, holding a wad of letters and telegrams in his hand, which he was crumpling angrily.

Harry asked timidly why his father as upset.

"I'm furious," said William Dorgan. "Certainly, I recognize that your brother Joe, since he returned from his captivity among the bandits of the Red Hand, has shown a crushing superiority in business matter..."

"Undoubtedly."

"Yes, he's a first-rate financier, a speculator of genius, that's agreed—but he's truly taking too many liberties with me. He doesn't even bother to consult me any longer before making considerable purchases. He scarcely has the politeness to inform me after the deal is done."

"It's true," said the engineer, not without irony, "that he has behind him, to advise him, Dr. Cornelius Kramm and his brother Fritz, who are certainly very clever...."

"Too clever! Too clever by half!" cried the billionaire, furiously. "Their persistent and rapid success in every kind of speculation is beginning to make me anxious. At the end of the day, is it the Kramm brothers or me who is directing the Trust? Now, I no longer count...I can see the moment coming when those gentlemen throw me out, like an old fogy, if I don't pull myself together..."

Harry Dorgan thought that his father was too well-disposed not to try to take advantage of it.

"You know, Father," he said, "that Joe and I don't see eye to eye. You have only one means of proving to the Kramms and my brother that you're still in charge."

"What's that?"

"Make a deal with Fred Jorgell. I know that he's ready to sign his Trust over to you, with enormous potential profits for you."

William Dorgan started in surprise. "But I know that his back is to the wall," he said. "Wouldn't it be better to wait a little, to crush him completely?"

"You're wrong, Father. Fred Jorgell might, as you've done yourself, find backers at the last moment, in which case the battle would begin all over again. By making a deal with him now, without taking advice from anyone, you'd make less profit, but it would be more reliable. And, in sum, you'd have attained the end you had in mind, in becoming the sole owner of the Trust."

William Dorgan did not offer any response, but he was struck by that reasoning.. "What you say is true," he murmured. "I'll think about it." And he left the engineer, not wanting to continue the discussion.

The following morning, Harry went to visit Isidora, whose improvement was marked. The young woman was able to get up and sit down on the veranda decorated with climbing plants that was adjacent to her room.

Her first concern was to ask the engineer whether he had seen his father.

"Yes," said Harry, perplexed, "but I haven't yet found any solution and I can't promise you anything. Tomorrow, perhaps, or even this evening, I hope to have some firm information."

Isidora did not persist, but all her joy had collapsed; the engineer's doubtful tone had plunged her back into cruel anxiety.

In the afternoon, Fred Jorgell came to his daughter's room, where William Dorgan was not long delayed in joining him. As on previous days, the two billionaires engaged in a courteous conversation.

"I'm glad to observe," said Fred Jorgell, "that thanks to your generous care, Isidora is now entirely well. I think that it's not quite safe to transport her, and that she can return to the paternal residence this evening."

"So you want to deprive us of such a charming companion already?" William Dorgan replied.

"It's necessary; it only remains for me to thank you again..."

"There's no need; you've already thanked me. Anyone, in any case, would have done the same in my place. But let's leave it at that. I'd like to have a few words with you in private."

Fred Jorgell made a gesture of surprise, but he followed his interlocutor silently.

Once they were alone in the Gothic study with the precious sculptures, William Dorgan said, without any preamble: "I want to talk to you frankly. I know that you're out of cash."

"That's true," said Fred Jorgell somberly. "What are you getting at?"

"Wait a minute. You're going to be forced to sell your Trust?"

"What point is there is hiding what I'll be forced to confess to everyone in a few days' time?"

"Well, if you'd like to show a little good will, we can still come to an understanding, to your complete satisfaction."

Fred Jorgell opened his eyes wide, finding his adversary once again as he had known him before—which is to say, honest and accommodating. The negotiations begun in such a clear and categorical fashion had to be concluded without the slightest delay. Isidora's father had the satisfaction of seeing that by accepting the conditions that were offered to him, he could still save nearly two thirds of his fortune.

The Yankees handle transactions of that nature rapidly. After two hours of discussion, William Dorgan was henceforth in possession of all the stocks of cotton and corn that had belonged to Fred Jorgell, and he later had received, as the price of that cession, several checks of considerable value drawn on the most solid banks in the Union.

Isadora was proud of having saved her father, but she was almost as glad to have obtained that result thanks to Harry's mediation.

When they took their leave of one another, the two young people promised to meet again from time to time. It was tantamount to a tacit admission that neither of them had renounced their most cherished hopes.

VII. A Failed Experiment

Baruch and his two accomplices, the Kramm brothers, were firmly convinced that William Dorgan's billions, further augmented by speculation, were on the point of falling into their hands; they regarded them as already theirs.

As they left on their tour of inspection, all three of them in an automobile driven by Leonello, Cornelius' laboratory assistant, they had the sentiment that the immense extents of corn and cotton through which they were traveling were their personal property.

They no longer counted the billionaire William Dorgan as anything at all, or anything very much, and it was only for form's sake that they bothered to inform him by letter or telegram of the more or less advantageous deals they concluded on the way.

If the brother Kramm had the secret intention of getting rid of Baruch once they had made use of him as a docile instrument, nothing in their conduct gave rise to any such suspicion. Everything in their speech and actions tended to prove to the fake Joe Dorgan that his accomplices had frankly associated him with their plans and their most secret resources. Baruch had not retained any suspicion of them and was almost proud to count himself among the three Lords who commanded the bloodthirsty companions of the Red Hand.

In the course of the journey, moreover, Fritz and Cornelius seemed to be making every effort to acquaint their new colleague with the secret resources of the mysterious organization.

Once, while Leonello was replacing a tire on the edge of a forest, the automobile was suddenly attacked by two bandits armed with enormous Brownings. Instead of responding to the menacing objurgations of the two thieves, Fritz contented himself with blowing two or three strident and specially-modulated notes on a silver whistle that he wore suspended on a cord round his neck, and the two tramps fled as fast as their legs could carry them.

Not a day passed without the Kramm brothers giving Baruch a further unexpected proof of the extent of their power and the number of their affiliates. It was a veritable army of malefactors, cleverly organized, that they had at their orders. But although Fritz applied himself to showing off the innumerable and powerful ramifications of the Red Hand, the doctor appeared to attach scant importance to it. One day, he went as far as to say: "I'm almost of the same opinion as Baruch—why not set aside this whole romantic organization, the direction of which gives us so much trouble and exposes us to so many dangers?"

"Certainly," Fritz replied, swiftly, "the role of Lord of the Red Hand is no sinecure, but we can't abandon it until we're rich enough." And the art dealer imposed silence on his brother with a gesture; he did not want a discussion of that sort to be carried out in the presence of Baruch, who was fundamentally of the same opinion as the doctor.

One day—it was a Saturday—the automobile was traversing an ocean of verdant crops, which belonged to the Trust as far as the eye could see. Baruch felt surges of pride rising to his head at the right of those earthly riches, that visible and palpable opulence.

"You must agree," he said to the Kramm brothers, "that you've joined the Trust"—he did not dare to say *my* Trust—"at the most opportune moment. The enterprise is completely established, the major capital has been disbursed, and now, thanks to your contribution, you'll collect the lion's share of the profits. Fred Jorgell has been driven to the worst expedients. His defeat is no longer anything but a matter of weeks, perhaps days..."

"I know that as well as you do," murmured Cornelius, hypocritically. "I even know that the charming Miss Isidora has been deeply affected. I think it will be hard for that elegant young woman to be reduced to indigence."

Baruch twitched nervously. His sister Isidora was perhaps the only person in the world for whom he had conserved a kind of affection. "Don't worry about Isidora," he muttered, discontentedly. "I'll be able to help her out, if necessary."

"She is, moreover, a very good person," the doctor added, with an atrocious irony. "I was told, during my last visit to the Lunatic Asylum, that she has given a pension to her brother, Baruch Jorgell, the unfortunate madman of whose story you can't be unaware."

Baruch ground his teeth. "Not one word more about that!" he roared.

"Yes," said Fritz, with a beaming smile, "it's a painful story; let's talk about our Trust instead. I think that it will be easy, thanks to the Red Hand, to make Fred Jorgell capitulate rapidly. A few fires lit, as if by chance, in his docks or his plantations, could accelerate the inevitable denouement."

The doctor shrugged his shoulders. "Fritz," he said, "you have a constant preoccupation with the Red Hand; you're deluding yourself with regard to the power of the tramps, who are, fundamentally, vulgar criminals. When will you understand that there's a bloody past behind us with which it's necessary break all connection as soon as possible."

"The Red Hand is a triumph!"

"Agreed, but it won't last forever. It's necessary to set those sorts of means aside. Personally, I want to become one of the masters of the world. Any other ambition is paltry—but to attain such a goal, it's billions that are necessary, not dollars stolen on the highway by cut-throats."

"The doctor is right," said Baruch, proudly. "No paltry ambitions, no petty means. It's not wretches or fools but individuals of my energy and intelligence that you need as collaborators, you see."

"We could dispense with your collaboration," replied Fritz, with a hint of mockery.

"No!" exclaimed the doctor, swiftly. "Baruch has proved himself. He'll have his share of our triumphs, but one essential condition of success is that our entente is never troubled."

"Our unity will ensure our power," said Baruch, enthusiastically. "Let no quarrel ever trouble our alliance. The Red Hand, Science and Speculation, united, ought to give us the mastery of the world. But I have a surprise for you today. I'll give you proof that I've attempted something for the common endeavor."

"What is it?" asked Fritz, exchanging an astonished glance with Cornelius.

"I've simply found a method thanks to which we can multiply the production of our acreage and corn and cotton tenfold."

Cornelius reflected momentarily. "I'll wager," he said, "that you've employed some of Prosper Bondonnat's procedures. He's the only man I regard as my equal in science—Bondonnat was Marbreuil's friend.

What good is it to rake up memories," said Baruch, without anger. "All that's in the past. I knew the French naturalist quite well, you now, And I believe I've appropriated some of his more astonishing methods for augmenting the vigor of vegetation."

"And when shall we see it?" asked Fritz Kramm, a trifle skeptically.

"Today," said Baruch, and lapsed into silence again.

The automobile was traveling at high speed through the high fields of corn, which were bizarrely rippled by the breeze from time to time, like ruffled silk. It was stiflingly hot. The sky, a leaden white in color, was stained here and there with yellow and red-brown tints, which advertised the imminence of a storm.

Leonello increased the vehicle's speed even more; the nickel-plated vehicle flew like a meteor, level with the verdure, interrupted here and there by a few clumps of slender palm-trees.

Finally, small houses roofed with corn-leaves or red tiles appeared on the slope of a hill overlooking the plain.

Looming above the houses were strange metallic devices, electric hail-cannon very similar to those invented by the naturalist Bondonnat, thanks to which a perpetual spring reigned in his gardens.

The automobile stopped in front of the largest of the cottages, and an army of black and mulatto servants ran to meet the owner of the Trust and guide them to a whitewashed room where a comfortable lunch had been set out.

The menu was one of those frequently encountered in the Southern United States: an appetizing stew of peppered river crabs; a roasted sucking-pig surrounded by fried bananas, and hedgehogs seasoned with ravensara, the flesh of which was as white and tasty as that of young chickens.

While the three bandits did honor to that collation, the sky had become as black as ink. Bruch hastened to give orders to the black men who were to operate the recently-installed machines.

Suddenly, the storm burst with an abruptness particular to tropical climates.

Large blue, green and violet lightning flashes tore through the mantle of clouds; the wind blew in a tempest, making the huts of the farm-workers creak lamentable, as if it wanted to tear them from their foundations; the corn-stalks were bent over and spread out by the blast, and their foliage waved turbulently, like the waves around a reef.

The thunder growled majestically in the distance.

Baruch remained silent; he seemed much less certain than he had an hour before about the effect of his apparatus. The brothers Kramm waited in patient silence for the advertised experiment.

At that moment, the hail-cannon resounded, but their detonations did not succeeded in dominating the din of the thunder; they remained ineffective against the terrible power of the tropical storm.

Furious, Baruch realized, too late, that his apparatus was not proportionate to the effect he had expected of it. What would have been sufficient in the clement climate of France became ineffective in this torrid region.

Angrily, he ordered the black man to cease firing at the victorious clouds. Politely, Cornelius and Fritz tried to console him for his disappointment. Baruch remained silent, having great difficulty containing his range and distress.

Meanwhile, the storm redoubled its fury, as if it had been attracted by the machinery installed on the hill. At one moment, hundreds of lightning-flashes were deployed like the bouquet of a gigantic firework display. The lightning-conductors were crowned with long livid flames.

There was a mighty crack. Lightning had just stuck the hut next to the one in which the three accomplices were standing.

Baruch and the Kramm brothers remained plunged in fearful silence. Already, though, the clouds disintegrated by the thunderbolts were bursting in a diluvian downpour, and a torrential rain that came down from the neighboring heights with the rapidity of a liquid avalanche drowned the crops, threatening to turn the fertile plain into a lake.

"A lamentable failure," murmured Baruch, dejectedly.

"It's lucky that we weren't struck by lightning," added the doctor, with the malicious composure that never deserted him.

"We must hope," Fritz said in his turn, "that Monsieur Bondonnat obtains better results with his apparatus."

"That what I find profoundly humiliating. I'm nothing but an ignoramus, by comparison with that old man, who can transform the seasons at whim, and make vegetables do whatever he pleases..." And Baruch, with a contraction of the features that returned his true physiognomy momentarily, shed tears of rage.

"Console yourself," said Cornelius. "Bondonnat is one of the most illustrious meteorologists and naturalists in the world. You can't hope to match him.

Oh, if I had him as an associate, how easily he would multiply the profits of out Trust tenfold, or a hundredfold!"

"That's an idea," said Fritz. "Why not have him come?"

"He wouldn't accept," Baruch murmured, shaking his head.

"What if we offered him a great deal of money?"

"He's rich."

"Let's kidnap him and imprison him, then," sniggered Cornelius. "He'd be obliged to work for us then."

The three accomplices looked at one another; the plan amused them, precisely because of its audacity and difficulty.

"We'll talk about it again," Cornelius murmured. "I'll examine the idea. For the moment, I think it's time to go to bed."

All three of them were preparing to go to their rooms when the telephone rang furiously.

"Hello?"

"Hello? Who's speaking?"

"Your father, William Dorgan. Is that you, my dear Joe?"

"Yes. What is it?"

"Good news! We've triumphed all down the line."

"Fred Jorgell is vanquished?"

"Entirely. He's sold everything, stocks and land, to me. We're the masters; tomorrow, our shares are going to go up..."

Baruch was exasperated. *It's stupid*, he thought, *to make a deal just as Fred Jorgell was about to go under. Once again my vengeance escapes me. I shouldn't have come away. Harry Dorgan has taken advantage of it—it's him, certainly, who's planned all this! But now I think of it, if the signatures haven't been exchanged, there might still be time...*

But no, there was nothing more to do, and William Dorgan was telephoning him to tell him, triumphantly, that everything was in order and that the sale, so advantageous for the Trust, was a *fait accompli*.

Baruch had to make an immense effort of self-control to stammer a few banal congratulations into the telephone.

"A bad day," he said to the Kramm brothers, who had heard everything, "but I'm wondering how my two fathers, the false and the true, were able to find common ground. Harry Dorgan will pay for all that, once and for all!"

Fritz and Cornelius did not share their accomplice's bad mood at all. They did not have the same reasons as Baruch to hate Fred Jorgell and, in sum, the affair had worked out excellently for them; the capital they had engaged or arranged to be engaged in the Trust would reap a handsome profit.

Baruch wished them good night and went to his room, cursing.

He told himself, as he went into the small room where a full-length mirror seemed to be waiting for him, that the night was not going to be tranquil. After such an agitated day, he was expecting a terrible visit from the nightmare that came to haunt his sleep every Saturday.

VIII. The Fairy Ring

There was to be a party that evening at the home of Prosper Bondonnat, the famous French naturalist. The villa he possessed at Kérity-sur-Mer resounded with the joyful preparations for a family banquet. The old scientist was celebrating the engagement of his daughter Frédérique to his collaborator, the naturalist Roger Ravenel, and that of Andrée de Maubreuil to his other collaborator, the engineer Antoine Paganot. The double wedding, which would realize one of the aged scientist's dearest wishes, had been arranged for the month of September, but it was not yet the end of June.

Such a solemn occasion created a great stir in the villa, from the bedrooms, where the young women were unwrapping, with joyful cries, dresses, lingerie and hats sent from Paris, to the kitchen, to which the local fishermen were bringing monstrous lobsters and giant sole.

In his study, Monsieur Bondonnat could hear the cheerful rattle of crockery and the young woman's bursts of laughter, and could not help smiling. Beside him, an adolescent, slightly hump-backed but mischievous in his expression and mannerisms, was busy cleaning the lenses of a large microscope, but he seemed as distracted as his master.

"Go on, Oscar," said Bondonnat suddenly. "It's five o'clock; we've done enough work for today. I'm going to take a walk along the cliff; you can come with me if you like."

"Gladly, my dear master," the young man murmured. In the blink of an eye he had tidied up the books and papers and put the scientific and mathematical instruments back in their places, while the naturalist put on a broad-brimmed hat and picked up a solid walking-stick with an ivory handle.

Bondonnat was overflowing with joy, swimming in felicity. Andrée's fiancé and Frédérique's were men of great heart and high intelligence. The naturalist was sure that with such husbands, the two young women would be happy.

If Maubreuil were here, he thought, *he'd certainly approve of the choice I've made.*

Bondonnat, followed a few paces behind by Oscar, went down into the gardens, whose foliage and flowers were sparkling with an almost fantastic gleam, due to the electric currents and stimulating gases that bathed their roots and stems. He went past the greenhouses fitted with colored glass, which served for his experiments on the influence of light, and he opened the door of the elevator that permitted access to the top of the cliff.

At that moment, a black long-haired barbet dog came to join the master and the disciple, barking joyfully.

"Are we taking Pistolet?" asked Oscar.

"Certainly; he'll be delighted to stretch his legs running across the heath."

The dog had leapt into the elevator, which, within a minute had reached the summit of the rock that formed a kind of circular path overlooking gardens, bordered by a high wall. It was there that the complicated apparatus loomed up that the meteorologist had invented to capture ambient electricity, condense the ozone and nitrogen that exist in large quantities in the atmosphere of storms, and which are the principal factors of the fertility of the soil. This was the apparatus that Baruch Jorgell had vainly tried to imitate in America in order to increase the Trust's yields. As we have seen, the crude counterfeit that he had attempted had failed pitifully.

At the moment when Pistolet leapt out of the glazed cage, however, he suddenly started barking furiously and scratching with his paws at the small door that gave access to the heath from the circular path.

"That's strange," said Oscar. "I've never seen him act like that before."

The adolescent opened the door. Immediately, Pistolet raced off across the heath, still barking.

"We need to follow him," declared Bondonnat. "The attitude of that animal—which I consider to be endowed with a near-human intelligence—seems to me to be quite extraordinary."

Oscar, who was following the naturalist at a distance, launched himself in pursuit of the dog.

The adolescent had only taken a few steps when he perceived two men of strange appearance who were defending themselves with forceful blows of their canes against Pistolet. The dog, his eyes bloodshot and his tongue hanging out, was trying to bite one of them.

The unknown man, clad in a green suit and a cyclist's helmet, had already had his trousers torn by the dog's teeth. His thin face was white with fear. Finally, as Bondonnat arrived at the scene of the drama, the man succeeded in retreating, took a Browning out of his belt, and took aim at the animal.

"Don't touch my dog!" shouted Bondonnat.

Oscar had already grabbed Pistolet by the ring on his collar, and was dragging him backwards forcibly, while stammering vague excuses addressed to the stranger.

But the latter, in a strange and hoarse voice that caused Bondonnat and Oscar to shiver, replied coldly: "That beast is rabid." And, at the risk of wounding Oscar, he fired.

"Monsieur," said the naturalist. "I apologize profusely; I'm ready to compensate you. The animal is a little wild, but I'd be grateful if you didn't kill him. We're very fond of him."

Without paying any heed, the unknown man was getting ready to shoot again, this time at point-blank range, when his companion said a few words to him in a low voice. Immediately, the man put his Browning back in its holster, and they both drew away without paying the slightest attention to Bondonnat and Oscar.

"Singular individuals," murmured the naturalist. "Tourists, no doubt—Americans, I think."

"They're rogues!" Oscar exclaimed, indignantly. "Did you hear the voice of the one who wanted to kill Pistolet? It resembles that of the murderer Baruch."

"I thought so too," said Bondonnat, shivering in spite of himself.

"Then again, poor Pistolet never barks at anyone..."

"There's something inexplicable about this. Those strangers ran off very promptly."

They both remained pensive. Oscar hastened to put a long and solid chain on the dog—an indispensable precaution, for Pistolet continued to howl with rage and did not seem ready to calm down.

The naturalist and his companion ended up forgetting about the incident, however—which, after all, was one of those that might happen any day, and continued their stroll across the heath as far as a place that was known as the Fairy Ring.

There was a vast area there that was completely sterile, covered with a sand as fine as if it had been evened out with a rake. The peasants claimed that it was in this deserted spot that the fairies, korrigans and spirits of the heath devoted themselves to their games and dances.

The old scientist rested for a while on a sandstone block; then, looking at the sun, which appeared to be on the point of disappearing over the horizon in a cloud the color of blood, he said: "It's time to go back. It's indispensable to be on time on a day like this."

"I'll show you a new trick of Pistolet's," said Oscar, taking a box out of his pocket that contained an alphabet of movable letters.

"We know that your pupil can form entire words, and that he can almost read fluently."

"Yes, but this time I've taught him a compliment to the fiancés—a surprise..."

He did not finish; the dog, his neck, extended toward the sky, had started barking again.

They both raised their heads and soon perceived the cause of the animal's fury.

In the sky, an airplane of considerable tonnage was tracing wide circles, as if its pilot intended to land on the top of the cliff.

"That airplane has frightened Pistolet," said Bondonnat. "You need to keep a tight hold on him—the animal has caused us enough trouble."

"But look!" said Oscar, in anguish. "The airplane's coming straight down—one would think it's going to crash on top of us."

The old scientist recoiled instinctively, but at the same time, two men—the same ones that had wanted to kill Pistolet—launched themselves from behind a clump of gorse, knocked Bondonnat down and threatened him with their Brownings.

"Help!" shouted Oscar, running forward courageously to defend his master—but a blow from a gun-butt knocked the boy over. He fell to the ground with his forehead covered in blood, his skull fractured.

At the same moment, the plane landed on the sandy track forming the fairy ring.

"Quickly, Baruch!" shouted the pilot.

"No names, no noise," riposted the other, bad-temperedly. And he grabbed Bondonnat, who was half-dead with shock, in a brutal fashion, and threw him into one of the machine's four bucket-seats.

Suddenly, however, Pistolet, of whom Oscar had let go at the beginning of the action, leapt on to the old man's knee with a single bound, just as the machine started to move off again.

Already, the airplane, whose engines were throbbing vertiginously, was rising into the air, heading toward the sky, where the first stars were beginning to shine.

Soon, it was no more than a white dot, which disappeared in the direction of the open sea.

N° 5. CHAQUE RÉCIT EST COMPLET EN UN VOLUME 25 Cent.

GUSTAVE LE ROUGE

LE MYSTÉRIEUX DOCTEUR CORNÉLIUS

Le SECRET DE L'ÎLE DES PENDUS

LA MAISON DU LIVRE 28 RUE MONSIEUR LE PRINCE PARIS

5. THE SECRET OF THE ISLAND OF HANGED MEN

I. The Seeker of Rare Sensations

It was two o'clock in the morning.

The clients of the Lapin Rouge, a tavern situated near Les Halles and frequented solely by the dregs of the Parisian population, were crowded tumultuously in the main room on the ground floor. Absinthe and white wine were flowing in waves over the zinc counter, around which pimps with gaudy cravats and shifty, shiny gazes were jostling one another, mingling confusedly with honest workers who were occupied every night unloading vegetables and fruit.

There were some rag-pickers there whose cart, hitched to a scrawny donkey, was waiting in the street; there were collectors of cigar-butts with canvas bags stuffed with "fag-ends"; there were newsvendors laden with heavy bundles of evening newspapers; there were Arabs and negroes, sellers of olives, pistachio-nuts or gimcrack jewelry, and beggars counting their day's harvest of copper coins in corners: a nocturnal and fantastic race that only emerges from its lairs when the sun sets and only finds itself at ease after dark.

Among all the rubicund or pallid faces, everyone was laughing, singing, whistling, or making a racket, to the strains of a guitar that a female musician in rags was strumming vaguely, in spite of the landlord's prohibitions. Everyone was also eating, with a hearty appetite, sausages sprinkled with vinegar, cornets of fries, or portions of appetizingly pink horsemeat. There was a deafening racket, a swarming mob reminiscent of ancient sabbats.

From the threshold of the door, an individual whose thin figure was draped in an ample cloak in yellow and blue checks, coifed in a felt hat tilted over one ear in a cavalier fashion, contemplated this scene for some time with a smile that as philosophical, but still young and naïve, in spite of his long gray hair and bushy beard. He perceived a soup-merchant under an awning, in the open air, busily occupied in serving her ragged clientele, and, mechanically, he began to sing the couplets of a old Latin Quarter song:

When you run through the market in the morning
And smell, rising from the greasy pavement
The odor of lilacs and the odor of cod,
Toward your great banquet of two-sou soup,

All we ruined gamblers disembark![15]

The unknown man shook his head sadly, as if to chase away importunate memories, and then, after a momentary hesitation—not without verifying the presence of a five-franc piece in his waistcoat pocket—went into the dive, cleared a path through the malodorous crowd and went to sit down at one of the dusty marble tables on the far side of the room.

"I'm beginning to get devilishly hungry," he murmured to himself. Leaning toward the kitchen door, which stood ajar, he shouted loudly: "Émile!"

A waiter with athletic shoulders, a low brow and the neck of a bull appeared, laden with bottles and trays.

"What can I do for Monsieur?"

"You can get me a rare steak, fries, half a liter of wine and a two-sou loaf of bread."

"And a napkin?"

"Of course."

As soon as his meal was served the unknown man set about eating, with a hearty appetite.

At that moment, a luxurious automobile stopped outside the drinking-den. An impeccably-dressed gentleman got out of it. He had a monocle in his eye and an orchid in his buttonhole. Silently, he came to sit down at the table next to the one occupied by the man in the cloak.

The newcomer displayed features of perfect regularity, and his clean-shaven face had the neat profile of an antique medal, but he was mortally pale, his green eyes had a dull gleam and that handsome face expressed a profound indifference; it seemed fixed in a marmoreal impassivity that nothing would be capable of moving.

With sniggers that were nevertheless edged with something resembling respect, the poor people had moved aside, murmuring: "Look, it's Milord Bamboche!" And they stared, with eyes ablaze with cupidity, at his fingers laden with rings and the large pearls that served him as shirt-buttons.

A pregnant silence reigned for some time in the tavern, and then the conversations gradually resumed, in low voices.

The man referred to as Milord Bamboche had not seemed to be aware the attention of which he was the object for an instant. Émile, the waiter, without waiting to receive any order, respectfully brought him a bottle of champagne,

---

[15] The author includes a reference identifying this song as "Two-sou Soup" by "the regretted poet Dalibard." That title produces no hits on Google and there is no trace of any poet named Dalibard, but Le Rouge hung around with the down-at-heel poets of the Latin Quarter for several years, and doubtless knew many who never reached print. The probability is, however, that the lines and the pseudonym are his own.

which the strange customer began to drink in small sips, after having lit a gold-ringed Havana that he took from a box ornamented with precious stones.

The solitary diner could not help darting a curious glance at the unexpected neighbor who seemed to be as much at ease and as tranquil in that hovel, in which murderers were not scarce, as he would have been in the smoking-room of the château that he doubtless possessed somewhere.

Milord Bamboche calmly contemplated the ragged crowd, which sniffed the odorous perfume of the champagne avidly.

"An odd specimen!" muttered the man in the cloak. "Some eccentric, no doubt."

His modest meal was concluded; he called the waiter and handed him his sole five-franc piece, negligently. Émile had a pencil behind his ear and added up the bill on the marble of the table.

"Sixty for the portion, ten for the bread, ten for the napkin, thirty for the wine—that makes twenty-two sous!"

To test the coin, Émile had placed it between his teeth, but with a brutal gesture he threw it on to the marble, where it rendered a dull sound. "Old fraud!" he sniggered. "The thune's lead—and I didn't suspect. You nearly put one over on me."

The man had gone pale. "But, Monsieur Émile," he stammered. "I don't have any other money...I...I was taken in first."

"Don't M'sieur Émile me—it's all lies. Cough up your twenty-two rounds or I'll call the cop on the corner. When one doesn't have the cash, one doesn't get the crust—that's all I know."

The unfortunate man, whose good faith was evident, seemed to be prey to a convulsive tremor. He darted around the desperate gaze of a drowning dog, but did not encounter any but the hostile, implacable faces of the poor. They were all on the side of the waiter.

"Émile's right, of course," they murmured. "The old man will finish his night in a cell, and it's only right."

The proprietor, enthroned behind the zinc, shouted in a surly tone: "Go on, get it over with! These things interrupt consumption. Fetch a policeman, and hurry up!"

At that moment, Milord Bamboche, who had observed the entire scene without a muscle in his face quivering, threw a louis on to the table.

"Take your money," he said, "and leave the gentleman alone."

No one flinched. Émile returned the change with an obsequious smile, while Milord Bamboche, silencing his debtor's expressions of gratitude with a gesture, said to him in a blank, extinct and seemingly distant voice: "No need to thank me, Monsieur; it's quite unimportant. Anyone might receive a false coin."

"Monsieur," stammered the man, whose face was red with shame. "I'm confused by this adventure..."

"Don't go on," replied Milord Bamboche, with the same imperious gesture. "Waiter! Champagne, and a glass for Monsieur..." He paused, and repeated interrogatively: "Monsieur...?"

"Agénor Marmousier."

"The poet?"

"The very same."

This time, Milord Bamboche manifested some astonishment. "Extraordinary!" he said. "My name is Lord Astor Burydan."

"The eccentric millionaire?"

"Yes—the same one that the French rabble have nicknamed Milord Bamboche. But—pardon my frankness—how is it that I encounter you in a state of fortune so ill-befitting your talent? In England, you'd be poet laureate, with a royal pension!"

Very simply, and also with dignity, Agénor explained that in France, poets are very badly paid, and that glory and wealth rarely march in step. His verses were admired, but he remained poor. He recognized, moreover, quite frankly, that it was his own fault, to some extent, that he had not been able to cash in on his genius. He lacked the practical skill and urbanity that is the prerogative of the mediocre. Then too, he was proud, and, he had to admit, fond of leisure.

Still impassive, Monsieur Bamboche heard him out, thoughtfully.

"A confidence for a confidence, my dear poet," he replied. "Personally, I'm always bored, and I get bored everywhere. I've tried in vain to distract myself with all kinds of eccentricities, but nothing works."

"Eccentricity is always interesting; it's one of the forms of lyric poetry, after all."

"The day after I came into my fortune I hosted a subterranean tea-party in a diving bell. The following day, I invited two hundred cesspit-emptiers and their wives to a banquet; the dress code required, smoking-jackets and work-boots for the men, and low-cut dresses for the women."

"Not bad," said the poet, smiling.

"The banquet caused a certain sensation. The next day, I married a negro process on an airplane. I'd asked the minister who was to bless our union to stand on the highest platform of his church, brilliantly illuminated for the occasion."

"Better and better."

"The marriage also caused a certain sensation," Lord Bamboche continued, with an expression of ennui. "The following day I went with my young wife into the cage of an Abyssinian lion, which I killed with revolver shots after a frightful struggle; then, without delay, in the presence of a enthusiastic crowd, I skinned the animal and transformed its flesh into appetizing sausages, which I distributed to the spectators free of charge."

"That's a veritable lesson in life."

"The next day, I had to go to the funeral of one of my aunts, Lady Esther Burydan. I followed the coffin, weeping. I had dressed for that solemn family occasion in a black silk leotard sown with white tears. Twenty of my trusted domestics were following me, dressed as clowns and crowned with funereal violets..."

The poet Agénor Marmousier burst into sonorous laughter. "You're truly an admirable man, Milord! I'll dedicate one of my poems to you. In the meantime, permit me to drink to your health!"

"I'm boring you," murmured Lord Burydan, sulkily.

"Not in the least, I assure you. Your eccentric exploits cause me a veritable joy. Continue, I pray you; it's a long time since I've laughed so wholeheartedly."

"You're very indulgent. A little while after that, I organized automobile and musical dinners for proletarians and the disinherited. At a quarter to noon, seven enormous automobiles left the courtyard on my town house. The first contained thirty musicians alternately playing *God Save the King, Home Sweet Home, Rule Britannia* and other classic melodies dear to all English hearts. The second was loaded with three thousand kilograms of rare roast beef, the third was constituted by a gigantic cooking-pot containing goose with turnips, and was as big as a locomotive."

"I'm listening to you with the most palpitating attention..."

"The fourth car offered vast baskets of hot potatoes and the chauffeur was wearing a dressing-gown. The fifth carried a plum pudding as big as a house, flanked with lackeys armed with cutlasses."

"To slice it?"

"Of course! The next car was loaded with Cheshire cheeses, and the last with superb Canadian apples."

"It must have been an appetizing cortege."

"Everything calculated to tease the palate. At every crossroads, the orchestra played a national anthem; then the crowd approached and everyone received a share of the lunch, very comforting fare. Then, a new aubade, and off to the next junction."

"It must have cost a great deal."

"A trifle. I'm very rich. I've tried to ruin myself, but I had to give up."

"And how did the musical automobile banquets end up?"

"Badly. The population pillaged my culinary vehicles, and I was once almost stoned with the dessert apples and the potatoes, still hot, that accompanied the roast beef I had paid for. After the lamentable failure of that endeavor, I had myself buried alive. Then I hosted a ball for undertakers and wet-nurses, the black and the white, Life and Death! It was superb! And now I'm bored..."

Lord Bamboche yawned like a tiger, and then ordered a third bottle of champagne.

"I fear that my weak head can't tolerate..." stammered the poet Agénor.

Milord was not listening; he had just called the waiter back, and, in his eternally world-weary manner, he said, nonchalantly: "Émile, bring me a hundred meters of black pudding."

Émile thought he had misheard, and straightened up in alarm.

"You said...?" he stammered.

"Exactly. A hundred meters of black pudding, top quality. I'll pay cash, but I insist on one thing: that the black pudding should be a single string."

"But Milord..."

"Pull yourself together! Put links in the sausage-skins. Call a sausage-maker, if necessary—but if I'm not served in ten minutes, I'll never set foot in this dive again!"

After having conferred briefly with the proprietor, who was as alarmed as he was, Émile raced outside as if he had the Devil at his heels.

A profound silence had fallen in the tavern. Very calmly, Milord Bamboche had taken out another gold-ringed Havana; then, having placed his chronometer beside him, he waited.

Agénor felt twenty years younger; he had never been at such a party.

The ninth minute had not expired when a gigantic rumor rose up. Through the morning mist a file of men advanced, young and chubby-cheeked like the true butcher's boys that they were, bearing on their shoulders an interminable black cable. At their head, Émile was advancing, his face radiant with just pride.

"Milord is served," he said, simply.

"Good. Fetch me a knife."

Gravely, milord sliced a minuscule portion of the black pudding and tasted it, in the midst of a profound silence.

"It's not bad," he pronounced. "And now..."

Outside, the rumor of an ever-increasing multitude could be heard, which three platoons of town sergeants, arriving at the double, could not succeed in dissipating.

"Now," the Englishman continued, "Émile will distribute, to anyone who asks, twenty-five centimeters of black pudding and a glass of champagne. Do you have a double decimeter, Émile?"

"Long live Milord Bamboche!" howled the crowd.

This distribution commenced in the most orderly manner, but at that moment a police commissaire wearing his sash came into the room. He looked furious.

"Milord," he said, "you promised to behave yourself. You're causing a veritable riot. I can see myself being forced to put you under arrest."

The Englishman drew himself up to his full height. "I'm not committing any offense, Monsieur," he declared, in a roguish tone. "I merely want to give the good people of Paris comestible proof of British sympathy. I want to tighten the *entente cordiale*, and if a hundred meters isn't sufficient, well, we'll send for two hundred meters!"

After long negotiations, the commissaire resigned himself to organizing an orderly service, and the distribution continued amid the cheers of an idolatrous crowd.

Milord Bamboche had already got to his feet, however, and had thrown the waiter two or three blue bills. Turning to Agénor, he said: "Come on, let's go. I'm bored."

The poet, who thought he was living an absurd and marvelous dream, followed his new friend without saying a word. Both of them, thanks to the protection of the police, were able to climb into the automobile waiting a short distance away, which sped off in fourth gear.

They had already left the Opéra and the Trinité behind and were descending the Avenue de Clichy like a bolide when Agénor asked timidly where they were going.

"Home," replied the Englishman, absent-mindedly.

The automobile had just passed through the fortifications.

"It's just..." Murmured the poet, slightly anxiously.

"Don't worry. I have a proposition to make to you. You're a poet, and, as such, a man of imagination."

"So what?"

"Prevent me from getting bored. Find me new sensations. Put me in extraordinary and perilous situations. In a word, be the author of the play in which I shall be the actor, and which will be my life. Try to realize the impossible for me."

"But how shall I do it?"

"I'll open unlimited credit for you. You'll be able to spend as much as you please, provided that you manage to drive away the hideous phantom of neurasthenia. In any case, you can fix the level of your remuneration yourself."

"But what if I don't succeed?"

"Well, too bad—but I'm sure you will."

Agénor was violently tempted. What magnificent feasts, what admirable artistic solemnities might he not organize thanks to the millions of this eccentric, who seemed to have fallen from the sky for the sole purpose of realizing the craziest dreams?"

The automobile flew through the dormant streets of Clichy like a gust of wind.

"Is it a deal?" asked the Englishman, impatiently.

"Well, so be it!" said Agénor. "I accept, but I need to have complete liberty in the choice of means I employ. It will be necessary nor to be astonished by anything..."

"Agreed."

"Don't worry, I promise you that you'll have excitement. Oh, I forgot— I've left a few manuscripts in the hotel room where I live, near the Panthéon..."

"Someone will fetch your manuscripts. Your debts will be paid, if you have any, but from now on, you're on duty. Here's a book of blank checks, and above all, don't think about money—I have a horror of parsimony."

The automobile stopped abruptly on the banks of the Seine. Along the quay the slender silhouette of a yacht was outlined in the morning twilight.

"You're in my home," said Milord Bamboche, helping his guest over the gangplank. "Good night, and try to me up with some new idea."

"Bonsoir, Milord—have no fear on that subject."

A neatly-dressed domestic conducted the poet to a luxurious cabin and retired, after having asked him respectfully whether he needed anything.

Agénor threw himself on to the maple-wood and mahogany couchette fully dressed, and did not take long to fall sound asleep.

When he woke up the next day, he could scarcely take account of where he was, his ideas still being confused by the fumes of the champagne, and he pinched himself until he drew blood to prove to himself that he was not dreaming. As he recalled all the scenes that had unfolded in the course of the previous night, he uttered exclamations of wonder.

His surprise reached a peak when he perceived, clearly visible on the side-table of the cabin the morocco briefcase containing his unpublished poems, which had been transported there as if by magic.

At that moment the domestic came in, carrying a gentleman's suit perfectly tailored to that fit Agénor, tussore silk shirts and pigskin boots—an entire elegant outfit, not forgetting a Russian leather wallet that contained the famous book of blank checks.

The poet was utterly amazed. He resigned himself, however, to playing his part in the fantastic adventure. After a long sojourn in the bathroom adjoining the cabin, he put on the sea-blue suit, abandoning his yellow and blue check cloak without regret, and went up on deck.

There he stood still in astonishment. While he was asleep, the yacht had been traveling; the sparkling bell-towers of the city of Rouen were outlined in the distance, and the verdant banks of the Seine appeared, with their décor of châteaux and picturesque ruins.

For some time, the poet contemplated the admirable landscape. It seemed to him that a new soul had entered into him; songs rose to his lips; delightedly, he breathed the pure air, embalmed with the odor of foliage and fresh water, and his heart was penetrated by a profound gratitude for the neurasthenic lord who had suddenly entered into his humble and needy existence, like a genie in a fairy tale.

Lord Burydan, he thought, *is a good companion, in spite of his lugubrious expression; he's had a god idea; it's now a matter of showing him what I'm capable of. He wants to have extraordinary sensations; well, he shall have them...*

The poet rubbed his hands; original ideas occurred to him in abundance; he felt inspired.

At that moment, a steward, as correct and ceremonious as an old diplomat, came to announce that lunch was served.

Agénor went down joyfully to the yacht's dining room, where his host had already preceded him.

II. Dramas

Six months had gone by; the poet Agénor had realized—and to excess—the hopes of Lord Burydan, whose existence was now a veritable series of enchantments, sometimes as terrible as a drama, sometimes as comical as a carnival farce. The scene-setter of all these events deployed an inexhaustible imagination and, distributing gold by the handful, achieved the most fantastic results.

The Englishman was obliged to admit that he had not been bored for a minute. Every day brought some disconcerting surprise. With a veritably Shakespearean genius, Agénor paraded all the countries of the world, all the epochs of history, including those of the future, all dramas and all comedies before his friend. Lord Burydan might wake up securely tied to the lightning-conductor of a tall cathedral, or enclosed in a barrel floating in the open sea, or tied up in a cripple's box at the door of a church, or riding a racehorse in the midst of a battle. The poet's inventive mind was never found wanting, and he was passionate about his work, incessantly repeating that the adventures of Milord Bamboche were the best poem he had ever composed.

The Englishman had as much amity as admiration for him.

"Spend!" he said to him. "Spend! We still have millions in the bank. It's only since you've taken on the direction of my amusements that I've been truly happy."

Lord Burydan repeated that statement for perhaps the thousandth time while leaning on the balustrade of a luxury train that was carrying the two friends through the grandiose solitudes of the American West.

Agénor Marmousier was now completely transformed. No one would have recognized the gray-haired Bohemian that we once saw devouring a meal in a low tavern in the brilliant gentleman with the pink and freshly-shaven face, and the robust and youthful stance who was nonchalantly savoring the perfume of a first-rate panatela beside the famous Lord Burydan. While struggling every day with the drama of life, the poet had grown twenty years younger.

"I believe," he said, "that I'm sufficiently prodigal, but if you insist, I could do more..."

"Do as you please. I've told you, once and for all, that you have *carte blanche*."

"You don't need to challenge me..."

Lord Burydan went back inside the salon-car. "I'll wager," he said, after a pause, "that our journey will take us peacefully all the way to San Francisco—the Yankees' beloved 'Frisco'?"

"It's necessary not to swear to anything," the poet relied, with an ambiguous smile.

"Bah! You have too much good taste to regale me with a vulgar railway crash, Besides, we've already seen that half a dozen times."

"Who knows?"

"Me. I know perfectly well that, in spite of your genius, nothing will happen today."

Lord Burydan rang for the barman and ordered a sherry cocktail, which he drank slowly with the aid of a long straw. Agénor followed his example, except that it was a mint julep that he savored in slow sips.

The two friends were on their second cigar when the train conductor came into the saloon car looking distressed.

"What's happening?" asked Lord Burydan.

"Something terrible, gentlemen: the engineer and the stoker are dead drunk and have passed out. A frightful catastrophe is inevitable!"

"But it seems to me," replied Agénor, tranquilly, that that's your responsibility. We've paid to be transported, in total safety and without delay, to San Francisco. Do whatever is necessary."

"That's easy to say!"

"Apply the brakes," suggested Lord Burydan.

"Which would lead," the conductor replied, "to a stoppage in the middle of the prairie. The cowboys and the bandits of the Red Hand would have murdered us all in no time, ten miles from any habitation. Then again, there's another express due in half an hour."

"Damn! That's serious," muttered Lord Burydan, vaguely alarmed. "You haven't foreseen this, my dear Agénor, and it's one danger that's not in the program."

The poet reflected. "There is one thing we can do," he said, finally.

"What?"

"I can drive a locomotive. In my youth, I was an assistant engineer at the Gare du Nord for three years. Milord, if you'll consent to serve as my stoker, I'll answer for everything!"

The conductor sighed, profoundly relieved. "Gentlemen," he said, "there are ninety-two passengers on this train; their lives are in your hands!"

"Don't worry."

"It's just that there isn't a moment to lose! I haven't said anything to the other passengers, in order not to frighten anyone. Follow me."

"Very amusing," declared Lord Burydan. "You see, my dear poet, that in spite of your imagination, hazard is still our ultimate master."

Agénor smiled without making any reply, and the two of them, going from carriage to carriage thanks to mobile gangplanks, reached the baggage car, situated at the front of the train; from there, it was easy to climb into the tender that was immediately behind the locomotive.

"Good luck!" the conductor shouted to them. "If the situation becomes urgent, make the signal and I'll apply the brakes."

Lord Burydan and Agénor shoved aside the inert bodies of the engineer and the stoker, both dead drunk, turned up the collars of their fur coats—which they had been careful not to forget—over their ears, and set to work courageously.

Manipulating the wheel controlling the steam, Agénor succeeded in modifying their frightful speed somewhat, while Lord Burydan hurled lumps of greasy coal into the ardent fire. They were both sweating in spite of the icy wind lashing their faces.

Night was falling rapidly, and the train flew like a phantom through an immense deserted plain, in which the melancholy lowing of wild cattle resounded in the distance. The train was traveling at about a hundred and twenty kilometers an hour.

An hour went by in that fashion. There was not a sound from the interior of the train. The passengers ought now to be sound asleep in the bunks of sleeping-cars. Lord Burydan could not help feeling excited.

The night was now black; they passed like a gust of wind through a little station whose lights appeared in the space of a lightning-flash only to disappear again immediately into the moving darkness.

The powerful electric headlights mounted on the front of the locomotive revealed cultivated land; they went through sleeping villages; the lights of crossing-barriers appeared and disappeared; the line had been separated from the fields by a kind of fence for a quarter of an hour.

"Courage, milord," said the poet. "We're nearly there. In half an hour, we'll reach the station in Jorgell City."

Lord Burydan, simultaneously roasted by the incandescent fire and frozen by the wind, replied in a growl: "Jorgell City—the city founded by the billionaire whose son murdered a French scientist?"

"That's right. It's said that it's cursed. In the beginning, there was a series of murders that no one has ever been able to explain."

Lord Burydan felt himself shiver, and fell back into silence. The speedometer indicated a hundred and ten.

Suddenly, Agénor uttered a dull exclamation. With his finger, he pointed at a heavy cart harnessed to eight horses, a few hundred meters away, which had just moved on to the track and was blocking it completely.

"Reverse the engine!" stammered the Englishman, whose teeth were chattering.

"Too late!"

"What are you going to do?"

"Too bad—I'll risk everything."

Nervously, Agénor had rotated the wheel; the steam filled the cylinders, the plates grated, the train acquired the frightful speed of a hundred and sixty kilometers an hour, flying along the rails like a meteor.

Lord Burydan closed his eyes at the moment when the cart, loaded with heavy blocks of granite, appeared in the full glare of the lights; he waited to die.

There was an impact, but it was scarcely sensible; whinnies of agony were lost in the night. The enormous mass of the cart and the horses had been swept away, knocked sideways off the track. The train passed by, blazing through the stations with a thunderous noise.

"That's good," murmured the poet. "We had a narrow escape."

Lord Burydan mopped his forehead, incapable of pronouncing a single word.

Already, the horizon was catching fire.

"Jorgell City," said Agénor. "It's time to slow down."

He maneuvered the wheel vigorously; the vertiginous speed was moderated to the placid rate of an omnibus: sixty kilometers an hour. A few minutes later, the train stopped in the glazed hall of the main station, constructed by Harry Dorgan.

The driver and stoker were carried to a camp bed; the locomotive, whose front end was staved in, was taken to the workshops and replaced by another.

Warmly congratulated, Agénor and Lord Burydan were free to go back to their sleeping-car, which they did, but not without comforting themselves with a hot toddy.

The next day, at about noon, they arrived in San Francisco.

Lord Burydan took pleasure in visiting that astonishing city, destroyed so many times by earthquakes, and reconstructed in steel, where all the races of the world are crowded together.

The day after their arrival they were walking on the quayside, after an excellent lunch at the France and Albion Hotel, admiring the port full of ships.

"What magnificent weather," said Agénor, suddenly. "The Pacific is as calm as a lake. Not a breath of wind, not a ripple..."

"Shall we take a little sea-trip?" Lord Burydan proposed. "Seen from the bay, the panorama of the city is splendid."

"As you please; there's a boat that will serve our purpose very well." And the poet pointed at a slender rowing boat in which two sailors, siring astride a bench, were nonchalantly playing cards while smoking their pipes. The bargain was quickly concluded; Agénor and Lord Burydan took their places at the rear, the mariners took hold of their oars and the light vessel drew away from the shore. Everything augured well for the excursion.

After traversing the harbor full of ships, they headed north along a deserted coast. The sky was still perfectly clear and the sea was calm, as smooth as the surface of a pond.

The city of San Francisco was already far away when Lord Burydan observed that perhaps the excursion had lasted long enough. "If we want to get back before nightfall," he said, "it's time to turn round." And he added: "I can say, of course, that its one of the nicest excursions I've had, but if I compare it to other days, I'm beginning to get bored. In fact, I'm already bored." And Lord Burydan stifled a long yawn.

"That's truly very regrettable," Agénor replied, with a singular smile—and he ordered the two mariners to turn round in order to return to San Francisco.

At that moment, however, a canoe emerged from a small marshy bay and headed out to sea. The sight of the craft immediately excited Lord Burydan's surprise; the slender hull was made in a single piece, hollowed out from the trunk of a gigantic cedar; it was decorated in gaudy colors—red, orange, black and blue—and manned by eight Indians wearing the classic costume of their race and armed with long paddles with sharpened points.

The faces of the savages were hideous, thanks to the tattoos and war-paint with which they were covered. They wore large head-dresses of eagle-feathers, and their opossum-fur mantles were flapping in the wind. They had knives and tomahawks in their belts, but their bows and arrows had been replaced by Winchester rifles and triple-banked cartridge-belts.

Lord Burydan admired them naively. "They're magnificent," he said, "but I thought that their race had been almost obliterated, or herded into reservations."

"You're mistaken," Agénor replied. "A few wild and untamable tribes still exist, in the Rocky Mountains and all along the coast that extends to the north of San Francisco, who have conceived an implacable hatred of white men. I fear that these might belong to an unsubmissive tribe."

"Damn!" murmured Lord Burydan, anxiously.

Impelled by the eight robust paddlers, the canoe was getting closer with prodigious rapidity. It seemed to be gliding like a bird over the surface of the tranquil waves. In vain, the two American sailors hauled on their oars. In less than three minutes, the canoe came alongside the rowing boat. Abruptly, two of the Indians let go of their oars and raised their rifles. Lord Burydan realized that all resistance was impossible.

"We'll get out of it by paying a ransom," he said, confidently.

"If they'll consent to that," murmured the poet, uncertainly.

Already, two of the Redskins had jumped into the rowing boat, and without wanting to hear any argument, with the dexterity of conjurors, they had bound the two tourists and the two sailors with slender bark cords. Then, methodically, they stripped Agénor and Lord Burydan of their purses, their watches and even their cigars and pocket handkerchiefs. While perpetrating these depredations, they made hideous grimaces and indulged in a simian pantomime.

Suddenly, they grabbed Lord Burydan, undressed him completely, and, after having passed a stout rope under his armpits, threw him into the sea. The rope was attached to the rear bench of the canoe. At a sign from their chief, the paddlers went to work rhythmically, the canoe resumed its swift course, dragging the unfortunate lord behind it, who was comparing himself mentally to Queen Brunhilda, tied to the tail of a wild horse.[16]

The situation was, in fact, just as painful and almost as perilous. The cords binding him cut into his flesh, and it was only with great difficulty that he was able to raise his head out of the water long enough to catch his breath. In his terror, he realized that after a few minutes of that diabolical sport, he would no longer have the strength to make the efforts necessary to breathe, and that he would drown by degrees, suffering the most odious and slow death. Agénor, bound and lying in the bottom of the canoe, could not help him at all. For a moment, Lord Burydan had the sensation that the savages with demonic faces were dragging him alive into some maritime inferno unsuspected by Dante.

Five minutes went by like that, seeming like five centuries.

The hectic pace of the canoe had relented somewhat. Lord Burydan was able to breathe. He began to hope that the torture he was enduring was only a brutal joke, and that it might soon come to an end. Suddenly, however, the marrow froze in his veins and his hair stood on end. Through the limpid blue water he had just perceived a large shadow, a sharp black silhouette that was gradually drawing closer to him.

"A shark!" he screamed. "Help! Agénor! Help!"

The poet only replied to that desperate appeal with a dull groan. The shark was getting nearer and nearer, beating the water with its formidable tail. Lord Burydan could see its mouth armed with a triple row of teeth, and its tiny eyes, ferocious and malign. The Indians had stopped paddling, and they were contemplating the spectacle with as much pleasant satisfaction as if they were watching a boxing match or a contest between a dog and rats.

Lord Burydan no longer had a drop of blood in his veins. With the super-acute clarity of sensation experienced by all those exposed to an imminent peril, he followed the movements of the shark. He saw it swerve in order to seize him, and he lost consciousness.

At that moment, however, one of the Indians, precipitately getting rid of his rifle, his tomahawk and his opossum mantle, dived into the sea brandishing a long knife. At the precise moment when the shark, as it swerved, exposed its long off-white underbelly, the Indian struck it full in the heart. The water turned red with blood, and in response to a curt order from the courageous Redskin, the Indians hauled the inert body of Lord Burydan aboard.

A little further away, the shark was writhing in the last somersaults of its agony.

---

[16] After an exceedingly colorful career, including two royal marriages and three regencies, the Visigothic princess Brunhilda—Brunehaut in French—(c. 543-613) was allegedly either dragged to death or torn limb from limb by wild horses as a punishment for her crimes.

III. Into the Unknown

When Lord Burydan came round, he found himself in the rowing boat alongside the poet Agénor, who was rubbing his temples vigorously with vinegar. The Indians and their canoe had disappeared, except for the one who had killed the shark, who was sitting placidly in the stern. The two American sailors, relieved of their bonds, were rowing calmly, as if nothing extraordinary had happened. It was almost dark, and a short distance away, the hull of a small steamship was visible, which seemed to have stopped to wait for the small boat.

"Where am I?" stammered Lord Burydan, in a weak voice.

"You're safe," Agénor told him. "The Redskins were put to flight be the arrival of the steamer that you can see, on which we'll shortly take passage."

"But what about that one?" asked the lord, darting a fearful glance at the impassive Indian.

"He's the one who saved you. I thought it worth taking him into your service, at a high price. His name is Kloum. He speaks very good English, and his was employed for a long time in an electric power plant in Jorgell City. But drink this, Milord, and you'll feel much better."

Agénor handed his friend a small goblet filled with old whisky. Lord Burydan drank it, and felt better. Abruptly, he uttered a loud burst of laughter.

"Agénor," he cried, "you're a marvelous man! For I'm sure now that it's you who organized and scripted the Redskins' attack, like a skillful director. The shark must have been some mechanical animal, such as I've seen in the theater at Covent Garden in London."

Agénor contented himself with smiling, without offering any explanation. "It's possible," he said, "that I might have had a hand in all that, but hazard also collaborated in the little drama. Don't seek to know any more. Are you satisfied?"

"Infinitely."

"That's the essential thing."

During this brief conversation they had almost reached the steamship; ropes were thrown down and Lord Burydan, Agénor and the impassive Kloum soon set foot on the *City of Frisco*, a seven-hundred-ton steamer whose captain, Mr. Hopkins, kindly put himself at the disposal of his passengers.

Everyone went to the ship's dining room, where a restorative meal was served. With his scarlet face, his bushy eyebrows and his bulbous nose, the captain bore more resemblance to a pirate than an honest trader. He wore little gold ear-rings and continually had a pewter mug filled with a mixture of whisky and soda-water within arm's reach. After the previous conservations it had been agreed between Agénor and Mr. Hopkins that the latter would take the aristocrat and his secretary back to San Francisco. The latter went to their respective cabins where they did not take long to fall into a deep sleep.

On going up on to the deck the following morning however, they experienced a violent surprise on observing that the coast had disappeared; in whichever direction they looked there was the limitless sea. Agénor immediately went to find Captain Hopkins in order to demand explanations.

The old sea-dog did not seem at all troubled. "I deeply regret it," he declared, in a peremptory tone," but there's no means of returning to San Francisco."

"But it was agreed..." said Agénor.

"That's as maybe, but one can't always do as one wishes. Know that my ship is exclusively laden with the coffins of Chinaman deceased in America, who have expressed the desire, like all good Chinamen, to rest in their native soil. Now, that's a kind of merchandise that it's forbidden to transport, and I learned at the last moment that I've been denounced."

"With the result that...?" Lord Burydan interjected, impatiently.

"With the result that it's impossible to go back to port before having unloaded my cargo, which I can only do at Nagasaki. If you wish, I can drop you off at Easter Island or in the Marquesas, where I'll be calling in."

"You've deceived us odiously!" Agénor exclaimed.

"It's not my fault. Anyway, I'm prepared to give your money back."

The poet was consternated. This was an incident he had not anticipated. Lord Burydan was the first to accept his part in the bizarre situation cheerfully.

"Well, too bad," he declared. "Since that's the way it is, we'll go to Nagasaki with Mr. Hopkins, and do our best to keep boredom at bay during the voyage."

"This is my fault," Agénor murmured. "I should have obtained more information."

"Don't have any worries on that account. I don't regret the obligatory voyage, and we have a unique opportunity to visit the Pacific islands."

"At any rate," said the captain, delighted to see things arranged so easily, "the *City of Frisco* is abundantly provided with food-supplies; she's a first-rate ship."

In that, the honorable captain was exaggerating slightly; the City of Frisco was an old rust-bucket whose engine, repaired twenty times over, could only render a speed of ten knots at best. Besides which, Mr. Hopkins, for reasons of economy, only burned cinders and coal debris, and hoisted his emergency sails every time the wind was favorable. For rapidity of transport, the ship was more akin to a diligence than an express train.

Twenty-four hours had not gone by when Lord Burydan had relapsed into neurasthenia. In spite of all his imagination, Agénor could not succeed in distracting him. Only the Indian Kloum, who had traded his dazzling costume for a simple sailor's reefer-jacket, seemed perfectly as ease, eating his four meals a day with a magnificent appetite and spending the rest of the time strolling on deck at a steady and rhythmic pace, smoking his black clay pipe.

On the second day the sea became heavy. The City of Frisco was only advancing with extreme slowness, and although the captain declared with an imperturbable assurance that his ship's solidity was proof against anything, no one was reassured.

By nightfall, the wind was blowing at gale force. The old steamer, whose fire had been put out as a precaution, was at the mercy of the waves. She was pitching and rolling drunkenly and the bolts in her disjointed carcass were groaning in a lamentable fashion. Soon, it was realized that the tiller had been carried away by a wave.

With remarkable imprudence, Mr. Hopkins had declared at first that it was only a squall, but he was soon shaken out of that aplomb. At about ten o'clock in the evening, the ship began to take on water. Everyone manned the pumps, not excepting Lord Burydan, the poet Agénor and Kloum. They worked all night without any appreciable result. By daybreak, the tempest had not calmed down, and there was a second leak.

Already, two sailors had been drowned. Captain Hopkins, who had gone up on to the poop deck, was swept away by a wave himself. The situation was desperate. In a few more minutes, the *City of Frisco*, whose framework was completely dislocated, was about to sink.

Assisted by Kloum, Agénor and Lord Burydan got into the smaller lifeboat, leaving the large launch to the crew. They had just taken their places when the old steamer, under the impact of a more forceful wave, opened up with a sinister cracking sound; the sea was covered with the coffins of the Chinamen and flotsam of all kinds. After a further minute, there was nothing more where the *City of Frisco* had been than a large whirlpool, which nearly dragged the lifeboat down.

Still silent and impassive, Kloum had taken the oars while Agénor took charge of the tiller. The frail boat was lifted up like a feather on the crests of enormous waves, then tumbling into foaming abysms; surges of sea-water continually filled the boat, while Lord Burydan bailed out the water with his hat as best he could.

A quarter of an hour had not gone by after the shipwreck when the three passengers in the lifeboat saw the launch go by, floating upside-down with its keel in the air.

At that moment, one of the oars that Kloum was holding snapped, as cleanly as if it had been made of glass. The lifeboat spun and started to dance like a cork, and the sudden shock caused Agénor to lose his balance; he was carried away by a gigantic wave.

Lord Burydan made a gesture of despair. He would certainly have risked his life willingly to save his friend, but in the middle of such a cataclysm, it was impossible to help the poor poet, who had already disappeared in the torment.

Once again, Lord Burydan understood the futility of his millions, and, forcing back a sob, came to sit down in the place designated to him by Kloum, who had not lost his composure for a second. Making use of the only oar remaining to him as a scull, the old Indian succeeded in preventing the dinghy from capsizing, but the wind carried them away at a furious speed. They were utterly drenched, cold and hungry. They clung on desperately to the boat's benches, by virtue of an almost unconscious impulsion.

Toward midday, the storm began to calm down. Kloum took advantage of it to bail out the water that was filling the boat, and he offered Lord Burydan half of a mouthful of whisky that remained in his flask.

By mid-afternoon the sea was completely calm. Kloum succeeded in fishing out an armful of seaweed, to the strands of which a few bivalve mollusks were attached. That paltry meal fortified the two men, but they were exhausted. They agreed to sleep in two-hour shifts, and it was thus that they reached nightfall, prey to the most terrible dread, for the wind was getting up again and the waves were swelling, already almost as furious as the previous evening.

Lord Burydan was at the end of his tether.

"We're doomed!" he murmured. "I ought to throw myself into the water right away, to get it over with."

"Don't do that, Milord," said the old Indian, swiftly. "Kloum knows that we aren't far from land."

"How did you figure that out?"

"Listen!"

Lord Burydan pricked up his ears. Through the howling of the wind he perceived a kind of funereal croaking.

"Those are the cries of sea-birds," Kloum explained, "and when there are birds, land isn't far away."

"What does it matter?" murmured the Englishman, completely demoralized. "I'm collapsing with fatigue and dying of the cold. Soon, I'll no longer have the strength to cling on to my bench...the next wave will carry me away..."

"It mustn't, Milord—and look, there's a means to prevent it. I'll tie you on." And he made use of the anchor-rope to attach his companion solidly to the bench.

The night went by in mortal terror. The wind had dropped slightly, but the cold was glacial. Finally, dawn broke. When the first rays of a pale sun has cleared away the mist, Kloum discerned, in the distance, a huge dark mass, which was undoubtedly a cape formed by rocky cliffs.

"Saved!" cried the Indian.

He woke Lord Burydan, whom the sight of the shore was scarcely able to extract him from the torpor into which he had plunged. Kloum had forgotten his fatigue; he maneuvered the lifeboat dexterously through a series of petty reefs that defended the shores of the unknown land. The mist had dissipated completely. The castaways found themselves confronted by a high granite wall that did not seem to have any gap in its continuity. At the bottom of the cliff there was a shingle beach, violently assailed at present by the surf.

Kloum attempted to land, but the enterprise was full of difficulty. Every time he tried, the waves threw him back toward the ring of reefs that he had had so much difficulty getting through.

Suddenly, men with long beards clad in leather and shod in immense boots emerged from a fissure in the cliff. They were armed with gaffes, grapnels and hooks. In a matter of minutes, they had hauled the boat to the shore. Lord Burydan and his companion were getting ready to thank them when one of the men drew a Browning from his belt and took aim at them.

"What do you say, Slug?" he said, turning to the one who appeared to be the leader. "Should we blow their brains out?"

"In truth," said Slug, hesitantly, "I don't know."

"You know that the Lords orders are strict. No strangers, no spies."

At that moment, a cannon-shot was heard in the distance, soon followed by a second, and then a third.

Slug's expression had changed. "It's the Red Hand's yacht," he said, respectfully. "It's up to the Lords themselves to decide the fate of the prisoners."

IV. The Island of Hanged Men

The shore on which the castaways had just landed was an island situated some way south of the Aleutians, about a hundred kilometers from Sakhalin.[17] It had been discovered in the eighteenth century by German navigators, who called it St. Frederick Island. Since then, as it was not on any shipping route, it had been completely forgotten, not only by mariners but by the majority of geographers. At one time, it had been an object of dispute between Russia and the United States, but the icy territory seemed so uninteresting that the matter was only settled in 1901. At that time it was officially attributed to America, and was almost immediately bought by a rich art dealer, Fritz Kramm, who, it was said, wanted to carry out an experiment in breeding fur-seals there.

After that, no further mention was made of the island, which all practical men regarded as a useless and sterile block of ice. In that, the practical men were much mistaken. St. Frederick Island was interesting from a number of viewpoints. Surrounded on all sides by high cliffs, which sheltered it from the glacial polar winds, it had fertile grasslands in its center, which were swarming with reindeer, elk, musk-deer, beavers and Arctic foxes. It was traversed by freshwater streams filled with salmon and trout; cod and crustaceans were abundant around its coasts; and its beaches were ideal for the breeding of fur-seals, which, being undisturbed, were extremely numerous there. On the summits of its cliffs the nests of eider ducks could be collected, with valuable plumage.

Unknown to anyone, the owner of the island had constructed vast and solid buildings, which sheltered a fairly considerable number of inhabitants. It was in one of these edifices, fitted out with a certain luxury and surrounded by a double circular pathway incessantly patrolled by sentries of criminal appearance, that Lord Burydan and Kloum now found themselves.

They had been given the job of serving as aides to a strange aged scientist, for whose use a superb laboratory had been installed. Thus far, however, they had only been able to exchange a few words with the old man with the venerable side-whiskers. All that they knew was that he was French.

All three of them were in a room especially equipped for experiments with hydrofluoric acid when the old scientist suddenly burst out laughing, and, after having rapidly bolted the communicating doors, said to his two companions: "My friends, you must have been surprised by my silence—but it's necessary to tell you that if I haven't treated you more politely, it's because I had my reasons. We're being monitored. All the walls here are fitted with microphones and eve-

---

[17] This implies that the castaways have travelled more than 4,500 miles in three days, having started out in a ship that could only travel at ten knots and ending up in a storm-tossed dinghy.

rything we say is recorded—but I've taken precautions. The microphones here are no longer working, and won't be working for some time. We can therefore talk quite safely. First of all, who are you?"

Lord Burydan and Kloum told him their names.

"My name is Prosper Bondonnat," said the old man. "I'm a meteorologist."

"What!" exclaimed the Englishman, in surprise. "You're the man whose mysterious disappearance caused such a sensation six months ago?"

"That's me," murmured the old man, whose face expressed a profound sadness. "The way I've been treated is abominable."

Lord Burydan had become attentive.

"The strangest thing of all," Bondonnat continued, "is that I don't know exactly what they want from me, and why I've been so brutally snatched away from my friends and my children. No, truly, I wouldn't have believed that such a crime was possible."

"But where are we, in fact?" Lord Burydan put in, anxiously.

"I don't know. I was brought here after forty-seven days of travel. One thing of which I'm sure, though, is that the island is the principal lair—the capital, so to speak—of a gang of redoubtable bandits. In spite of my captivity, I've ended up discovering numerous things."

"Before anything else," said the Englishman, "tell us how you came to be here."

"You know my name, Milord. You know that I've always led the sheltered existence of a man who has dedicated his life to science. No adventure had ever befallen me, personally, before this. The only drama in my tranquil existence had been the murder of my friend Marbreuil by an American, presently confined to a lunatic asylum. Andrée de Marbreuil and my daughter Frédérique were friends, almost sisters. I loved them both equally, and had resolved to marry them to two of my collaborators, two young scientists for whom I had as much esteem as amity."

"But the double marriage didn't happen?"

"Patience! On the eve of the engagement, I was walking peacefully, about a kilometer from my home when an airplane landed on the heath. Men got out, threw me into one of the bucket-seats after having struck down and perhaps murdered a child who had accompanied me on my walk. My dog Pistolet jumped in with me. I defended him so fiercely that they didn't dare kill him."

On hearing his name, the large barbet with the curly black hair got up from underneath one of the tables and came to his master, looking at him with his large moist eyes, as expressive as hose of a human being. Bondonnat stroked the animal, which immediately lay down at his feet with a growl of pleasure.

"After scarcely an hour's flight," the old scientist went on, "the airplane deposited me on the deck of a yacht and I was immediately shut up in a cabin with my dog. I only came out to change prison. I'm kept out of sight in this laboratory, and I knew that if I attempt to escape I'll be shot without mercy by the sentinels who operate in hourly shifts."

"That," murmured the Englishman, with a kind of satisfaction, "is even stranger than anything that has happened to me." And he added: "Have you been able to divine the objective of this extraordinary sequestration, Master?"

"I didn't take long to find out. I had only been in possession of the comfortable, almost luxurious, wooden house that serves as my prison for two days when a man came in one morning, his face covered by the thin rubber mask that disguises all of those who deal with me directly. In his accent, and even in his mentality, I recognized a Yankee. 'Monsieur Bondonnat,' he said, brutally, 'you're a great scientist; we don't want to take your life, but we demand that you reveal all your discoveries to us, without exception, and that you put yourself entirely at our disposal for further inventions.'"

"Naturally," said Lord Burydan, "you protested."

"Indignantly. Then the American—I'm sure that he's an American—replied, tranquilly: 'As you please. Except, in that case, you can consider yourself a prisoner in perpetuity; you'll never see your daughter, your ward, or your friends again. On the other hand, if you put your intuitive genius at our service, you'll be royally rewarded and you'll be set free as soon as we have no further need of you. In addition, you can—under certain restrictions—let your daughters know that you're still alive, and you'll have news of them from time to time. Oh, I forgot one more thing: if you prove recalcitrant, the first measure we'll use against you will be to kill your dog.'"

"And you agreed?"

"Yes," murmured Monsieur Bondonnat, lowering his head. "I was afraid for my daughter—for both my daughters, for I regard Andrée de Maubreuil as my child. I feared that these wretches, who seem to be all-powerful, might take reprisals on those innocent children or their fiancés. I set to work."

Lord Burydan clenched his fists with a generous anger. "Monsieur Bondonnat," he said, "I'm rich and powerful too; I swear to you that once I get out of here, I'll take a terrible vengeance on these people!"

"What's the point of vengeance?" murmured the old man, sadly. "I don't wish harm upon any of my enemies. Then again, these bandits, who believe themselves to be so clever, might unwittingly be serving the eternal cause of the Progress, always on the march, that advances indefatigably through a thousand avatars toward a better future, a more perfect society."

"What do you mean?"

"They're demanding from me formulae that permit the multiplication, between twofold and tenfold, of crop yields. What I had realized on a small scale in my gardens, ought now to be possible on a large scale in plantations of cotton and corn. I would probably have needed millions to popularize my discoveries; the bandits, undoubtedly billionaires, who have captured me are taking charge of that work. They think they're robbing me, but they're carrying out, without knowing it, the work of which I've dreamed: the intensive production, at a low price, of all nutritive substances, and the disappearance of hunger and poverty from the world."

Lord Burydan remained silent and pensive. The old scientist's words had opened a luminous widow on the future for him. "But why tell me," he said, after a momentary pause, "that this island is a lair of bandits? That billionaires, the directors of some Trust, have abducted you in order to steal your discoveries is plausible—but bandits?"

"I haven't told you everything yet," the old man replied. "It was agreed, from the day of my arrival, that the materials, apparatus and personnel necessary to my experiments would be furnished to me in unlimited quantity; the promise has been kept. I only have to say the word for the rarest metals and the most costly machines to be put at my disposal; I've been given as assistants athletic individuals with long beards, perfectly docile in spite of their criminal appearance, but those aides have talked, and this is what I've ended up learning..."

"The Red Hand," murmured Kloum, who had remained still and silent until then.

"Yes," said Bondonnat, lowering his voice, "the Red Hand. There exists in the United States an extremely powerful association of pickpockets and murderers, and this island is their place of safety, their capital. Do you know what they call it, between themselves? The Island of Hanged Men."

"Why?"

"Because it appears that taking refuge here, until they've been forgotten, are all the malefactors that have been duly executed, but whom the physicians of the Red Hand have succeeded in snatching from the jaws of death. Hanging, as in well known, is not mortal if certain precautions are taken before the suspension. The name must already be old, going back to the era when electrocution had not yet been adopted in America for capital executions. In sum, this island is populated by individuals whose death certificates have been officially issued."

"It seems to me to me a bad dream," said the Englishman, shivering. "But what do they want of me? I'm not a great scientist like you?"

"You're rich," Bondonnat replied. "They'll doubtless be content with demanding a large ransom from you. They won't kill you if they haven't already done so. It seems that here, on the Island of Hanged Men, they're so sure of their impunity, so much at home, that they have no reason to be needlessly cruel."

At that moment Pistolet stood up and started barking furiously.

"Someone's coming," murmured the old scientist, not without a certain anxiety.

Almost immediately, the doors of the laboratory were thrown open, giving passage to a disquieting cortege. At the head marched two men of Herculean stature, entirely dressed in red and carrying woodcutters' axes. Their broad-brimmed gray hats, turned up at the edges, were decorated with a red hand; behind them came three individuals wrapped in luxurious cloaks of black fox-fur, who were not carrying any weapons; their fur bonnets were surrounded by gold rings from which rose a multitude of little ruby hands, forming a veritable crown. Their clean-shaven faces were covered with thin rubber masks that, while hiding them completely, allowed the play of the features to be discerned. One of them was wearing gold-rimmed spectacles.

Six hirsute Hercules with long beards formed a rearguard, armed with rifles and Brownings. They wore the gray hats ornamented with red hands, but their garments were black leather and they were shod in knee-length boots.

The eight men of the escort arranged themselves in a semicircle near the door, while the three masked individuals advanced toward Monsieur Bondonnat. They greeted him with arrogant nods of the head.

The old man understood that he was in the presence of the bandit chiefs, the redoubtable Lords of the Red Hand, who had held the police and government of the Union at bay for so many years.

Pistolet, simultaneously fearful and furious, had taken refuge beside his master, from where he continued to bark dully at the newcomers.

"Monsieur Bondonnat," said one of the masked men, in a mocking voice, "you're ingenious and cunning, but you omitted to disable some of the microphones, and we've had the pleasure, just now, of listening to your conversation. Be wary of becoming too well informed regarding this island and its inhabitants—it could be dangerous for you."

As the old scientist remained silent, the masked man continued: "First of all, we're going to deprive you of the services of Lord Burydan; dangerous conspiracies might result from your association with him. While waiting to settle the question of his ransom with us, he'll work in the fur-seal park, where there's no shortage of things to do. Until further notice, Monsieur Bondonnat will content himself with this worthy Redskin—the honest Kloum, whom I don't believe to be capable of any evil design—as a laboratory assistant."

Lord Burydan tried to protest. "This is shameful!" he exclaimed. "By what right...?"

Already, however, two of the long-bearded bandits were dragging him out of the laboratory.

"Having said that," the man in the mask continued imperturbably, bringing a wallet out from beneath his cloak, from which he took a wad of banknotes, "Here, as the first installment of what you've been promised, is a hundred thousand dollars."

"I don't want it!" cried the naturalist, angrily. "In surrendering my discoveries to you, I've only yielded to violence. I have nothing in common with you; you're criminals, merely a little richer and bolder than others. Keep your money."

"I'll leave the banknotes here. You have too much common sense not to decide to keep them, after having reflected for a while."

"Never!"

"Take it easy. I've already decided, in accord with my colleagues"—the other two Lords of the Red Hand bowed—"that you'll renounce all questions of agricultural meteorology from now on."

Bondonnat made a gesture of protest.

"That's how it is. We're going to direct our efforts to another goal. You're going to study the means of rapidly destroying ships of heavy tonnage. Try to find something better than banal torpedoes."

"You want me to be an accomplice to your piracies, then?" the old scientist exclaimed, indignantly. "Never, you hear, never, will I put my knowledge in the service of such banditry. I'm your prisoner, do with me what you will—my life is in your hands—but I won't attempt the slightest experiment."

"Think about it," replied the Lord of the Red Hand, with a frightful calm. "But if you haven't given us a favorable response three days from now, your dog will be killed. And if you haven't yet decided at the end of a week, it'll be Mademoiselle Frédérique Bondonnat and Mademoiselle Andrée de Marbreuil against whom we'll take measures."

The old man had become very pale; he lowered his head, defeated. Suddenly, however, his face brightened with a half-smile. "All right," he said. "I give in. I'm the weaker, I'll do what you want of me. I'll start studying the question tomorrow..."

The three Lords of the Red Hand looked at one another with a certain astonishment; they had expected a longer resistance on the part of the old scientist.

"Above all," the one wearing the gold-rimmed spectacles continued, "don't try to deceive us, Monsieur Bondonnat. You're dealing, you can be sure, with scientists who are as eminent as you in their own specialty."

"Messieurs," said the scientist, with a perfect good grace, "you shall see me at work."

V. The Three Lords

Once they had emerged from the ring of palisades that surrounded the laboratory, the three Lords of the Red Hand dismissed their escort, took off their masks and went into a single-story house of wood and brick that was almost elegant in its appearance. It was surrounded by a garden in which all the vegetables capable of resisting the rigors of the climate had been gathered. There were sorb-trees, pines and arctic willows, around which were plots of heather and Alpine plants.

The three Lords went into a room heated by a large porcelain stove and comfortably furnished with leather armchairs and cupboards in varnished pine and beech. A silver samovar was exhaling the odorant vapor of yellow tea. Piles of caviar sandwiches were heaped up on old Saxe plates.

"Gentlemen," said the man in the gold-rimmed spectacles, "that old French scientist seems to me to be as cunning as the Devil. We can't trust him."

"My dear Dr. Cornelius," replied another—the one who had been the spokesman for his colleagues with regard to Monsieur Bondonnat—"I believe you're mistaken. The Frenchman's afraid for his daughters; with that argument, we can make him do anything we want."

"That's not certain."

"Yes," said the third interlocutor, "Baruch's right. Bondonnat adores his daughters. Anyway, he's given us serious pledges. He application of his methods has multiplied the yields of our acreage of cotton and corn tenfold."

"That's possible, my dear Fritz," Cornelius said, "but what we're asking of him now goes against his prejudices, and he had a strange smile. I'm not confident."

Baruch raised his fist. "Whether Bondonnat likes it or not," he said, "he'll do as he's told. We have him, and our grip is secure."

"That doesn't alter the fact," said Cornelius obstinately, "that he had a bizarre smile. He agreed very easily to work on an invention that he must regard as abominable. The old fox will do us some bad turn. I have a presentiment, and I'm rarely mistaken."

Baruch shrugged his shoulders. "Bah!" he said. "I don't see that poor Bondonnat, caught as he is, can do anything against us."

"If necessary," said Fritz Kramm, "we'll kill him."

"Never!" exclaimed Baruch, passionately. "I'm in love with Andrée de Marbreuil, and I'm convinced that with my new face, I can please her!"

"In spite of the murder!" exclaimed Fritz and Cornelius, simultaneously amazed.

"Perhaps because of the murder..."

There was a pause.

"So be it," said Cornelius, laughing diabolically. "We'll respect the life of her adoptive father. Let's put the subject aside."

"Yes," Fritz approved. "The yacht's leaving this evening; it's as well to employ the hours that remain with one last severe turn of inspection. Don't forget that this island—the Red Hand's capital, the legendary Island of the Hanged Men about which all the tramps talk without believing in it—is a vital trump card in the hand we're playing. It's our reserve, our warehouse, our secret laboratory and our fortress."

"Admirable!" said Baruch. "You talk like a true poet. A knight of the Middle Ages couldn't have made a better eulogy to his castle. Today, everything's changed."

"Why is that?"

"Let an ironclad cruiser come within sight of the island, or a mere torpedo-boat, and you'll see your arsenal blown to smithereens, your soldiers—your tramps—put in the hold in handcuff..."

"It wouldn't be as easy as that," Cornelius put in. "To begin with, the Island of Hanged Men is surrounded by a ring of torpedoes and floating mines; no ship, even a first-rate ironclad—a dreadnought—could get close without sinking. That protective ring extends over a three-mile radius around the island. Inexplicable shipwrecks often take place in the open sea in these parts. Do you understand? It would take an entire fleet to take possession of the Island of Hanged Men. It's the city of the Red Hand. It's our capital."

Baruch said nothing. Cornelius continued, with an enthusiastic verve: "Do you think that even if a detachment of sailors managed to disembark, their victory would be assured? Not at all. We have fences with electrified bars that will electrocute anyone who tries to get through them, and ditches mined with dynamite, capable of reducing a regiment to dust. Finally, our men, all of whom have been condemned to death, have nothing to lose in fighting to the last drop of blood."

"If the government of the Union were aware of that state of affairs..." Baruch murmured.

"Of course!" aid Fritz, "but our strength resides precisely in the fact that no one is aware of us, that we're disdained. So far as the world is concerned, the Island of Hanged Men is nothing but an icy rock, only good to serve as a reserve for fur-seals..."

"Have you noticed," Baruch suddenly interjected, "how the old Frenchman's dog detests me? It's not deceived. It recognizes Baruch Jorgell under the features of Joe Dorgan."

"What does it matter?" said Cornelius. "The dog is staying on the island, and you don't often have any reason to come here."

"It would give me pleasure to kill it myself, as I tried to do before."

"Impossible," said Fritz, "Bondonnat has a very great affection for the animal; his fear of seeing it perish is one of our means of leverage against the Frenchman."

"So be it," muttered Baruch, getting to his feet and looking at his chronometer, "but it's getting late—we only just have time to carry out our tour of inspection."

All three put on their masks and their cloaks and went out of the house. Outside the garden they found the bandits who served as their bodyguard.

First they visited the northern region of the island, which was entirely abandoned to the fur-seals, and which included a large bay strewn with rocky islets. The animals, which no one molested, were not wild; they could be seen lying on the sand in groups of five or six, warming themselves in the sun, or playing with one another, making the guttural cries that are reminiscent of barking. Half a dozen Eskimos were in charge of watching over them and supplying them with fish. Beside he Eskimos' huts there was a hangar for the preparation of skins; it was here that Lord Burydan would be employed until the Lords of the Red Hand had made a decision in his regard.

Baruch and his accomplices only cast a distracted glance over that installation. From there they went on to the store-rooms that formed a kind of village in the center of the island, which contained an abundance of food-supplies, clothing and the weapons and ammunition necessary to a garrison composed of a hundred bandits. The latter occupied a kind of barracks maintained with the utmost cleanliness, where a severe discipline reigned.

When the Lords went into the main room that served as a refectory, the bandits lined up in two rows, bare-headed, observing a respectful silence. All the men had the same physical appearance: savage faces, long beards, broad shoulders and gnarled hands. All of them were wearing the same leather costume, with felt hats turned up at the brim and ornamented with red hands. At the back of the room there as a weapon-rack in which Winchester rifles and Brownings, perfectly maintained, were symmetrically aligned.

Cornelius turned to one of the bandits clad in red—a uniform that served to distinguish the leaders of the army of malefactors. "Captain Slug," he said, "We're about to leave; have you any special communication to make to the Lords of the Red Hand?"

"No, Your Honor," the bandit replied, with a profound bow. "I hope that the Lords are satisfied with the maintenance and the discipline."

"Quite satisfied –so, henceforth, I authorize a double ration of whisky every Saturday. In the next few months, the Red Hand's yacht will come to fetch the men whose presence in the States of the Union has become possible again. The situation's still good from the sanitary viewpoint?"

"Excellent, except that Jackson, since he was electrocuted, is always agitated by a nervous tremor that will doubtless never be cured. As for Moller, he was so brutally hanged in Canada that his neck, in spite of all the massage, will never be straight again. Berval, who was lynched and half-roasted on a heap of oil-soaked faggots, had to have his arms amputated. Apart from that, there are no invalids."

"I'll go to the infirmary myself," said Cornelius gravely. "As for Berval, I'll have him repatriated as soon as his papers have been forged, and he'll collect the pension to which he's entitled." In the midst of a profound silence he added: "The Lords of the Red Hand never abandon their friends, or their enemies."

Afterwards, Cornelius passed along the ranks, addressing a few words to each of the bandits.

"Why are you here?" he asked one.

"Electrocuted," the man replied, "And recalled to life in the amphitheater by a doctor belonging to the association."

"And you?"

"Escaped from the penitentiary."

"And you?"

"Hanged."

"You?"

"Electrocuted."

"You?"

"Hanged."

"You?"

"Hanged."

The replies were invariable; all the wretched had been submitted to the ultimate penalty and had survived it, thanks to the accomplices that the Red Hand had everywhere. The sinister capital had not stolen the name of the Island of Hanged Men.

Of all the bandits present, only two had not been hanged, electrocuted or lynched; one had been garroted in Spain, the other had escaped from the verdigris mines of Siberia after having been subjected to the punishment of the knout.

Having arrived at the far end of the hall, Cornelius had stopped in front of an old bandit with a long white beard. "Well, Father Marlyn," he asked, "is your health still good?"

"Yes, Your Honor. I'm almost eighty-two, but it doesn't prevent me from having an appetite and liking whisky."

Fritz Kramm leaned toward Baruch. "You see that old man," he said, "he's a veritable patriarch, the doyen of tramps without a doubt. Since his earliest childhood he's been attacking people on the highways; he's been hanged twice and lynched so many times that he can no longer even remember the exact number. He's always been lucky enough to get out of it safe and sound. He's famous throughout America; he's been sentenced to a hundred years in prison that he's never served."

That review of sorts concluded the visit. Captain Slug broke up the ranks and the three Lords, after having gone through a tall palisade, went into the third subdivision of the island, which consisted of five or six wooden houses distributed along the banks of a stream.

The interior of one of these residences was vaguely reminiscent of the office of a notary or an advocate. All the walls were covered with pigeon-holes arranged in scrupulous order. In the center of the room, two men were copying an official document, which appeared to be a birth-certificate.

"You haven't seen our offices," Fritz said to Baruch, laughing. "It's here that we fabricate all the false documents that the members of the association require when it becomes necessary for them to change their identity. We possess an assortment of official paper stocks and imprints, a collection of seals and stamps, inks of every color, and chemical products like calcium hypochlorite and hydrogen peroxide for changing dates."

"From what I can see, you're admirably equipped," said Baruch.

"Nothing is lacking. In an hour, I can have a death certificate or birth certificate—any kind of certificate at all—bearing all the marks of authenticity.

The two forgers had stood up when the Lords arrived, and remained silent, their heads bare. "Sit down," said Cornelius. "We don't want to disturb you at your work."

The doctor had picked up a few documents from the table at hazard; he showed them to Baruch, who could not help admiring the perfection of the work.

"It's not bad, is it?" said Fritz. "The Red Hand has won many trials, including civil suits, thanks to these skillful artists. Now, if you wish, we'll go see the factory of false banknotes."

"It's not functioning at the moment," Cornelius objected. "Our coffers are full and our workshops are idle, but I can still show you Julian and Johnnie, two engravers of genuine talent who have made a specialty of reproducing, with no flaws, the banknotes of all the civilized nations."

While conversing they had arrived alongside a long building surmounted by a brick chimney. They went through two or three rooms in which there were typographic presses, and then Cornelius called a halt in front of a door pierced by a judas-hole.

"Look," he said, lowered his voice.

Baruch leaned over, and almost uttered a cry of surprise. He had just seen two men studiously occupied in engraving a plate—but one of the men resembled Dr. Cornelius, feature by feature, while the other's physiognomy offered the exact image of Fritz Kramm.

The doctor had closed the judas-hole again, quietly. "What do you think of that?" he said.

"I'm amazed."

"You must understand, my dear Baruch, that in life one is sometimes very glad to have a double, even if it's only to establish an alibi in some unfortunate circumstance."

"Those two honest engravers," Fritz explained, "bore a certain resemblance to us. The doctor has contented himself with finishing off the work of nature; once again he has shown that he really is the sculptor of human flesh."

Baruch remained silent; he was frightened, and simultaneously wonder-struck, by the power that his accomplices appeared to have over everything around them.

The rest of the inspection tour of the Island of Hanged Men was completed without any incident worthy of remark.

At dawn the next day, black flags bearing a bloody hand in the center were hoisted above all the island's buildings. The official flag of the Red Hand was also fluttering on the mizzen mast of the yacht anchored in the bay directly opposite the tramps' barracks.

In order to embark, the three Lords went through a double line of armed men, and when they reached the deck of the yacht, the battery of cannons installed on the cliff-top saluted them with an eleven-shot salvo, to which the tramps replied with three cheers, as the mariners of any national navy would have done.

The yacht lifted anchor; at first it maneuvered prudently through the floating mines that garnished the vicinity of the island; then, the danger zone have been crossed, it put on steam. Soon, it was not more than a black dot in the gray-green sea.

On hearing the cannon-shots that announced the departure of the Lords of the Red Hand, Monsieur Bondonnat uttered a sigh of relief, and turned toward the Indian Kloum.

"For the two of us, now, my dear fellow," he said, "it's a matter of staying for as short a time as possible on this accursed and devil-led Island of Hanged Men."

"For the three of us, rather," the Indian replied, indicating the dog Pistolet, who was looking at his master at that moment with eyes so intelligent and so profound that one would have sworn that he understood what they had just said.

VI. An Idyll

An English schooner, the *Pink Pearl*, coming from Australia with a cargo of copra and heading for San Francisco had a macabre encounter two days before its arrival in the great American port. One morning, the crewmen saw that the ocean was covered after as the eye could see with oblong boxes, the majority painted bright red or blue, and a few of them covered with gilded inscriptions.

The captain of the schooner thought that he had made a rich find; he immediately ordered that a launch be put to sea to fish out a few of the elegantly-painted boxes. He was obeyed with ardor, but imagine the anger and disgust of the first mariner to prize off the lid of a beautiful gilded box on observing that it only contained a withered yellow cadaver—the cadaver of an old Chinaman.

A second, then a third and a fourth box were examined, but their contents were always the same. The *Pink Pearl* was sailing through a veritable floating cemetery.

The captain, infuriated by this disappointment, was about to order the launch to return to the ship without paying any more heed to the Chinese corpses when the mariners perceived a shipwreck-victim, unconscious and perhaps dead, who was attached to one of the coffins, It was soon realized that he was tied to it by a rope around his waist. The rope was cut and the man was hoisted aboard. It was observed that he was no longer showing any sign of life; his extremities ere icy and his heart was no longer beating.

The captain was about to order that he be thrown back into the sea when a physician, who happened to be aboard as a passenger, had the idea of applying artificial respiration and rhythmic tractions of the tongue. After three house of energetic attention, the shipwreck-victim gave some feeble signs of life. When they reached San Francisco, he was still in a coma, but the doctor had declared that he would come out of it. Not knowing what to do with him, the captain had him transported to a French hospital, where he remained for an entire month.

He had declared that his name was Agénor Marmousier, a French poet, but when he recounted that he was in the service of a millionaire aristocrat, in which he had no other function than to find extraordinary ideas and invent perilous and dramatic situations, it was thought that the suffering he had undergone had addled his brain, and no one believed a word of his marvelous stories.

The director of the hospital got rid of him be giving him a letter of introduction to the French consul. The latter had, luckily, heard of Lord Burydan, the famous eccentric, the Milord Bamboche of whom he columns of the French newspapers still made mention. He was touched by pity on seeing the sad situation to which the poet had been reduced, deprived of his sole protector and aged ten years by suffering and illness. He comforted him with a few kind words and gave him enough money to get to New York and to embark there for France.

Agénor was unfamiliar with New York, through which he had only passed rapidly on his previous travels. He decided to spend three days there, as much to rest as to form an opinion on the monstrous city in which thirty-story skyscrapers seemed to be throwing down a challenge to the sublime architects of Egypt, India and the Gothic Middle Ages, and where the struggle for existence takes on such a savage and inexorable form.

Agénor promised himself that he would not stay long in the city, where he felt an indescribable mental malaise, and sought information about the departure of the Transatlantic Company's liners, aboard which he wanted to book his passage.

As he was going along the quays of Brooklyn in order to complete this indispensable formality, his foot collided with a voluminous object; he tripped and nearly fell flat on his face. The obstacle that had caused his unfortunate stumble was nothing but a wallet.

The poet picked it up.

"Well," he murmured, examining his find carefully, "it's crocodile-skin, with the initials F.J.. It must belong to some rich fellow."

Agénor opened the wallet and was literally dazzled; it was crammed with five-hundred- and thousand-dollar banknotes.

"There's a genuine fortune here!" he said. "What a pity it's not mine!"

In spite of his poverty the thought never occurred to him of taking possession of the sum. He had only one concern: to discover the name of its owner. That was easy enough; as well as the banknotes, the wallet contained several letters addressed to Mr. Fred Jorgell, a rich speculator, well-known in New York and throughout America, of whom Agénor had heard mention many a time. Immediately, the poet leap into an electric cab and, placing his precious find on his knees, gave the driver the billionaire's address.

Fred Jorgell was not at home; it was a trusted manservant, an old Irishman named Paddock, who received the aged poet and, on learning the objective of his visit, congratulated him cordially.

"You merit being complimented all the more," he said, "because you could have kept the banknotes without my master mounting any search to discover their possessor. For him, such a sum is quite insignificant..."

Agénor interrupted the Irish butler brusquely. "It seems to me," he said, "that returning a found object to its legitimate owner doesn't warrant such exaggerated eulogies. Adieu, Monsieur, I'm a little pressed for time."

The poet had taken a step toward the door, but the honest Paddock barred his way. "You can't go like that," he said. "Mr. Jorgell would reprimand me severely if I let you go without giving you a reward proportionate to the magnitude of the sum."

"I don't want anything," Agénor declared, going red. "That's not customary in my country."

Agénor was about to leave in spite of all the Irishman's efforts when the door to the reception room opened abruptly. A young woman with a harmonious stride and a serene and grave beauty appeared.

"What is it, Paddock?" she asked. "I thought I heard the sound of an argument."

"Miss Isidora," the old Irishman relied, "it's this French gentleman, who has just brought back the wallet full of banknotes that your father lost yesterday, and who doesn't want to accept any reward."

"That's all right," said the young woman, after having heard the butler's explanation. "You can go, Paddock; I'll take care of it."

And, indicating a seat to the discountenanced poet with a gracious gesture, she said to him in French, which she spoke in an admirably correct fashion: "Sit down, Monsieur. It's necessary to forgive Paddock, whose intention was excellent; he didn't know with whom he was dealing. Fortunately, I'm a little less ignorant of French manners. On hearing your name pronounced, some of the beautiful verses that you've written came to mind."

"Thank you, Miss," said Agénor, blushing again, this time in confusion, "for your indulgence."

"I hope that now," the young woman added, with a charming smile, "you won't leave so promptly. You won't refuse to accept a glass of champagne in my company?"

The conversation, commenced in that cordial one, soon took on a more confidential turn. Isidora asked her guest a host of questions, first about France and then about himself. Agénor, whom the frankness of the young billionairess had caused him to relax, did not have to be begged to offer her a brief account of his recent adventures.

The story was not yet concluded when Fred Jorgell came in; he was in an excellent mood that evening, because he had just concluded a very profitable deal. Isidora brought him rapidly up to date and introduced him to the poet.

"My God!" cried the billionaire, with a hearty laugh. "Permit me to shake your hand!" And he gratified the poet with a handshake that made his joints creak. "It isn't every day," he continued, "that one has the pleasure of shaking the hand of an honest man. I hope you'll give me the pleasure of staying for dinner."

Seduced by these slightly brutal but entirely frank manners, Agénor accepted the invitation. A quarter of an hour later he sat down with Fred Jorgell and Isidora in the luxurious dining room, where the service was contrived automatically, without a glimpse of any servant. Ingenious electrical apparatus caused the plates to circulate and took away the dessert; it was as if he were in some enchanted dwelling.

Although he normally ate very soberly himself, the billionaire had wanted the menu to be worthy of his fortune. Among other gastronomic rarities, Agénor savored an exquisite turtle soup, fried oysters, truffled bear-paws and Javanese crayfish, which were simply marvelous.

"What do you think of my cuisine?" the billionaire asked, suddenly, turning to the poet, who, with a convalescent appetite, had done honor to every dish.

"Delicious," Agénor replied. "it would truly be difficult not to find it so."

"Then you're pleased?"

"Rather say delighted."

"That's perfect, then. That's already an important point of order; I'm sure that we're going to understand one another."

"I confess that I don't know what you mean."

"You will, after a brief explanation. I know that you no longer have any family or friends in France..."

"I still have many friends there, but..."

"Don't interrupt. I need a man I can trust, a private secretary who speaks good French and English. You seem entirely suitable. The work won't be crushing; you'll have two thousand dollars a month..."

"And, of course," Isidora put in, laughing, "you'll eat at our table."

"That goes without saying," said Fred Jorgell. "Will you accept my proposition?"

Agénor was disconcerted by this promptitude in matters of business. "Your offer is very seductive," he replied, "but I confess that you've taken me somewhat by surprise..."

"That's Yankees for you," replied the billionaire. "We don't waste time hesitating and dilly-dallying like you folk in the Old World. Come on, make up your mind. I'll give you five minutes to think about it."

And the terrible man took out his chronometer and put it on the table in front of him.

"It's a great service that you'd be doing my father and me," added Isidora.

"Well, so be it—I accept," murmured the poet, nonplussed.

"It's agreed, then—someone will show you to your apartment; you'll start work tomorrow, after having received three months pay I advance.

Thus, in the most unexpected fashion, the poet Agénor Marmousier became the private secretary of the billionaire Fred Jorgell.

He had, in addition, ample reason to be pleased with the decision he had made. He was considered by Isidora and her father as more of a friend than an ordinary employee, and the work of correspondence with which he was charged was neither complicated nor difficult. But for the chagrin caused to him by the death of the eccentric Lord Burydan, Agénor would have considered himself perfectly happy in the billionaire's house.

VII. Harry and Isadora

For a long time, Fred Jorgell had shared the royalties in corn and cotton with the speculator William Dorgan, but the latter had, as we know, won the battle. Fred Jorgell had been obliged to liquidate the stock comprising his Trust and sell it at a loss to his adversary. He might even have been completely ruined but for the intervention of the engineer Harry Dorgan, who had convinced his father to moderate his demands.

Harry had once been Isidora's fiancé, but, even though their marriage had been indefinitely postponed, the two young people had maintained a sincere affection for one another.

One morning, Agénor was coming back from the Post Office, where he had just carried out a few commissions on Fred Jorgell's behalf, when he suddenly found himself face to face with Harry Dorgan. The two men were acquainted, and they greeted one another courteously.

"Is Miss Isidora well?" asked the engineer.

"Marvelously. But you seem preoccupied, Mr. Dorgan?"

"Yes, I'm in a very bad mood. I've just had a violent argument with my brother Joe. We definitely can't reach an understanding. It's necessary to put an end to it…"

Agénor was about to continue on his way, without saying any more, out of discretion, when the engineer called him back.

"I need to ask you to do me a favor," he said. "I know that you get on well with Mrs. MacBarlott.

The poet blushed, because it was claimed that he was discreetly paying court to Isidora's widowed lady companion. "Entirely at your service," he replied. "What do you want me to do?"

Harry Dorgan took a letter from his pocket. "I'd be very grateful if you could give this to Miss Isidora, in person."

"Of course," said Agénor, smiling. "Your commission will be carried out faithfully." And he took his leave of the engineer.

A quarter of an hour later, Isidora, not without a certain emotion, broke the seal on Harry Dorgan's letter.

My dear Isidora, he had written, I have already told you about all the annoyances that my brother Joe had caused me, but his animosity towards me has been further exacerbated since then, and his underhanded methods are becoming intolerable. He has never forgiven me for the part I played in the arrangement made between your father and mine in the matter of the liquidation of the Trust.

237

I must say that Joe is being very badly advised by the Kramm brothers—Dr. Cornelius, the so-called sculptor of human flesh, and Fritz, the art dealer. Those two men have obtained, I don't know how, an extraordinary ascendancy over him. He has made several mysterious voyages in their company, and since then, his hatred for me seems to have been augmented. He scarcely speaks to me.

I thought momentarily that I had recovered my influence over my father; with his naïve honesty, he was glad of my initiative in the affair of the liquidation of the Trust, but Joe has quickly regained the ground he lost. By means of malevolent insinuations, he has almost made my father detest me; my advice is no longer heeded, and when it's a matter of any serious business, they don't even take the trouble to consult me any longer before making a decision.

I'm certain that my father has, deep down, the same affection for me that he had before, but he must have been misled by lies, and that is visible in the constraint that he show me, instead of the frank expansion of old, and a little while ago.

You know, my dear Isidora, how energetic I am, and even brutal, every time I find myself in the presence of an injustice, whether it's me or someone else who is the victim. I couldn't help telling Joe, in a very forthright fashion, what I thought, and I have, in my father's presence, severely criticized the dishonest methods of which your father was a victim in the Agricultural Trust.

At any rate, life in the paternal house has become untenable for me. I'm going to put an end to the situation.

At the moment when you are reading this letter, I shall ask my father for the authorization to marry you. Whether that authorization is granted or refused, I shall not spend another day in the company of a brother who detests me and a father who disdains me and takes no account of my loyalty or me efforts.

To tell you everything that is in my heart, my dear Isidora, my brother Joe is no longer the same since his captivity among the bandits of the Red Hand. His ideas and behavior have changed so completely that there are times when I wonder whether it is really him who is expressing himself in that arrogant, imperious and brutal fashion.

I have only one hope left, and that is in my father's loyalty. He must consent to our marriage. Your esteem and your heart, of which I'm sure, encourage me.

Your,

Harry Dorgan

Isidora read and reread those feverish lines, scribbled in the grip of a generous anger, with a profound emotion, but she dared not confide her secret to Fred Jorgell or to the poet Agénor, or even her lady companion, the devoted Mrs. MacBarlott.

As the latter was becoming anxious at Isidora's silence, having taken note of her preoccupied manner, the young, the young woman made an impatient gesture.

"I'm a little nervous today, my dear MacBarlott," she murmured, by way of an apology. "I feel the need to get some fresh air. Would you like to take a turn in the auto?"

"Gladly, Miss," the governess acquiesced, respectfully. "I'll give the order to the chauffeur."

A quarter of an hour later, the two women were traveling at top speed in the superb hundred-horsepower vehicle that Fred Jorgell had had constructed in France especially for Isidora's excursions.

While the young billionairess was seeking a distraction from her mortal apprehension in that excursion, a violent scene was taking place in William Dorgan's study between him and his son, Harry.

The young man had promised himself to expose his marriage plan frankly and honestly, with no prevarication. William Dorgan, very coldly, let him speak without interrupting, but scarcely had he finished explaining his intentions in respect of Isidora than the old billionaire gave free rein to his anger.

His face became congested, his fists clenched, and the veins in his head swelled as if to burst.

"Harry," he stammered, furiously, "your brother Joe was right when he told me recently to mistrust you! You're betraying my most cherished hopes; you're dishonoring me; you're making common cause with my worst enemies!" When the engineer tried to protest, he went on: "Shut up! You're dishonoring me! You'll never marry the sister of that murderer Baruch, or it will be in spite of me!"

"Father!"

"Never, you hear, will you become the son-in-law of a man whom my pity alone prevented the irreparable ruin!"

Harry Dorgan made an enormous effort to remain calm. "Father," he replied, slowly and moderately, "I shall marry Isidora!"

"I forbid you to!"

"Whatever it costs me, I shall be obliged to disobey you. Isidora has my word, and it was even with your consent that I once..."

"When I consented to that marriage in Jorgell City, Baruch hadn't yet murdered anyone; I couldn't foresee...."

"Isidora, who is an exemplar of virtue and filial devotion, cannot be held responsible for the crimes of her wretched brother!"

"Oh, I know that you're madly in love with Miss Jorgell; already, thanks to your cunning, I've sacrificed the interests of our Trust to your passion for the murderer's sister—but you won't marry her, I swear!"

Harry Dorgan fell silent.

"I forbid you to mention this marriage to me again," roared the old billionaire. "I forbid you to pronounce Miss Isidora's name in my presence. If you ever dare to do so, I shall curse you, I shall kick you out, and you won't have a single dollar of my inheritance."

"Well, so be it!" exclaimed the engineer, furious in his turn. "I can do without you and your billions. My brother Joe and his accomplices, the Kramm brothers, can share it without a contest. From today onwards, I'm resolved to no longer be responsible to you. I'll be able to make a fortune of my own, without doing any wrong to anyone, and without employing dishonest means!"

"I'm a dishonest man, then?" cried the billionaire, at the peak of his rage. "You've insulted me! You're a wretch, well worthy of entering the family of Baruch the murderer. Get out! I never want you see you again!"

"Please, Father!"

"Not another word! Get out, and take my curse with you. Oh, your brother Joe was right—you're a scoundrel!"

Harry Dorgan went out, exasperated, swearing to himself that he would never return. In the street he hailed a cab and gave the driver Fed Jorgell's address.

Harry was still feeling the effects of that terrible scene when he went into the billionaire's study. In a few short sentences he brought the latter up to date with events, not even hiding from him that his projected marriage to Isidora had been the principal cause of the quarrel. Fred Jorgell heard the young man out in complete silence.

"Al this is very regrettable, my dear Harry," he said, finally, "but what are your plans? How can I help you?"

"I'll tell you very frankly," the engineer declared, "that I've thought of finding a job in one of your enterprises that would ensure my independence. Although I'm the son of a billionaire, I'm capable of earning an honest living. I am, as you know neither an idler nor incapable."

"I now that," Fred Jorgell replied, smiling. "I've seen you at work and I have the highest opinion of your talents and your energy. Your collaboration will certainly be precious to me."

As decisive as ever, Fred Jorgell immediately assigned the engineer a respectable salary, then brought him up to date with a new project he was launching with a thoroughly youthful ardor. The cotton and corn Trusts now being in the hands of William Dorgan and the Kramms, his associates, it was a matter of an enterprise in a new kind of navigation. The steamships that Fred Jorgell had under construction would be able to travel between Le Havre and New York in less than four days.

Harry Dorgan listened with profound attention, immediately entering into the details of the project and already glimpsing possible improvements. When he took his leave of the billionaire, he had resolved to set to work without losing a moment.

The engineer had only just left when Isidora appeared, her features still agitated by anxiety.

"Guess who just left?" said the billionaire, almost joyfully.

"Harry Dorgan," replied the young woman, without trying to hide her emotion. "I've just come back from an excursion in the company of Mrs. MacBarlott, and I overheard the end of your conversation from the corridor."

"Then you know that Mr. Dorgan, improbable as it might appear, is now one of my collaborators?"

"I know that, but…"

"But what? I'll wager that you're dying to question me."

Isidora blushed, without making any reply.

"I can guess what's tormenting you," the billionaire went on, affectionately. "You want to know whether William Dorgan agreed to the projected marriage between you and his son?"

"Yes, Father," the young woman murmured, trembling with emotion.

"I'm opposed to all dissimulation on principle, and I've no reason to hide the truth from you in a matter in which you, in sum, have a greater interest than anyone else. William Dorgan threatened his son with his curse if he married you, and the argument that took place between them on that subject was so violent that they're now mortally at odds."

Isidora had gone mortally pale.

"Once," the billionaire went on, without seeming to perceive the young woman's distress, "I would have taken such an insult badly and would have forbidden my door to the engineer, but I've given it a great deal of thought."

"And?" asked Isidora, anxiously.

"For love of you, Harry did me a great service in the affair of the Trust. I know that you share his affection and I don't see that I have any right, in spite of the bloody stain that the wretch Baruch has imprinted on our name, to deprive you of the happiness you deserve."

"So you consent to our marriage?" exclaimed the young woman, her beautiful face lighting up with joy.

"Don't go to work so quickly," said the billionaire, more emotional himself than he wanted to appear. "I haven't yet promised anything to Mr. Dorgan. I'll grant him your hand, but on one condition, which is that he merits it."

"What do you mean?" asked Isidora, gripped by anxiety again.

"I have a very high opinion of the engineer Harry, but I want him to prove himself, so to speak. I've only accepted his services in order to study him at closer range. I've often told you, my dear, that I'll only grant your hand to a man who has enough energy and intelligence to defend my billions when I'm gone."

"I'm certain," the young woman relied, smiling and blushing, "that my dear Harry will realize all the hopes that you've founded on him."

"I believe so too, but let's not rush things. What I've just told you must remain between the two of us until further notice. Don't forget that I've given my consent to your marriage under the express condition that Mr. Dorgan gives me full satisfaction."

Isidora threw her arms around her father's neck affectionately, her heart overflowing with gratitude and happiness; now she was sure that nothing would prevent her from becoming the engineer's wife. After the departure of her father, obliged to return to the shipyard, Isidora went back up to her room to reread her fiancé's letters and savor in advance all the happiness that she glimpsed in the imminent future.

After the terrible argument that he had had with his son, William Dorgan had had a terrible fit of anger. It was not until evening that he recovered a modicum of calm; the engineer's reproaches had cut his self-esteem to the quick and he imposed silence of Joe rudely several times, when he pretended, with his customary hypocrisy, to defend his brother.

"Never mention Harry to me again," he said. "He's an insolent, arrogant ingrate, and I never want to see him again."

The next day, however, after a night of reflection, the billionaire was far from finding his determination so grim. He took account of the wrongs that he had done himself to the engineer, and, without admitting in consequence that Harry was right, began to regret the previous day's scene.

For the rest of the day William Dorgan was troubled and agitated; he began to lead the cause of the absentee himself, and began to deplore the surge of unreflective anger that had driven him to kick his son out.

I showed myself to be as callow, as angry and as obstinate as him, he thought. *Fundamentally, however, I know that Harry is very honest and good...*

When he was not under the immediate influence of the hypocritical Joe, the billionaire had a very real affection for Harry. He wondered now what would become of the young man, and thought about the amusement of the other billionaires when they heard about the quarrel between the father and the son. Twenty times, William Dorgan was on the point of giving the order to send someone in search of the fugitive, but twenty times pride held him back. He was doubtless about to triumph over that unfortunate shame when Joe—or, rather, the man he took to be Joe—came into his study, with a mocking smile on his lips.

"I've been thinking," said the old man, after a slight hesitation. "Doesn't it seem to you, as it does to me, that I treated your brother a little harshly? I'm sorry that, for the sake of a moment of bad temper, he'll be reduced to earning a living in some manner unworthy of him or me."

Joe had a Mephistophelean smile. "You can see, Father," she said, sardonically, "that I was right yesterday in preaching indulgence."

"Indeed, I agree..."

"Except," Joe continued, in an ironic and mordant tone, "you can be sure that my brother Harry has had no difficulty in getting out of trouble; he's already found a new situation."

"You have news of him?"

"Very fresh. I've just left our excellent friend Dr. Cornelius Kramm, who has informed me fully."

"Well?"

"Harry, as it was necessary to expect, has found shelter with our enemy—I mean the father of the charming Isidora. I understand that the ex-fiancé has been welcomed with open arms; a young woman whose brother is a murderer is not always easy to marry off..."

William Dorgan had changed color; all his anger had flooded back. He struck his desk with a mighty blow of his fist.

"That's too much!" he cried. "To go take refuge with Fred Jorgell, whose daughter he's doubtless going to marry! That wretched Harry is dishonoring us!"

"You see," Joe persisted, insidiously, "that you were quite wrong to have any anxieties on the subject of my brother. I've always told you that he was in league with Mr. Jorgell. Remember his conduct during the affair of the Trust..."

William Dorgan was no longer listening. He was striding furiously back and forth in his study, a host of contradictory thoughts crowding his overheated brain. Joe followed him with his eyes, convinced that the rupture between the father and the son was irremediable this time.

Suddenly, however, an abrupt reversal took place in the millionaire's mind. He stopped dead, suddenly becoming calm, and said to the amazed Joe: "Obviously, Harry was wrong, but up to a certain point, he has an excuse: he's in love. I'm not saying that he's right, but on the other hand, I don't want it said that my son needed to rely on the charity of one of my enemies to live..."

Joe was exasperated. "You're going to give in, then!" he exclaimed. "That would be the worst of weaknesses; it would even be acting contrary to the real interests of my brother, whose pride needs to be severely punished. By making the first move, you'd render yourself ridiculous. Leave him where he is, and you'll see that he'll come back, humble and repentant; I know him well enough to know that he's too fearful of being disinherited to break with you completely."

"My decision is made," said William Dorgan, coldly. "Nothing will change it."

Joe saw that his perfidious insinuations were completely futile, and did not persist. "Since that's the way it is," he said, "I'll go look for my brother and give him your apologies."

"I didn't say that," the billionaire replied, impatiently. "All that you have to do is find Harry, give him a check for four hundred dollars on my behalf and tell him that he'll receive a similar sum every month. Try, in sum, to make him understand that I don't have anything against him and only want to be flexible. I'm convinced that Harry will be touched by my generous move."

"I'll follow your instructions to the letter," Joe murmured, with a sly smile. "Let's hope that the result will be in conformity with your desire. I'll set out in search of my brother without delay."

This search, let us say, did not take long. In his capacity as a Lord of the Red Hand, Joe had spies at his disposal who had been watching the engineer's every move closely for a long time. Joe Dorgan already knew the address of the furnished apartment that Harry had rented, a short distance away from Fred Jorgell's palace.

It was Harry himself who came to open the door to his brother. On the threshold the two of them exchanged glances charged with hatred.

"What do you want?" the engineer demanded. "What are you doing here?"

"It's not on my own account that I've come," Joe replied, with a mocking smile. "I've been sent by our father."

"My father has expelled me from his house; we no longer have anything in common." He added, in a softer tone: "Unless he wants to admit that he went too far in his anger. I got a little carried away myself..."

Joe sniggered in a sinister fashion. "Ha ha! You're very naïve if you think I've come to attempt a reconciliation. You're beginning to regret your insolent conduct, and you've realized, a little belatedly, that you've been stupid. My father has not changed his opinion in your regard..."

"What do you want, then?" retorted the engineer, feeling anger invade him.

"Patience. My father has thrown you out, but as he doesn't want you to be begging on the streets of New York, he's instructed me to bring you alms, a small allowance that will be renewed monthly." Joe handed Harry the check he was carrying.

"Know," cried the engineer, half-suffocated by indignation and fury, "that in order to live I have no need of your charity or my father's. Get out. I disown you as my brother. Go, or I might be capable of doing something extreme."

With a brutal gesture, Harry ripped up the check that Joe was holding out in his fingertips and stamped on the fragments. Then, with an abrupt shove, he knocked his brother backwards and forced him to retreat on to the landing.

Joe, all of whose words were calculated to exasperate his brother, maintained an absolute self-control. "Better and better," he sniggered. "I'll tell my father about the amiable fashion and the exquisite politeness with which you welcome his generosity. I warn you, of course, that it's the last time I shall attempt such a step in regard to you. I day will come, I predict, when you'll bite the fingers of your arrogance."

"Get out!" shouted the engineer, utterly exasperated. "My patience is at an end. Go to the Devil! You're not my brother!"

At that cry, sprung from Harry's lips without him taking any account himself of the implication of his words, Joe had gone pale. "That's good," he growled, between his teeth. "I'm going—but we'll see one another again, and you'll pay me for all those insults..."

He went down the stairs precipitately and went back to the automobile that was waiting at the door.

I'm not his brother, he repeated to himself anxiously. *What did he mean by that? Does Harry suspect the diabolical metamorphosis that, thanks to the genius of the sculptor of human flesh, has made the murderer Baruch Jorgell into the billionaire Joe Dorgan? Oh, if I thought that he had the slightest presentiment of the truth, he wouldn't have long to live.*

The bandit ended up reassuring himself by reflecting that if Harry Dorgan had had such a terrible weapon in his hands, he would have made use of it long ago, but he remained pensive. He did not like to suppose, even for a moment, that his true identity could ever be discovered.

When he got out of the car he went to see William Dorgan, who was waiting for him in the small drawing room on the ground floor.

"Well?" asked the old man, anxiously. "Did you find your brother?"

"Very easily. It was only necessarily to look for him in the vicinity of Fred Jorgell's palace, and that's what I did."

"You've seen him? You've given him the check?"

Joe assumed a contrite expression. "It pains me to hurt you," he said, "but my brother heaped me with insults, tore up the check you sent him before my eyes and threw me out, howling like a madman that he had no need of you or anyone. I'm not mistaken; henceforth, Harry is lost to us."

William Dorgan remained plunged into a silence full of dejection for some time. Joe thought it appropriate to lavish hypocritical consolations upon him.

"Don't take it too hard, Father," he murmured. "Harry is full of arrogance at present because he feels that he has the support of Fred Jorgell, but I'll wager that the latter has only welcomed my brother in order to annoy you. When he knows that Harry can no longer count on your inheritance, he'll soon throw him out; then the fugitive will return to us, humble and repentant, and I'm sure that you'll still be willing to forgive him."

William Dorgan's only reply to that exhortation was a profound sigh. The departure of his son Harry had struck him in the heart.

In spite of all Joe's efforts, weeks went by without the billionaire being able to console himself for his son's absence; he even wrote to him twice in secret, promising him complete forgiveness of he would consent to return. Unfortunately, the letters were intercepted by Joe, whose diabolical vigilance did not relax for an instant. Seeing that his son did not even deign to rely to his affectionate missives, William Dorgan felt his prejudices revive, and strive to banish his ingrate soon from his memory forever. The rancor he retained against him was in proportion to the chagrin caused to him by his flight.

The billionaire would have been singularly astonished if he had known that Harry bitterly regretted having quarreled with him and reproached himself every day for his violence and lack of respect toward his father. If he had dared, the young man would have attempted a reconciliation; what held him back was the thought of finding himself once more in association with Joe. He had understood once and for all that his brother and he would never reach an understanding, and could not help hating the hypocrite to whom he attributed, not without reason, all his troubles.

At any rate, Fred Jorgell was delighted with the services of his new engineer, and was already treating him, in many circumstances, as if he were his own son.

The Lightning Steamship Company—that was the name Fred Jorgell had given his navigation enterprise—was prospering. Half-ruined by the liquidation of the cotton and corn Trust, his speculation was triumphant again. The high-speed steamers that he had launched, as he had announced, made the journey between Le Havre and New York in less than four days. The first-class passengers had adopted them and were booking their cabins a long time in advance.

How had Fred Jorgell achieved this almost-incredible abbreviation of the journey time? Simply by reducing the weight of the ships in considerable proportions, and simultaneously equipping them with much more powerful engines, while according considerably less space to fuel.

With the aid of the engineer, the billionaire had solved that triple problem by replacing the steel ordinarily employed in the construction of the hulls by a light an extra-slid alloy of nickel and aluminum; he had renounced coal and only gasoline or naphtha oil for his engines, much less bulky combustibles, which permitted the use of smaller generators.

Joe took a hateful pleasure in keeping William Dorgan up to date with all these matters on a daily basis, and needling his dormant rancor.

"Do you know what is going to happen, Father?" he said "Provided that the success continues to increase, Fred Jorgell won't take long to form a Trust of his navigation companies, and then we'll be obliged to submit to his tariffs to transport our corn and cotton. The battle between us will begin again, as fast and furious as ever, for you'll have before you as an adversary the son who detests you, who abandoned you and betrayed you.

"How has Harry betrayed me?" asked the billionaire, timidly.

"You're asking me that? If he hadn't interceded, in my absence, on behalf of Fred Jorgell on the affair of the Trust, we'd have finished off that redoubtable adversary long ago. I was right then to advise you not to give in. You can see that now."

One morning, Joe appeared before his father with his face illuminated by an evil joy. He was brandishing a copy of the *Herald*.

"Well," he cried, as soon as he perceived the billionaire, "It's complete! My most pessimistic anticipations have been realized. In a month's time, Harry is going to marry Isidora Jorgell. The news is official. You'll soon have the joy of being thee father-in-law of the sister of the murderer Baruch!"

"Are you sure of what you're saying?" asked the old man, sadly.

"There's no talk of anything but the marriage in New York. All the newspapers are talking about it and publishing portraits of the future spouses. Look!"

William Dorgan did not reply; this final blow had struck him full in the heart.

The information was, in fact, perfectly correct. The marriage of Isidora and Harry Dorgan had been decided.

A few days before the news became public, Fred Jorgell had summoned Harry to his study and had said to him, simply: "My dear Harry, you're almost replacing the son I've lost. You've proved to me, abundantly, that you're capable of conserving and even augmenting a fortune as considerable as mine. I no longer have any reason to delay your marriage to Isidora, who, I know, loves you as much as you love her."

Too emotional to assure Fred Jorgell of his devotion and energy, as he wanted to do, Harry shook the hand that the billionaire held out to him.

The same day, the engagement of the two young people was celebrated solemnly in the course of a splendid banquet, witnessed by the poet Agénor, the steward Paddock and Mrs. MacBarlott, embellished and as if rejuvenated herself by the happiness of her young mistress.

In Fred Jorgell's hospitable abode, Agénor had finally found repose and security. Only one thing cast a shadow over his happiness: the death of his friend and benefactor Lord Burydan, for which he could not console himself.

N° 6. CHAQUE RÉCIT EST COMPLET EN UN VOLUME — 25 Cent.

GUSTAVE LE ROUGE

LE MYSTÉRIEUX DOCTEUR CORNÉLIUS

LES

CHEVALIERS DU CHLOROFORME

LA MAISON DU LIVRE 28 RUE MONSIEUR LE PRINCE PARIS

6. THE KNIGHTS OF CHLOROFORM

I. The Bandits of Chinatown

Although the Grizzly Club had installed its premises on the thirty-second and topmost floor of a recently-built skyscraper, its members had the enjoyment of a magnificent garden that could, in some respects, be compared to the Hanging Garden of Babylon constructed by Queen Semiramis. The garden had, in fact, been installed on the roof itself, disposed in terraces and covered with a thick layer of bitumen.

For weeks on end the elevators had hoisted crates full of rich soil. Finally, by courtesy of money and patience, shady arbors now extended over the pale green lawns that separated the sandy pathways. A lively spring snaked through the plots of grass, where rhododendron bushes, camellias and orange-trees grew.

Even on the hottest days of summer, an exquisite freshness reigned in the garden, magically blooming at the summit of the monstrous edifice of brick and steel, Nonchalantly lying in their rocking chairs or sprawling in colored rattan armchairs, the club members could admire, in the verdant frame of foliage, the vast panorama of New York bay, the city's gigantic edifices and the Hudson, covered in ships and the grandiose Statue of Liberty, whose torch was illuminated at dusk.

It was in the evening especially, when the bushes were illuminated by thousands of little blue and green electric bulbs, that the garden of the Grizzly Club presented a magical appearance. Leaning on marble balustrades, the clubmen were then able to admire the titanic accumulation of edifices whose silhouettes stood out against a background of raw light, while, in the distance, the waves of the immense Atlantic sparkled softly in the moonlight, and the innumerable fleet anchored near the shore swayed at the whim of the nocturnal breeze, the forest of masts illuminated by multicolored beacons.

To the attractions of that unique panorama other, less poetic, temptations were added. White-clad waiters as grave as diplomats circulated with silver trays marked with the club's emblem decked with the entire redoubtable pharmacy of American drinks: the "mint julep," perfumed like bouquets of wild flowers; the treacherous "mother's milk"; the "prairie oyster," the providence of drunkards; and the infallible and definitive "nightcap."

Such was the place occasionally frequented by the billionaire Fred Jorgell, the director of the Lightning Steamship Company.

That evening, he had gone there in the company of his private secretary, a Frenchman celebrate in his homeland as a poet, and who, after numerous adventures, had ended up attaching his fortune definitively to that of the billionaire. Fred Jorgell had the utmost confidence in Agénor Marmousier, and treated him more as a friend than an employee.

Both of them were installed under a magnolia, to either side of a small marble table, playing a game of checkers while savoring a glass of extra-dry champagne. That meditative game was the only one that the billionaire ever played. He found a distraction in its simplistic strategies from the fatiguing calculations necessitated by his speculations.

Besides which, Fred Jorgell and the poet were equal in strength, and sometimes succeeded in prolonging a single game almost indefinitely.

They had already been playing for half an hour, savoring the beauty of the warm evening, when a sudden agitation became manifest among the clubmen installed here and there beneath the shade of the garden. A copy of an evening newspaper was being passed feverishly from hand to hand.

"What's going on, then?" Fred Jorgell asked one of the waiters, who came in response to the electric bell.

"It's another exploit of the Knights of Chloroform, sir."

The billionaire could not help shuddering.

"Can you get me a paper?"

"Right away, sir."

He soon returned with a copy of the *Night*. The poet took possession of it and read aloud the article that was causing so much emotion among the members of the Grizzly Club.

HOTELIER MURDERED

As we go to press, we learn that a murder has been committed in mysterious circumstances, the victim of which is the honorable Mrs. Griffon, who has been the owner of a boarding house at number 93 Thirtieth Avenue for ten years.

After taking tea in the company of her boarders, as she did every evening, Mrs. Griffon, who is Scottish by birth, went to her room to look for some postcards reproducing views of Edinburgh, which she wanted to show to a friend. When she did not come down again, her boarders feared that she had had an accident and decided to go see what had become of her. Having knocked for some time without receiving any reply, they broke down the door, and a horrible spectacle appeared before their eyes.

Mrs. Griffon was lying on the bed, fully dressed, her face covered with a rubber mask, giving no sign of life. The sickening odor of chloroform that filled the room left no doubt about the fashion in which the crime had been committed. The celebrated Dr. Cornelius Kramm, whose residence is not far away, was summoned in haste, but his cares were in vein; he could only certify the death.

The affair presents many mysterious features and it will doubtless not be soon that the New York Police will put their hands on the guilty parties. The victim's body bore no trace of a struggle or violence; no one had heard the murderer come in or go out or furnish the slightest information on that account. Finally, the furniture in the room had not been disturbed and no precious object appears to have been stolen. The police and district attorneys are reduced to conjectures regarding the motive for the audacious murder.

Only one hypothesis is plausible, in our opinion. Our readers will remember that it was in Mrs. Griffon's establishment that the famous murderer Baruch Jorgell was arrested, who has long been supposed to belong to the association of the Red Hand; it would, we believe, not be extraordinary if the death of the honorable lady were a revenge on the part of that redoubtable secret society.

This murder by chloroform in the third committed in a month; the population of our capital is terrorized; it is already designating the members of this mysterious gang, whom no one has been able to capture, as "the Knights of Chloroform."

Let us recall, in conclusion, that Baruch Jorgell, presently interned in a lunatic asylum, is the son of the well-known billionaire Fred Jorgell and the brother of the charming Miss Isidora, whose portrait we published a few days ago, and who is soon due to marry the distinguished engineer Harry Dorgan.

In order not to annoy Fred Jorgell, Agénor had skipped the final paragraph, but the billionaire read it over the poet's shoulder and swallowed the affront to the hilt. His face went lividly pale and his hands trembled. He crumpled the newspaper violently and threw it on the ground.

"So they're still talking about that wretch Baruch!" he exclaimed, despairingly. "Just as long as Isidora and Harry don't see it. It would be stab in the heart!"

"Mr. Dorgan is so busy at present that he scarcely has the time to read, and I'll make sure that Miss Isidora doesn't see this unfortunate paper, or another like it."

"Thank you," replied the billionaire, sadly. "I can count on you, can't I?"

There were a few minutes of awkward silence.

"Shall we go on with the game?" Agénor asked, finally.

"No, I'm no longer in the mood for games; that accursed article has spoiled my evening. Besides which, it's getting late."

"A few minutes past midnight."

"Shall we go home?"

"As you please."

A minute later, they took their places in the electric elevator that terminated in the center of the aerial garden and deposited them a few yards away from the billionaire's electric coupé.

The chauffeur opened the door respectfully, but Fred Jorgell waved him away. "It's such a beautiful evening," he said, "that I'd rather go home on foot; it will clear my headache—unless Monsieur Agénor prefers to go back by car."

"Not at all," the poet replied, with his customary courtesy. "I'll accompany you."

They both set out at a tranquil pace, following a broad avenue in which the nocturnal crowd was already thinning out.

They had been walking for less than a quarter of an hour when Agénor, on turning round, thought that he perceived suspicious shadows.

"It seems to me," he said to the billionaire, "that we're being followed."

Fred Jorgell shrugged his shoulders, smiling. "You're probably right," he said. "It's rare that I don't have a few spies on my heels, but I'm so used to it that I don't pay them any attention."

"Spies?"

"Exactly. I'm not unaware that my financial rivals have all my actions and movements watched by special agents. I confess, moreover, that I do the same with some of them—William Dorgan and his son Joe, for example. In addition, as is usual among billionaires, I pay the New York Police a certain number of dollars every year for special protection. Finally, I'm not afraid of professional malefactors, specialists in nocturnal attacks; I'm a man of action, and I've often cleared a path through life with revolver shots, and even with my fists."

As is evident, a measure of braggadocio was mingled with the billionaire's authentic bravery. Agénor could not help smiling.

They continued on their way, chatting about other things. Fred Jorgell seemed to have completely forgotten the surge bad temper that he had experienced on reading the article in the *Night*. He had not, though.

Suddenly, a newsvendor ran out of a deserted street and crossed the avenue, shouting: "Get the fifteenth edition of the *Night!* Get this exciting edition! New details of Mrs. Griffon's death!"

"Here! Here!" cried the billionaire—but the man did not hear and drew away rapidly. "Be good enough to run after him, my dear Agénor, and try to catch up with him. No matter what I do, this crime interests me. I'll follow the avenue at a moderate pace; you won't have any difficulty rejoining me."

The poet launched himself in pursuit of the newsvendor and followed him into an ill-lit street. He only had time to take a few more steps, however; without him being able to see anyone a mask was clamped over his face and he fell to the ground, unconscious, without having been able to utter a cry.

His attacker, a kind of Hercules with a long beard, leaned over the body of his victim and, with a sureness of hand that denoted long practice, planted a dagger in his heart, took off the mask and disappeared, not without having taken possession of a wallet.

That horrific scene had unfolded with lightning rapidity. A few seconds had sufficed to turn the joyful, intelligent and honest poet into an anonymous cadaver abandoned at the foot of a boundary-marker, his head in the gutter, in a deserted alley.

Meanwhile Fred Jorgell slowly continued on his way. After a quarter of an hour, however, having not seen his companion return, he began to get anxious and abruptly turned round.

"I'm so stupid," he murmured, "to have charged Agénor with such a mission. Stupid, too, not to have come back by car. I'd already be at home and I could have sent a domestic to fetch the evening papers for me."

The billionaire returned to the spot where Agénor had left him, and went in his turn into the network of side-streets. As he went forward he observed that the district was unfamiliar to him and that everything had a strange character.

Paper lanterns were swaying above multicolored shop-fronts; tailless dogs and fat rats, occupied in rummaging in heaps of filth, were fleeing in all directions, and the houses had a sordid and leprous appearance that Fred Jorgell had only ever seen in the Orient. In addition, all the shops being closed, only a few beams of light filtered through the ventilation-shafts of cellars or between the cracks of poorly-fitted shutters.

As he passed in front of an obscure alley in the depths of which the red light of a smoky lantern was glowing, Fred Jorgell's nostrils were assailed by an acrid, nauseating and bizarre odor. It was like a powerful perfume that had gone bad. He recognized the stink that identifies at a distance the dens where the black poison is sold.

"Opium," he murmured, with a gesture of disgust. "It reeks of opium. I'm in Chinatown."

However, he could not find any trace of Agénor and was beginning to feel seriously anxious. He explored a whole block of rickety buildings sweating dirt and poverty. Agénor remained undiscoverable.

The diabolical Frenchman must have learned some news that demanded instant action, the billionaire thought. *Perhaps he's gone to the offices of some newspaper without telling me, in order to put a stop to the insulting articles that are being published about me. I'll doubtless find him when I get back home.*

After three-quarters of an hour of futile searching, Fred Jorgell decided to go back to his house, very discontented and, deep down, more alarmed by his secretary's disappearance than he wanted to admit.

He therefore headed back in the direction of the avenue that he had quit, walking uneasily through the side-streets and alleyways—but it did not take him long to perceive that he was not going the right way. The further he went, the more hideous the neighborhood became, somber and stinking.

"I believe, by Jove," he muttered, "that I'm lost. Chinatown is like a labyrinth that I can't seem to escape from. Bah! The simplest thing to do is to walk in a straight line. I'll end up reaching an avenue or I'll find a cab rank and policemen to show me the way."

Having reassured himself twice over that no one was following him and that his Browning was within easy reach of his hand in his overcoat pocket, he set out again at a long and rhythmic stride. Fred Jorgell was not afraid; he was merely furious at having wasted so much time and vexed at having got lost like a simple cockney fresh off the boat.

He would have been much less confident if he had perceived a rogue of gigantic stature who was clinging obstinately to his tracks, creeping along the mute façades, hiding in dark corners, where he remained motionless every time the billionaire turned round. The determined tracker was the same bandit that had just murdered the unfortunate Agénor.

Fred Jorgell, whose bad mood was increasing, was beginning to feel the fatigue of the long march through badly-paved back-streets when he arrived at the entrance to a street where the shop-fronts of a few all-night bars were still illuminated. People in rags were coming and going along the sidewalk or jostling in the doorways of drinking-dens.

"Finally!" the billionaire exclaimed, "I'm in a more civilized neighborhood. I'll be able to find someone who can give me directions."

He increased his pace joyfully, and went deliberately into the first bar he came to, where he ordered a glass of whisky.

A profound silence had descended as he entered upon the clan of paupers gathered along the counter or perched on high stools. They were all studying, with gleaming eyes, the well-dressed stranger who had not fear of venturing into such a place at such an hour. Fred Jorgell seemed so calm and so sure of himself, however, so perfectly at ease in that atmosphere polluted by tobacco and alcohol, that he was assumed to be some high dignitary of the police. No one budged, and the conversations soon resumed their course, as before his arrival.

Without even moistening his lips with the nauseating liquor that had just been served to him, he asked in a tranquil voice which was the quickest way to reach Tenth Avenue. A bearded Hercules who had come into the bar immediately after him obligingly gave him the information.

He paid, left without any unfortunate incident occurring, and set out on this way, impatient to put an end to the forced excursion in a malodorous district. It did not take him long to perceive that in the street into which he had turned, following the directions given to him by the man with the long beard, all the gas lamps had been broken by hurled stones. A profound obscurity reigned there, but he did not attach any importance to that detail, which was not out of the ordinary in such a neighborhood.

Half way along the street he turned round and then perceived that he was being followed by the very same man that had given him directions, and who was not even taking the trouble to hide.

Perhaps, after all, the billionaire thought, *the fellow is simply going in the same direction as me.* And he continued walking, but more slowly, with his hand on the butt of his Browning.

Suddenly, however, he uttered an exclamation of fury and disappointment. The street had been indicated to him as a thoroughfare, and which, naively, he had assumed to be one, was actually a dead end.

"My God!" he groaned. "The blackguards have caught me like a rat in a trap. But we'll see!"

He turned round abruptly, the Browning in his hand.

The giant with the long beard was standing in the middle of the street, barring his passage, his hand clutching the naked blade of a Bowie knife almost as long as one of the immense cutlasses that are used to butcher whales. Another bandit, emerged from who knows where, was standing behind the first, ready to come to his aid.

Fortunately, Fred Jorgell was no novice in such adventures; he did not lose his imperturbable composure for an instant, and, with a sure and precise gesture, without waiting to be attacked, he raised his Browning, took aim and fired.

The bearded giant fell to the ground howling, his leg broken.

"I aimed too low," the billionaire murmured, coldly. His eyes searched for the second bandit, who had disappeared.

"These scoundrels are singularly cowardly," said Fred Jorgell, smiling. "As soon as someone stands up to them, they're no longer there!"

With no other emotion, he was about to continue on his way when a vigorous arm seized him from behind and squeezed his neck to the point of strangling him.

"Kill him!" cried the hoarse voice of the man on the ground. "You know that's the Lords' orders."

"Hurrah for the Red Hand!" replied the other, enthusiastically. At the same time, he struck Fred Jorgell, a furious dagger-blow, fortunately deadened by the check-book that the billionaire habitually carried in his inside jacket pocket.

With a desperate surge, the billionaire broke free and, half-strangled, with blood in his eyes, he fired three times in succession.

"Kill him, then!" repeated the voice of the wounded man, this time in a menacing fashion.

At the same moment, Fred Jorgell, knocked down by a terrible head-butt in the stomach, fell to the ground and dropped his Browning. He was doomed.

"Cut his throat—that's best!" said the wounded man again, who had succeeded in propping himself up on his elbow and who appeared to be the leader of the gang.

Fred Jorgell could no longer feel a drop of blood in his veins; his attacker had put a knee on his chest; it was all over.

He saw a glint of steel before his eyes: the blade of the knife was interrupted momentarily by the thickness of the collar, which, in accordance with that year's fashion, was high and firm, the blade grating against the large diamond ornamenting the pin of his cravat.

In that second, the billionaire lived a century of anguish.

The wounded man, in spite of his broken leg, was crawling closer.

"Hurry up, then!" he howled. "Do I have to kill him myself? The police will come. Windows are opening! I'm losing blood—my leg's hurting like hell."

"But Slug," the other stammered, "I'm going as fast...!"

He could not say any more. A fourth person, emerging abruptly from a dark alley, had just smashed his skull with the blow of a cudgel. He fell like an inert mass on Fred Jorgell's body, two trickles of blood emerging from his nostrils.

The newcomer was short, deformed and slightly hunchbacked. He was bizarrely dressed in an old naval reefer-jacket and a jockey's cap. He immediately hastened to help Fred Jorgell to his feet.

"Well, sir," he said, in bad English, "I hope you're not completely dead and that I got here in time."

"Just in time," the billionaire replied, taking a deep breath.

"You're not wounded?"

"No. My neck was only nicked by the villain's blade, and I was hit in the stomach."

"That's nothing. Do you want to go to a pharmacist's?"

"Yes—but there's still this murderer"—he pointed to the wounded man—"who seems to be the leader of the gang."

Fred Jorgell picked up his Browning, and methodically, like a man doing his duty, shot Slug twice—after which he put the weapon back in his pocket and held out his hand graciously to his savior.

"You're a good lad," he said. "Will you have a glass of wine with me?"

"Gladly, sir," the hunchback replied, "But don't you want to go to the pharmacist's—or, as they say here, the chemist's—first? There's one only a short distance away, which stays open all night."

"I would, for I perceive that I'm spitting blood—that head-butt has injured my stomach."

They both set out, and reached the shop of the "chemist and druggist," the flamboyant bottles of whose window-display could be seen from a distance, without any further incident.

There was a crowd of about twenty people outside the shop, and Fred Jorgell learned that a wounded man found by policemen at a street corner had just been carried into it.

As in all Anglo-Saxon countries, the "chemist" was also a "medic"—which is to say, a doctor. He wore blue-tinted spectacles and a long pale brown moustache. He bandaged the cut that the would-be murderer's blade had made in the billionaire's neck and assured him that, given certain precautions that he indicated, the head-butt he had received would not have any serious consequences.

Fred Jorgell, who had just been overtaken by an ominous presentiment, then asked the chemist for some details regarding the wounded man that the police had just brought to him. To justify his question, he gave a brief account of his own adventure.

"Do you want to visit the wounded man?" the doctor asked, obligingly. "You'll be able to see right away whether or not he's your friend."

Fred Jorgell accepted and went into the back room, at the back of which a man was lying on a bed, watched over by a policeman. The billionaire started in dolorous alarm; he had just recognized the poet Agénor, immobile and pale, showing no sign of life.

"I hope he's not dead?"

"He's gravely wounded. He hasn't recovered consciousness since he was brought here."

"Is there any hope?" asked Fred Jorgell, anguished.

"I can't say as yet; it didn't reach the heart, though."

Prey to a violent emotion, the billionaire strode back and forth in the room at a jerky pace.

"Doctor," he said, agitatedly, "I'm Feed Jorgell the billionaire. The wounded man is one of my friends. Save him, and I'll reward you royally."

"I'll try."

"I confide him to your care, but telephone me an update on his condition at hourly intervals, and as soon as he can be moved, warn me, and I'll have him taken to my home."

"Well, sir..."

"I forgot; here's a payment on account."

The doctor took the banknote that Fred Jorgell held out to him, bowed deeply and escorted his illustrious visitor to the door.

The billionaire was about to climb into a cab of which the hunchback had hastily gone in search, but before then he wanted to inform the policeman in the shop of what had happened.

The latter departed in all haste for the spot where the attack had taken place. They found nothing but two large pools of blood. The bodies of the bandits had disappeared, doubtless carried away by their accomplices.

II. Oscar Tournesol's Story

With an authoritative gesture, Fred Jorgell had made the ragged hunchback climb in beside him on to the pneumatic cushions of the taxicab, which immediately set off in third gear in the direction of the city center.

"You're a brave lad," said the billionaire to his bizarre companion. "You saved my life, and you have my sworn word that you won't have wasted your time tonight. First of all, what's your name?"

"Oscar Tournesol."

"You're not American?"

"No, sir, I'm French, Parisian by birth."

"And what do you do?"

Oscar Tournesol lowered his head, blushing. "I'm a shoeshine boy," he replied, a little ashamed of such a humble profession.

"It's not necessary to be ashamed of one's profession," Fred Jorgell said, severely. "It's never shameful to work. I polished the shoes of sailors for a long time myself on the quays of San Francisco, and yet I'm now a billionaire." As Oscar opened his eyes wide, he added: "that's the way it goes, my boy—but first, tell me what inspired you to come to my rescue."

"It's quite simple. I lodge, at two dollars a week, in a sort of cellar that opens into the dead end were you were attacked. It's not rare for me to hear revolver shots in the vicinity, but I've never been able to get used to the noise. When you fired at the man with the long beard, I woke up with a start, jumped out of bed and quickly got dressed..."

"You did well to hurry," murmured the billionaire, with a grimace of retrospective fear, "but go on..."

"I looked out of the ventilation shaft of the cellar, and when I saw that it wasn't a matter of a battle between apaches but a genuine murder, I didn't hesitate. I picked up a club, the only weapon I had at my disposal, and I lay in ambush in the corridor, waiting for the right moment to intervene."

"But you might have been killed..."

"In truth, I didn't think of that. Anyway, if I'd allowed someone to cut your throat before my eyes like that, I'd have suffered from remorse all my life; it would always have seemed to me that I'd been an accomplice."

At that moment the cab stopped in front of an edifice with a brightly-illuminated façade.

"We've arrived," the billionaire declared. "This is Delmonico's restaurant; I thought it would do us both good to have something substantial after such a scare."

"But I'm not very presentable," Oscar stammered. "People will think you've invited a dog-clipper or—which is exactly accurate—a boot-black to supper with you."

"That's okay by me," said Fred Jorgell, with superb nonchalance. "I have the most complete indifference to what people might say."

While speaking, he pushed the confused Oscar in front of him into a vast hall with a gold ceiling, tables scintillating with flowers, silver-plate and crystal glass.

At the sight of the boot-boy the cashier and the steward had exchanged bewildered glances, and a certain amount of discreet laughter circulated among the customers, but that was all. The billionaire was well-known and none ventured to make any observation. More than that, some of the diners thought that eccentricity a bold and sterling quality, on the very day in which Baruch's name had resurfaced along with the bloody allusions of the newspapers.

Fred Jorgell and Oscar Tournesol took their places at an isolated table and the billionaire immediately picked up the menu. "We need," he said to Oscar, who made no protests, something simple and filling. In consequence, here's what I'll order: three dozen Kankal oysters; lobster salad with celery hearts and a few truffles; Kentucky chicken with trust sauce; and, as you're French, escargots with vanilla and sugar. Then desserts, coffee and Canadian Club whisky. Is that all right?"

"Admirable—and it will go down all the better because I've eaten very lightly today. *J'ai la dent*—and how!"

"What's a *dent*?"

"It's a French expression—it means that I'm hungry."

"Very good. Do you drink wine?"

"With pleasure, especially when it's from my homeland, Monsieur le Billionaire."

"You'll be satisfied."

While Fred Jorgell asked the waiter for a wine list, Oscar promised himself secretly not to touch the escargots with vanilla and sugar, which he considered, without having tasted it, as an abomination invented by Yankees to dishonor Burgundy.

The supper was soon served; the hunchback ate like a hungry wolf. The billionaire watched him clear the plates and mop up the sauces with his bread, in veritable delight. He refrained from troubling his guest with untimely questions, first allowing him to sate his appetite in peace. It was only during dessert that he began to speak again.

"Now, my brave Oscar, I'd like to have a brief account of your past life, and, if you're worthy of it—as is my firm conviction—I promise to create a truly enviable position for you here."

"Sir," the hunchback replied. "I don't have any reason to hide my antecedents from you, and you shall know them in their entirety. As I told you, I was born in Paris; my father was a poor cabinet-maker in the Faubourg Saint-Antoine. I was five years old when my parents died, within the space of a fortnight, in an epidemic of typhoid fever. The neighbors wanted to hand me over to the Assistance Publique, but I was so afraid of being locked up that I fled, with twenty sous that my poor mother had given me a few days before her death. After that, I lived on my wits of the streets of Paris, following all the petty trades of those who have none."

"You were a street-hawker," said the billionaire.

"That's right—I sold evening newspapers, tricolor flags on national holidays, Armenian paper and furry monkeys at fairgrounds; I sold olives from a little cedar basket on the terraces of cafes, picked up cigar butts, helped unload carts of fruits and vegetables. I never think of those days without feeling sad. How many times I was forced the sleep under bridges or on building sites! Then again, everyone made fun of me because of my hump and my yellow hair. When I was over fifteen I still looked under twelve, I was so small and puny."

"Poor devil," murmured Fred Jorgell. "Then, doubtless, you came to America to seek your fortune?"

"Wait a little—we're not there yet. One night when it was cold enough to split stones, I had no shelter, didn't have a sou and hadn't eaten since the day before; half dead with hunger and cold, I took refuge under the arch of a coaching-entrance on the Quai de Tourelles. I was found there the next morning, unconscious and half-frozen. The owner of the house, a famous scientist, took pity on me, cared for me, fed me, and finally kept me in his home.

"What was the worthy gentleman's name?" asked Fred Jorgell, very interested.

"Monsieur de Marbreuil."

When he heard that name, which brought back such terrible memories, Fred Jorgell's face fell, and he put down the glass that he had just lifted to his lips without touching its contents. He needed all his strength of character not to give any indication of what was passing through his mind.

"Go on," he said, in a dull voice, to Oscar—who, absorbed in his story, had not noticed anything.

"Monsieur de Maubreuil and his daughter, Mademoiselle Andrée, were very generous to me; they treated me almost as if I were their own child. My misfortunes seemed to be over. I was clothed, fed and educated like a true son of the family. When Monsieur de Maubreuil, losing his taste for Paris, went to live in Brittany, he took me with him to his château, which people called the Manor of Diamonds. I would doubtless still be there if, unfortunately, an American named Baruch Jorgell hadn't come to live with us..."

"I know that story," the billionaire interjected, brusquely. It was in all the newspapers. What became of you after the death of your protector?"

"I went to live, along with Mademoiselle Andrée, with an old friend of Monsieur de Marbreuil's, Monsieur Bondonnat."

"The famous naturalist?"

"Exactly—but imagine my bad luck! My second protector suffered almost the same fate as the first."

"Murdered?"

"No, but abducted by unknown men in an airplane, without anyone being able to discover what has become of him. It was the same day that the engagement of my master's daughter, Mademoiselle Frédérique, was to be celebrated, and Mademoiselle Andrée's as well. Before the meal, I went for a walk on the heath with my old master. We were taken absolutely unawares, and that was foolish, because there were strangers—Englishmen or Americans—of suspicious appearance on the heath, who had already tried to kill our guard-dog Pistolet."

"That ought to have put you on your guard."

"Undoubtedly, but we were a thousand leagues from suspecting that such a thing was possible. Monsieur Bondonnat was amusing himself watching the dog, to whom I had taught some surprising tricks, when an airplane suddenly landed on the heath like a vulture falling on its prey. Two American got out— the same ones that had tried to kill Pistolet. Brownings in hand, they knocked Monsieur Bondonnat down and threw him into the airplane. I tried to defend my master, but I was knocked down by a blow with a gun-butt, which fractured my skull. Since then, it's been impossible for me to discover what became of Monsieur Bondonnat. He must be still alive; if they had wanted to kill him, that would have been easy to do."

"That's a strange story," the billionaire murmured, pensively. "But what became of you?"

Oscar displayed a large scar striping his forehead. "They didn't kill me, the swine," he said. "I hovered between life and death for a month. Mademoiselle Andrée and Mademoiselle Frédérique cared for me with enormous devotion, better than if they were my true sisters. When I was able to get up, though, when I was regarded as out of danger, what sadness! What heartbreak! Monsieur Bondonnat's villa, once so joyful, was sad and silent, like a house in which someone has died. Mademoiselle Andrée and Mademoiselle Frédérique seemed completely changed. The beautiful botanical garden, left to itself, resembled a thicket; the apparatus that my master had invented to change the seasons at will was rusting on the cliff-top. It was a land of desolation!"

"What about the two young ladies' fiancés?"

"Monsieur Ravenel and Monsieur Paganot, for reasons of propriety, had, in accord with the demoiselles, postponed the marriages until later. They had gone back to Paris, while waiting for Monsieur Bondonnat's fate to be ascertained. It was a situation with no exit. To complete the misfortune, the physician caring for me detected the early signs of tuberculosis. I'd never been very sturdy; that long illness was seriously debilitating..."

Oscar's voice became troubled; one might have thought that he was trying to hold back tears that had risen to his eyes.

"I couldn't stay at the villa any longer. Mademoiselle Frédérique sent me to a sanitarium at Berck-sur-Mer, where I was very well cared for, and every week, the two demoiselles sent me a comforting letter, always accompanied by some gift or money order. I was very glad of what they were doing for me, but I was bored to death. Finally, after two months of treatment, the senior doctor declared me completely cured..."

"And you returned to the villa?"

"Well no. During my long hours of solitude, I'd had time to reflect. What future did I have with two young women plunged into grief? Was it worthy of a man of courage to remain with them, when I had an imperious duty to fulfill? After Monsieur de Maubreuil, Monsieur Bondonnat was my benefactor; I swore to myself that I would find him, to bring him back safe and sound to his daughter."

"That's very noble, my dear chap," murmured the billionaire, sincerely touched, "but you scarcely see to me to be equipped to succeed in that difficult quest."

"That depends, sir. I've already proved to myself that I'm capable of anything. I came to New York without paying for my passage."

"How did you do that?"

"I'd carefully saved up the small sums that my benefactresses had sent me. As soon as I was cured I took the train to Le Havre. The transatlantic liner *Touraine* was about to leave. While prowling around the ship I chanced to meet a young mariner I'd known in Brittany. Thanks to him, I was able to get hired as a galley assistant—or, to be exact, a dish-washer. That was how I got to New York."

"But they wouldn't have let you disembark," said Fred Jorgell, suspiciously, "since all immigrants are required to prove that they have means of support, in the form of a deposit of five hundred dollars."

Oscar Tournesol winked mischievously. "I was warned about that," he said, "so I carefully refrained from saying that I wasn't keeping my employment as dish-washer aboard the liner; I passed myself off as a crewman and was allowed to disembark; that was all I wanted. Once on the streets of New York, where the police don't interfere much, it would have taken a clever man to find me. I set myself up as a shoeshine boy and immediately began my investigations."

"And have you discovered anything?"

"Nothing at all, alas," said the hunchback, with profound discouragement. "I perceive that the task I've undertaken is full of difficulties."

"Are you discouraged already?"

"Not at all! I'll go on until the end. I've sworn to do that, and I promised Mademoiselle Andrée and Mademoiselle Frédérique."

The billionaire remained silent. In spite of all the sympathy that Oscar Tournesol inspired in him, he hesitated between two courses of action. A great conflict took place within him. Finally, in spite of his pride, he came to a decision.

"Do you know who I am?" he asked the hunchback, abruptly.

"No sir—you haven't yet judged it appropriate to tell me your name."

"I'm Fred Jorgell."

Oscar changed color. "Baruch's father?"

"Yes," the billionaire replied, his sadness and secret humiliation hidden behind a mask of glacial indifference, "I'm that wretch's father, and it's necessary that I tell you that, although it will never come up again in our conversations. I no longer have a son—it's as if I never had a son."

Oscar remained silent, utterly nonplussed by that unexpected revelation.

"You've saved my life," Fred Jorgell went on, "and what's more, you're an energetic and honest fellow. That's two reasons for me to be interested in your future; it will only depend on you whether it will be as brilliant as it can be, and furthermore, I promise that I'll do everything in my power to find Monsieur Bondonnat."

Oscar, marveling at the bizarre chain of events that was doubtless about to make the father of Baruch Jorgell into the benefactor of Andrée and Frédérique, dissolved in thanks, but the billionaire cut off his emotional expressions of gratitude.

"That's okay," he said. "It's late—it's time, for you as well as me, to go to bed. Let's talk practically. Here's a five-hundred-dollar bill; it's yours, on account, until I can do something serious for you. Tomorrow, dress a little more decently and present yourself at the offices of the navigation company of which I'm the owner—here's the address. There, you'll be given suitably-paid employment while I reflect on the best means to employ to find Monsieur Bondonnat. Is that agreeable?"

"Very. It's more than I would have dared to hope for."

"We can go, then. You'll climb into a car with me, and I'll drop you at the door of some decent hotel."

Fred Jorgell threw a banknote to the waiter and, without paying any heed to the malign smiles that strayed over the lips of some of the diners at the sight of his strange companion, he went out of Delmonico's and climbed into a cab.

Half an hour later, Oscar Tournesol, who had not yet recovered from the night's adventures, was installed in a comfortable room at the Preston Hotel—electricity, central heating, elevator, telephone, etc. A word from Fred Jorgell had changed the arrogant expression of the hotel manager, who was initially reluctant to admit such an ill-clad client, into obsequious salutations.

Before going to bed, the hunchback leaned on the balcony of his room for a few moments, which overlooked the completely deserted Thirty-third Avenue.

At that moment, an automobile came down the avenue at high speed. By the light of the electric streetlights, Oscar clearly distinguished three individuals who, judging by the vivacity of their gestures, were plunged into the most animated argument.

Suddenly, he uttered a cry of surprise.

In one of the three individuals, he had just recognized a man whose physiognomy was indelibly engraved in his memory: the man who had wounded him, almost mortally, with a blow from the butt of his revolver on the Breton heath; the man who had wanted to kill the dog who could read; one of the three bandits who had cooperated in the abduction of Monsieur Bondonnat by airplane.

Oscar would have liked to launch himself in pursuit and have him arrested, but the automobile had already disappeared like a nocturnal meteor, and its dazzling headlights were no more than little patches of light, almost effaced already at the far end of the immense avenue.

III. To New York

Since Monsieur Bondonnat's disappearance, the magnificent gardens that he had created at Kérity-sur-Mer had almost reverted to the lamentable state of uncultivated land. In the midst of that sadness and abandonment that possessed the villa, once so joyful, two young women were watching the days go by in despair and in tears.

Frédérique and Andrée, by virtue of a kind of superstition, had not wanted to leave the residence where misfortune had fallen upon them at the very moment when a happy future was opening up before them. They had both confined themselves to a profound retreat. They did not see anyone except their fiancés, the engineer Antoine Paganot and the naturalist Roger Ravenel, who made every effort to console them and to attenuate their immense dolor as much as possible.

That day, the weather was somber; the sky, veiled with large funereal clouds and striped by fine rain, added its own melancholy to the sadness of Frédérique and Andrée.

"It seems to me," murmured Mademoiselle de Maubreuil, "that my life is over; that, in spite of my fiancé's love, I shall never be happy. The death of my father, so cruelly murdered, has struck me a blow from which I shall never recover. I've tried to forget, but I can't. And the disappearance of my poor dear guardian has rendered my pain even more acute. Fortunately, dear Frédérique, misfortune has not afflicted you so gravely; you can still hope to see your father again someday."

"I no longer dare believe that. I even strive not to think about it any longer, for if I think about it a little, I ask myself, with anguish, whether my father has suffered the same fate as yours."

"Don't think that. Don't entertain black ideas." After a moment's silence, the young woman added: "Haven't I told you that every Saturday, as before. I'm tormented by a nightmare? I watch the scene of the murder, I see that wretch Baruch again. Do you know what I think? It's that I'll only be free of these frightful apparitions when the murderer..."

"Let not talk about that any longer. We've treated that terrible topic of conversation too often, and I've said everything I have to say about it. Do you know what I was thinking jut now?"

"I'll wager that you were thinking about Oscar."

"You're not mistaken. Where is the poor boy at present? Weak and ill, without any money, he had the courage to go forth alone to search for my father."

"Perhaps he'll find him. I have a conviction, my dear Frédérique, that if Monsieur Bondonnat is being held prisoner, it's not to do him harm. Someone doubtless is doubtless trying to steal his discoveries. I've always thought so."

"For me, there's not a shadow of doubt about it, but there will come a day when all will be revealed. Monsieur Paganot and Monsieur Ravenel are familiar with my father's endeavors. When the day comes when someone tries to utilize one of his discoveries, they'll know."

"Yes, that's true, but a lot of time might pass between now and then."

A violent ringing of the doorbell snatched the two friends from their melancholy reflections. From the window close to where they were sitting they perceived Benjamin, the village postman, who was sliding a letter into the box fitted to the tall wrought iron gate that was some distance in front of the main building of the villa.

Frédérique observed immediately that the envelope bore a New York postmark, and Andrée exclaimed that it must be a letter from Oscar.

She was not mistaken. The missive was from the little hunchback, and Frédérique read it aloud.

Mesdemoiselles,

Excuse me for having taken so long to write to you, but a host of more or less bizarre adventures have happened to me recently, some of which have been very fortunate. At any rate, I'm very well and I've become the protégé of a rich American, whose life I had the good luck to save while rolling around the land of billionaires and bandits.

(At this point Oscar gave a detailed account of the manner in which he had saved Fred Jorgell from death, although, for reasons that are easy to understand, he did not name the American.)

The only thing that annoys me, he continued, *is not having any good news to give you on the subject of Monsieur Bondonnat. I ought, however, to let you know two interesting facts.*

The first is that my employer, the billionaire, has promised to mount a serious search throughout America, The second is that I believe that I recognized, in an automobile that was passing by at high speed, the authors of the abduction that had plunged us all into desolation.

The police here are very active—on condition, of course, that one pays them well—and with luck, we shall soon be on the trail of the bandit of the bandits who have caused you so much chagrin.

To conclude, it would perhaps be good if you were to decide to make the voyage to New York and come to join me here, in the company of Messieurs Ravenel and Paganot.

The letter was terminated by various indications relating to the times of trains and liners, and the hotel at which the valiant hunchback suggested that his friends stay when they landed in America.

"Oscar's right," said Mademoiselle de Maubreuil. "We don't have the right to hesitate any longer."

"Yes, we ought to go," added Frédérique, with an energetic gesture. "Oscar has set us an example, and our duty is clear. It's not up to that poor hunchback, devoted as he is, to go in search of my father alone; it's my job."

"And mine, as your best friend and adoptive sister; I ought to be at your side ad to share the dangers and fatigues of your voyage."

"But wouldn't it be as well to warn those we love?" said Frédérique, with a melancholy smile. "We can't decide anything before asking their advice."

"You're right," said Andrée, throwing a mantle over her shoulders. "I'll run to find Monsieur Paganot at the Tête-de-Pie inn. He certainly won't have gone out yet. I'll leave it to you to write the letter to Oscar and tell Monsieur Ravenel about our determination; he won't be long in coming, as he does every day."

After an affectionate kiss, the two young women parted.

Frédérique did not have long to wait. Scarcely a quarter of an hour had gone by before the naturalist appeared at the gate, carrying a bunch of wild flowers that he had brought for his fiancée, as he was accustomed to do every morning.

"Well, my darling," he said, "have you some good news to tell me?"

"No, Roger, not yet. However, I've received a letter from Oscar. Read it, and tell me what you think."

The naturalist scanned the missive at a glance, but lingered at greater length over the final paragraph.

"Frédérique," he murmured, "I love you so much that all my future happiness must come from you. I'm only happy when you're smiling. I'll do anything you wish. Let's go search for your father, since that's your wish."

In a surge of enthusiasm, he drew the young woman on to the terrace that overlooked the sea. Extending his arm toward the distant horizon, he said: "That's where we'll go! It's out there that we'll find your father; it's out there that we'll be able to love one another without any afterthought, without sadness."

"Yes, it's out there," murmured another voice, behind them. It was that of the engineer Paganot, who had arrived in company with Andrée. "The die is cast," he said. "We'll leave for New York. A secret voice tells me that we're awaited there with impatience."

A profound emotion had taken hold of the two young women. They contemplated their fiancés with ecstatic gazes. How handsome they seemed, the two young men, in the enthusiasm of devotion! Andrée and Frédérique felt that they were truly beloved. Their fiancés could not have even them greater evidence of attachment than to abandon their work, their studies and their homeland in this fashion, in order to go with them to a foreign land, where they might perhaps be exposed to many dangers.

Paganot had already made a number of transatlantic trips. He knew the best means of locomotion and the least expensive tariffs. He was the one who took charge of drawing up a list of expenses and the itinerary of the voyage.

Thanks to information extracted from directories and timetables, they decided that the simplest thing would be to leave for Paris the next day, where they would spend a day making the purchases indispensable for a long journey.

Andrée and Frédérique went to bed late that evening. Before quitting the family home, they wanted to put the objects that were most dear to them and their most precious souvenirs in order; then it was necessary to pack their trunks. Although very simplified, the luggage was still rather voluminous.

Early the next morning, they set out in quest of a god carrier and went to see a former servant of Monsieur Bondonnat's, Eric Marsouan, whom they asked to take care of the dwelling they were about to leave during their absence.

At noon, everyone met up at the villa, where the luggage was loaded on to a truck that would take it to the nearest railway station, and two hours later, the four travelers, installed in a first class carriage, were heading for Paris, from which they would embark on the transatlantic train for Cherbourg.

The journey from Paris to Cherbourg was uneventful, and the four young people took their places in the cabins they had reserved telegraphically aboard the *Kaiser Wilhelm*, which soon emerged from the harbor and headed for the open sea.

The crossing was rather painful for the young women, to whom seasickness showed no mercy, and when, six days later, they set foot on the quays of New York, they were so pale that their fiancés were alarmed—but they quickly recovered their color.

Oscar Tournesol, who had come to meet them, and took charge of guiding them to the Preston Hotel, only found that chagrin had caused them to grow thinner.

Since he had been in America, the hunchback had not experienced an emotion as acute as that which the arrival of his friends caused him.

"I told you to come to the Preston Hotel because it's an establishment with which I'm familiar, and I know that you'll be comfortable there."

In spite of Oscar's assurances, the four French people were slightly surprised by the organization of the American hotel. At the entrance door, a lady installed in a glass-fronted cage gave each of them a piece of cardboard on which a number—that of the room—was inscribed. An electric elevator deposited them at the very threshold of their rooms, all four of which were on the same corridor.

What surprised the visitors most was perceiving in each of the rooms an immense enameled dial placed directly above the fireplace opposite the window; in its center was a nickel lever activating a long gilded needle. They were then able to read, instead of hours, on that strange disk, which scintillated in the electric light, words repeated in several languages indicating everything of which they might have need, such as wax, brush, comb, hot water, cold water, coffee, chocolate, tea, masseur, physician, midwife, chicken, cutlet, dinner, breakfast, shower, slippers, waiter, chambermaid, etc. It was sufficient to place the needle over the word designating the desired object to be served with marvelous rapidity.

Andrée and Frédérique, who both being a little fearful, had decided to occupy the same room, pivoted the needle in order to order dinner. They were served in a matter of minutes; the meal was copious and delicate, but the physiognomy of the two waiters who served them seemed extremely uncongenial, not to say disquieting. At one moment, when she held out her plate to one of them, Andrée shivered, intimidated by the effrontery of two eyes as yellow as a cat's, and she thought she detected a malicious smile on the man's lips.

For her part, Frédérique had the same impression.

Once the table was cleared, the two young women talked about the impression they had felt.

"Did you notice, Frédérique, their criminal appearance. I don't know whether it's because I'm not yet used to the people of this country, but that individual frightened me. He seemed to be threatening me, as if he wanted to do me harm."

"My poor Andrée, I'm as anxious as you are. This hotel is very luxurious, but I don't feel at ease here. I might be wrong, but those two waiters—one in particular—have the faces of bandits."

"Come on, don't worry," said Andrée. "After all, why should anyone threaten us or have anything against us? We've scarcely arrived, and no one knows us."

"Yes, we must be reasonable. Let's not forget that we have a sacred duty to fulfill. We don't have the right to lack courage. Besides which, Oscar told us that the establishment is honorable. Let's go to bed. We need rest; tomorrow, we set out on campaign."

The two young women went to bed and slept peacefully in spite of their fears. That was the first night they spent on American soil.

Their instinct, however, was not mistaken. The two waiters who had frightened them so much were, in fact, agents of the Red Hand—but the bad impression they had made dissipated during the following days. The two young women were entirely devoted to the pleasure of getting to know the New World, which bore no resemblance at all to Europe.

After having made the indispensable visits to the French consulate and the most notable people in the French colony, the four young people set about collecting information that might facilitate their task, but their research was in vain. The investigation they were making to locate Monsieur Bondonnat did not advance by a single step, in spite of the zeal deployed by Oscar Tournesol.

"Do you know what we ought to do?" the hunchback said one day to Frédérique. "We ought to go to the madhouse where Baruch is imprisoned."

269

"No," the young woman murmured, "that's impossible."

"Why?"

"I have a horror of that wretch."

"You have to overcome your repugnance. You know what mystery surrounded the trial, and even the arrest of the murderer. No one has ever been able to clarify that sinister affair. I'm sure that there must be a correlation between the two events—Monsieur de Maubreuil's murder and his friend's disappearance."

"That's also Andrée's opinion," murmured Frédérique, becoming thoughtful.

"I'm sure," said Oscar, "that Baruch, whether he's completely mad or whether he retains a few glimmers of reason, will be able to give us precious clues."

"Perhaps you're right."

"I'm sure that I'm right, and I'll wager that Monsieur Paganot and Monsieur Ravenel, if they were consulted, would think the same."

Oscar Tournesol was not mistaken; the engineer and his friend thought the idea excellent, and it was decided that everyone would go to the Lunatic Asylum at Greenaway, where Baruch was detained.

IV. A Sensational Arrest

Beneath his inoffensive and good-natured appearance, the director of the Lunatic Asylum was a veritable bandit. The association of the Red Hand, which had affiliates in the highest strata of American society had in him the most devoted of servants and the most faithful of agents.

Closely linked to Dr. Cornelius, who was in control of the Lunatic Asylum's fortunes, Johnson was, however, unaware that the sculptor of human flesh was the leader of the Lords of the Red Hand and the grand master of the terrible association. Cornelius had known what he was doing when he had abandoned the pseudo-Baruch—which is to say, Joe Dorgan—in a street in New York. He knew that the unfortunate would end up in the establishment run by Dr. Johnson and that there, under the eyes of such a chief, he would certainly be well-guarded. And, indeed, under the pretext of experimentation, it was Cornelius who directed the patient's treatment himself, in a manner that is easily imaginable.

That day, Dr. Johnson was in a very bad mood. A rather disagreeable adventure had befallen him, and he could foresee that it might cause him a host of troubles.

In return for a substantial wad of banknotes, he had consented to receive at the Lunatic Asylum a rich businessman from Chicago, Mr. Hirchmann, whose heirs wanted to get rid of him. The businessman had died two months later, but, unfortunately for Dr. Johnson, troublesome rumors had soon begun to circulate regarding that strange and excessively rapid decease. There was talk of sequestration and murder, and the newspapers had announced that the police were going to investigate the affair.

The director was in the process of reflecting on the best course of action to adopt in such an awkward circumstance when someone knocked on his study door. He went to pen it and found himself confronted by one of the establishment's overseers, a former convict who was, like his master, affiliated to the Red Hand.

"What is it, Stop?" asked Dr. Johnson. "Why are you disturbing me at such an hour?"

"Excuse me, sir. I only wanted to tell you that Baruch Jorgell, the patient on whom we were asked to keep a special watch, has been giving manifest signs of logic and common sense since yesterday."

"That's very singular," murmured Dr. Johnson, becoming pensive.

"Yes. By taking a gentle approach, I've succeeded in getting him to talk, and among the things he said, one in particular struck me: 'Whatever the difficulties are against which I have to struggle, and whatever it costs, I'll get out of this infernal prison.'"

271

"He said that?"

"Yes, sir. You can easily make sure for yourself."

"Yes—that's interesting."

Dr. Johnson had already risen to his feet when the door gave passage to Dr. Cornelius Kramm, who had come precisely to seek information as to the patient's condition. The two physicians exchanged a cordial handshake.

"You know," said Johnson, eventually, "the care you're lavishing on one of our inmates, the famous Baruch Jorgell, seems to be on the point of being crowned by success."

Cornelius started. "You don't say!" he said. "I'm surprised by that."

"It's as I have the pleasure of telling you. Baruch is well on the way to recovery—isn't that so, Stop?"

The warder replied to his employer's question with an affirmative nod.

Cornelius' ordinarily pale face became even paler, but he did not allow any anxiety to show, and it was in a tranquil voice that he replied: "What you say is very interesting. I'll go to make sure of the condition of our patient myself."

"As you wish. Would you like me to accompany you?"

"There's no need. Until later, my dear colleague."

"Until later, my dear master."

Cornelius, who knew every inch of the establishment, had no need of any guide to reach the large and well-illuminated room occupied by his victim. Sitting by the window with his head in his hands, Joe seemed to be plunged in profound reflection. He was making desperate efforts to reconnect the uninterrupted chain of his ideas and reasoning. He greeted Cornelius, to whose visits he was accustomed, politely.

"Well, how are you doing?" asked the sculptor of human flesh, in a tone full of benevolence.

"Much better, sir. It seems to me that my memory is slowly disengaging from a fog. I've succeeded, with a great deal of effort, in remembering certain facts."

"What, for example?" asked Cornelius, not without a slight emotion.

"I recall quite clearing having taken part in a bloody battle with bandits. Then again, I can clearly remember my brother and my father—it's just the names that I can't succeed in putting to them."

"That will come, but you mustn't tire yourself out. Make as little effort as possible. I can see today that your condition is obviously better. You're conscious that you've lost your memory—that's already a big step."

"Yes, and I'm even conscious, quite clearly, of the very slow but progressive and regular return of that vanished memory." And he added, with a naivety that drew a nervous snigger from Cornelius: "I'm sure that if you told me my name, and those of my parents, and if you told me in what circumstances I came to be here, it would focus my ideas and hasten my complete recovery."

"I shall refrain from giving you that information," the sculptor of human flesh, raising a finger in a doctoral manner. "It's indispensable that it's your own brain that accomplishes that mnemotechnical reconstitution on its own; that's a necessary effort."

"While bemusing his victim with all sorts of specious reasoning, Cornelius reflected. A violent conflict was taking place within him. He observed, to his great humiliation, that the delicate operation he had carried out on Joe Dorgan's brain had only succeeded incompletely, and that, if things were left to follow their natural course, the patient would not take long to recover his memory along with his reason. The destroyed cells were being reconstituted, the disjointed circumvolutions reconnecting; a cure was imminent.

We'll have to get rid of him, he thought—but then he had second thoughts, rebelling against the idea. *No*, he went on. *Joe is my masterpiece, I'm sure. I don't want to destroy him! Besides which, isn't he the living proof I'm keeping of Baruch's culpability, in case he takes it into his head to betray the Red Hand? No, decidedly, it's necessary not to kill him—but it's necessary to prevent the cure, and that's easy.*

While talking to himself, Cornelius groped in the pocket of his overcoat for a case that contained a Pravaz syringe.

"My dear friend," he said to Joe in his most cordial tone, "I've come today precisely to give you an injection of a cephalic serum that will produce a rapid improvement in your condition."

"Oh, if that were true!"

"Be certain of it. You've been able to observe for yourself the efficacy of my treatment."

Cornelius had opened the case and, after having filled the syringe with a colorless liquid contained in a phial, he fitted a new needle to the instrument and then asked Joe to lean his head forward slightly.

"In order for the injection to be effective," he said, "it has to be made behind the ear."

The young man obeyed, and bore the slight pain for the injection courageously.

"There, that's done," Cornelius murmured, with a sardonic laugh. "Now, I'll answer for the result."

Joe did not say a single word in reply. The effect of the serum—or, rather, the poison—had been immediate. Already, the patient's eyes had become vague and haggard, and he was tilting his head wearily. Then he put his hands to his forehead with a bewildered gesture, and collapsed on his bed, uttering a stifled sigh.

"Good," said Cornelius. "There's someone who'll leave us tranquil for a long time, I hope."

He wiped the tip of the syringe, carefully replaced it in its case, and left the room at a tranquil pace in order to rejoin the director, who as waiting for him in his study.

After some hesitation, Dr. Johnson, although he was unaware that Dr. Cornelius was part of the Red Hand, confided to him what he referred to as his imprudence in the matter of the sequestration and murder of the unfortunate Hirchmann.

The two bandits were able to understand one another readily. Cornelius reassured Johnson, suggested what he ought to say in the case of an investigation, and assured him of his valuable protection.

The director of the Lunatic Asylum was beginning to breathe more easily when the sudden sound of shouting voices caused him to leap to his feet and run to the door.

"Open up in the name of the law—and no one is to leave!"

Those words were still echoing when the man who had pronounced them—who was none other than Mr. Steffel, the New York Police Chief—irrupted into the room, followed by a troop of detectives armed to the teeth.

He marched straight up to Dr. Johnson, who had gone as white as a sheet. "Sir," he said, rudely, "a complaint has been made against you. You are accused of having illegally sequestered and subsequently murdered the honorable Dr. Hirchmann, former fur trader. I arrest you in the name of the law."

Three shots rang out. Two bullets whistled past Mr. Steffel's ears and the third went through the leather cap of a policeman. It was Johnson who had just made use of his Browning and was trying to get to the door—but several vigorous hands had taken hold of him and he was reduced to impotence in no time.

Cornelius, who had not lost his composure for a moment, went to the prisoner. "Dr. Johnson," he said, "If the accusation made against you is true, you have brought shame on our profession." Confronted by Johnson's fearful expression, however, he immediately added in a softer tone: "However, the fact that you've been arrested doesn't mean that you're guilty. These gentlemen will admit themselves that in New York, as in Paris or London, the law isn't always infallible. If you're innocent, as I hope, you were quite wrong to offer resistance to the agents of authority."

Cornelius went to the police chief, bowed to him and said: "My compliments, Mr. Steffel. The name of Dr. Cornelius Kramm is doubtless not unknown to you."

"Indeed, no. I've read several interesting pamphlets he's written, including *The Rational Esthetics of the Human Body*."

"Well, you have before you Dr. Kramm in person."

The physician handed his card to the policeman, who bowed respectfully, apologizing for not having recognized him sooner, for he had often seen his picture in the newspapers.

Then, going back to the director of the Lunatic Asylum, who cut a pitiful figure between two policemen, Cornelius whispered in his ear "Be discreet, and I'll do my best to get you out of this." Aloud, he said: "My dear colleague, I can't believe that you're guilty. We scientists have preoccupations that are too noble to allow us to be agitated by the paltry passions that lead common men to crime. Here's my hand—I offer it to you without hesitation, for I believe you to be innocent."

He gratified Johnson with a vigorous handshake, under cover of which he slipped him a small phial, which the director of the Lunatic Asylum dexterously caused to vanish into one of his pockets.

Then Cornelius drew away tranquilly, after having taken his leave of Mr. Steffel.

As he was going through the asylum's visitors' room, he was approached by a young man who had detached himself from a group that included two young women in mourning.

"We've come from France," said the visitor, who was none other than Antoine Paganot, accompanied by Roger Ravenel, Mademoiselle de Maubreuil and the naturalist's daughter, "and we'd like to see, if it's possible at this time, one of the unfortunates incarcerated here, Baruch Jorgell."

Cornelius stated slightly on hearing that name, and, having darted a glance at the people surrounding him, soon deduced what was going on. He realized that he was dealing with relatives and friends of Monsieur Bondonnat. With lightning rapidity, he realized the danger of a visit to Joe, and in order to prevent that, he said, coldly: "I'm the director of the asylum. Baruch is permanently deprived of reason. He has become very dangerous, and I cannot permit any visit." Then he drew away, leaving the four young people, who had founded a good deal of hope on the interview, in consternation.

Cornelius took his seat in the automobile that was waiting for him at the fate of the asylum and ordered his laboratory assistant Leonello, who was serving as his chauffeur that day, to take him home. Suddenly, however, he changed his mind and took Leonello's place.

"I'll drive myself," he said. "Do you see those people coming out of the asylum?" He pointed at the two young women and their companions. "Follow them. It's absolutely necessary that you find out where they're staying."

The Italian bowed respectfully, while Cornelius set off at top speed, heading for the nearest telephone booth.

V. The Council of the Lords

On the evening of the day when the dramatic arrest at the Lunatic Asylum had taken place, Dr. Cornelius waited with feverish anticipation for his brother and the fake Joe Dorgan—the sinister Baruch—whom he had summoned by telephone.

The three of them formed the directive council of the Red Hand. It was necessary that on the eve of engaging in a perilous combat, at the moment when redoubtable adversaries were emerging from all directions, the cynical trio should hold a meeting.

Several discreet raps on the door announced the arrival of those he was expecting.

"Well," said Fritz, who came in first, "it appears that the director of the Lunatic Asylum has been arrested and is under lock and key?"

"Yes, several hours ago."

"Do they have proof of his guilt, then?" said Baruch, appearing in his turn. "He won't, I suppose, commit any indiscretion? One never knows what a man might say when he's grilled by the police."

"The situation might get complicated," Fritz added, "and the Red Hand might be brought into it at any moment."

"That affair," said Cornelius, "isn't the only cause of the urgent summons you received. If you think the Dr, Jonson will spill the beans, you're mistaken. Sure as he is of our support—which I promised him in the presence of Mr. Steffel, the police chief—he'll keep quiet about the Red Hand, whatever means the police use to make him talk."

"Obviously," Fritz said. "Johnson isn't an imbecile."

"He's got himself pinched, though," said Baruch, "And that doesn't indicate any great intellectual capacity on his part."

"Let's leave Johnson aside for a moment," said Cornelius. "Once again, that isn't the direction from which I can see danger coming. It's necessary, to have an exact idea of the situation, to get into a luxury hotel in the center of New York, in which Fred Jorgell is a major shareholder."

"The Preston Hotel?"

"That's right."

"Is my father up to his old tricks again?"

"No, not him, the dear fellow. His own business affairs are keeping him too busy to think about ours."

"Well then?"

"Well, there are four new guests in that hotel whose mere presence in New York must have some significance for us. As in the song, they're birds that come from France."

"From France?"

"The charming village where you left rather bloody memories in a certain manor."

"Mademoiselle de Maubreuil and her fiancé are here?"

"Yes; they've crossed the Atlantic in order to search for the excellent Monsieur Bondonnat."

"And they're not alone?" exclaimed Fritz, who was beginning to experience a slight anxiety.

"As you can imagine, the naturalist's daughter has accompanied her friend, and as the demoiselles can't travel without protectors, needless to say, Monsieur Ravenel wouldn't allow Monsieur Paganot and his lady friends leave without him."

"Which raises the number of our enemies to four," said Baruch.

"That makes one more than there are of us," added Fritz Kramm, philosophically.

"Oh, they're young people who are prompt to get down to work. Having arrived yesterday on the *Kaiser Wilhelm*, they've already crossed the threshold of the Lunatic Asylum."

"They've seen the madman?" said Baruch, his eyes opening wide with anxiety.

"No, not yet."

"So much the better—one never knows, with madmen, what might happen."

"In truth, you're right—one never knows. The proof is that as recently as this morning, our lunatic was beginning to reason in a rather sane manner."

"He's recovered his reason?"

"Don't use the present tense, but he might yet. Anyway, I gave him an anesthetic and stupefying injection, which will rid us of him for a long time, I guarantee."

"Admirable, my dear fellow."

"Yes, Cornelius, I admire you too—which doesn't prevent me from feeling rather ill at ease at present in the new envelope you've so graciously granted me."

"Know, Baruch, that one ought never feel ill at ease in a epidermis offered by the mysterious Dr. Cornelius. My science has got rid of the one that was an obstacle to us, and my science will liberate you this very day from the four pawns that are barring the route we want to follow in the great game of chess in which we've engaged."

"And you have the ability to get rid of these troublesome individuals without too much inconvenience?" asked the younger Kramm brother.

Getting up slowly from the seat he occupied, the chief of the Lords of the Red Hand went to a mahogany cupboard in which, behind the glass panels, bottles, retorts, glass syringes and various objects designed for uncertain purposes could be seen. The light door of the cupboard grated slightly. The doctor up his hand through the gap and took hold of an object that he came to show to his accomplices.

"Look, gentlemen," he said. "This is the simple apparatus that will help us clear the road to success."

"It's just a vaporizer," said Baruch.

"Indeed, it's merely a kind of bicycle pump. I don't, however, advise you to make use of it personally."

"From a master like you, it's necessary to expect anything."

"Even death, or at least sleep."

"It's a soporific?"

"Yes, gentlemen—from this pointed metal nozzle, whose interior walls are lined with glass, a kind of semi-sleep emerges at will—sleep or death. You operate this lever, and immediately, those who breath the gas emitted by the tube slowly fall asleep, and, according to the dose, will either eventually wake up, or not."

"And may one know what the strange product in with which the tube is filled?"

"It's simply chloronal."[18]

As if he were giving a lecture at the Faculty, Dr. Cornelius furnished all the desirable explanations relative to that dangerous product. He explained the manufacture of the liquid, gave extensive details regarding the calculation of dosage and the different methods employed for increasing its efficacy, and ended up by saying that it was purely and simply a powerful successor of chloroform.

"You see," he concluded, "It's chloroform reduced to its optimum state of volatility, chloroform from which it has been possible to remove the penetrating and revealing odor. I have no need to explain its applications to you. You've even guessed that tonight, the Preston Hotel will receive a visit from men devoted to the Red Hand, who will introduce the metallic nozzle of this minuscule apparatus through the keyholes. When one is in the presence of four adversaries, a weapon of quadruple efficiency is required.

"But how are they going to get into the hotel?" Baruch asked.

"As one gets into a house whose doors are opened to you."

At that moment the door opened and Leonello came toward his masters. "I've just seen Burman and Gelstone at the Preston Hotel," he said. "They've told me that everything is ready, but it's necessary to be cautious, for the young women they were serving in their rooms decided that they didn't like the look of them and asked to be served by someone else."

"These slaves of the Red Hand are stupid!" exclaimed Cornelius, striking the table with his fist. They're signally maladroit, and they'll be punished for

---

[18] Le Rouge improvised this term; he could not know that it would subsequently be reinvented for application to a kind of disinfectant.

their incompetence within twenty-four hours. Go to the place immediately, Leonello, and gather all the useful information you can about the situation. The scientist Bondonnat is ours; no one is going to steal him from us. The Red Hand, which extends its claws over the best part of America, won't succumb to the groping of a handful of Frenchmen."

The doctor, generally so calm and measured in his enthusiasm, had taken on a wild and excited expression, the sight of which caused a certain anxiety to his listeners, Striding back and forth in the laboratory, one might have thought him a terrorist conspirator making a speech.

"The Red Hand," he proclaimed, "is your entire life and my entire life. No audacious individual will stand up against it with impunity. The Red Hand has built its fortune on blood; the Red Hand will continue to create life and death, according to my will. Let everyone be ready this evening. Do you hear, Fritz and Baruch? It isn't a wisp of straw that will divert the great river of gold on which we're sailing to conquer the world."

Gradually, Dr. Cornelius calmed down and recovered his composure. He shook his companions' hands successively and left them, saying: "This evening will be decisive. Let's be equal to our task..."

VI. The Knights of Chloroform

Since the arrival in New York of Andrée de Marbreuil, Frédérique and the young women's fiancés, Oscar Tournesol's heart had been swimming in joy. It had been a long time since the hunchback had felt as happy. He found himself reunited with the people who constituted his true—or, to put it better, his only—family, and he was firmly persuaded that Monsieur Bondonnat was sure to be located and liberated soon.

That evening, Andrée and Frédérique had gone to bed early, still not completely recovered from the fatigue of a long voyage. The engineer Paganot and the naturalist Ravenel had not taken long to retire to their rooms in their turn.

Oscar did not feel at all sleepy; he had the idea of going to get some fresh air on the terrace of the hotel, which, without being as sumptuously fitted out as that of the Grizzly Cub, was decorated with orange-trees and laurels in pots, in the shade of which garden benches had been disposed.

Disdaining the use of the elevators, the hunchback went up the three flights of stairs that separated him from the terrace and soon found himself in the aerial garden, which was utterly deserted.

He installed himself on a bench and began tranquilly to contemplate the panorama of the giant city.

He had only been there five minutes when he heard the elevator door open.

"Who can be coming here at this hour?" he wondered, anxiously.

Unthinkingly, he hid behind a large pot in which a laurier-rose was planted and remained still. Two men entirely dressed in white had come out of the elevator; they were doubtless hotel employees, bell-boys or stewards.

"No one about," said one of them. "We can talk freely.

"At this hour, unless it's very hot, there's not so much as a cat on the terrace; all the guests are in bed."

Without relying, the other darted a circumspect glance around in order to reassure himself. "No," he said in his turn, "there's no one here. Anyway, I've been watching the elevator; no one's come up for an hour. Everyone's asleep."

"The Frenchies too?"

"Yes, the lights went out in their rooms some time ago."

Oscar pricked up his ears; he knew that there were no other French people in the hotel than the two young women, their fiancés and himself. What interest could the two hotel employees have in whether the French guests were asleep or not?

"Is the hunchback asleep too?" asked the first speaker.

"Oh yes, he must be asleep—there's no light in his room and I heard him wish the others good night. They're all at home; I think it's a good time."

"It's this evening then?" said the other, lowering his voice.

"Yes, Tom, I've received instructions from the Lords of the Red Hand, and the instrument is fully loaded."

Now, Oscar was transfixed; he knew that he was in the presence of two bandits in the process of hatching some sinister plot against his dearest friends and himself. At the risk of being discovered, he advanced his head slightly out of his hiding place, to see what kind of fully-loaded instrument the two rogues were examining in the moonlight.

To his great surprise, he saw a metallic apparatus similar to a bicycle pump, terminated at one end by a wooden handle at and the other by a sharp nozzle.

"You see," explained the one addressed as Tom to his accomplice, "it's simple and easy to handle. This is the best was of making use of it: first you make sure that there's no light on in the room; you listen, if necessary, to make sure that the people are asleep; then you introduce the nozzle, which is pierced by a number of little holes, like the head of a watering-can, into the keyhole; then you pump gently, until the lack of resistance tells you that the tube is empty."

"And that's all?"

"That's sufficient. The tube is loaded with a kind of poison that ends those who breathe it to sleep permanently; it has no odor and leaves no trace."

"That's marvelous. And this is why they call us the Knights of Chloroform?"

"Yes, with the difference that this is much superior to the chloroform that has been used until now, which has a very strong odor without taking effect so rapidly. It appears that it's an invention of the Red Hand's scientists." And he added, in a tone penetrated with respect: "They're powerful people; it's better to be with them than against them."

"For sure. Then all the Frenchies are for it?"

"No, just the two young women…those are the orders. The Red Hand wants the chambers to give the appearance of having been robbed, of course, all the baggage searched, to make it look like an ordinary robbery."

The two bandits continued their conversation for some time, organizing in advance the slightest details of the crime they were about to commit, like men accustomed to such expeditions. It was thus that Oscar learned that, as soon as their crime was complete, they would leave the hotel and go to an auto that was waiting for them, ready for any eventuality, in a neighboring street.

Behind the pot, the hunchback, more dead than alive, wondered what he could do to prevent the murders. He thought of jumping the bandits unexpectedly and frightening them, but reflected that he had no weapon, and the two scoundrels were Herculean in stature, Poor Oscar was prey to an inexpressible anguish; his stomach was constricted and he was choking. Every second that went by seemed as long as a century

Finally, the two affiliates of the Red Hand, whose plan was now settled, installed themselves placidly in the elevator. They had scarcely disappeared when Oscar launched himself out of his hiding place and ran to the door to the stairs.

He uttered an exclamation of rage and despair; the door was locked. Either the bandits had heard a noise, or it was a simple measure of prudence on their part, but the brutal fact was there. While Andrée and Frédérique were being murdered, the adolescent would be forced to remain on the terrace, where no one could hear his cries for help.

"What can I do?" he cried, furiously, digging his fingernails into his flesh until he drew blood. "I ought to have let myself get killed rather than let those wretches go down. I have to find a means of raising the alarm."

Suddenly, an idea dawned in his feverish brain. He had just perceived, in the gloom, the gray mass of a twill awning under which the guests of the hotel could shelter from the ardor of the sun. In the blink of an eye, he took possession of the ropes that served to hold up the awning. He knotted them together and lengthened the improvised cable further with the aid of a long strip of twill which he succeeded in tearing off.

Without wanting to think for an instant about the vertiginous height at which it was located, he attached his cable to the balustrade of the terrace.

He knew that the rooms situated three floors below were equipped with spacious balconies, and his plan, bold to the point of insensate temerity, was to slide down to one of those balconies, at the risk of breaking his neck twenty times over.

Once on the balcony, he thought, *I'll knock on the window and whoever is in the room will come to let me in! The worst that can happen is that I'll be mistaken for a malefactor myself and stop a couple of bullets. Too bad—I don't have any choice.*

Breathless with anxiety, a trembling lest he arrived too late, Oscar tested the solidity of the knot attacking his cable to the balustrade one last time, and let himself slide down, not without cruelly grazing his hands and thighs. Finally, he set foot on a balcony.

As long as the room's occupied! he thought, gripped by anxiety. *It would be the worst of luck to accomplish such a feat only to reach an empty room!*

Fortunately, the shutters were not closed. He rapped rudely on the glass. The occupant of the room, doubtless not caring for a visit at that hour, especially given that the visit was arriving via the window, protested energetically and, rapidly switching on the electric light, appeared to Oscar in underpants and a night-shirt, with a Browning in his hand.

Oscar uttered a cry of joy; his lucky star had not abandoned him entirely. As the summarily-clad guest came forward, he recognized Antoine Paganot, Mademoiselle de Maubreuil's fiancé.

At the sight of Oscar, the engineer manifested extreme surprise, but, understanding from the hunchback's imperious gestures that something extraordinary was happening, he hastened to open the window

"What's the matter?" he demanded, as soon as Oscar was in the room.

"Quickly, give me a revolver—any weapon whatsoever! Hurry—they're in the process of killing Mademoiselle Andrée and her friend."

In three rapid sentences he explained the situation to the engineer, whose face covered in cold sweat. An instant later they launched themselves into the corridor, Brownings in hand, shouting for help with all the force of their lungs.

Disturbed in the middle of their criminal operation, the two bandits fired their revolvers at random, ran to the elevator and disappeared.

Already, at the noise of the cries and the gunshots, doors were opening and the guests of the Preston Hotel appeared, snatched abruptly from sleep, some of them furious and other terrified. Roger Ravenel, Frédérique's fiancé, immediately ran toward Oscar, whose voice he had recognized, and the latter quickly brought him up to date.

"Look," he said, in a voice breathless with emotion, showing him the bizarre instrument, reminiscent of a bicycle pump, which he had just snatched from the keyhole of the room where the two young women were sleeping. "This is the murderous implement of which the Knights of Chloroform make use!"

The three Frenchmen did not lose a moment. They had knocked loudly on the door of the room and, having received no reply, tried to break it down

"I dread that we might have arrived too late," stammered the engineer, all of whose limbs were agitated by a convulsive tremor.

"We have to get in, at all costs!" roared the naturalist.

With a formidable thrust of his shoulder he broke through the door, whose hinges creaked lamentably, and went into the room.

The electric bulb in the ceiling revealed the two young women, whose faces displayed a livid pallor, lying motionless, eyes closed, in their bed.

"They're dead!" cried the hunchback, with a sob.

"Open the window," the engineer ordered. "The first thing to do is to renew this poisoned atmosphere! Hurry! If we breathe this vitiated air for a few minutes more, we'll be poisoned ourselves."

Oscar hastened to obey, and then ran to fetch the hotel doctor. In the meantime, the engineer moistened Mademoiselle de Maubreuil's temples with cold water and made her breathe in smelling salts, while Roger Ravenel lavished the same care on Frédérique, The revulsives, however, ordinarily so powerful, had no effect. The two young women, whose pulses were only beating imperceptibly, maintained their immobility and their alarming pallor.

"It's maddening!" growled the engineer. "Nothing works! Their heartbeats are getting weaker and weaker."

"Time's passing and the doctor hasn't come," added Roger Ravenel, scarcely suppressing a sob. "If we wait any longer, they're doomed—we can only count on ourselves."

"You're right," said the engineer, who had already ripped a page out of his notebook and was scribbling a prescription. Here, Roger, run—don't lose a second."

Antoine Paganot, we have omitted to say, had concluded his medical studies in a brilliant fashion, and it was not long since he had abandoned his practice in favor of pure science.

The naturalist raced outside. He had no sooner left than the hunchback came back, accompanied by an individual of crafty appearance who as none other than the doctor. The individual had given evidence of evident reluctance; Oscar had almost been obliged to resort to threats to make him get out of bed and come.

"There's been no poisoning," he declared, at once, in a peremptory one. "I don't observe any odor of chloroform here; we're simply in the presence of a natural faint that will dissipate of its own accord."

"That doesn't make sense!" cried the engineer, angrily.

"I've given you my opinion," replied the Yankee, insolently. "There's nothing more for me to do than retire."

"Yes, get out!" shouted the engineer, clenching his fists. "I don't know what's keeping me from giving you a good hiding, for one of two things must be true: either you're an ignoramus who doesn't know your trade, or you're an accomplice of the Knights of Chloroform!"

The final phrase, which the engineer had pronounced at hazard in the fury of his wrath, appeared to have a considerable impact on the physician. "I don't know who the Knights of Chloroform are," he stammered, his expression changing, "but I'm ready to try a revulsive to bring these charming young ladies round."

"Futile, Monsieur. Get out—I have no further need of your services, but be warned that I'll be making a complaint against you tomorrow."

The Yankee fled without saying another word, just as Roger Ravenel returned laden with phials and boxes from the pharmacy.

With feverish haste, the engineer immediately gave the two invalids an injection of caffeine, whose effect was immediate. They opened their eyes almost right away, and looked around dazedly—but they were not yet conscious of what was happening around them; they had only partly escaped the influence of the mysterious poison.

It was only after inhalations of pure oxygen and further injections that they finally recovered consciousness completely. Then they blushed, distressed to find themselves in simple night-dresses and lying in their beds in the presence of their fiancés.

"Mesdemoiselles," Roger Ravenel explained, smiling, "You must excuse our intrusion, but you were in grave danger, and without the courage and ingenuity of our friend Oscar, I dare not think what would have become of you."

"What's happened, then?" asked Andree, with ardent curiosity.

"We'll tell you when you're better, when you're completely recovered from this alarm."

"We're ready to hear anything," Frédérique retorted. "I can already deduce that it's not a matter of any ordinary accident; we must have been victims of some criminal attack."

"There's nothing extraordinary about that," added Andrée. "Our presence must certainly have alarmed the wretches who have abducted Monsieur Bondonnat, and has driven them to further crimes. Speak, Monsieur Ravenel; we're ready to hear anything..."

In prudent terms, so as not to upset Amedée and Frédérique excessively, the naturalist recounted the night's drama, stressing the real heroism that Oscar Tournesol had shown on this occasion.

"You know, Monsieur Ravenel," said Frédérique, once the story was concluded and the hunchback had received his fair share of thanks and praise, "what's happened is rather encouraging."

"How so?"

"Yes—if my father's abductors weren't afraid of being discovered, they wouldn't have made the attempt on our lives. If they want to get rid of us, it's because our research is inconvenient for them, and because we might, perhaps, be close to achieving a result."

"But how can we be sure," Andrée objected, "that we're not just dealing with vulgar criminals?"

"No, my dear Andrée—what our brave Oscar heard on the terrace is, I think, explicit enough."

"Remember," added the engineer, "that it wasn't long ago that Mrs. Griffon, the owner of the boarding house where Baruch was arrested, also fell victim to the Knights of Chloroform; the similarity between the events is, it seems to me, significant. It might be that we'll soon have an explanation of the bloody mystery that surrounds us."

Paganot, who had remained silent until then, rose to his feet abruptly. "I too," he said, "think that we're close to a solution. But before anything else, it's necessary to analyze the redoubtable liquid contained in the device that the knights of chloroform abandoned when they fled."

"I put it there, on the sideboard," said Oscar.

"It's no longer there."

They searched the room thoroughly, but the device had disappeared. Evidently, the bandits had accomplices in the hotel.

The engineer, secretly alarmed, had the sensation that the bandits were all around them, invisibly listening in on all their conversations. Needless to say, all attempts made to find the two malefactors were fruitless.

VII. On the Island of Hanged Men

While his daughter and her friends were devoting themselves to indefatigable and perilous research, the situation of the naturalist Prosper Bondonnat—still alive and well, fortunately—was exceedingly singular. Often, the illustrious old man wondered whether he might be dreaming while awake, or whether he had suddenly gone mad.

What the Lords of the Red Hand wanted from him now, it will be remembered, were torpedoes of a new kind: machines capable of destroying big ships without leaving any trace, by means of powerful artificial whirlpools.

Obliged to yield to constraint, Monsieur Bondonnat had pretended to agree to what was demanded of him, but he had promised himself secretly that the apparatus constructed according to his plans would, once realized, present such inconveniences that they would never attain sufficient practical utility for the bandits to be able to make use of them in their piracies.

In appearance, he gave evidence of the greatest docility. His fecund imagination gave birth to one project after another. Every week, bundles of drawings were handed to the representative of the Red Hand, who immediately sent them to workshops on the continent.

The bandits were very satisfied with their prisoner; he had begun to dazzle them, to amuse them and to inspire their trust, and he was counting on convincing them in a short time to build an apparatus that he might be able to use in order to escape. In the meantime, he distracted himself by teaching Kloum to speak French. He believed he could count on the Indian, who was very attached to him and had an extraordinary confidence in him.

With the skill and patience of his race, Kloum had succeeded, in spite of the sentinels, in sawing through two planks in the palisade, and every night he escaped into the island and brought back precious information to Monsieur Bondonnat.

In the course of these nocturnal excursions he succeeded in reaching Lord Burydan, who, by virtue of the isolated situation of the fur-seal reservation, was not watched nearly as closely. From then on, a regular correspondence was established between the Englishman and Monsieur Bondonnat.

The eccentric lord was dying of boredom. Obliged to serve brutal and coarse individuals, he became neurasthenic, and in each of the pencil-scribbled notes that he confided to Kloum he announced his imminent suicide to Monsieur Bondonnat, if the latter did not find a means of escape soon.

The old scientist urged him to be patient, repeating to him that the escape plan he had made was soon sure to end in success, but time went by without bringing any apparent change in the prisoners' situation.

Bondonnat, naïve and sentimental by nature, like many scientists of genius, obtained a certain consolation from the amity of his dog Pistolet. The old man amused himself by carving the twenty-four letters of the alphabet into a plank of soft wood; patiently, he continued the barbet's education, so brilliantly commenced in France by Oscar Tournesol.

Meanwhile, in the presence of the results obtained by Bondonnat's labors, the Red Hand bandits had relaxed their surveillance somewhat. One day, the scientist obtained access to a cupboard full of scientific instruments that had previously been carefully hidden from him, and discovered a telescope and a sextant.

"Now," he exclaimed, joyfully, I can find out where I am. With the second hand of my watch, this is enough to discover the exact latitude and longitude of the island."

He took a bearing immediately, and his calculations gave him 47° north latitude and 161° west latitude.

"In consequence," he reflected, "the Island of Hanged Men must be somewhere between the Aleutians and the port of Vancouver. We're entering the warm season; it's a good time for an escape."

He did not mention his discover to Kloum, for whom the words longitude and latitude had no precise meaning, but by virtue of a bizarre whim—a true scientist's caprice—he amused himself by patiently teaching Pistolet the precious geographical formula and to compose it with his mobile letters, although it would doubtless never be any use to the poor quadruped.

At any rate, thanks to those daily lessons, the barbet had made surprising progress. He now knew more than fifty words, and was never mistaken with regard to their exact significance.

A little while thereafter, the Red Hand's usual emissary, a taciturn and morose individual who answered to the name of Sam Porter and possessed a genuine knowledge of mechanics and chemistry, asked Bondonnat whether he might be capable of producing plans for an airplane superior to all those thus far constructed.

The scientist thought about it briefly; the bandit's question had opened up unexpected perspectives.

"There's something better than airplanes," he said. "I can furnish you with the plans for a flying machine that will combine the advantages of the dirigible and the airplane. I call it an airship."

The bandit could not help being surprised by the willingness that the scientist seemed to be showing to deprived himself of such an important discovery.

"Give us the plan for your airship," he replied, "And I promise you that you'll be rewarded."

"Will you finally set me free?"

"Not yet, but I promise to get a letter from you to your daughters—provided, of course, that it doesn't contain any information that could compromise us or make your whereabouts known."

"Well, all right," the scientist acquiesced. "I agree to that, although I don't have enormous confidence in the fashion in which my letter will reach its destination. But my airship is a delicate machine and it will require the assembly and the trials to take place before my eyes."

"You're not hoping, perhaps, to make use of it to make your escape?" Sam Porter darted a suspicious glance at the old man through the eye-holes in his rubber mask.

"Don't worry," sighed Bondonnat, hypocritically, deeply annoyed that his thoughts had been read. "One can't take up aviation at my age."

"Besides which, I'll be there to prevent you from escaping."

Three days later, Bondonnat handed over the plans for his airship, which excited the Lords of the Red Hand with a real enthusiasm.

This is, in brief, what Monsieur Bondonnat's airship looked like. Imagine two gigantic mattresses, one vertical and one horizontal, both filled with hydrogen gas. Solidly stitched seams prevented the enveloped from distending and resuming an oval form. A cross-section of the apparatus offered the form of a cross with arms of equal length. Maintained by an aluminum carcass with hinges and pulleys, the vertical plane could be folded back to the horizontal one, and vice versa. That ingenious arrangement, completed by two propellers, permitted the practical assurance of the vehicle's direction. In a favorable air current it presented itself vertically and moved like an inflated sail. If it was necessary to head into the wind it become horizontal, and progressed like a fixed wing.

A cabin was suspended from the framework at the rear, to which five small gondolas were attached, one of which contained a powerful electrical motor. The passengers would take their places, one by one, in the other four. By the combination of angles, planes and the rudder, the airship progressed like a veritable bird, following or going against the air currents, rising or descending against the wind.

Sam Porter was so satisfied with the plans for the apparatus that he authorized Monsieur Bondonnat to write to his daughters, promising him that the letter would reach its destination.

In the letter, all the terms of which the bandit carefully laid down, Bondonnat simply explained that he was alive and well, but detained by capitalists who were keeping him prisoner in order that nothing leaked out regarding the secret inventions on which they were making him work. Without being able to specify an exact date for his return, he announced that it was imminent.

Bondonnat felt calmer after giving that letter to Sam Porter. As one can imagine, he only had a very limited confidence in the bandits' promises, but he told himself that would not have been made to write the letter if they had not the intention of enabling it to reach its addressees.

The construction of the airship proceeded with a feverish activity. Every week, the Red Hand's yacht brought the separate pieces, which were immediately assembled, under Bondonnat's direction, by Kloum, assisted by four robust bandits.

A month to the day after handing over his plans, Bondonnat had the satisfaction of seeing the airship swaying lightly in the breeze, retained by a solid steel cable, moored to a turnstile set outside the double circular path. A sentinel armed with a rifle mounted guard next to the cable night and day.

The old scientist resolved not to wait for the day when the decisive trials were to be held, and he let Lord Burydan know, via Kloum, that he must be ready for anything.

"My brave Kloum," said Bondonnat, one day, "it's tonight that we're leaving the Island of Hanged Men. The accumulators are charged, the gondolas stocked with food-supplies, and the propellers, which I checked this morning, are functioning marvelously."

Kloum, ordinarily so grave, manifested his joy with a host of grimaces and bizarre contortions. Even Pistolet joined in, barking joyfully, to his master's satisfaction.

At about ten o'clock in the evening, as usual, the bandits made a round armed with lanterns. Then the lights were extinguished, and in the silence of the dormant island, nothing more could be heard but the rumble of the waves and the measured footsteps of the sentinels.

"Now's the time, Kloum," said Bondonnat suddenly to the Indian, who had followed him into his bedroom. "Go out and fetch Lord Burydan."

"Yes, sir."

"When he's succeeded in getting out of the seal enclosure without difficulty, head toward the sentinel placed beside the cable and..."

Kloum, taciturn by nature, used the flat of his hand to make the gesture of cutting someone's throat.

"No, not that!" the old man protested, severely. "I don't want to buy my liberty at the price of a man's life. Let Lord Burydan be content with stunning the man with a blow of his fist, without giving him time to cry out. When that's done, treat the man standing guard on the circular path the same way. Then come to fetch me, and we'll go."

Bondonnat repeated these instructions twice, to be sure that the Indian had understood them fully. Finally, Kloum slid silently outside the residence and was lost in the darkness.

Half an hour went by. Bondonnat was violently excited. It seemed to him that Kloum had already had time to come back. Suddenly, however, Pistolet stood up as if he had scented an enemy—and the old man, palpitating with anguish, immediately thought he could make out the sound of footsteps and a struggle in the distance, and something like a dull groan.

Then everything became silent again.

A moment later, Kloum and Lord Burydan came into the room like a gust of wind. Their clothes were soiled with mud and a little blood was visible on the eccentric aristocrat's fists.

"Are you wounded?" asked Bondonnat, anxiously.

"Oh, it's nothing," said the Englishman. "A mere scratch. One of the rogues tried to gratify me with a thrust of a Bowie knife to prevent me from wringing his wreck, but I was the stronger, and I believe I've strangled him for good.

"Let's go, quickly," murmured the old scientist. "In half an hour they'll relieve the sentries; we don't have a minute to lose."

All three of them—or, rather, all four, for it is necessary not to forget Pistolet, left the laboratory and slipped cautiously toward the narrow exit that Kloum had contrived by sawing through some of the planks in the palisade. They arrived without a hitch as far as the place where the airship was moored, which they saw bobbing in the sky in the moonlight, like a grotesque dreambird. Combining their efforts, the three fugitives managed to maneuver the turnstile, and the airship slowly drew nearer to the ground.

As soon as it had made contact, the embarkation commenced. Pistolet was placed in the highest gondola first. Kloum climbed into the second and Lord Burydan into the third.

Bondonnat had reserved the fourth for himself, for it was him, with the aid of the solid ax with which he was equipped, who had to cut the metal cable.

"Let's get a move on," said Lord Burydan. "It seems to me that I can see lights moving back and forth on the other side of the island."

Bondonnat started striking the cable with mighty blows, whose sonorous cable vibrated tumultuously in the darkness, like the string of an Aeolian harp.

In response to that noise, gunshots burst forth from all directions. Electric searchlights were switched on, revealing to squadrons of bandits advancing at a run.

Bondonnat continued to strike the cable desperately—which, fabricated in threads of top-quality vanadium steel, would not yield without difficulty. It was only half-severed when Sam Porter appeared, breathless and furious, at the head of his men.

"Ha ha!" he laughed. "Monsieur Bondonnat is trying to get away from us—but one doesn't leave the Island of Hanged Men as easily as that." At the same time, he seized the old man around the waist and tried to pull him out of the gondola. He clung on to the rim desperately—but the struggle did not last ten seconds.

Suddenly, there was a screech of shearing metal, and the airship leap up toward the clouds with a mighty bound, vainly saluted by the bandits with a volley of rifle shots.

Bondonnat and Sam Porter, who had not let go, had fallen to the ground, tipped over by the violence of the shock.

The audacious attempt had failed. The old man would remain for a long time, perhaps forever, a prisoner of the bandits of the Red Hand.

**TO BE CONTINUED IN VOLUME 2:
THE ISLAND OF HANGED MEN**

SF & FANTASY

Adolphe Alhaiza. *Cybele*
Alphonse Allais. *The Adventures of Captain Cap*
Henri Allorge. *The Great Cataclysm*
Guy d'Armen. *Doc Ardan: The City of Gold and Lepers*
G.-J. Arnaud. *The Ice Company*
Charles Asselineau. *The Double Life*
Cyprien Bérard. *The Vampire Lord Ruthwen*
S. Henry Berthoud. *Martyrs of Science*
Aloysius Bertrand. *Gaspard de la Nuit*
Richard Bessière. *The Gardens of the Apocalypse*
Albert Bleunard. *Ever Smaller*
Félix Bodin. *The Novel of the Future*
Louis Boussenard. *Monsieur Synthesis*
Alphonse Brown. *City of Glass; The Conquest of the Air*
Emile Calvet. *In a Thousand Years*
André Caroff. *The Terror of Madame Atomos; Miss Atomos; The Return of Madame Atomos; The Mistake of Madame Atomos; The Monsters of Madame Atomos; The Revenge of Madame Atomos; The Resurrection of Madame Atomos; The Mark of Madame Atomos*
Félicien Champsaur. *The Human Arrow; Ouha, King of the Apes; Pharaoh's Wife*
Didier de Chousy. *Ignis*
Jules Clarétie. *Obsession*
Michel Corday. *The Eternal Flame*
Captain Danrit. *Undersea Odyssey*
C. I. Defontenay. *Star (Psi Cassiopeia)*
Charles Derennes. *The People of the Pole*
Georges Dodds (anthologist). *The Missing Link*
Harry Dickson. *The Heir of Dracula*
Jules Dornay. *Lord Ruthven Begins*
Alfred Driou. *The Adventures of a Parisian Aeronaut*
Sâr Dubnotal *vs. Jack the Ripper*
Alexandre Dumas. *The Return of Lord Ruthven*
Renée Dunan. *Baal*
J.-C. Dunyach. *The Night Orchid; The Thieves of Silence*
Henri Duvernois. *The Man Who Found Himself*
Achille Eyraud. *Voyage to Venus*
Henri Falk. *The Age of Lead*
Paul Féval. *Anne of the Isles; Knightshade; Revenants; Vampire City; The Vampire Countess; The Wandering Jew's Daughter*
Paul Féval, *fils. Felifax, the Tiger-Man*
Charles de Fieux. *Lamékis*
Louis Forest. *Someone is Stealing Children in Paris*
Arnould Galopin. *Doctor Omega; Doctor Omega and the Shadowmen* (anthology)
Judith Gautier. *Isoline and the Serpent-Flower*
Léon Gozlan. *The Vampire of the Val-de-Grâce*

Jean Richepin. *The Wing; The Crazy Corner*
Albert Robida. *The Adventures of Saturnin Farandoul; The Clock of the Centuries; Chalet in the Sky; The Electric Life*
J.-H. Rosny Aîné. *Helgvor of the Blue River; The Givreuse Enigma; The Mysterious Force; The Navigators of Space; Vamireh; The World of the Variants; The Young Vampire*
Marcel Rouff. *Journey to the Inverted World*
Han Ryner. *The Superhumans*
Brian Stableford. *The New Faust at the Tragicomique;The Empire of the Necromancers (The Shadow of Frankenstein; Frankenstein and the Vampire Countess; Frankenstein in London); Sherlock Holmes & The Vampires of Eternity; The Stones of Camelot; The Wayward Muse.* (anthologist) *News from the Moon; The Germans on Venus; The Supreme Progress; The World Above the World; Nemoville; Investigations of the Future; The Conqueror of Death*
Jacques Spitz. *The Eye of Purgatory*
Kurt Steiner. *Ortog*
Eugène Thébault. *Radio-Terror*
C.-F. Tiphaigne de La Roche. *Amilec*
Louis Ulbach. *Prince Bonifacio*
Théo Varlet. *The Golden Rock. The Xenobiotic Invasion; The Castaways of Eros; Timeslip Troopers* (w/André Blandin); *The Martian Epic* (w/Octave Joncquel)
Paul Vibert. *The Mysterious Fluid*
Villiers de l'Isle-Adam. *The Scaffold; The Vampire Soul*
Philippe Ward. *Artahe*
Philippe Ward & Sylvie Miller. *The Song of Montségur*

MYSTERIES & THRILLERS

M. Allain & P. Souvestre. *The Daughter of Fantômas*
A. Anicet-Bourgeois, Lucien Dabril. *Rocambole*
A. Bernède. *Belphegor*; *Judex* (w/Louis Feuillade); *The Return of Judex* (w/Louis Feuillade); *The Shadow of Judex*
A. Bisson & G. Livet. *Nick Carter vs. Fantômas*
V. Darlay & H. de Gorsse. *Arsène Lupin vs. Sherlock Holmes: The Stage Play*
Séamas Duffy. *Sherlock Holmes in Paris*
Paul Féval. *Gentlemen of the Night; John Devil; The Black Coats ('Salem Street; The Invisible Weapon; The Parisian Jungle; The Companions of the Treasure; Heart of Steel; The Cadet Gang; The Sword-Swallower)*
Emile Gaboriau. *Monsieur Lecoq*
Goron & Emile Gautier. *Spawn of the Penitentiary*
Rick Lai. *Shadows of the Opera: Retribution in Blood; Sisters of the Shadows: The Curse of Cagliostro*
Steve Leadley. *Sherlock Holmes: The Circle of Blood*
Maurice Leblanc. *Arsène Lupin vs. Countess Cagliostro; Arsène Lupin vs. Sherlock Holmes (The Blonde Phantom; The Hollow Needle); The Many Faces of Arsène Lupin*
Gaston Leroux. *Chéri-Bibi; The Phantom of the Opera; Rouletabille & the Mystery of the Yellow Room; Rouletabille at Krupp's*
Richard Marsh. *The Complete Adventures of Judith Lee*

William Patrick Maynard. *The Terror of Fu Manchu; The Destiny of Fu Manchu*
Frank J. Morlock. *Sherlock Holmes: The Grand Horizontals; Sherlock Holmes vs Jack the Ripper*
Jean Petithuguenin. *The Adventures of Ethel King*
. Antonin Reschal. *The Adventures of Miss Boston*
P. de Wattyne & Y. Walter. *Sherlock Holmes vs. Fantômas*
David White. *Fantômas in America*
Pierre Yrondy. *The Adventures of Thérèse Arnaud*

SCREENPLAYS

Mike Baron. *The Iron Triangle*
Emma Bull & Will Shetterly. *Nightspeeder; War for the Oaks*
Gerry Conway & Roy Thomas. *Doc Dynamo*
Steve Englehart. *Majorca*
James Hudnall. *The Devastator*
Jean-Marc & Randy Lofficier. *Royal Flush*
J.-M. & R. Lofficier & Marc Agapit. *Despair*
J.-M. & R. Lofficier & Joël Houssin. *City*
Andrew Paquette. *Peripheral Vision*
Robert L. Robinson, Jr. *Judex*
R. Thomas, J. Hendler & L. Sprague de Camp. *Rivers of Time*

NON-FICTION

Stephen R. Bissette. *Blur 1-5. Green Mountain Cinema 1; Teen Angels*
Win Scott Eckert. *Crossovers* (2 vols.)
Jean-Marc & Randy Lofficier. *Shadowmen* (2 vols.)
Randy Lofficier. *Over Here*

ART BOOKS

Jean-Pierre Normand. *Science Fiction Illustrations*
Raven Okeefe. *Raven's L'il Critters; Rave's Faves*
Randy Lofficier & Raven Okeefe. *If Your Possum Go Daylight...*
Daniele Serra. *Illusions*

HEXAGON COMICS

Franco Frescura & Luciano Bernasconi. *Wampus*
Franco Frescura & Giorgio Trevisan. *CLASH*
L. Bernasconi, J.-M. Lofficier & Juan Roncagliolo Berger. *Phenix*
Claude Legrand, J.-M. Lofficier & L. Bernasconi. *Kabur*
Franco Oneta. *Zembla*
L. Buffolente, Lofficier & J.-J. Dzialowski. *Strangers: Homicron*
Danilo Grossi. *Strangers: Jaydee*
Claude Legrand & Luciano Bernasconi. *Strangers: Starlock*

www.ingramcontent.com/pod-product-compliance
Lightning Source LLC
Chambersburg PA
CBHW030348020726
47493CB00003B/734